Praise for the novels
of Mindy L. Klasky

The Glasswrights' Journeyman

"A fast-paced adventure series featuring a passionate, heart-winning heroine."　　　　　　　　　　　*—Booklist*

"The best book in the series . . . a juicy epic fantasy that will appeal to fans of Mercedes Lackey."　*—Midwest Book Review*

Season of Sacrifice

"A fine story of magic and adventure, this is a wonderful coming-of-age tale, too."　　　　　　　　*—Booklist*

"Entertaining, with a spectacular climax and satisfying conclusion."　　　　　　　　　　　　　　　*—Locus*

"A very creative and colorful high fantasy novel [with] action and drama. . . . Klasky proves she is a supertalented author."
　　　　　　　　　　　—The Midwest Review of Books

"Klasky summons a medieval flavor for her descriptions of the kingdom, and she allows her well-rounded characters to display both frailties and courage."　　　　　　　　　*—VOYA*

continued . . .

The Glasswrights' Progress

"A strong follow-up to Klasky's debut novel, building on the strengths of the first book without succumbing to repetition."
—SF Site

"This sequel . . . stands alone but will compel readers to read the first book."
—*VOYA*

The Glasswrights' Apprentice

"I wouldn't be surprised at all if Klasky moves quickly to the front rank of fantasy writers."
—*Science Fiction Chronicle*

"A fun and colorful adventure, and a solid first novel."
—*Locus*

"A fine fantasy novel . . . a fast-paced action thriller that has wide appeal . . . this novel is a winner."
—BookBrowser

"Klasky's future novels . . . will be worth waiting for."
—SF Site

"Ms. Klasky creates remarkably shaded characters. . . . The result is an absorbing reading indeed—look for this author to develop in fascinating ways."
—*Romantic Times*

"This is a splendid tale, one which captured me from start to finish. Bravo—nicely done."
—Dennis L. McKiernan

"From its rich imagery to its all-too-believable class system, this first novel will absorb and intrigue you, right up to the unexpected ending."
—Nancy Kress, author of *Maximum Light*

THE GLASSWRIGHTS' TEST

Mindy L. Klasky

A ROC BOOK

ROC
Published by New American Library, a division of
Penguin Group (USA) Inc., 375 Hudson Street,
New York, New York 10014, U.S.A.
Penguin Books Ltd, 80 Strand,
London WC2R 0RL, England
Penguin Books Australia Ltd, 250 Camberwell Road,
Camberwell, Victoria 3124, Australia
Penguin Books Canada Ltd, 10 Alcorn Avenue,
Toronto, Ontario, Canada M4V 3B2
Penguin Books (N.Z.) Ltd, Cnr Rosedale and Airborne Roads,
Albany, Auckland 1310, New Zealand

Penguin Books Ltd, Registered Offices:
80 Strand, London WC2R 0RL, England

First published by Roc, an imprint of New American Library,
a division of Penguin Group (USA) Inc.

First Printing, June 2003
10 9 8 7 6 5 4 3 2 1

PUBLISHER'S NOTE
This is a work of fiction. Names, characters, places, and incidents either are the
product of the author's imagination or are used fictitiously, and any resemblance to
actual persons, living or dead, business establishments, events, or locales is entirely
coincidental.

To Mark,
who had no idea what he was getting into
when he replied to that first e-mail

ACKNOWLEDGMENTS

The Glasswrights' Test would never have been completed without the help of many people: Richard Curtis (my agent) and Laura Anne Gilman (my editor)—who answered the frantic e-mails and provided the never-ending words of advice and support; Bruce Sundrud—who once again read too many chapters in too short a time; Bob Dickey and the rest of the Arent Fox Library staff—who remained flexible and supportive during Writing Marathon and other insanities; Jane Johnson—who provided eternal telephonic support; the Washington Area Writers Group and the Hatrack Tuesday night gang—who have remained enthusiastic and good-humored throughout all the readings and signings and discussions of where we go from here; to my family (Mom and Dad and Ben and Lisa)—who have always been there for desperate phone calls and frantic tears; and to Mark, who kept me from writing *Test* but helped me to finish it.

If you would like to learn more about the Glasswright Series, participate in my newsgroup, or send me e-mail, come to my Web page: www.sff.net/people/mindy-klasky.

1

Rani Trader gazed out over the hall, catching her breath as a ray of sunlight streamed through a window to illuminate a stack of undyed silk as high as her head. She turned to the tall player who stood beside her. "Tovin! It's beautiful!"

"Money always is." The player nodded as he looked around the hall, obviously noting which merchants were ready to trade. The auction would begin at noon, and the tension was palpable in the spacious room. Rani followed Tovin's gaze to a cluster of men in shimmering white cloaks, garments that collected the brilliant summer sunlight and cast it back in jeweled glints.

She indicated the visitors with an arch of one eyebrow. "So, the spiderguild sent five masters."

"They want to see just how damaged they will be by your Halaravilli's market."

Her Halaravilli. Rani nearly objected to the words. Hal was not hers. Had not been for nearly three years, if he ever had been. Hal belonged to Morenia. He belonged to Queen Mareka.

Tovin was only petulant because Hal had sent three messengers to her in as many days. The king had insisted that he must discuss an important matter with her, and yet when she had attended him dutifully, his attention had been stolen by the new silk hall, by the auction, by the embassy from the Liantine spiderguild. The last time he'd summoned her, she had spent an entire afternoon waiting for him to spare her a few moments, only to leave the audience hall in a flurry of skirts and speculation when Hal needed to devote his attention to a minor border dispute among his lords.

She remained curious about Hal's demand, but she had other things to attend to—glasswright things, merchant things, player things. The king would speak to her when he was ready. For the present, she'd try to forget his requests; there was nothing she could do, in any case, and she disliked subjecting herself to the edge in Tovin's voice while she waited. She chose to let his current comment pass.

Even as she made that conscious decision, Hal stepped into the sunlight that pooled on the dais at the front of the room. He was resplendent in his crimson robe, a garment cut from the first silk harvested from his octolaris spiders. With Rani's help, Hal had spirited the creatures from their home in Liantine, breaking the longtime monopoly of the distant spiderguild. He had distributed them among his nobles, giving them to the newly created Order of the Octolaris and collecting valuable gold bars in exchange.

The spider gold had secured Hal's throne, keeping him safe from powerful forces that fought to destroy his kingdom. It had warded off the voracious church, which had lent money to the crown. Even more importantly, it had forestalled Hal's yielding to the Fellowship of Jair, a secret, shadowy organization that lurked on the edges of Morenian politics, that threatened to control all relations between the crown and other nations.

Rani and Hal—and Tovin too, now—were members of that secret organization. Rani glanced about the hall, wondering how many of the others present at this first silk auction were members of the cabal. How many had attended meetings of the secret brotherhood, shielding their faces behind black masks? How many would buy silk today and use it to fashion a Fellowship mask, turning the crown's new-found wealth into a symbol of secret power?

Before Rani could continue her thoughts, Hal raised a hand. The gesture commanded instant silence. Every eye in the hall was directed to the dais, waiting for the bids to begin.

"Honored merchants," Hal said, "welcome to the silk hall. Welcome to the first new market established in our fair land since the dread fire of three years' past. May Lor look kindly upon all our dealings here."

Lor. The god of silk. Never had one of the Thousand Gods risen to such prestige in so short a time.

Hal continued. "When I first brought octolaris to fair Morenia, many said that we could not build a silk trade, that we could not rival the great masters of Liantine. We could not challenge our neighbors to the east." Hal inclined his head graciously toward the knot of master spiderguildsmen, and one, the oldest, narrowed his eyes to accept the salute.

"And yet," Hal said, returning his attention to the gathered luminaries, "you have surpassed my greatest expectations. In three short years, you have grown the silk trade. You have bred your octolaris and fed them their precious markin grubs. You have harvested their silk, spun the thread, woven the cloth. You have built a guildhall in the center of a city that was in ruins, a hall worthy of our finest masons and sculptors. And now, a mere three years since the first silk spiders arrived in Moren, we stand ready to auction off the fruits of your labors."

A roar of approval tore through the crowd, and Hal smiled patiently as he waited for silence to return. "Before we open the auction, there are a few individuals whom I must recognize—people without whom we would not be present today. First and foremost, always in our thoughts is Queen Mareka, the woman who had the courage to give us our octolaris even when she risked her own power and prestige. Of course, my lady cannot stand beside me today, but nonetheless, I raise this cup in her honor and drink to her glory."

A cheer echoed in the hall, obliging and obedient, but lacking the same unbounded enthusiasm that Hal had commanded for himself. Morenia had accepted Mareka because Hal had presented her, but the kingdom had no love for its queen. It did not like the fact that she was a mere guildswoman, even if she came from an exotic guild in a foreign land. It did not like that she had tricked their king, that she had manipulated him with the oldest of a woman's wiles, snagging her crown by sparking a king's heir inside her womb.

Still, the kingdom had mourned when Mareka lost that child in her sixth month, when her infant son was born too soon to breathe the bitter winter air. And they mourned the daughter that she had borne, the tiny girl who had not lasted a single night.

But now Mareka was once again with child. Eight months along, and all seemed fine. The royal physicians had confined the queen to her chambers, demanding that she rest and conserve her strength, that she drink the blood of new lambs throughout the spring, that she make offerings to Nome, the god of children. Mareka said that she could feel her child stir within her, that she could feel him kicking strongly, all through the long nights. She was certain that she carried a boy, the heir that Halaravilli needed so desperately. She husbanded her strength, fed her considerable will into the child growing within her, and she waited, waited, waited.

No, Mareka could not be at the silk hall. And she might not be pleased with what she saw, even if she had attended. Mareka had been a promising apprentice in the distant spiderguild, a willful girl intent on serving her guild with all her might. Her loyalties might be tested too much by seeing the accumulation of silk, the vast wealth that her former masters would despise. Better, Rani thought, that Mareka not attend this first silk auction.

As if Hal were setting aside the memory of his queen's torn loyalties, he swallowed the wine from his toast to his lady. Then he looked out over the hall and said, "It is fitting that we bless this market before we earn our first profits here. That blessing might be done by any priest, but we know another who is well suited to invoke the Thousand Gods on this auspicious day. The octolaris that have brought us to this momentous occasion came from Liantine, and the blessing should come from there as well. My lady? Will you invoke the gods' good graces upon our ventures?"

Berylina Thunderspear. Rani had not realized that the Liantine princess was attending the auction. Following the line of Hal's gesture, Rani saw the dark corner where he settled his gaze. Berylina took a hesitant step, moving as if her king's gesture pulled her from a pit of shifting sand.

The princess had grown in the three years she had spent at court. She had slimmed away her childhood roundness, melted into the softer curves of womanhood. She had gained more poise as well, become almost accustomed to the glare of public attention. She made her way to Hal's dais without blushing, without fidgeting, without clutching at her simple gown of grassy green.

Some things about the princess, though, would never change. Her teeth still jutted out over her lower lip, lending her a horselike expression. One of her eyes wandered, so that even now Rani could not tell if the girl looked out over the assembly or gazed privately at her adopted king. Berylina's hair had escaped her demure braids, and it billowed about her face like unruly straw.

And yet there was a peace about the princess, a confidence that she had never shown in her native land. When she stood at the front of the dais, her voice was quiet, so soft that the assembly needed to catch its collective breath. But her words were calm, certain. Her voice was steady as she said,

"May Lor watch over all the dealings in this hall and guide all men to truth and justice. May First God Ait guide all who traffic here. May Pilgrim Jair appear before us as a guide and model of all that is right and good, for all the days to come. In the name of all the Thousand Gods, let us pray for guidance and success forever and ever. Amen."

"Forever and ever, amen," Hal repeated, smiling kindly. Few present knew the full risk that he had taken accepting Berylina into his house. Few knew that Berylina's father, Teheboth Thunderspear, had threatened war, had promised to harry Morenia's coasts with all the ships at his disposal. Hal had managed to negotiate a sort of peace, reminding Teheboth that the king had not placed any value on the princess when she lived in his palace, had not honored her in any way. Ultimately, at Rani's prompting, Hal had resorted to one great negotiating maneuver, offering to return Berylina to her father, to send the princess back to Liantine against her will.

Teheboth had retreated from his negotiation then. After all, what did the house of Thunderspear want with an ugly daughter, a damaged girl, a religious fanatic who followed the paths of the Thousand Gods even when those paths led her into shame and poverty in the Morenian court? Hal had bristled at Teheboth's dismissal, but he had let the final correspondence go unanswered. Berylina was safe, and war had been averted. What more could Hal truly demand?

In the silk hall, Berylina completed her whispered blessing and stepped down from the dais, immediately retreating to her darkened corner. Rani noted that Father Siritalanu waited for her there. The priest had been instrumental in the princess's escape from Liantine, and he had overseen her religious instruction here in Morenia. The man was loyal to her beyond all reason, consistently claiming that he loved her spirit, her pure faith. Rani shrugged. Spirit, faith, lust for her body . . . What difference did it truly make? The man had helped the awkward Berylina settle into her new home.

From the dais, Hal recognized others, raising his cup to salute the master mason who had built the silk hall. He recognized Davin, the ancient retainer who had designed an irrigation system for the delicate riberry trees that hosted the octolaris' sole source of food. He recognized the hordes of workers that tended to the octolaris, feeding the spiders their grubs, tending to their cages. He also recognized the seven workers who had given their lives in the past three years, succumbing to the spiders' deadly poison as the Morenians learned the dangers of their newfound commodity.

And then Hal turned toward Rani. His eyes sought her out in the crowd, honed in on the crimson that she wore in his honor. Her throat constricted at his serious gaze, and she could not keep from clutching Tovin's arm.

"And," Hal said, "we recognize Ranita Glasswright, without whom we could never have raised the octolaris to success. Ranita brought us the riberry trees; she conceived the strategy for breaking the spiderguild's monopoly, and she followed through when all action seemed impossible." He lifted his golden cup and stared at her over the rim. Rani swallowed hard and raised her chin. It felt as if she were answering Hal with proud defiance, challenging him to count out all the costs that had been paid that day in Liantine. She had bargained for the trees, but her bidding had cost Morenia—cost the kingdom—a brave soldier who had stayed behind at the spiderguild.

Rani drove away thoughts of Crestman, forcing herself not to dwell on the fate that the young soldier had chosen. Not to dwell on his enslavement in the spiderguild. Not to dwell on the look of betrayal on his face as she closed the deal for the trees.

Instead, she gazed into her king's eyes and folded herself into a decent curtsy, looking for all the world as if she had been born to a life of finery and pomp. Hal acknowledged her obeisance, and then he sipped from the goblet. Of course, he gave no clue to the reason he had summoned her earlier in the week, no hint about that mystery.

"And, my lords and ladies," he continued, "there is one more whom I must recognize, one more who made today possible. I would not stand before you without the help of Baron Farsobalinti, Grand Master of the Order of the Octolaris." Farso had been the first of Hal's knights to don the brooch of the Order, and he had led the way to Hal's financial success. The baron had presented his ten bars of gold; he had cajoled and shamed and bullied his fellow nobles into doing the same. But Farso had done even more than that—he had explored trade routes for Morenian silk, rooting out merchants who would trade in the new goods, discovering guildsmen who would adapt their broader woolen-goods looms into narrower, sturdier silk machines. He had hired the foremen for the silk hall's construction, supervised the workers who had carted straw and clay, lumber and stone. Farso had worked tirelessly for the past three years, giving of his days, his nights, his heart, and his soul.

The steady labor and constant worry had taken their toll on the young nobleman. Gone was the sunny youth who had served his king with a child's dedication. Instead, Farso's hair had begun to tarnish with untimely silver; fine lines spread out beside his eyes, as if he had strained them poring over account ledgers in the dark of night.

Nevertheless, Farso stood straight and tall on this victorious day, and even as he stepped forward to accept the king's accolades, he flashed a grin at the woman by his side. Mair's response was a smile of her own, an expression that only broadened when the babe in her arms began to fuss. Mair shifted Laranifarso, Farsobalinti's own son, and cast her glance from her husband to her king.

Even with the pressures of the silk trade, Farso had found time enough to marry. Over a year had passed since he had vowed to honor his wife, and still Mair and Farso gazed at each other with the fierce eyes of new lovers. Lovers, that was, until Mair decided that Farso had done something foolish, had overstepped his bounds in some way. Then her tongue was as sharp as ever, full of the screeching condemnation that she had mastered as a leader among the Touched, the casteless poor who filled the streets of Moren. For now, though, she stepped back, offering up the moment of public recognition for her beloved to receive the honor of his king.

Despite Mair's best efforts, Laranifarso continued fussing, and the Touched mother shifted him from arm to arm. Rani knew that Mair was fully aware of critical eyes in the silk hall. Some of the elite watchers might condemn her for bringing her son to the auction. Some might question her ability to manage her own child, to stop the fussing that threatened to grow into a full squall. Nearly every person in the hall scorned Mair merely for her marriage to Farsobalinti, for daring to create a union between a nobleman and a Touched girl. In fact, Halaravilli had presided over their union, attempting to deflect vicious gossip by invoking his title Defender of the Faith to bless them.

Rani shook her head as she watched her oldest friend ease back from the dais. Mair had been realistic about the courtly bias against her. She had never expected to be anything more than Farso's mistress, nothing more than his cherished leman. Even though Farso insisted that she meant much more to him, the past three years had not proven easy. They had not flowed smoothly, despite all of Mair's seeming blessings.

The Touched woman's struggles for acceptance had tainted the way that Rani thought of the Morenian court. Of course, Rani had no hopes for marrying into the noble caste herself. She knew that. She knew that the only man who might have had her, Halaravilli, had other obligations—to the kingdom, to the court, to his queen. Besides, Rani had her own responsibilities. Not only was she growing her fledgling glasswrights' guild, but she was also responsible for the players.

At Tovin's urging, Rani had become the players' sponsor throughout all of Morenia. She had tried to explain to him that such recognition was not necessary in her homeland, that Morenia did not have Liantine's restrictions on travel and trade. But Tovin had shaken his head, holding to his own traditions. Despite Rani's repeated attempts to dislodge the limitations in the usually creative player's mind, he would have nothing of her arguments.

The players needed sponsors, Tovin had explained at last. They needed to be subject to rules, to restrictions. Only with such limitations would good people accept the traveling acting troop. Only with such reassurance would people open their homes and their hearts to scoundrels on the high road, to folk who had no home beyond the tents they carried with them, who had no history in the castes of Morenia. Only with a sponsor would people agree to Speak to the players.

Despite the warmth in the silk hall, Rani shivered when she thought of Speaking. Her tremor was not from fear but rather from naked longing. Only that morning, she had Spoken with Tovin, telling him of the merchant ceremonies that she had witnessed in her youth. Tovin's voice had woven a curtain around her, spinning a cottony nest of safety and security. Even now she could feel his words thrumming through her chest, taking her deeper, deeper, into her knowledge, into her memories. . . .

Swaying, Rani forced her attention back to the present, back to the silk hall and the dais where her king proclaimed: "And now, let the bidding begin. Our first lot is this bolt of crimson silk, the first ever spun in Morenia, dyed in honor of our crown. What am I bid for fair Morenia's venture into the silk trade?"

"One gold bar!" Farso cried out, and the crowd took a collective step forward. Three merchants shouted over themselves, topping the bid, and Hal graciously nodded toward each successive bidder, gesturing toward them with the ceremonial baton of the auction conductor.

Rani looked at the excitement on Hal's face, at the energy that thrummed across his shoulders. He had waited for this day impatiently, harrying the octolaris wranglers, demanding that silk be collected twice daily, bullying Davin constantly into building bigger looms and better ones. He had paced in front of the breeding spiders' cages like an expectant father, waiting with frozen breath as he learned that the first clutch of spider eggs had hatched successfully on Morenian soil, that the riberry trees had borne fruit, that the markin moths had spun their clumsy cocoons, produced their sightless white grubs. Long days and longer nights had slipped away as Hal pinned his kingdom's hopes on the poisonous spiders, and now he hoped to gather in his reward.

It appeared that both merchants and noblemen were willing to oblige their king. Twelve golden bars were bid on the bolt of cloth. Thirteen. Fourteen.

"Twenty-five bars of gold!" Tovin shouted into the hall, his player's voice rising to the rafters. The strength of his bid shattered the air, silencing the buzzing watchers.

"What is that, Tovin Player?" Hal turned to the broad-shouldered man, taking only an instant to flick his eyes over to Rani. She understood the momentary question there, the flash of doubt as he demanded to know if he were being mocked. She could only meet Hal's gaze steadily. She knew nothing of Tovin's intentions.

"Twenty-five bars of gold, Your Majesty. The players bid twenty-five."

Rani ran her merchant's mind over the figure. Tovin could pay it. The players had more than that in store after three years of touring Morenia. Exiled from their homeland, they had proven thrifty, relying on existing costumes and curtains. The players' only cost had been a score of new glass panels, and Rani had been more than happy to supply the glass for those, to supply the lead and paint and silver stain. After all, she sponsored the players. She supported them. And she learned from them, all for free.

Rani closed her hand on Tovin's forearm, feeling the energy pulse through the man's taut muscle. She watched Hal measure her motion, watched him calculate the genuine offer behind the player's words.

"Very well. Twenty-five bars of gold. Is there anyone who will bid more? Is there anyone who places greater value on the first fruit of the Morenian looms?"

Merchants looked at each other, fingering the pouches of gold at their waist. One man shook his head and eyed the other bolts of cloth, bolts that would not command the same premium as the first. A nobleman cleared his throat, drawing attention, but then he flushed and stepped backwards.

"Very well, then," Hal proclaimed. "Twenty-five bars of gold from Tovin Player! The first bolt of silk is sold!"

Cheers rang out to the hall's ceiling, and the crowd surged even closer to the dais. Hal acknowledged the enthusiastic congratulations, and then he stepped down, handing the traditional baton over to the silk official who had been appointed to conduct the body of the trades. Another lot—this one of undyed silk—was displayed before the crowd, and bidding began anew.

Hal worked his way through the crowd, touching one man on a shoulder, leaning down to listen to the hearty words of another. He was in his element, Rani thought. He was happy and comfortable—his land was thriving for the first time since he had taken the throne. The northern kingdom of Amanthia was paying tribute as expected. Poor Moren was springing back to life after her devastating fire—whole quarters of the city were nearly rebuilt, with wide avenues and sturdy new buildings. The spring had been warm, and plants had gone in early. The early summer had boasted days of gentle heat punctuated by long, soaking rains. All was well in Morenia.

Rani became aware of the clutch that had gathered around Tovin, of the men who collected to congratulate him. "A fine gesture, Player!" Count Jerumalashi was saying, one of Hal's own councilors. "I should like to see what you do with that silk, in my own court. Speak to my chamberlain, when you have a moment—let us know when you'll be able to play for us."

"Of course, my lord," Tovin said. "I would be most honored."

"And when you've played for Count Jerumalashi, you can present your work for us," Farsobalinti said, muscling his way through the crowd and offering a hand to Tovin. "You're a good man, Tovin Player."

"Aye," Rani heard at her elbow, and she turned to meet Mair's amused glance. "A grand man that Tovin Player is."

Rani stepped to the side, the better to converse with her friend. As she moved away from the nobles, she heard the silk master declare another bolt of silk sold, realized that he was beginning the auction of yet another lot. "What do you mean by that?"

Mair shifted the burden of her son to her left shoulder, taking care not to wake the now-sleeping babe. "Only that Tovin Player is a shrewd bargainer. You must have taught him a thing or two about driving a deal."

"I hardly needed to do that!" Rani said, automatically springing to the man's defense, as if he needed it.

"I meant no insult, Rai! I only meant that the man made a good bargain. Twenty-five bars he'll pay, and the story will be all through the city by the end of the day. Every person in Moren will pay a gold crown to see the next players' show, and when the troop announces that it has made costumes with the king's silk . . . He's no fool, your Tovin."

The excited buzz of merchants bidding on silk rose higher as Rani thought, *He's not my Tovin.* She glanced at the man's copper eyes, at his unkempt curls, and a flash of longing curled through her belly—longing for the Speaking that they had shared, for the quiet days when they had first returned to Moren. Days without Tovin pressuring her to wed. Days without the obligations of studying glasswrights' lore, of plotting to rebuild her guild. Even as Tovin darted a smile to her across the hall, she thought of the argument they'd had the night before.

"Ranita, it should be enough!" he had said. "You have studied the books. You have learned new techniques. Announce that you're reopening the guild and be done with it."

"It isn't enough." She had pulled away from him even as she was reluctant to leave the warmth of his palms across her back. She had settled her silk dressing gown around her shoulders, jerking the sash tight as she crossed to the window. The Pilgrims' Bell had tolled across the city, steady and secure in the moonlit night. "It isn't enough at all."

She'd heard him sigh from the bed, realized that he was biting back a dozen arguments. He had come to stand behind her, folding his arms around her and pulling her to his chest. She could make out the crisscross of glass scars on his fingers, perfect white in the moonlight. "Tell me, then. Tell me why. Tell me why you cannot declare the guild rebuilt and your obligation paid."

Tears had welled up in her eyes. If she leaned forward, she could see the executioner's block in the courtyard. She could see the stone that had cradled her brother's neck before he paid for his treason, before he yielded up all that he had to give. She could see the iron grate that led to the dungeons, to the dank stone corridors where prisoners awaited their fate. Where glasswrights huddled in terror and rage, masters and journeymen and apprentices imprisoned for their imagined crimes against the crown.

She forced words past her tightened throat, forced a confession from her choked misery. "The obligation is not paid. I don't know if it ever can be." She swallowed hard. "After Prince Tuvashanoran was slain, I hid. I did not come forward, even to explain my innocence, even to say that it was all a terrible mistake. I did not say that I never meant to call the prince into range for the arrow that took his life. The glasswrights bled for me, Tovin. They paid a blood debt each time they were interrogated, the masters and the journeymen. The apprentices were maimed, *for me.*" *Maimed.* That word was not enough. That single sound could not capture the horror, the brutality. The apprentices had been culled methodically, one each day—for the entire time that Rani had remained loose in the city streets. Every sunrise a child was torn from the pack, dragged to the courtyard, forced to the block.

Was it the executioner who did the job? Or was there another master, a butcher who specialized in hands?

Each apprentice had been forced to kneel, forced to splay trembling fingers on the thirsty, frozen stone. Each was asked to confess, ordered to divulge secrets. Each was commanded to disclose Rani's whereabouts, Rani's allies, Rani's plans. And each remained silent, unable to craft a reply that satisfied old King Shanoranvilli.

The blade fell. The thumbs rolled. The blood flowed and flowed and flowed. . . .

And Rani could not repay the guild for that. Even though she had been innocent—she had been a victim herself—she could not declare the balance sheet even, the debt paid. Not yet. No matter how much she longed to be free from her past. No matter how much she longed to move into the future . . .

She had forced herself to speak to Tovin in the night, to feel her words vibrate against his broad chest even as the doleful Pilgrims' Bell counted through the night. "I cannot mark the bill paid yet. The old guild must do that. The old masters and journeymen. The apprentices. The ones who survived."

"You do not even know where they are," Tovin had said reasonably.

"They are not in Morenia," she agreed. "But I have sent messengers, trackers. Some glasswrights have returned to their homelands, to their villages. Others have gathered in other lands, in courts that are kinder than Morenia was." In

Brianta, she thought as she listened to the Pilgrims' Bell. In the homeland of Jair, where there was mercy for all.

Tovin had pulled her closer, settling her head against his throat. She could feel the steady pulse that beat there. "You are too harsh on yourself."

"I am not harsh enough." She held out her hands in the moonlight, turning them to capture the eldritch glow. A trick of the light made her bones stand out, as if her flesh had melted away.

"You cannot undo the past," Tovin murmured.

She clenched her hands into fists, and her tears finally slid down her cheeks. *I know,* she thought. *Oh, how I know.* She let him fold his fingers around the knots of her own. She let him turn her toward him. She let him guide her back to the shadows of the curtained bed that they shared.

And in the summer light of morning she had pushed away the despair, the sorrow, the hopeless mourning. She had dressed in her finest crimson and attended the first silk auction in Morenian history.

"Your Tovin will turn a profit on this one in less than a season," Mair crowed, completely unaware of Rani's drifting thoughts. "By Jair, he's a wise one!"

"By Jair . . ." Rani heard an echo before she could reply, and she looked up to find Princess Berylina standing before them. There was an intensity in the girl's face, as if she listened to voices from afar, voices that whispered above the rising bids from the dais.

"Your Highness," Rani said, automatically dropping into a polite curtsy. Beside her, Mair ducked as well, simplifying the maneuver in light of her son. She kept her head up, her eyes on the princess. Rani, too, watched the girl warily, as if she were a wild creature trapped in a stable.

"Ranita Glasswright. Lady Mair." The princess managed to meet Rani's gaze for a moment, a quick dart of her own right eye as her cast left eye roamed. Then she inclined her head, studying her fingers clasping and unclasping her gown. "I am glad that you could be here today."

"We would not have missed the first sale of Morenian silk," Rani said, trying to warm her voice. She had no reason to dislike the princess, no reason to take exception to the girl at all. Nevertheless, she was uncomfortable around Berylina. The princess's roaming eye made it difficult to talk to her directly, and Rani could remember too clearly the child who had stammered and blushed, unable to string together three consecutive words without a fit of shyness.

Of course, three years in Moren had changed that. As had the normal maturation of a young girl. And the attentions of Father Siritalanu.

The priest was never far from the princess, and Rani glanced up to see that he was now a mere two steps away. He kept his gaze on the princess, steady and calm, like a hound awaiting its master's bidding. As Rani always did when she saw the pair, she wondered how the priest could divide his loyalties—how he could maintain his pledge to the church and to the crown and his adoptive princess. The man's intensity gave no clue to his balance.

"The first silk," Berylina said, and her voice was shadowed by surprise, as if she had not realized that the auction was under way. "Yes, that is important."

Rani started to shake her head and turn back to the bidding, but Berylina took a step closer. For the first time that Rani could remember, the princess set a hand upon her arm. The girl's short fingers were stained by charcoal, red chalk, and ink. The palace rumors were true, then. Berylina continued to spell out her devotion to the Thousand Gods, to illustrate the deities as they came to her, as they spoke inside her mind. "I am grateful to you, Ranita Glasswright."

"Grateful?" Rani repeated the word like one of the players' talking birds, and she cast a quick glance toward Mair. The Touched girl shrugged minutely, clearly as confused as Rani was.

"For agreeing to travel with me to Brianta. I recognize the gesture as a sign of respect for my homeland, for all the Thousand Gods."

"My lady!" Hal's voice was falsely hearty, and he startled Rani by seeming to appear from nowhere. Even one who did not know him as well as she did would have understood that he was forcing the smile onto his face, pounding bluff good nature into his tone. He waved jeweled fingers toward the dais, toward the excited clutch of merchants who fought to outbid themselves on a particularly fine lot of undyed silk. "We were honored by your prayer before the auction."

"Anything that I can do in the service of the Thousand Gods, Your Majesty." Berylina sank into a curtsy, making a holy sign across her chest. "May Lor look upon this day with endless mercy, my lord."

Hal automatically reached out to raise up the princess, and then he looked about him, clearly wanting to hand her off to another. He avoided Rani's gaze as he maneuvered the girl, avoided the demand she had yet to voice.

Agreeing to travel to Brianta . . . Rani had done no such thing. In fact, she could *not* travel now—she was sworn to make a dozen screens for the players. She had obligations—to her players' troop, to Tovin, to herself. Besides, there was Mair to assist, Mair and little Laranifarso.

Hal said, "I see that Princess Berylina has managed to speak with you when I could not."

"My lord?" Rani froze her voice, and she felt Mair stiffen beside her.

"Aye, Rani." Hal's eyes snared hers, and she read the message there—he was pleading. Asking her not to protest. Asking her to agree meekly, to concede.

Berylina spoke, apparently unaware of the silent conversation that passed between them. "The gods have spoken. They are pleased that you will accompany me to Brianta."

"They are—" Rani started to say, but Berylina continued.

"I am summoned, you know. The Thousand have ordered

me to journey to the homeland of First Pilgrim Jair. I am to undertake the complete pilgrimage, that I might hear the gods' voices uninterrupted."

Rani's mind reeled. Hal had not spoken to her, had not found the time to issue his orders to her directly, and yet he had shared them with the *princess.* He had listened to the Liantine woman's mysteries and her secret plots, to the truths that the gods whispered to her when she knelt in prayer. Hal was ordering Rani to act, to do something she was not prepared to do, all on the basis of the princess's visions.

Even as Rani's anger rose bitter at the back of her throat, she registered the rest of Berylina's message. The girl was going to undertake a complete pilgrimage. Every Morenian desired to make such a journey in his lifetime, such a grand declaration of faith. Rani's brother, Bardo, had planned to travel to Brianta. The family had saved for his pilgrimage, setting aside silver coins from their shop. But those coins had been traded to the Glasswrights' Guild instead, buying Rani's advancement.

Rani's entrance to the guild had cut off all of Bardo's hopes. He had rebelled in his own way, seeking out dark counsel, finding sinister allies in the city of his birth. If Bardo had been able to travel to Brianta, he might never have fallen in with the evil Brotherhood. He might have continued to live and work in the Merchants' Quarter. He might have commandeered the family business, led the Traders to wealth and glory within their caste. He might have lived.

And now Berylina proposed taking the trip that had been denied to Bardo, traveling to Brianta with all the wealth and pomp of a princess. . . .

"I wish you a safe journey, Your Highness," Rani choked out, raising an angry hand to dash away the tears that had somehow appeared on her cheeks.

Berylina looked at her and glanced away, her eyes as

quick as swallows at sunset. She clutched at her simple green robe, the caloya costume that marked her as a devotee of the gods. "I—" she started to say, but she lost herself in her former shyness, unable to bring herself to form coherent words.

Hal stepped closer, coming between Rani and Berylina. The movement brought him too near for comfort; Rani fought the impulse to step back. "Princess Berylina has envisioned herself on the road to Brianta, where she will serve the Thousand Gods with pride. She has also seen you, Rani, honoring Lor and Clain and First Pilgrim Jair himself."

"Sire—"

"We are honored by your accepting this duty, Ranita Glasswright." The royal command was unmistakable—Hal used the traditional plural. He called her by her guild name. He spoke to her here, in the silk hall, where she could not express her misgivings. Where she could not refuse.

"The gods have spoken," Berylina announced with a child's simple confidence, rising out of her shy whirlpool long enough to flash a trusting smile at Rani.

"Your Highness," Rani said, barely managing to keep her tone even, her words patient. "You do not understand. I have other work here."

"Alas, my lady," the princess said, and her soft voice conveyed a true sorrow that was older than her years, "I fear that *you* do not understand. Clain has spoken to me. If you do not travel to Brianta now, you will never achieve mastery in your guild. You will never bring your glasswrights back to Morenia."

Rani turned to Hal, pinning him with a heated gaze. Surely he could have made time in his busy schedule to tell her of his command. He must have known that Rani would rebel against the princess's vision. If he had wanted to, he could have spared her this unsettling public display. "Sire?"

"Rani." He closed the distance between them once again,

coming near enough that he could rest a hand on her shoulder. "Ranita. We all have obligations."

"Yes, Sire. And all of my time is spoken for!"

"You will find time. You will travel to Brianta to watch over Berylina as steadily as I would myself if I could go."

"Sire—" she began, but she let the word trail off. Could she upset Hal's balance? Should she disrupt the power that he was exercising, the success he was at last enjoying? He was her king, after all. She was his vassal.

She bowed her head. "Aye, Sire. I will go with Berylina to Brianta."

Tovin stepped up beside her as she spoke, returned from harvesting his new commissions. She felt the warmth of his body through her crimson gown.

"I will travel with you, Ranita," Tovin said as easily as if they spoke of an afternoon's outing beyond the city walls.

Hal said, "Player, you are not required to accompany Ranita Glasswright in this task."

"Nevertheless, I feel the call," Tovin responded immediately, moving his hand across his chest in a fluid holy sign. If Rani had not known the player's skill, she would have thought him struck with sudden religious fervor, with a stunning insight into the Thousand Gods and all that they intended to work in the lives of men. Tovin pressed: "Your Majesty, the players came to Morenia to serve you. Do not hamper our work. Do not order me from the side of our patron."

"Sold!" rang out the silk master, crashing his baton against the wooden podium. Another lot of spidersilk. More gold for the royal coffers.

Rani watched Hal make up his mind. She saw him nod at Tovin, absorb the player's untold promises. She saw him glance at Berylina, note the princess's whispered prayer of gratitude to Lor, gratitude for another lot of successfully auctioned silk. She saw Hal turn to her, to Rani, take her measurement to determine what she desired.

Of course Rani wanted Tovin's companionship. She wanted the player beside her, sharing with her, teaching her. She wanted his devotion. His dry humor. His glasswright's knowledge. If she were bound to travel to Brianta, better to work with Tovin than without. She nodded her head, ducking her chin in barely perceptible agreement.

"It is settled, then. Tovin Player, you shall go." Hal started to reach for Tovin's hand, to seal the bargain with a royal clasp, but before he could move, the door to the silk hall crashed open. Sunlight streamed into the building, spilling across the floor like golden milk.

The silk master stopped his bidding, cutting off his recitation of the glories of the cobalt silk now on the dais. All eyes turned to the doorway, to the frantic palace messenger who sprinted into the hall.

"Your Majesty!" the boy gasped. "Come quick! Queen Mareka has fallen! The midwives stand ready—your child is about to be born!"

2

Parion Glasswright touched his head to the altar in the corner of his study, automatically muttering a prayer for forgiveness to all the Thousand Gods. Forgiveness for all the mistakes that he had made in his life, for all the wrong words he had said, the ones that he had failed to say . . .

Why were the unspoken words the ones that he remembered most clearly? Why was his silence the thing that haunted him most often? Not his rage, not his ranting. Rather, the times when he could have said something, could have done something to change the world around him but had waited too long.

Years had passed in stasis, but Parion was ready to act now. He was ready to speak his mind, to take mastery over his fate and the fate of all the Morenian glasswrights under his control. Parion rested his fingers on the glass medallion that was centered on his altar—glass for Clain, the glasswrights' god. Glass for Morada, the lost love of Parion's life.

A knock on the door pulled the master to his feet. Three sharp raps. Of course the priest had come. The priest came every morning.

"Father," Parion said, as he opened the door.

The young man hovered on the threshold, clad in the spring-green robes that marked him as devoted to all the Thousand Gods. Not that such robes made him anything special in Brianta . . . Half the people in the streets wore the green garments—if not the priests, then the women who served them, the caloyas who made certain that the religious colonies were provided for, wanting neither food nor clothing nor any other material thing. Elsewhere in the world, one needed to be born into the priestly caste, but here in Brianta, converts were accepted freely. Converts with money, that was—gold could pave a thousand roads.

The priest intoned, "May the Thousand Gods bless all of your endeavors."

"And yours, Father," Parion replied automatically. "May First Pilgrim Jair watch over you with favor." Every single morning he exchanged benisons with a representative of the church; he was awakened by their cries in the street: "Blessings of the Gods! Praise be the Gods! All sing praise to the Thousand Gods!"

Shrugging, Parion crossed to his broad worktable, automatically fumbling for the gold coin he had set aside for the guild's daily offering. He placed it in the priest's outstretched hand, making a holy sign across his own chest. "Pray for us, Father. Pray for Clain to bless our glasswrights' guild."

"In the name of Clain," the priest replied promptly, "may your day bring you joy and prosperity." The priest aped the sign that Parion had made, and then he bowed his way out the door.

The master glasswright shrugged as the latch snicked closed beneath his hand. At first the priests' constant begging had annoyed him, but he had grown accustomed to the Briantan tradition. After all, if he had been back in Morenia, he would have delivered gold once a week, when he gathered with all the other guildsmen for a service in the cathedral. He would have bundled up several coins, traded them for tapers to place on Clain's altar. What difference did it make if the priests came to him, here in Brianta? What difference did it make if Parion worked his business away from the church?

At least here, the guild owed no taxes to a king. Briantan royalty understood that it was second in importance to the church; the king did not attempt to fill his treasury from the glasswrights' tattered pockets. No, Briantan royalty was . . . restrained. Weak.

Things might have been different if the Briantan princess had successfully married Halaravilli—what was it?—three years before? The royal house here might have grown in prestige. But ben-Jair had scorned the woman, sent her away without ceremony before he went and found himself his spiderguild queen.

Yet another reason for the glasswrights to stay in exile, then. There was no love lost between the ostensible rulers of Brianta and cruel Morenia. The weak Briantan king would not mind if Parion's guild grew to power, used that power against the house of ben-Jair. Parion had watched the Briantan nobility fade in the past three years, as if the return of their princess was the final plucking of fading petals.

As the king had weakened, religious factions had gained power throughout the city, throughout all of Brianta. Priests issued decrees as if they were nobles. Religious fraternities had begun to demand stricter rules—pilgrims were forbidden to walk through the streets without long robes and cloaks. Preachers had begun to cry out from street corners, expounding on the actions of loyal worshipers, dedicated pilgrims. People had begun to whisper of witches, of travelers who masqueraded as people of faith only to undermine the true foundation of Brianta.

Parion could ignore all of that religious claptrap. He had brought the glasswrights to Brianta for one simple reason: Here he was safe from rendering any payment to the house of ben-Jair. He did not need to fund royal soldiers, beasts who would trample through a guild's gardens, tear down kilns, maim and murder innocents. . . .

"Clain preserve us," Parion muttered out of habit, and then he recited the Guildsman's Prayer, the familiar words that had begun each day of his craftsmanship since he was a child. "May all the gods look upon my craft with favor, and may they take pleasure in the humble art created by my hands. May Jair himself be pleased with the humble offering I make, and may the least of my works bring glory to the world. May my works guide me to the Heavenly Fields in my proper time, as the gods do favor. All glory to the Thousand Gods."

His fingers fumbled for the glass medallion that rested in the center of the altar. Raising it to his eyes, he gazed at the morning light that streamed through his window. The sunshine set the emblem sparkling, dancing through dust motes like the pilgrims' chants that rose from the street on the Briantan breeze.

The medallion was flawed in the middle—a jagged crack ran through its vortex of black and white. Black and white, like Morada's hair. Black and white, like the battle that raged in Parion's heart, the struggle for revenge, for stability. Despite eight years of handling the cracked medallion, it remained unbroken. He muttered a grateful prayer without specifying one of the Thousand, and he laid the glass against his forearm. The cool round drew the fire from the livid scars that laced his flesh, scars from his sworn fealty, from blood oaths strewn with salt in ben-Jair's dungeons.

Even now, after all this time, his veins heated at the memory of the instructor who had fashioned the glass piece, at the woman who had given him the final token of her undying love.

Undying *love* perhaps, but not an undying body.

Eight years ago, Morada had been executed by Shanoranvilli ben-Jair's torturers. She had been taken by the crown as a pawn in a game that she had not begun to understand. Why hadn't she listened to Parion when he tried to warn her? Why hadn't she protected herself when he told her that no sane glasswright would toy with politics?

He could still remember how Morada had turned from him that night, the first time that she'd lied to him. Even then, she had plotted her escape from the guild's watchful eye, from Parion's arms. She had gone to some secret meeting, some clandestine assignation that had promised her the power that she craved. Desperate to create something beyond test pieces for apprentices, Morada had used her considerable glasswright skills to create a mosaic for some noble faction, to decorate their secret den.

Parion could remember the first time, months later, that he had seen the entwined snakes tattooed across her arm, twisting about themselves viciously. Hungrily. Hopelessly. She had admitted that the design was the same that she had done for the secret cabal, the same that she had set in tile in their hidden meeting place.

And yet, Clain save him, he had not ordered her to abandon the noble power struggles. A master in the glasswrights' guild, he had thought that he understood her connection to those villains. Morada was merely mourning the life that she had lost, the adventures that she was denied because of her promise to stay at the guildhall and teach. After all, instructors often embraced extreme fashions—clothes or mannerisms or wild, extravagant feasts. They needed something to break up the monotony of their guild-bound days.

Morada! Parion thought as he polished the medallion. *If only I had known! If only I had saved you from the political fray, from the vengeance of ben-Jair when he learned of the plots against him!*

He had not seen her head on a pike. For that, he was grateful to all the Thousand Gods. If he had witnessed that last indignity, he might have been broken. He might not have managed the journey to Brianta. He might not have set up the new guild, gathering in his apprentices and journeymen and masters. Plotting his revenge.

Of course, many of the Morenian glasswrights never made it to Jair's distant homeland. Madness claimed some, hopelessness others. Sheer distance proved a barrier, and Parion had been loath to advertise his presence, lest misguided royalists continue to measure out revenge for the death of Prince Tuvashanoran, for the murder that had not been the guild's fault.

Nevertheless, Parion had gathered nearly four score glasswrights in his hall. Eighty guildsmen, all dedicated to Clain and craft. Some were Morenians who had built a new life in this distant land. Others were Briantans, drawn to the fine art of the guildhall. Yet others came from distant lands, drawn by the magic of the First Pilgrim's birthplace. Many pilgrims came to Jair's homeland, but not all left.

A knock sounded at the door, rousing Parion from his bitter memories. "Come!" he called, automatically covering Morada's emblem with a sheet of parchment. He scarcely realized that he was shielding the precious thing, protecting one of the few tangible reminders of his Morenian life.

The door swung open silently, as if the gods themselves controlled the hinges. As Parion watched, a black-hooded figure entered the chamber. One gloved hand—a woman's? A man's?—reached out to the prayer bell that hung beside the door. The fingers brushed against the bronze surface, eliciting a soft jingle. "In the name of the First Pilgrim," the newcomer whispered, the sound almost lost as the figure glided over the threshold.

"Welcome, in the name of Jair," Parion said automatically. Which one of the Fellowship was this? Would Parion recognize the face inside the hood? His heart beat faster as the visitor closed the door.

It had taken Parion years to build tenuous ties with the Fellowship. Only in the past six months had he determined a reliable system for sending messages, for requesting a visit from the shadowy faction. In Brianta, even more than in Morenia, the Fellowship of Jair held power. The organization had its roots here in the Pilgrim's homeland; it sent out its tendrils of power to the rest of the world.

Priests made offerings to the Fellowship, saluting the clandestine organization through scarcely veiled sermons. The Briantan king was rumored to pay tribute on a monthly basis, offering up gold and jewels for the right to keep his throne. The Fellowship determined the raising of masters in at least three guilds, and the captain of the City Guard was widely rumored to be a member.

Parion swallowed audibly, his throat suddenly dry. "Would you share a glass of wine with a humble glasswright master?"

"Nay," the visitor replied, carefully pitching the single word to a tone that defied Parion's perception of gender. Male or female, this secret Fellow was determined to remain anonymous. "I haven't much time."

"You've brought the Hand, though?" Parion could not keep the eagerness from his voice. He had worked his first business transaction with the Fellowship almost six months before, and he had spent nearly all of his limited patience waiting for fruition.

"Aye."

When the figure did not move forward promptly enough, Parion fought the urge to rush across the floor. Instead, he said hoarsely, "Let me see it, then!"

"All in good time. All in good time, Glasswright."

Parion's curiosity gnawed at him like acid. He had promised much to the Fellowship for this new device. A message had been slipped beneath his door the day before, an unsigned slip of parchment that stated only, "Liantine riches have arrived."

Who *did* the Fellowship deal with in that distant land? The Liantines could have no use for the First Pilgrim, not with their worship of the ancient goddess the Horned Hind. The Fellowship of Jair would have no easy time snaring power from the house of Thunderspear. Someone, though, had joined them. Someone had come to recognize their power.

And that someone had sent the precious goods that Parion needed, that the glasswrights craved. Trying to mask his eagerness, he crossed to the window, but he could not keep from making the Briantan sign of gratitude. The ritual gesture recognized the power of Jair's favor upon his people. "Let me see the Hand."

The Fellow took a moment, raising gloved fingers to adjust the deep hood. Parion wanted to bellow, *I won't look at your cursed face! Just show me the goods!* but he managed to restrain himself. Instead, he muttered a prayer for patience. May Plad keep him on his true course and guide him in the ways of waiting.

The visitor stepped up to the window and produced a silk-swathed bundle from beneath the disguising black robe. Plad be damned—Parion snatched the roll of cloth. As he unwound the soft, undyed fabric, his breath came fast. Twice, his agile fingers nearly let the precious thing slip to the floor.

Careful! he tried to warn himself. *You've waited for six months. Surely you can wait a few more heartbeats.*

Turn the cloth. Shift the burden. Position his fingers beneath the Hand; cradle it. One last twist of fabric. One last turn.

And there it was.

An iron bracelet wrapped in softest spidersilk. Silk bands looped over the iron, hinting at the shape of a palm, of vital, bending fingers. Long, shimmering thread—no, not thread—ribbon, fashioned from the same precious silk, weaving from finger to finger, looping across the shimmering sunlight. Carefully oiled metal levers, weighted with a jeweler's precision.

Parion glanced at his visitor, annoyed that he must share this treasure with anyone, even with a silent guest, even with the person who had brought it. Turning his back on the

black-robed figure, Parion faced the window. He clenched
his own fist—his four functional fingers, his thumb—and
then he slipped the leather cuff over his hand.

It was light. Flexible. He guided his fingers into the loops
of spidersilk, adjusted the ribbons. Folding his working
thumb against his palm, he lined up the metal jaws with the
edge of his hand, pretending as best he could that he had no
digit, that he was as maimed as his poor guildsmen.

He wiggled his fingers, manipulating the metal jaws with
the silken ribbons. The motion was smooth, but his hand rebelled against the strange balance. He felt the tremor of a
cramp skirt across his palm. Squinting in concentration, he
reached toward the large earthenware pot on the edge of the
table, closest to the window. Baubles of glass filled the container—one thousand plus one, for each of the gods and
First Pilgrim Jair. It had taken Parion a year to assemble his
offering in a manner acceptable to the Briantan priests.

He reached toward the pot, catching his lower lip between his teeth in concentration. If he could just manipulate
the ribbons . . . If he could pull the jaws open . . . There . . .
There. . . .

He brought the metal teeth closer to a glass bauble, to a
glinting bit of crimson on the top of the pile. Despite his intense concentration, he was distracted by a flash of light on
the pebble, the smallest reflection of sunlight from the metal
jaws. Which god had he saluted when he presented that trinket to the offering pot? Which of the Thousand had he recognized as he added the glass to his stash?

Concentrate. Focus. Move the fingers. Right—no, left!
Easy. Easy. Close the jaws by edging his fingers closer to his
palm, by folding them over his own thumb, his real thumb.
Slowly . . . Slowly . . .

He caught his breath as he lifted the crimson glass. Using
the Hand, he brought the treasure up to his face, looked
through it at the morning sunshine. The Briantan street outside his window turned to crimson, washed in bloodred as if

a sudden sunset had descended upon the city. Parion turned to his visitor and barely caught a laugh against the back of his throat. "It works!"

"Of course it works," the hooded figure whispered. "You asked the Fellowship, and we delivered. It could do nothing less than work."

"There are more? I asked for two score, left and right."

"There will be more. The others will be delivered in a fortnight."

"We cannot wait!" Not now. Not when Parion had seen how well the Hand could be manipulated.

"You must." The visitor stepped back from the window, retreating into the room's deep shadows. "The Fellowship demands it."

"I have a guild to manage!"

"Your guild has waited eight years. It can wait another fortnight."

Parion wanted to howl against the injustice. Didn't the Fellowship *know*? Didn't they *understand*? The glass-wrights needed these Hands, they *deserved* them. Nevertheless, there was nothing he could say. Nothing he could do. The Fellowship held all the cards. He took a deep breath and forced himself to say, "A fortnight, then."

"We will expect full payment before we deliver the goods."

"Of course."

"Full payment, in gold. And in service."

A shiver ran down Parion's spine, as if the Hand's iron jaws had stroked his jugular. "What service can you need of me?"

"Nothing you will mind giving." The hooded figure took a single step forward. "Only that you summon one here, to Brianta."

"Summon one? Who?"

"The one you call the Traitor."

Parion's reaction was automatic; his unbound hand

moved in the ritual gesture of cleansing. "You cannot ask that of me."

"The Fellowship does not ask. It demands."

"I will not communicate with her. You demand too much."

"We offer much. Forty Hands, Glasswright."

"She is the very reason that we need the Hands! She is the one who destroyed us."

"All the more reason for you to send for her, then. Get her to Brianta. Her fate awaits her here. Get the Traitor to our land, and the Hands will be yours."

Parion opened his mouth to protest. Anything but that. Anything but reaching out to that one, welcoming her in, bringing her back to the good glasswrights that she had betrayed. Before he could speak, though, the hooded figure turned and crossed to the door.

From the threshold, a heavy whisper carried across the room: "Send the message today, Glasswright. In a fortnight, spidersilk can burn. Iron can be reforged."

The Fellow glided out the door even as Parion started to protest. The master glasswright stretched his right hand toward the door, toward escape, toward a fleeing dream. The monstrous metal jaws gaped as Parion drew back, as he lowered the device to his side.

He sighed. Contact the Traitor. Invite her to Brianta. Could he force himself to write the letter?

Parion turned back to his window. Reaching across his body with his left hand, he unfastened the spidersilk ribbons that nestled the Hand against his flesh. When the contraption lay on the table, the metal jaws pointed up, accusing him with their smooth surfaces. How could he let his pride interfere? How could he imagine *not* inviting the Traitor to Brianta if that was the payment the Fellowship demanded? He owed all of his glasswrights, all of the children who had grown into competent journeymen, actual masters, despite their injuries in service to the guild. He must swallow his pride, his wrath. He must send the letter.

Parion reached into his offering basket and palmed a bauble of glass, cool blue this time. He rolled it across his flesh and felt the trinket absorb the heat from his skin. Over his fingers, under his fingers, across the white-gleaming cicatrices of his craft. This, too, was a meditation on Jair. This, too, was worship of the Thousand Gods. Without consciously planning, he muttered a prayer to the Pilgrim, words that passed his lips a hundred times a day. "May First Pilgrim Jair intercede for all my prayers in the true course of time."

Somehow, Brianta had converted him into a religious man. At first he had adopted the Briantans' complicated prayers because he wanted to prove his fitness for their society. He wanted to illustrate that he was safe, that they could trust him. He needed the security of a land where the king held little power, where the glasswrights could lick their wounds and recover. Over time, however, Parion had grown to find comfort in the prayerful words, refuge in the familiarity. His mind glided over the religious salutations like a blind man striding along a familiar path. Briantan worship had become a salve. A support. A guide.

Parion's reflections were interrupted as the door to his study opened yet again. No knock this time; no request for admission. One of the glasswrights, then. One who expected to be welcome in this chamber.

He glanced up in time to see Larinda Glasswright slip into the room. She reached out automatically for the prayer bell, passed her palm across the surface with a smooth touch that set the chimes to jangling. The action was reflexive for the girl. After all, she had spent nearly one-third of her life in Brianta, eight years surrounded by the paraphernalia of First Pilgrim Jair.

Parion forced a patient smile onto his lips. "Blessings of the Pilgrim, Journeyman."

"Blessings of the Pilgrim, Master," she responded immediately.

"How fares the guild this morning, Larinda?"

"Well, Master." She ducked her head in the traditional salute. "The apprentices are counting out the new shipment of Zarithian glass. Our silver stain arrived this morning as well; it is already placed in the treasury."

"And Instructor Tanilo?"

"He remains in the infirmary. He has not awoken yet. Sister Domira fears for him. She says that the instructor's fits had been growing worse before he was found in the garden yesterday. It is not good that he has not regained consciousness."

"May Yor bring strength to the man."

"May Yor bring strength," Larinda repeated, making a gesture to summon the protective attention of the god of healing.

Ironically, the motion was nearly impossible for the girl to complete. Her own hands had been maimed in Morenia, destroyed by the King's Men when the Traitor worked her evil upon the guild. Larinda wore a crude Hand, one of the first that Parion had ever commissioned for his charges, but the tool was heavy and lacked both grace and ease of use. In fact, she winced as she twisted her wrist in the complicated salute to Yor.

"Does your hand pain you, Larinda?"

"No, Master," she responded immediately, but he saw the way she cradled her right wrist with her left.

He made a decision. Stepping over to his worktable, he waved the journeyman to his side and lifted the spidersilk shroud that covered the new device. "You should see this, Larinda Glasswright. You should know that we will soon have new Hands for you and all the wounded guildsmen."

For just an instant, suspicion clouded the girl's face. She glanced at the table, as if she were afraid of trickery, as if she feared that her hopes would be destroyed in a flicker of cruel fire. She could not keep from gazing on the Hand, though. She darted a look at Parion, silently asking for permission. He nodded, and she lifted the new Hand in her heavy, awkward grip.

She ran her fingertips over the silk covering, and a look of awe spread across her face. She straightened the ribbons, twisting them so that they fell in their proper configuration. With two fingers, she manipulated the metal jaws, catching a gasp against the back of her throat as she discovered the smooth motion, as she measured the increased gripping strength.

"Master, it's amazing!"

"We'll have forty of them within a fortnight. Left and right—they're on their way to Brianta now."

"All thanks go to the Pilgrim," Larinda said. Parion swallowed a grimace. All thanks did *not* go to the Pilgrim. In fact, some thanks should go toward him, toward Parion.

After all, he was the one who had negotiated with the Fellowship. He was the one who was letting Larinda view the treasure now, letting her realize the riches that she would soon have at her disposal. Nevertheless, he was not surprised that the journeyman's first instinct was to salute the Pilgrim. Better to bathe in the stream of Brianta, than . . . He let the old proverb trail off in his mind.

"May I, Master?" The longing on her face was naked, and she nodded toward her crippled hand, then toward the wondrous new tool.

"Yes, Journeyman. I would like to see how it works. Let me help you with that." He reached out to unfasten the heavy metal Hand that already closed about her wrist.

Larinda merely eyed him with steady accusation. Of course she did not need help with her existing Hand. She had spent eight years mastering the tool. If she could not tame the straps and buckles herself, she could hardly profit from their use.

Parion stepped back, darting his agile fingers in the ritual symbol of apology, offering up his mistake to all the Thousand Gods. He winced as Larinda set aside the precious new armature and waved her own fingers through the traditional acceptance of an apology. She made the motion without seeming to realize how awkward it was, without appearing to be aware that it required both thumbs to gather in this gesture, to reply in the traditional way.

He shook his head, knowing that he rebelled against the Briantans' strict rituals so that he did not have to pay attention to Larinda's actions. The girl began removing her older Hands, settling the heavy structures on the table. As he watched her painful progress, he remembered that she had been the first apprentice maimed in the old guildhall. A soldier's knife had flashed and left her with her without a thumb, with her right hand suddenly seeming too long, too thin. The resulting limb would have been eerily graceful, if blood had not pumped from the wound.

Others had suffered once the apprentices were herded into the king's dungeons. There, more apprentices lost first one thumb, then the other. He could still remember how the soldiers had come for Larinda in the grey light before a winter dawn, come to destroy her other hand. They had dragged her from the squalid holding cell, bullied her into the courtyard. She had fought like a wildcat, twisting, turning, biting the soldiers who sought to overpower her. Four men had forced the hysterical child to the ground, and a fifth had raised his fateful blade. A single flash, which Parion had glimpsed from the barred dungeon window, and then Larinda had been tossed back into her cell, shivering, whimpering, unable to catch her breath against the pain and the shock and the blood. So much blood.

If Larinda resented the fact that she had nearly been spared the second amputation, she never spoke of it. She never outwardly mourned the cruel twist that had deprived her of her left thumb on the very day that the old king declared the forlorn guildsmen free to go. But Parion knew that *he* would have hated the happenstance. It would have settled in his belly like a burning stone, and he would have raged against the world even more than he already did—he would have despised the Traitor with a passion hotter than a glass kiln.

But who knew how Larinda Glasswright's mind worked? Who knew what thoughts coursed behind her eyes as she stared at the new armature? She caught the tip of her tongue between her teeth as she studied the contraption. She rotated her wrists, as if measuring the best approach. She was a general, calculating the superior placement of troops; she was preparing to do battle with a new and untested army.

Only when she had studied the tool from every possible angle did she spare him a tight nod. "Very well, then. Let us see how this one works."

And she reached out for the Hand. He knew not to help her. He knew that he would only make things worse if he held the device, if he offered to tighten one of the straps. She would have to work the buckles her own way, tighten down the device with her own ingenuity.

And, of course, she did. He should not have been surprised by the creativity she applied; after all, he'd seen her solve more complex problems every day of her Briantan life. Nevertheless, he admired the way that she cut through the confusion of the new tool, the way that she turned it about, maneuvered it, made it her own.

Ah, Morada, Parion thought. *If you could have been here to train this one, if you could have passed on your knowledge and your wisdom to one as deserving as she* . . . But Morada was dead, of course. Executed because of the Traitor.

The Traitor that the Fellowship wanted him to summon.

Parion shook his head, shying away from the letter that he had pledged to write. He spoke to fill the awful silence, to distract himself from the pained expression on Larinda's face as she worked the silken ribbons, as she struggled to find the new balance in the tool that would be her life. "What other news, Larinda? What is happening in fair Brianta this summer morn, outside our own guildhall?"

"The priests prepare for the feast of the Pilgrim's birth." She answered immediately, but her tone was distracted. She was moving her wrist against the silken padding, reaching out with the fingers of her left hand to smooth the cuff. "We journeymen will be ready to show you our glass designs by noon."

Parion was surprised. He had not expected to see the sketches for another week. He nodded, though, as Larinda tightened two of the ribbons. The metal jaws flashed open. "And have we decided which cycle we will tell?" He tried to make the question casual, tried to seem as if he weren't hanging on her every action with the new Hand.

After all, he had listened to hours of debate among the glasswrights about the new commission. Some thought that the guild should create works depicting Jair's life in Brianta—six panels, one for each of the castes and one for the holy, overarching status of Pilgrim. Others, though, believed that the glasswrights could better serve their purpose by imagining on a larger scale. One journeyman had argued eloquently for the six windows to depict the five great kingdoms, with Brianta taking precedence, of course, as the land of Jair's birth.

Larinda glanced up from the mechanism, blinking her eyes as she focused on Parion's question. "I should not tell you, Master. You should see the designs for yourself."

"Aye, and I will. But you can tell me the direction that the discussions have taken."

Larinda looked uncomfortable, and she let her gaze return to the Hand. She flexed her wrist to close the jaws, then arched her palm to settle the iron bracelet more comfortably against her flesh. She chose her words with care as she found a better balance with the tool. "One of the journeymen hit upon a solution, Master. A combination of the various plans that had been discussed."

"Yes?" he prompted when she fell silent.

"Jair's life should be depicted—each of the castes. But he should be linked with a kingdom for each of the stations. With Brianta, we'll focus on his life among the Touched. With Liantine, his merchant days, for the goods he traded in that land. For Sarmonia, we'll show him in the weaver's guild. In Amanthia, he'll be a soldier, and in Morenia, a nobleman, a priest. The last window will show him in his true guise, in his overarching presentation, as First Pilgrim."

Parion heard the pride in Larinda's voice, and he knew that she must have devised the plan. "You think, then, that all will be pleased if we follow this path."

"Of course not. We will never find a design that pleases *everyone.*" Her disdain was palpable. "I think, though, that this is a good plan."

Parion nodded. "Very well, then. I will look at the designs. We'll see what works."

"The guild is honored by the master's attention."

"Noon, then? I'll come to the hall and view the drawings."

"Noon, Master." She nodded and returned her attention to the Hand. This time, however, she slipped her fingers out of the silken ribbons. She wriggled her wrist through the cloth-covered band and returned the treasure to his work-table. "That is a good tool, Master. A great tool for your humble glasswrights."

He heard the longing in her voice. Curse the Traitor! Why should a glasswright as good and loyal as Larinda be reduced to pining after a twisted pile of silk and iron?

"Two weeks, Larinda," he said. "Two weeks, and it shall be yours."

"Clain smiles upon us, Master."

"Aye. Clain smiles upon us."

He waited for Larinda to take her leave, to let him return

to his work. She did not make any motion toward the door, though, and she did not mutter one of the standard prayers to end conversation. "Is there something else, Larinda?"

"One thing more. We have completed our survey of the cavalcade points."

The cavalcade points. In the midst of all his other plans, Parion had nearly forgotten the basis for the upcoming glasswrights' test, for the journeymen's ascension within the guild.

The points were scattered throughout the capital of Brianta—one thousand of them. Each was dedicated to a different god, forming the start for pilgrims' journeys. A priest was stationed at each point, offering a parchment scroll and an ornate wax seal. Pilgrims planned carefully before beginning their travels, plotting a course through Brianta so that a personal series of gods watched over their journeys.

The lucky pilgrims, the ones who had both money and time, would leave Brianta then. They would travel to distant shrines made sacred to their chosen gods, or to places holy to the First Pilgrim. At each stage of their journey, they would add to their cavalcade, to the scroll that recorded their worship.

The most faithful of the pilgrims would make their way to Morenia, tracing Jair's own path. Jair had lived out the final decades of his life in Moren, and he had died in that city. Each year, hundreds of pilgrims arranged to be in Moren for the annual re-creation of Jair's arrival in the city, for the presentation of the First Pilgrim.

"So, the survey is finished," Parion repeated.

"Yes, Master. I have instructed one of the younger journeymen to copy over the figures. I'll deliver them to you before the end of the day."

"And what do they tell us?"

"Much as we expected. There are only forty-three cavalcade points that boast full churches."

Forty-three. That left hundreds of opportunities. Parion

forced himself not to leap ahead too far in his plans. "And are there windows in each of those churches?"

"Certainly. Some of them are quite good, in fact. We need not direct our attentions to them for a while."

"And the ones that are not churches?"

"There are four hundred and twenty-two buildings. Mostly single rooms, in priests' houses or in shops that are sacred to a particular god."

"Windows?"

"In a handful. Not many. The owners of the rooms would likely be grateful for anything that we offer."

"And the others? What about the other gods? It's what— more than five hundred?"

"Nothing."

"Nothing?"

"They have altars. Small shelters for priests, little more than single walls to protect a candle flame. The priests don't stay there on a daily basis; they visit only occasionally. Once a week, perhaps, to attend to pilgrims' needs, to stamp their cavalcades and send the faithful on their way."

"And those altars, are they decorated?"

"They have cloths. The faithful bring flowers in season, or other devotional offerings."

"And glass?"

"At none of them."

"None." Parion repeated the word, breathing in as if he spoke a prayer. None. The gods were being neglected. Eighty glasswrights here in Brianta. More than five hundred altars. They could craft symbols for the abandoned gods, Larinda and the other journeymen who were ready to rise to master status. They could recognize the power and the glory of each deity. Parion said, "I'll need the list."

"It will be done by this afternoon."

"Very good." Already, he could see the whitewashed tables, could imagine his people hard at work. The emblems they would create would be fine work, worthy of the accolade *master.*

The neglected third-tier gods would exalt in the attention. The priests would be grateful, eager to recompense such a pious guild. They would use the glasswrights' devotion to inspire activity by other guildsmen, more concrete examples of craft offered up in honor of faith. The priests would preach about the glory of the glasswrights who offered up their art and skill in service of the gods.

And even if the priests didn't pay for the new altarpieces outright, the pilgrims would. They would make offerings at the cavalcade points. They would seek out glasswrights to create replicas of the insignias, reproductions of the masterpieces. The guild could create a form book, a description of each piece and how it should be made. Apprentices could learn their craft by practicing on those forms. Journeymen could set the pieces, stain them, solder them. A master could certify them—yes, a stamp would be necessary. Each medallion would have a lead tag, an official designation, proving that it was issued by a master glasswright.

The guild could sell them at the larger cavalcade points— the more senior apprentices could work the transactions. The complete set would be available to interested pilgrims who visited the guildhall itself.

Would anyone want all of the medallions? Was there a nobleman in all the world devoted enough—and wealthy enough—to want one thousand emblems? One thousand and one, Parion quickly remonstrated with himself. He mustn't forget Jair. The guild would create a separate symbol for the Pilgrim, for the man who defined true faith in all the Thousand Gods.

"Very good, Larinda," Parion forced himself to say. "Send me the list as soon as it is complete, and we will begin to plot our course among the points. You'll be working on your masterpiece by the end of summer."

"Thank you, Master." The gratitude in her voice was palpable. "I look forward to serving the guild." Like a good journeyman, she bowed her head as she left his study, nearly managing to avoid a last longing glance at the Hand on Parion's worktable.

He waited until the door closed before he turned back to the window, to the view of all Brianta that spread before him. His fingers automatically pushed aside the piece of parchment, and he cradled the medallion that Morada had made so long ago, in simpler days.

"We'll have our vengeance yet, my love. We'll raise the glasswrights up. We'll turn our guild into an instrument of power. And when we have the money, when we have the dedication, when we have the zeal of hundreds of glasswrights, educated and true, then all will rue the day that our Morenian guild was destroyed!"

Parion bent his head and muttered a few formulaic prayers to Clain. It was a good thing that he had mastered the words as a young apprentice, for he would never have been able to repeat them otherwise, with his mind flying from topic to topic, from plan to plan.

"In the name of Clain, amen," he concluded, and he set Morada's gift upon the table.

It took him only a moment to find a bottle of ink. He tested his glass pen against his fingertip, then held it up to the golden sunlight that streamed through the window. It would do. He watched the ink drip from its smooth edge, leaving behind a perfect film. His hand was firm as he started to write to the Traitor: *From Parion, master of the Glasswrights' Guild, to Ranita, who once counted herself among our number . . .*

3

Berylina Thunderspear ran her tongue over her lips, knowing that the motion only emphasized the thrust of her jaw, drawing attention to the rabbit teeth that had plagued her for her entire life. She could not help herself. She licked her lips when she was nervous, when she fought for the courage to make an argument. And the current argument was worth fighting for.

She lifted her chin and said, "Father, we have discussed this many times. You agreed before. What made you change your mind?"

Siritalanu sighed and shook his brow. A frown creased his brow, adding unexpected age to the priest's round face. The familiar lines around his mouth were pulled down into an uncharacteristic frown, and beads of sweat greased his flesh. He refused to meet her eyes, directing his gaze to his hands, which clenched and unclenched in his lap.

Berylina rarely argued with her mentor. Generally, they both understood the importance of worshiping the Thousand Gods. They both knew the actions they must take to preserve their piety, to honor the gods. All the more reason for her to push him this time—she was certain that she was right, even if Siritalanu now thought otherwise.

"Your Highness," he began, but she cut him off before he could press his argument.

"I am not speaking to you as a princess. You may not put me off like that." The firmness in her voice astonished her. Nevertheless, if she allowed Siritalanu to address her as royalty, then he could claim moral superiority. He could claim greater knowledge of the gods, of their expectations. If the priest considered her a penitent, though, a loyal caloya . . . She had to swallow hard before she could say, "Father, I am speaking to you as one of the faithful."

"But no woman of faith would ever make your demand!"

Berylina shook her head. "Are you saying that none of the players have faith, Father? That is not the lesson that you've taught me in the past. The church says that all men and women have faith if they come to the Thousand Gods with open hearts and uplifted souls."

"You twist my words, my lady."

"Perhaps it is your *thoughts* that are twisted!" Berylina said bitterly, before she could stop herself. What was she doing? She must watch her tongue! She was speaking to a priest, after all, even if he *was* Siritalanu, the one man she trusted most in the entire world. What was she saying? "I'm sorry, Father," she whispered. "I did not mean that."

Shame washed over her, painting her cheeks with all-too-familiar heat. Why could she not speak to people properly? She was of the house of Thunderspear, after all. Any other princess would not hesitate to order a common priest to do her will! Any other princess would speak with command, with authority. She would stand tall and gaze coldly. She would keep her voice firm.

But Berylina had never been like any other princess.

Whenever she spoke, her voice broke against her rabbit teeth. Strangers looked away from her cast eyes, unable to stomach her shattered gaze. Her brittle hair stood out from her scalp, as if she had been caught in a windstorm. Everyone who saw her knew that she was flawed, that she was broken. People with the best of intentions believed that she was an idiot. Others claimed that she was evil, stricken at birth as vengeance for her parents' sins. No one believed that Berylina could have anything important to say or think or do.

"My lady . . ." But Father Siritalanu was different. He saw past Berylina's physical self. He looked beyond her face, beyond her hair. He understood the shape of her soul, the perfection that she offered up in her heart in service to all the Thousand Gods. He knew her perfect passion, the faith that burned inside her. "My lady, you must know that I do not mean to cause you displeasure."

"But it would please me beyond telling to offer up this worship to the Thousand Gods."

"My lady, what you propose may be heresy!"

"Is it heresy to find the depths of the gods within you? To travel the paths of our minds—minds that the gods themselves created—to find the way that they wish to be worshiped? Is it heresy to Speak to the Thousand Gods?"

"But you would not be Speaking with the gods, my lady." The priest answered her emotional outburst with quiet anguish. "You would be Speaking with me."

"And you are the messenger of the gods in this world!"

"A messenger, my lady! Not the gods themselves! What if I am flawed? What if I am not worthy to guide you on that path!"

Berylina heard the despair in the priest's voice, the raw fear behind his words. Father Siritalanu—the man who had rescued her from the shame of living in her father's home, the priest who had saved her from a kingdom that worshiped an unholy goddess of blood and death, who had kept her from being traded off as a chattel to Halaravilli ben-Jair— Father Siritalanu was *afraid*.

"Father!" Berylina exclaimed. "You cannot doubt yourself in this!"

"I doubt myself in all aspects of your spiritual life, my lady. Every morning when I rise, I ask if I am wise enough to guide your worship. Every evening, I question if I have kept you on the proper path."

"But you are a priest, Father Siritalanu. You are *my* priest."

"Nothing has trained me for such an honor, my lady. When I came to the priesthood as a boy, they trained me in the ways of ritual. They taught me formulas to honor the gods. They taught me traditions."

"But when the gods guide us, we create new traditions, Father."

"How am I to know, though? How am I to know if what you ask is guidance from the gods, or merely the voice of your pride?" She caught her breath at the accusation, and he hastened to add, "Pride most deservedly taken, my lady! In all my studies, in all my speaking to my fellow priests, I have never heard of a penitent who receives such inspiration as you. The gods speak to you in ways that most men only dream. Who am I to measure that? Who am I to direct it?"

"You trusted me enough to talk to the players when I asked, to learn how they go about their Speaking."

"My lady, I would talk to anyone, if you but asked me. You know that I am devoted to you."

"Then what has changed? Why are you now afraid to guide me down the players' path?"

"No one has ever done such a thing in service to the Thousand Gods."

Berylina took a deep breath, and her nose was filled with the perfume of lilac, the familiar signal of Hin, the god of rhetoric. She fought the urge to stretch her lips into a rabbity smile. With Hin guiding her, she knew that she would win this debate. She placed her words carefully, setting them between two lilac-scented breaths. "And if Speaking is new, then you think it must be evil?"

"I do not know, my lady!"

The fragrance grew even more intense. "What if the first priests had feared to raise up altars to the gods?"

"Don't be ridiculous, my lady."

"What if the first priests had feared to light candles for the gods?" The aroma was so intense that it seemed a physical structure in the air around her.

"My lady—"

"What if the first priests had feared to speak their prayers aloud?" Hin was beside her, *in*side her, crafting her arguments for her.

"That's absurd, my lady!"

"Is it? Can you say, in the name of Hin, that those arguments are absurd?"

Father Siritalanu sighed and shrugged, clasping and unclasping his hands. The motion seemed to free Hin, to let the god wander away, but the priest appeared unaware of the departure. "No, my lady. By Hin, I cannot answer those arguments with rhetoric."

Berylina pressed her advantage, silently sending a prayer of gratitude to the departed deity. "Then perhaps Speaking is merely the next form of worship that the gods desire. Perhaps it is like the prayers that people spoke within their minds, before they were moved to pray aloud."

"Perhaps . . ." The priest sighed.

Berylina sensed that he was nearly ready to concede. She pushed: "When you met with the players, did you feel that the gods were displeased?"

"No, my lady."

"Did the skies grow dark? Did the day grow chill?"

"Of course not."

"Did your body cramp up with pain? Did your mind seize so that you could not think of the words you wanted to say?"

"No."

"Then, Father, the gods were not disturbed by your learning to Speak."

"They have not shown their displeasure. Yet."

"Then we should try. We should attempt to add Speaking to the ways in which we honor the gods. Give yourself up to the Thousand, Father. If they want to change our actions, they have the power."

"Yes, my lady," the priest whispered, and Berylina swallowed a smile.

She was so certain that she was right. She had often heard Ranita Glasswright tell of Speaking; she understood the power of that state, the force of the mind. To harness that energy in service to the Thousand Gods . . .

Before Berylina could say anything else, though, a bell began to toll. Deep and steady, the tone sent a long shiver down her spine. Tarn's Knell. The largest of the cathedral's bronze bells rang only to summon the faithful to funerals, to the trying services before bodies of the faithful were committed to their pyres.

More time had passed in argument than Berylina had realized. Convincing Siritalanu had taken the entire morning. She should have been at the cathedral long ago. She had planned to offer up extra prayers before the day's service. Now she would be hard-pressed to summon even one of the gods.

"Come, Father," Berylina said. "We'll continue this later. We'll see what the gods think of Speaking after the funeral."

Berylina threw a cloak over her simple gown, taking only a moment to tuck her wiry hair beneath a veil. She still reveled in her green garments, in the bright declaration of her faith. She had not yet spoken her formal vows to the church—she was waiting to do that in Brianta, in the very homeland of First Pilgrim Jair—but Siritalanu had agreed that she might dress as a caloya, a woman sworn to give her life in service to the church. She had earned that much with her faith and devotion. She had been granted that much by the gods who came to her, presenting themselves with their wonderful and unpredictable presences, their scents and tastes and sights.

Siritalanu led her from her apartments in the royal palace, walking rapidly through the city streets. They passed few people, for Moren was officially in mourning. All of the shops had been ordered closed in honor of the day's grim business, and many homes were draped with somber black banners.

Berylina knew these Morenian passages well; she traveled back and forth to the cathedral several times each day. In fact, she had considered asking King Halaravilli to let her reside in the cathedral close, to live among the priests and their caloyas. She had not found the courage to make such a request, though. It would be easier after she had traveled to Brianta, after she had a stamped and sealed cavalcade to evidence the depth of her devotion.

The square in front of the House of the Thousand Gods was filled with mourners— nobles, merchants, guildsmen, soldiers, even a few Touched on the edges of the crowd. The cathedral itself would already be filled with nobles and priests, members of the royal family's own caste. Nevertheless, all the people of Moren felt their liege lord's pain; all wished to express their sorrow with prayer, with chanting, with offerings to the gods.

Berylina was not surprised when Siritalanu skirted the edge of the House, bringing her to the transept door. The crowds were thinner there, and people yielded to the power of their paired green robes. Berylina inclined her head in gratitude, keeping her eyes directed toward her feet. A flush spread across her cheeks as she thought of all the people who watched her. Suddenly, it was difficult to swallow. She fought the urge to clench her hands into fists, to shrink away to nothingness.

Without asking, Father Siritalanu understood where Berylina would like to offer up her special funerary devotions. He guided her to the large side chapel that was dedicated to Nome. On an ordinary day, the god of children was greeted by thousands of worshipers; his altar was broad, and the ceiling of the chamber was obscured with soot from the candles that burned to his glory. Today, every inch of altar space was aflame with lit tapers.

Berylina's hand trembled as she selected her own candle to add, forfeiting a heavy gold coin in exchange. She waited for a trio of women to edge away from the altar, and she ignored the pitying stares they cast upon her face. Instead, she moved forward to the empty space before the block of marble, dropping to her knees. She raised her candle to one that already burned, using the existing flame to kindle her own.

The wick caught and flared high, drawing Berylina's attention to the carved letters on the front of the altar. NOME. Each letter was carved deep, the marble rising into strong minims, curling into delicate horizontal strokes. As Berylina opened her mind to the god of children, she heard his name inside her thoughts, heard the jaunty piper's air that was his unique signature.

Of course, she could not *hear* all the gods. Some came to her as colors. Some were scents. A few were flavors, spread out across her tongue. Berylina knew that she was different, that her sensing the gods' physical presences was strange and wonderful. She pitied the other worshipers, the ones who saw only marble and paint, only candle flames left by petitioners. They missed so much. They never knew the true nature of the beings they prayed to.

Nome preserve us, she thought as she settled onto her knees. *Nome keep us safe from harm.*

That was a ridiculous prayer, though. *She* wasn't in any danger. She did not need Nome to watch over her. No, she should have prayed to the god of children a fortnight ago. She should have appealed to him when he first played a few notes for her on that sunny morning when she was walking to King Halaravilli's new silk hall.

She had heard Nome beside her then. She knew him well—he had come to her often when she still lived in Liantine. On the day of the silk auction, she had heard his piping air, like the songs that her nurses sang to her in her

Liantine nursery when she was a young child. Nome had played urgently the day of the silk bidding, pushing his notes into her morning prayers. She had heard him when she knelt at the prie-dieu in the corner of her room, and again when she passed the Children's Fountain in the middle of the Nobles' Quarter. The carved toys that were suspended from the ancient font had danced in the morning breeze, their jointed arms swinging, their heads bobbing as if they moved in time to the god's music.

Berylina had tried to silence Nome in frustration. She had been intent on reaching out to Lor, trying to gather in the peppery scent of the god of silk. After all, she was going to honor Lor in the name of King Halaravilli. She was going to invoke the god's blessing on the new guildish venture. She had thought that she had no time for Nome's frivolous games.

If only she had listened to Nome's music . . . if she had just let the god tell her all that he had to say! She had even been drawing that morning before she left for the guildhall. He could have folded his fingers around her own, guided her hand across the page. She might have depicted Queen Mareka's bedchamber, the tall window that looked over the town. She might have drawn the balcony, with its raised stone bench, with the curious, steep stairs that led from the queen's apartments to the balustrade. She might have seen the queen pacing outside her rooms, ignoring her physicians as she took the sun, as she leaned out to see the strong, proud lines of the distant silk hall.

In the days since the disaster, Berylina had told herself that things might have been worse. The queen could have toppled over the edge of the balcony, fallen into the court-yard below. If that had happened, Queen Mareka would have lost her own life along with those of the twins that she bore.

Instead, the queen had yielded to her chiding ladies-in-waiting. She had agreed to return to her curtained bed.

Blinded by the brilliant sunshine as she approached the steep stairs, the queen had turned to look over her shoulder, imagining that she could hear the silk master cry out "Sold!" for the first lot of cloth. She had placed her foot unsteadily on the stone edge, and she had turned her ankle, toppling on the joint that was swollen from pregnancy. She had reached out to catch herself, but she had missed the stone upright of the window. Six stairs. Six stone steps, and then the queen had fetched up sharply against the leg of a wooden table.

Even now, Berylina could imagine the flurry in the queen's chambers. She knew that the gods had been invoked: minty Zake for chirurgeons, salty Chine for mothers. Piping Nome, for children, of course.

And for several long minutes, those prayers had seemed enough. The gods had shifted to a new balance. They had spun about in their eternal dance, touching each other, moving into patterns, embracing and protecting the people who offered up prayers to them.

Queen Mareka had been eased into her bed, covered with woolen blankets. She had sobbed in frustration and pain, snapping at the noble lady who attempted to tend to her twisted ankle. One attendant ran for wine, another for water, to lay cool cloths upon the royal foot.

And then the birth pangs started.

When it was all over, Nome had come to Berylina, piping his lament. He had explained that the princes had come too soon. No god could work all miracles. Nome could not stop actions that had already begun. The queen's womb was injured by her tumble down the stairs, by her crash against the table—Nome could not stop that. The twins were startled to wakefulness by the fall—no god could change that, either.

If there had been one infant, Nome might have proven strong enough. But he'd needed to divide his attention between two young charges; he'd needed to breathe life into two fragile bodies. In the end, the princes were too small. There was nothing to be done.

Tarn gathered up the royal heirs. The god of death folded them beneath his green-black cloak, hiding the light of their souls under silk that shimmered like a beetle's wings. He carried them off before they ever tasted life in the palace, before they ever had a chance to live their royal lives. Nome had relinquished his hold with a sad shrug, a skirling of pipes that was almost lost on the summer breeze.

So why was Berylina lighting a candle to him now? Why was she trying to summon his music, to bring forth the god? She could not settle her reasoning into words. Nome would understand, though. He would know that she would not ignore his warnings again. She would not overlook his piping for thoughts of another god, even for Lor, the silk god.

She stayed on her knees until Tarn's Knell ceased its tolling, the heavy clang trailing off into murmur-dusted silence. Usually, Berylina loved the sound of a fading campanile—the cathedral bells summoned worshipers each week, ushering all the faithful into the House of the Thousand Gods. Hidden in the notes, Berylina could hear an entire symphony of gods, a thousand voices singing out amid the metal tones.

Tarn's Knell was different, though. It was lonely. Sad.

Berylina pulled herself to her feet, casting one last glance at the candle she had lit. Wax had melted around the wick, a clear pool that shimmered in the chapel's heat. She imagined submerging herself in the circle, searing away her human flesh until she was nothing but devotion to the gods, nothing but pure, unformed worship.

There was no time, though, for such fantasies of faith. She must attend King Halaravilli. She must offer up her prayers that the newest royal twins might be received beyond the Heavenly Gates.

Siritalanu was waiting for her, of course. He took her arm as she left Nome's chapel, and he eased her through the throng that filled the cathedral. The tall nave was crowded with folk who came to honor their king, to mourn with him, yet again, for lost heirs.

This time was the worst. Two sons gone. Two perfect boys—ten fingers each, ten toes. Flawless rosebud lips and ears that folded against their tiny skulls like wisps of parchment. They were so small. . . .

Berylina wished that she had not seen the children. She knew that the memory would haunt her dreams for months; the dead twins would hover in front of her eyes when she should be seeing the gods. She would smell the ladanum upon their tiny bodies when she should be breathing the fragrance of one of the Thousand. She would hear their tiny cries, the pitiful mews that they had managed before their chests fell still in the summer afternoon.

Now that they had lost their battle, Berylina must bear witness to their struggle. That was her fate, after all—to bear witness for the house of ben-Jair. The Thousand Gods had had a reason to raise her up from her own home, to carry her forth from her land of infidels. She had journeyed across the sea to this new home so that she could attest to the power of the Thousand Gods in the lives of men, in the lives of the royal family.

Father Siritalanu understood. That was why he brought her to the front ranks of the nobles. That was why he guided her to stand with the priests and the caloyas of the king's own household. She had a clear view of Holy Father Dartulamino when he stepped onto the dais in the middle of the transept.

The Holy Father's face was drawn, dark, as if the children he mourned were his own. Cloth of gold draped across his shoulders, weighing down his green robes. The priest's dark eyes were hooded, and his handsome face was grave. He raised a commanding hand, and all eyes followed the arch of his fingers, turning to look down the nave of the church.

The crowd parted slowly, as if people were reluctant to look upon unbridled grief. From Berylina's vantage point, she could see anxious faces; she could make out anger and sorrow and more than a little fear.

The king and queen were dressed in full mourning attire. Their robes were dyed deepest black, stiffened with somber embroidery that made each step seem like a rigid military march. King Halaravilli had placed a pounded iron crown upon his head, its heavy band his sole concession to royal status in the House of the Thousand Gods. He moved like a man defeated, like an ancient warrior bowed beneath a conquering army. His face was haggard, and Berylina wondered if he had slept in the fortnight since the silk sale. He should not be burning more babes; he should not be offering up more fallen heirs on funeral pyres.

Queen Mareka leaned heavily on her husband's arm. Her slight body nearly disappeared in her stiff mourning gown; the fabric swallowed up her slender limbs. Her face was pale as whey in the afternoon light, and her flesh took on an unhealthy glow as she passed through the jeweled tones of the stained-glass windows set high in the cathedral walls. Queen Mareka moved like a broken woman, like a grandmother tottering toward an unclean grave. She limped as she walked beside her husband, clearly favoring the ankle that had turned so cruelly, that had betrayed her so completely.

Holy Father Dartulamino waited until his king and queen stood before him. "Greetings to all in the name of the Thousand Gods."

"May all the gods bless you," Berylina responded with the crowd.

"I come before you with a heavy heart," the priest said. "Throughout our lives, we all must witness the work of Tarn. We all must greet the god of death and recognize the dominion that he holds over us, for Tarn will gather each of us beneath his cloak when our course is done."

Each time the priest spoke the name of the god of death,

Berylina saw a flash of green-black, the iridescence of an insect wing, hovering above King Halaravilli. Her heart went out to the man, and she wished that she could spare him, that she could shield him from Tarn's cold attentions.

After all, the king had tried to be kind to her. Even when he courted her. Even when he intended to marry her, beneath the hateful eyes of the Horned Hind. She could understand that now. She had grown so much since she left her father's court. Before, when King Halaravilli had wooed her, she had been so afraid. She had thought that he meant to have her only to bolster his own treasury, only to add to his store of gold.

Now she knew that Halaravilli was a religious man. He took his obligations as Defender of the Faith seriously. He extended his protection to her even though she had no gold left to give. He made sure that Berylina had parchment for her drawings, and chalk and ink and whatever else she required.

Holy Father Dartulamino continued with the funeral service. Perhaps it was easier for the king and queen, knowing that the prayers they spoke aloud were the standard prayers of death, the same words that had been choked out by grieving parents for centuries. In the eyes of the Thousand Gods, there was nothing special about the loss of the princes, no particular failure on the part of Queen Mareka or the king. Standing in the cathedral, they were not required to act as royalty; they did not need to lead all of Morenia. Rather, they could be parents—simple, grieving parents.

It was customary to display possessions of the dead upon the altar during a funeral service. The royal princes, though, had not yet owned a thing. They had been birthed so soon that they had not received a single gift from any lord or lady, from any distant land.

Berylina sighed. Ordinarily, eager nobles would have sent treasures to commemorate Queen Mareka's pregnancy. People had waited this time. They must have been uncertain, after the losses of the other babes. They had not wanted to waste their gold, their ivory, their gifts of greeting.

Nevertheless, two plaques sat upon the altar, hurried emblems that had been crafted to honor the children. One was carved with the arms of ben-Jair, the king's proud lion twisting in low relief. The other captured the queen's arms—or those of her former guild, at least. An octolaris spider rose from the wooden surface, its eight legs arched high above its back. A web traced across the wooden surface, symbol of the silk that Mareka had brought to Morenia.

Raising his hands above the plaques, Father Dartulamino intoned: "Hail Nome, god of children, guide of Jair the Pilgrim. Look upon these pilgrims with mercy in your heart and justice in your soul. Guide the feet of these pilgrims on righteous paths of glory that all may be done to honor you and yours among the Thousand Gods. These pilgrims ask for the grace of your blessing, Nome, god of children."

Once again, Berylina heard Nome's high pipes, but his tune was mournful now, fleeting. She could not help but look about the cathedral, to examine the other worshipers, to see if any of them heard the notes.

Apparently, none did.

After Holy Father Dartulamino completed the traditional death prayer to Nome, he moved on to summon other gods. There was Tak, of course, the god of spiders, in honor of the grieving mother. Berylina heard a clarion call, like a hunter's horn in the woods. There was Fen, the god of mercy. Berylina smelled fresh-baked bread, hot from the oven. The priest invoked Ote, the god of peace, and Berylina blinked against the shimmering gold of a summer sunset.

And then, of course, the priest summoned Tarn. Berylina fell to her knees with the other worshipers, buffeted by waves of green and black. She knew that she knelt on marble; she knew that she wore a dress of plain green silk. Yet everything before her eyes seemed different, shimmering, empowered by the god.

Berylina recited the familiar prayer, rolling the individual words over her tongue without paying attention to them. The final phrase echoed in the cathedral, breathed by hundreds of worshipers: "These pilgrims ask for the grace of your blessing, Tarn, god of death."

Through her shimmering fog, Berylina saw Queen Mareka topple to one side, overcome by great sobs. King Halaravilli tried to slip an arm around his lady, to ease her back onto her knees, but the queen was too distraught. The Holy Father set his jaw and made a subtle hand gesture for a pair of green-clad caloyas to step forward and assist.

"It is not fair!" the queen wailed from the marble floor. "Tarn takes too much! He has enough of my children! The Heavenly Gates are dripping with my children's blood!" The religious women gathered around the queen, patting her black-clad arms with their soft hands. The queen, though, recoiled from their green garments as if the women burned her. She struggled to her knees and raised a defiant fist to the Holy Father. "This is not fair, Priest! No god should ask this of a mother!"

Father Dartulamino pitched his voice softly. "The gods do not ask, Your Majesty."

"That, at least, is true!" Queen Mareka cried. "They ask nothing. They take! They steal! They murder innocent babes!"

"No one was murdered, Your Majesty."

"Tell that to my children! Tell that to the corpses that await the pyre outside. Tell that . . ." The queen trailed off, her words lost in hysterical sobs as she collapsed back to the marble floor. King Halaravilli hovered over her, trying to settle a soothing hand upon her brow. The queen twisted away from him, writhing as if she were a fish caught on a line. Her sobs rose to the transept vaulting, filling the church with the raw passion of a mother denied.

"My lady . . ." the king said. "Please, Mareka. Please . . ."

The queen, though, did not acknowledge her husband's

whispered words. King Halaravilli glanced wildly at the
Holy Father, at the caloyas who still clustered ineffectually
around his wife.

They did not understand. They did not know how Mareka
Octolaris's mind worked.

All of a sudden, Berylina's mouth filled with the taste of
peach. The flavor surged across her tongue, coating her
throat as if she had bitten into the ripest summer fruit. She
caught her breath at the purity of the flavor, at the sheer
force of the sensation. What god was this? She did not remember having felt his touch before, having swallowed his
intoxicating nature.

She reached inside her thoughts, calming the still, small
place inside her, as Father Siritalanu had taught her to do.
Taking a deep breath, she gathered in the essence of peach
once again, rolled it across the back of her tongue. There . . .
Almost . . . Nim! The god of wind.

Berylina hastily spoke a prayer in her mind. *Hail, Nim,
god of wind. Greetings in this house dedicated to all the
Thousand Gods.*

She scarcely hesitated as the power of the god enveloped
her. Nim reached inside her thoughts, gathering up her
prayer with his grasping fingers. He swirled through her
awareness, wrapping her in the flavor of peach, in the overwhelming essence of fruit.

Nim. The unbridled power of the winds that blew across
the high plains of Liantine. The force that made the long,
green grass lie down in rippling waves, like fold after fold
of softest silk . . . Nim, who had encircled the spiderguild in
Liantine, who had cradled the stronghold in the grip of
storm, in the flow of daily life. Nim, who would be the comfort of any member of the spiderguild, forever and always.
Nim, who had watched a young apprentice grow up in the
shelter of her family and her craftsmen, who had watched a
young woman discover and create the meaning of her life.

Berylina was barely aware of the crowd behind her as she

stepped up to the dais. She edged past the Holy Father, skirting the king of all Morenia. She scarcely saw her hands passing between those of the green-clad caloyas, only vaguely realized that she was kneeling before the altar. Kneeling beside her queen.

The flavor of peach was flooding her mouth, flowing through her body, commanding her heart and her lungs and her brain. "My lady," she whispered. "You must take strength, Your Majesty."

"There is no strength!"

"There is, my lady." Berylina reached out one hand, settled her fingertips against the desperate woman's lips. She felt the power of Nim flow through her, felt the touch of peach wash against Queen Mareka, as clearly as if nectar dripped onto the royal lips. "There is strength, my lady. Strength in Nim."

"Nim . . ."

"The god of wind, Your Majesty. He has watched you since you were a child." Berylina heard the god inside her head, understood the words that he whispered. "He has seen you stand strong before. He knows your core. He knows that you can conquer this loss. You can rise up now. You can do what must be done."

The queen merely cried out in agony, devastation etching her face, her hands, every fiber of her body.

Berylina closed her crossed eyes, drew her vision inside her mind. How often had she done this? How often had she closed out the distorted view of the world, the sights that passed unreliably through her skewed gaze? In the darkness of her inner sight, she could make out a child-Mareka huddled on a cot, a frightened girl, an apprentice away from her family for the first time. She saw the same child standing in the spiderguild's riberry groves, afraid to climb a tree. She saw the girl reaching out to feed a hungry octolaris. At each of these tests, the girl-Mareka had been surrounded by the wind, bolstered by Nim, even if she had been unaware of the god's presence.

Berylina forced her voice to be strong, let her inner conviction harden her words more than she had ever dared before. She proclaimed, "Nim has been with you, my lady. In the guild, he stood beside you from the first day that you took your apprentice oath. Think of the wind on the high plain. Think of the god's touch as he smiled upon you."

Queen Mareka quieted, her sobs dying off as she listened to Berylina's words. The queen darted her tongue across her lips, as if she were collecting the sweet nectar of Berylina's vision. "He has," she whispered. "He watched over my presentation to the guild."

"He has watched over all that you have done. All the difficult choices that you ever made. He came to me just now, Your Majesty. He came to remind me, to remind you, that you can do this terrible thing. You can find the strength. You *must* find the strength." The queen held out her hands to Berylina, and the princess helped the older woman to stand. "Nim will watch over you, my lady. He will not abandon you."

Mareka raised her eyes to the altar, to the wooden plaques that represented her lost sons. She drew one shuddering breath, and for an instant Berylina feared that the god might have played her false. She could still taste peach at the back of her throat, though. Nim was still in the cathedral. He still attended his neediest worshiper.

"Come, my lady," Berylina said. "Let us go with the priests to the courtyard."

"The pyre." Mareka's voice was dead as she spoke the two words.

"Aye, my lady. It must be done. But Nim will be there. He will carry your children to the Heavenly Fields. He will usher them into life everlasting."

"Nim will be there."

"He watches over you, my lady. He loves you."

"Nim . . ." Queen Mareka turned to the Holy Father as if she had only just discovered the religious man upon the dais. "I am sorry, Father. I meant no disrespect."

"The Thousand Gods are understanding, Your Majesty." Dartulamino delivered the benediction with an arched eyebrow, and he spared a long glance for Berylina.

Still hesitating, the queen turned to her husband. "My lord. I am sorry." She seemed to be speaking of more than the service, of more than her emotional collapse.

King Halaravilli's eyes filled with tears as he stepped beside his wife. He took her hands between both of his and said, "No apologies, my lady. None are necessary. Let us finish this grim business, that you may return to your chambers and get your rest."

Queen Mareka pulled free from her husband and closed both her hands around Berylina's arm. The bones stood out from her flesh as if she were a starving child. "Please! Come with us, Berylina. Come into the courtyard!"

"I will not leave you, my lady." Berylina helped the queen step down from the dais. Nim hovered nearby, filling the princess's mouth with peach as the procession edged out of the cathedral.

Outside the building, the summer sun shone, as if the day were made for a festival. The sky was blue. Birds sang from their perches on the marble roof of the House of the Thousand Gods. Queen Mareka clutched at Berylina's arm almost like a blind woman, as if she needed to draw from the princess's strength to set one foot in front of the other.

Berylina felt Nim's touch rise, a headier flavor, a riper taste. A breeze whipped around the corner of the building, bringing with it the smell of smoke. The queen stumbled, clearly not prepared to take these final steps, but Berylina said, "Hail, Nim, god of wind. He is come to us across the ocean, across the plain. Gather in the stories of your children, my lady, and bring them to Nim now."

The queen appeared to take comfort in the words. At

least, she managed to step forward, to move around the corner of the building. She could not keep from crying out, though, as she saw the pyre constructed in the center of the vast cathedral close.

The iron framework stood in the center of the charred circle, towering high enough for dried faggots to be placed beneath it, around it. Two linen-wrapped bundles were centered on the platform, standing out against the metal like nightmares leaping forth from sleep.

Bundles of wood were stacked against the frame, lengths of hard oak. Even across the courtyard, Berylina could smell the oil, the sacred chrism that would guarantee that the fire caught and burned hot. Two green-clad priests stood beside the pyre, each holding a flaming torch. The fire paled in the bright light of midday.

Holy Father Dartulamino crossed the close as if he were destined for some grim marketplace. King Halaravilli followed more slowly, his pale face falling as he neared the iron platform. Queen Mareka's grip tightened on Berylina's hand, cinching tighter, pulling the princess closer. Berylina wanted to protest, wanted to spare her crushed bones, but she could not abandon her country-woman.

"And so we gather beneath the eyes of all the Thousand Gods," Father Dartulamino intoned. "We gather before this worldly representation of the gates to the Heavenly Fields, this stand of iron and wood that seems for us, if only for a moment, to be a passage into the next world, into life beyond, where we will find peace and joy and life everlasting."

The priest knelt before the iron stand, inclining his head in silent prayer for a long minute. Berylina watched King Halaravilli fall to his own knees, his lips moving in some heartfelt salute. She wondered for a moment what gods the king might call upon to guide his children. Queen Mareka pulled the princess down beside her, and Berylina could just make out a single whispered word: "Nim . . ."

The Holy Father reached out to a golden plate that was embedded in the earth on the edge of the burned circle. His fingers closed upon a loaf of bread, a perfect circle that had been baked that morning in the priests' most sacred oven. "Prince Marekivilli ben-Jair, we present you with this bread to ease your journey to the Fields. Prince Halarameko ben-Jair, we present you with this bread to ease your journey to the Fields."

The Holy Father climbed to his feet and bowed deeply. Raising the perfectly round loaf above his head, he clenched his fingers, tearing the loaf into two equal parts. Turning to his king and queen, the priest offered up the funeral bread. Queen Mareka was unable to move, but the king stepped forward and took one of the pieces. He tore a morsel from the loaf and proffered it to his wife, setting it inside her open mouth when she seemed unable to handle it herself. King Halaravilli took a piece for himself, chewing slowly, as if he had never tasted bread before. Only when he had stretched his neck, swallowing audibly, did he return the loaf to Dartulamino. The priest stepped up to the iron framework, leaning the bread against each shrouded bundle.

Then the Holy Father stepped back and bowed again, rising with a golden cup in his hand. The blinding sunlight glinted off the rim of the goblet, sending a message to the heavens. "Prince Marekivilli, we present you with this wine to ease your journey through the Gates. Prince Halamareko, we present you with this wine to ease your journey through the Gates."

But first, of course, the priest presented the cup to his king and queen. Again, King Halaravilli helped his wife, holding the goblet so that she could swallow. For just an instant, Berylina thought that Mareka would not be able to act, but then she closed her eyes and gulped from the cup. Wine glistened on her lips as her husband followed suit, and the royal couple watched as the priest turned back to the pyre.

He poured the wine slowly, spilling half of it on one

shroud before turning to stain the other. When he stepped back, the crowd surged closer. They knew that there was only one prayer left to utter, one action left to take.

"May Nome watch over these children after they cross into the Heavenly Fields. May Gir wrap them in his robes of flame that they might reach the Gates with all possible speed. May Tarn gather them beneath his cloak and keep them safe from further harm."

A piped air indicated that Nome accepted his charge. Gir stepped forward with his gold-white robes, so cool for the god of fire. Tarn flashed again, green-black in Berylina's mind.

And then the Holy Father raised a hand. The two priests lowered their torches, thrusting the burning pitch into the stacks of oil-soaked wood. Flames leaped up immediately, orange and red and yellow tongues licking at the linen shrouds, the bread, the spill of wine.

King Halaravilli cried out, a wordless wail that carried across the courtyard like the fire stretching to the sky. Queen Mareka crumpled to her knees, her breath coming in short gasps as she sobbed, "Nim! Nim!"

Berylina sensed the presence of the god of wind and dozens of his brothers, all gathered to greet the royal princes. The taste of peach was overpowering, the flash of lights, the jangle of sounds. The princess caught her own breath, momentarily overcome by the visitation of so many holy beings.

And then she opened her eyes.

The gods had left. They had gathered up the spirits of the princes, begun the destruction of the physical shells that remained behind.

The cathedral close felt empty even though hundreds of men and women watched the pyre. Berylina heard the queen continue to call upon the god of wind, and she wondered that the woman could not tell that Nim had left. She thought about reaching out to smooth Queen Mareka's hair, to tell her that it was over, that the hard part was past, but there was no reason to steal away a comfort and a prop.

Instead, Berylina waited patiently, knowing that the shrouds would darken and curl, would crumble to ash. Then Berylina would return to the palace with the king and queen. She would kneel in the corner of her small room. Father Siritalanu would come to her, and she would share what she had seen, what she had felt, how she had come to know Nim completely.

And she would prepare for her journey to Brianta, to the homeland of Jair. She would make ready for her pilgrimage. She would submit to the Speaking, and she would open her heart to all the Thousand Gods.

4

Rani stepped from the shadows into the courtyard, blinking as her eyes adjusted to the brilliant summer sunshine. She was surprised to feel the heat radiating off the flagstones.

A chill had locked her spine when she read the urgent message that a page had carried to her tower chamber. She still held the parchment, curling the scrap between her fingers. She was surprised that the words excited her as much as they did—after all, she had spent more than ten years trying to convince herself that the glasswrights' guild did not matter, that she did not care.

Where was Tovin? What would he say when she showed him the message? She glanced about the courtyard but did not find the glasswright amid the working players.

The troop had taken advantage of the warm weather, stripping off their flowing cloaks and reducing their attire to their preferred tight jerkins and leggings. The simple clothes let them move more freely, tumbling and falling without fear of catching themselves on trailing sleeves and skirts.

Rani's first reaction was surprise at seeing the players in their practice clothes. After all, Hal's edict had been clear—there were to be no public performances of any kind for one year. One solid year, to mark the deaths of the princes.

Rani had tried to reason with him, had tried to explain

that an entire year was too long, would cost people too much. Hal had scarcely spared the energy to bridle at her; instead, he had sighed and asked her if her players needed a profit so badly that she was willing to risk offending all the Thousand Gods. Rani had been left spluttering an excuse.

So, whatever routine the players were practicing, it wasn't likely to be viewed by others for months. Nevertheless, the active performers could hardly do *nothing* throughout the official period of mourning. They needed to move; they needed to work; they needed to develop the diversions that would eventually help heal all of Morenia.

As Rani watched, four players climbed to the top of an iron cube. The structure was made from narrow metal bars; there were ample perches for feet and hands. The performers each selected a corner of the device, planting their bodies at unlikely angles. A player who stood on the ground began to count out an even beat, clapping her hands to set a rhythm. After a full count of eight, the players on the cube began their performance, springing from one bar to another.

The performers passed each other in the air. Sometimes, they merely flew like birds. Other times, they clasped hands, reversing the directions of their flights. Once, a pair of agile women twisted about a bar on top of the cube, rotating like fish leaping clear of the ocean.

All the time that the performers executed their leaps and lunges, the single woman stood on the ground, counting out the rhythm, controlling the performance, keeping the action steady and smooth. Rani caught her breath as all four acrobats completed an unlikely series of pirouettes in midair, and she took an involuntary step forward when one of the players slipped. The man caught himself easily, though, and he flew back into the routine, passing by his fellows as if he had not endangered the group's precarious balance.

All too soon, the players found themselves back at their original corners, clinging to the iron with hands that trembled from exertion. They waited until their entire company was steady, and then they shouted as one, pushing off the iron structure and landing on the flagstones. Each player tucked his head and tumbled forward, ending on one knee, with arms extended toward a supposed audience.

Rani threw back her head and laughed, clapping her hands together in sheer delight. "That was wonderful!" she exclaimed, looking at each of the performers. "I've never seen you practice that routine!"

The players rose to their feet, smiling to accept her praise. Even as Rani stepped forward to congratulate them further, the fifth player, the one who had counted out the pace, stepped up. What was her name? Rani knew it. . . . Ah, yes. Takela.

"That was all wrong!" the woman snapped. "Modu, if you take that much time to complete the circuit on the upper bars, Shareni will be stranded at the bottom. She needs the snap from your arms to send her back up to the top." Modu nodded, his handsome face dark as he stared at the iron stand. "And Shareni, you can't reach for the third bar on the last circuit. You won't leave any room for Robit's foot."

"But—"

"No argument. This is a matter of safety." Shareni swallowed further protest and nodded.

Rani felt sorry for the girl. Even she, untrained as a player, could see that there had been no other place for Shareni to rest her hand; she needed the third bar. Perhaps Robit should be asked to change *his* position. Or maybe they should add another beat to the rotation, give Shareni more time to find her place. Rani cleared her throat and stepped forward. "*I* thought that the balance was stunning. I thought that the piece was very well executed."

Takela looked up, as if she had just seen Rani for the first time. The player bowed deeply, crossing both arms over her chest in a theatrical flourish. The woman's blue-black hair rippled in the summer sunshine. "Ranita Glasswright. We

are honored that you've come to watch our humble practice."

Takela's use of the title brought back all the import of the
parchment that still curled inside Rani's hand. It also served
to drive a wedge between Rani and the players, to remind
them that she was their sponsor. Sighing as she watched the
friendly players transform into respectful professionals,
Rani reminded herself that she hardly had time for their diversions. She needed to speak with Tovin.

"Alas, Takela," she said, forcing her tone to be light, "I
fear I don't have time to watch your other routines. Is Tovin
here in the practice yard?"

"Aye, Glasswright. He's in the work shed." Takela nodded to the building that stood at the far end of the courtyard.
Rani offered her thanks and hurried across the flagstones. As
she reached the doorway of the shed, she looked back to the
players, noting that they had taken their places at the corners
of the cube once more. Takela was ready to start the count
again, to run them through the entire routine.

Before she could initiate the program, the sun passed behind a cloud, lending a sudden chill to the afternoon air.
Rani blinked, and the iron cube stood out in the new light,
harsh against the creamy flagstones. Rani was reminded of
the funeral pyre that had stood in the cathedral close, of the
bitter iron poles that stretched toward the Heavenly Gates.
She shuddered and thought a quick prayer for the dead
princes, the image of the funeral flames still fresh in her
mind after only four short days. Rani ducked through the
door of the shed.

Tovin was hunched over a table, peering closely at a
beaded mask. A brazier burned beside him, the contents of
an iron pot bubbling slowly atop the flame. He looked up as
she closed the door.

Rani heard Takela's steady clapping begin again, and she
said to Tovin, "Do you think the players are wise to create a
piece based on iron bars?"

He did not pretend to misunderstand her. "We cannot spend our lives afraid of iron."

"But it's so soon. The ashes have scarcely been raked."

"If the pyre had not burned for the princes, you would not question us. There are other mothers, other fathers, who lose their children every day."

He was right, of course. But the princes were different. Their loss belonged to more than just Hal and Mareka. All of Morenia suffered. She tried again. "But so many people saw this last pyre. So many came to honor the princes."

"And those are all the ones who will need assistance returning to their ordinary lives. They're the ones who must go back to the cathedral without fear, who must hear a child's cry without regret."

"But didn't you see the queen? She was destroyed by the princes' deaths."

"And you think that our players' roles will hurt her more? You think that we could add to the pain of a woman determined to feel guilt, determined to embrace responsibility for a foolish, terrible accident?"

"I think it would hurt her to see the production you plan."

"And since when do you live your life by what will hurt Mareka?"

She bristled at the coldness behind his words. "*Queen* Mareka."

"Aye. She bears that title."

"And King Halaravilli."

Tovin leaned his brush against the side of the boiling pot. "Then *that* is your concern? You fear that we players will hurt the man?"

Rani heard the transparent jealousy in Tovin's voice. How could she explain to him? How could she tell him that he had no reason to fear, that there was nothing, could never *be* anything between her and the king? She had recognized that hard truth three years before; she had built her life around that fact after Hal and Mareka had wed. Rani had chosen Tovin, but the player still did not trust her.

She made her voice steady. "I fear that you will hurt the king of all Morenia. I fear that you will cause him pain when it is not necessary to do so."

Tovin's eyes were copper pools as he studied her face. "Are you ordering your players not to practice this piece?"

"Of course not!"

"You are our patron here, Ranita. You have that power."

"I am not invoking that power. I am not speaking to you as the players' sponsor. I'm speaking to you as a Morenian. I'm speaking to you as a friend."

Tovin studied her earnest gaze, and then he nodded. "I'll think about your concerns."

"That is all I ask," Rani said. "That you consider the impact of what you do."

"The piece might not carry past the king's ban. We might tire of it by fall, or winter."

Consciously setting aside the debate, Rani stepped up to the table and peered at the brazier. She wrinkled her nose at the sharp smell. "What is that? What are you doing?"

Tovin smiled at her tone and waved at the viscous liquid. "That's glue. From rabbit skins. It has to be applied hot, but it will set fast and dry clear."

"And the mask?"

"We'll use it next summer. There will be four—one for each of the cardinal points."

"Then you've decided not to use panels any longer?" Rani could not keep the surprise from her voice.

"You have no need to worry about *that,*" Tovin said. "We'll have glass. Glass and costumes and music, too. The masks will only add to the production." He stirred the glue and sat back on his stool. "What is it, Ranita? You aren't usually so fearful about your status with the players. You're not afraid that I'll abandon you, are you?" He smiled wolfishly.

"I—" she started. "Don't look at me that way!"

"What way?"

"Stop!" She grimaced, and Tovin laughed.

"All right. I'll stop. What have you got there?" She started to hand him the parchment roll, but he shrugged and indicated his hands. "Glue."

She wrinkled her nose and unrolled the document. Her heart was pounding as she saw the bold letters once again, and she forced herself to take a deep breath. She cleared her throat and read, " 'From Parion, master of the Glasswrights' Guild, to Ranita, who once counted herself among our number.' "

She stopped and looked at Tovin, checking to see if he understood the import of the greeting. He raised his eyebrows and pursed his lips as if he were going to whistle. Satisfied that he knew what the letter meant to her, Rani continued: " 'The Glasswrights' Guild will count its masters in its home of exile. We are told that you claim the appellation journeyman. We therefore summon you to spend the summer in Brianta, demonstrating the skills that you have gained. Your test for entry to the rank of master must be completed in one day, on the feast day of our patron, Clain. Join us for the glasswrights' test, or be forever banished from the guild you once called home.' "

Rani looked up from the parchment, and she scarcely managed to take a full breath. "Tovin, do you understand? They want me to test for master! They want to recognize my rank within the guild!"

The player fumbled for a rag, wiping the glue off his fingers before he reached for the notice. He read the message, his copper eyes narrowing. "You 'claim the appellation,' then."

"Yes!"

"But they've never seen any need to take notice of you before."

"There's been no reason to." Rani sighed in exasperation.

"Tovin, you aren't paying attention. This isn't about my being journeyman! This is about being declared a master!"

"This is about your traveling to Brianta."

"And what is wrong with that?" He looked at her sharply, and she swallowed hard, softening the tone of her voice, explaining, pleading. "The guild is in Brianta now. They were forced there because of me."

Tovin sighed and rested his hands upon his thighs. "You still insist that you wronged them."

"I did, Tovin. I've told you many times. The guild was destroyed because of me."

"The guild was destroyed because of a mistake, a mistake made by your old King Shanoranvilli. The guild was destroyed because the Brotherhood murdered Prince Tuvashanoran. The guild was destroyed because Instructor Morada refused to come forward and confess her involvement."

Rani started to argue, to remind him that she had been the one to summon Tuvashanoran to his death, but then she realized instead that she could use Tovin's own words against him. "Yes," she said. "All that is true. And Parion Glasswright must now recognize what truly happened. That must be why he has written to me. He wants to make amends for all the past mistakes, for all our former misunderstandings."

"I wonder . . ."

"You wonder what?"

"I wonder why he contacts you now. When Berylina plans to travel to Brianta."

"What could a glasswright master thousands of leagues away possibly know about the plans of a fugitive princess in Morenia?"

"What indeed? . . ." Tovin twisted his question into a sigh. "Would you listen to me if I said this note holds danger?"

"How could it?"

"Would you listen if I begged you not to go to the guild?"

"Tovin, I—"

"What if I said that I'd come with you? That I'd enter the guildhall with you to keep you safe from harm?"

"Would you?" Surprising herself with the rush of relief that flooded her body, Rani realized that she had been denying her own fear. "You'd travel all the way to Brianta?"

Tovin reached out to the boiling pot, taking a long moment to stir his glue. "I might as well," he sighed. "As long as I'm already pledged to accompany you and Berylina."

Rani barely restrained herself until he had drawn back from the hot glue, and then she threw her arms around him. "Thank you! I'll be able to succeed now, knowing you'll be with me."

He folded his arms around her and rested his chin atop her head for just an instant. Then he pushed her back and cupped his palm against her jaw. "You understand that this will not be easy, don't you? They won't take kindly to the instruction you've gained from me. They'll treat every one of my glasswork lessons as suspect, challenge every method that I've taught you."

"We must convince them."

"They will not want to make you master in the guild."

"When they see my work, they'll have no choice."

"They will, though. Ranita, they have all the choices."

She laughed, refusing to acknowledge the warning behind his words. "Do you doubt your own skills, Tovin Player? Are you questioning if you've taught me well?"

He shook his head but smiled at her taunting. "I know just what I've taught you, girl. I know you'll pass any *fair* test that is set for you."

"Any one?" She took a step closer to his worktable.

"Any one at all."

Rani's laugh was lost against the linen of his tunic.

"Ye think ye'll meet up wi' th' Glasswright Guild fer *what?*" Mair's shriek awakened Laranifarso, who had been sleeping comfortably in his mother's arms. The child began to wail, clutching his hands into tight fists and squeezing his eyes closed. Mair clucked to him apologetically, raising him to her shoulder. "Now look wha' ye've made me do!"

"I haven't made you do anything, Mair." Rani shook her head, fighting the urge to laugh at her friend.

"At least this bairn 'as th' sense th' Thousand Gods gave 'im, t' stay safe 'n' warm i' th' city o' 'is birth." Laranifarso seemed determined to prove his mother a liar; he continued to wail as if he had no sense at all, no concept of any world beyond his own sorrow.

"I have sense, Mair. I have sense enough to know that this is the chance I've been waiting for." Rani paced beside the garden bench, oblivious to the roses that bloomed behind her friend. She watched as Mair stroked her son's cheek, saw that the baby was beginning to calm. She took advantage of the quieter moment to fumble for words. "It was one thing for Hal to declare me a journeyman in Liantine. The technical knowledge for that rank is important, but everyone knows that journeyman is truly a financial status. I made my donation to the crown, as expected, and so Hal had the authority to raise me in the guild."

"And if you give the crown enough gold now, he'll raise you up again. There's no reason for you to see the guild in Brianta." Mair had calmed down enough that she abandoned the Touched patois of her youth. Her relative peace seemed to extend to her son, who snuffled for a few more breaths and then stuffed one fat fist into his mouth, sucking industriously on his knuckles.

Rani closed her fingers in her skirts, clenching them tight as she tried to form her argument. "I don't expect you to understand. I don't expect you to place the same value on the guild that I do. I know that you grew up as a Touched girl. You think that our rankings and statuses are absurd."

"You were raised as a merchant girl, Rai."

"But my merchant family paid to see me enter the guild.

My parents hoarded their silver to see me advance. My own
brother passed up the opportunity to make his pilgrimage so
that I could join the guild. I have to make that sacrifice
worthwhile. I have to give it meaning."

"So that's what this is all about! You plan to make the pilgrimage that Bardo never made!"

Rani started to protest. She had never thought that at all!
It had never occurred to her that she might redeem her
brother so directly.

And yet had it not? Had she not envisioned her cavalcade, from nearly the first instant that she promised Hal
she'd accompany Berylina? She would already be in Brianta, after all. She would be at the shrines. How could she
visit Brianta and *not* make an offering to Hern, the god of
merchants? How could she ignore Bote, the god of silver,
and San, the god of iron? Her family had planted their roots
in those deities. No one could begrudge her offering up her
faith to the gods.

She swallowed hard. "There's nothing I can do for Bardo
now. He made his choices. I cannot redeem him."

"If I thought for one moment that you actually *believed*
yourself, I would not be half so worried."

"There's nothing to worry about, Mair."

"Except for why a master glasswright has contacted you
for the first time in eleven years. Why he has offered to let
you compete for the title you crave most in all the world.
Why he is willing to overlook the death and destruction that
he attributes to you, justly or no."

"Even mountains are worn away by time," Rani quoted.

"Not in eleven years."

"What else am I supposed to do, Mair? I've already
promised Hal that I'll go with Berylina. There's no reason
for me to rush home. You've heard Hal's proclamation.
There are to be no celebrations for an entire year, in honor
of the dead princes. No commitments for the players. No
commissions for my glasswork."

"The king intends to appease the Thousand Gods for any wrong he might have committed. He hopes to stop his stream of misfortune."

"I know *why* he does it! I just don't know how I am supposed to respond. I cannot sit and watch the seasons change, doing nothing. I don't have a household of my own to keep me busy!"

Mair gazed at her shrewdly. "Then accept your Tovin's offer and wed the man. Create your 'household,' if that's what you desire."

"That's not it!" Rani's answer was immediate, hot, and she was horrified to feel tears gather at the back of her throat. She swallowed hard and looked across the garden, focusing on the pond amid the grass, the birds that twittered in the oak tree to her right. She took a deep breath and forced herself to repeat, "That's not enough, Mair. I had a mission before Tovin came to Moren, and I've got a mission now."

"A mission to achieve master status in the Glasswrights' Guild."

"Or to fail trying."

Mair settled more comfortably on the bench, letting Rani's oath drift across the garden. Laranifarso had fallen back to sleep, his wet eyelashes dark upon his cheeks. "Farso had thought that I would travel with him when he rides home to supervise the harvest. He won't be pleased to have me traveling to Brianta."

"Oh, Mair, I couldn't ask you to come!"

"You couldn't ask, but I can choose."

"With the baby?"

"He's too small to leave behind with his father."

"But it would be madness to take him to Brianta!"

"Rai, the babe is traveling one place or another. Either he goes with his father and me to the Oaken Hall, or he goes with you and me to Brianta. It's not like we're off to join the Little Army."

"Would Farso ever agree?"

"I can convince him." Mair smiled archly. "He'll come to see my way of thinking. Do you think he could stop me once I've made up my mind?"

Rani resisted the temptation to tug at the hood that hid her face. She had not had time to gather her silk mask—the Fellowship would have to accept her well-intentioned effort to disguise her identity. After all, when she had first learned of the shadowy organization's structure, they had worn only black robes, hiding their faces in deep, peaked hoods. The masks were a new trapping, one that was not vital.

A message from the Fellowship had been waiting for Rani when she returned to her tower room after supper, a small scrap of parchment curling in the middle of her worktable. "Speak to Jair at midnight." Now that the night approached that hour, the Pilgrims' Bell tolled, its steady call muffled by the walls surrounding Rani. She shivered as she thought of other midnight assignations, other secret meetings that had resulted in death and chaos.

Nevertheless, a longstanding sense of obligation to the Fellowship drove her to the group's newest meeting place. Rani had made her way from the palace without divulging her destination, accomplishing her escape by ostentatiously displaying a pair of candles and whispering Nome's name. No one, not even the most zealous of the King's Men, would challenge a worshiper who seemed intent on saluting the lost princes.

Rani had kept her steps even as she headed toward the cathedral. It was only after the street curved and she was out of sight of the guards' hut that she picked up her pace and hurried to the Merchants' Quarter.

That part of Moren had been rebuilt in the last three years. Broad streets cut through the ancient section of town, taking advantage of the fire that had razed the former tumble of narrow passages. Rani missed the twisting byways of her childhood, the winding lanes that she had memorized even as she learned to walk.

The new quarter, though, boasted one of Davin's greatest innovations. The ancient inventor had suggested a system of alleys laid out behind each row of merchants' shops. The plan permitted private entrances for the families that lived above their stores. Deliveries could be made in secret, deterring both thieves and competitors. Slops could be thrown into the alleys, leaving the main streets cleaner, more inviting for the customers who supported the merchants.

Davin had argued with the city planners for days, insisting that his system was worth the extra space, worth the land lost to alleys. The Merchants' Council was divided; no one wanted to pay a premium for land that was not directly traversed by customers, but everyone agreed that merchants must keep potential buyers content. Ultimately, Hal himself had sanctioned the plan.

Rani wondered if the Fellowship had had a hand in the creation of the alleys. Three of their last meeting places had debouched onto one of the dark passages. Tonight's destination was no different—as she'd woven deeper and deeper into the Quarter, Rani had heard families at work and play around her. Nevertheless, she had been sheltered from witnesses who might have noted her passage if she'd been on the main streets.

She wondered how her own family would have reacted to the new design. Her mother would have loved the privacy of the back entrance, the ability to keep mud and muck from the rooms where goods were sold. Her father, though, would have grumbled about the lost land. Jotham Trader would have calculated just how many shops could have stood on all the alleyways combined. He would have reminded his wife precisely what her scrubbed floors cost. Rani's mother would have laughed at the teasing, would have told Jotham that cleanliness was worth three times the price. . . .

"Speak, Fellow."

Rani jumped. She had lost herself so completely in her memories, in her dreams, that she had not heard anyone approach. Nevertheless, she choked out her response: "The sparrow hides its heart within the clouds." Sparrow. Heart. Clouds. Not as grim as many of the Fellowship's passwords.

"Very well. Follow me." The command was whispered in a voice so soft that Rani was not certain if her guide was a man or a woman. The figure held a lantern that was nearly completely shuttered; only one narrow beam of light fell upon the floor, guiding Rani's feet down a narrow flight of stairs. She shuffled along a close corridor, ducking to pass through several low doorways.

Where were they going? How could this extensive system of tunnels exist beneath the new shops in the Merchants' Quarter?

At last, the guide stopped shuffling forward. The lantern was shuttered completely, and Rani blinked in the darkness. She heard a panel slide open, wood against wood, and the soft voice whispered, "The sparrow's heart is plucked by hawks amid the clouds." Sparrow, heart, and clouds again, but in a darker combination than Rani had contemplated.

She swallowed hard and heard a door open before her. The hooded guide stepped to one side, ushering Rani forward with a hand that gripped her forearm unerringly. Before she could turn around, before she could choke out a word of thanks, the door closed, settling into its frame like an axe into a chopping block.

"Ranita Glasswright."

Rani knew the voice before she turned around, recognized the speaker before his lantern was opened. "Holy Father Dartulamino." She took a step forward, but she did not fall upon her knees. There was no need to honor the Holy Father here, no need to kiss the ring that was cut with a thousand facets. Not when Dartulamino summoned her on Fellowship business.

Within the Fellowship, they were equals—in name, at

least. Dartulamino was closer to the core of the organization than Rani had ever hoped to be; he knew more of its clandestine plans. Rani lifted her chin and said, "I'd expected a gathering of the Fellowship."

"We have no need to summon all of our brethren. I wanted the opportunity to speak with you alone." Rani was scarcely comforted by that pronouncement. The Holy Father continued, "So you will stake claim to the name of Ranita Pilgrim. You plan to don the Thousand-Pointed Star and make your holy journey to Brianta."

"No, Father."

"No?" His surprise turned into a frown. "We were told that you travel west with Berylina Thunderspear."

"I travel with the princess, but not as a pilgrim." The Holy Father's eyes narrowed, and Rani stood straighter. She hardened her voice and said, "I go to see the masters of my guild. I go to face the glasswrights' test and craft my masterpiece."

"I see." Dartulamino gazed at her for a long moment, and she wondered what thoughts passed behind his shadowed eyes. What adjustments was he making in his calculations? How was he applying the facts that she had fed him?

Better to force his plan into the open. Rani settled for a direct question. "What interest does the Fellowship take in my journey, Father?"

He did not answer her question. "The time is drawing near when you must make a choice."

"A choice?"

"You have known of our society for ten years and more. We lifted you out of Shanoranvilli's dungeons, and we set you in a place of power."

"You witnessed my trial," she contradicted. "The trial when King Halaravilli learned the truth, when he discovered that I had no hand in the death of Prince Tuvashanoran. The Fellowship did not rescue me; King Halaravilli did, as the Chief Inquisitor."

"Why do you always fight us, Ranita?"

The question was deceptively mild, and she grasped for an appropriate answer. Fight the Fellowship? She did not do so consciously. She did not plot to rebel against its leaders, to topple them from power. She only fought the Fellowship when they seemed arrayed against her, when they appeared to act against her own interest and the interests of those she loved. She chose her words as carefully as she would stipple paint upon a pane of glass. "I do not fight the Fellowship, Father. I fight injustice and secrecy and wrong."

"Then do you trust your Fellows? You have no faith in our vision for Morenia?"

Rani bit off a harsh laugh. "How can I trust you, Father? How can I have faith in a secret, in plans that are always kept hidden from me?"

He clicked his tongue, shaking his head as if she were a much younger child. "But that is the meaning of faith, Ranita. You should not need to have *faith* explained to you, not at your age."

"I have faith in the Thousand Gods, Father. I have faith in First Pilgrim Jair. I have faith in the divine right of the house of ben-Jair to hold the throne of Morenia. But I cannot have faith in simple men and women who walk the earth and breathe the air unless they would tell me why they do the things they do, why they command the things they command."

"And yet you would do all the things your king commands, your king who is—within our Fellowship—a simple man."

Rani's rebellion was immediate; her words came out as hot as coals. "I will fight the Fellowship with my last breath if it moves against Halaravilli ben-Jair."

The Holy Father's laugh was dry. "Relax, young fighter. No one is moving against your king today."

"But once you did. In Amanthia. You let the assassin Tasuntimanu take up steel against my lord."

Again, Dartulamino laughed. "Not I, Ranita Glasswright. Years ago, one of our members thought to take matters into his own hands. One man. One crazed creature. The Fellowship as a whole never plotted against the king's life."

"Then why do you question my loyalty to the crown now?"

"Not just to the crown." Dartulamino took a step closer to her. All traces of levity had been washed from his face, scrubbed away in solemn darkness. "I question your loyalty to the crown, to the Fellowship, to the very guild that you have held so dear. I come to warn you, Ranita Glasswright."

Her palms were moist, even though her skin was deadly cold. "Warn me against what?"

"You will face choices in Brianta. You will need to make decisions. Lives will depend on the course you choose."

"What sort of course?"

"Our future. The future of the Royal Pilgrim."

Rani shivered. She had heard of the Royal Pilgrim. She swallowed hard and forced bravado into her words. "I've heard that prophecy before, but never from you. Never from one in power."

"Yet you know that the Royal Pilgrim will bind the kingdoms of the world together. The Royal Pilgrim will gather the Five Kingdoms under one ruler, unite them beneath the cloak of the Fellowship of Jair."

"Who is the Royal Pilgrim, then? Who will do these things?"

This time, the Holy Father's laugh was genuine. "If only I knew that, Ranita! If I could simply appoint the Royal Pilgrim, then the prophecy would be fulfilled. The Fellowship would complete its mission, and the Five Kingdoms would be at peace." He shook his head. "No, Ranita. The Fellowship's prophecy is like a pot that was cradled on a high shelf, a treasure set in a place of honor. The vessel was toppled long ago, and it was shattered. We must piece together what we can, and fill in all the bits that are missing."

The tolling of the Pilgrims' Bell lent an aura of mystery to the Holy Father's words, a grim air of danger. "But how do you think I can help? Why are you telling me this now?"

"To prepare you for your journey. We believe—the Fellowship believes—that your travels to Brianta will set our final story into motion. Pieces will be found in Jair's birthplace. We will bind our shattered vessel."

"It's all well and good to speak in poetry, but I travel for very specific purposes. I will accompany Princess Berylina to keep her safe, and I will test for the rank of master within my guild. I will not be working any mysteries for the Fellowship. I won't be searching for hidden prophecies."

Holy Father Dartulamino shook his head as if she were a reluctant child slow to master her letters. "You will meet many Fellows in Brianta. Our people are able to move more openly there, where the name of Jair is spoken with faith and courtesy by every living soul. You will meet the core of the Fellowship, and you will receive your orders. You will understand what you must do to work toward the unveiling of the Royal Pilgrim."

"That is why you summoned me in the middle of the night? To tell me to watch for Fellows in Brianta?"

The Holy Father's eyes glinted at her rebellious tone. "I summoned you, Ranita Glasswright, to warn you about the importance of your journey. Do not assume that you can return to Morenia unchanged. Do not assume that you can set aside lightly the burdens that you take on in Brianta. Do not assume that your path will be easy. And do not assume that the Fellowship will let you shirk your duties. You are bound to us by sacred oaths. You are required to uphold your vows. You go to take the glasswrights' test, but you will be challenged by the Fellowship as well."

"And if I fail?"

"Ahhh," the Holy Father sighed, and Rani could almost believe that he was saddened by the words that he was forced to say. "If you fail the Fellowship, you will be cast out from our number."

"Cast out? Forbidden to attend meetings?"

"Forbidden to speak of all you know."

"The Fellowship cannot bind my tongue!" Rani answered hotly.

"Not while you're alive, no. There is nothing we can do while you're alive."

She heard the threat, blatant as a player's spoken piece. She started to protest, but she knew that she would gain nothing by squabbling with the priest. Instead, she bowed her head, swallowing hard and fighting to quench the flame of rebellion.

"Is that all, Father?"

"That is all that I can tell you now. Travel safely, Ranita Glasswright. May Jair keep you always in his sight."

The cathedral bells chose that moment to toll the hour after midnight, a solitary bronze clang that drove down Rani's spine like a pike. Before she could speak, Dartulamino made a holy sign, and then he disappeared in the shadows at the far end of the chamber. Rani was left to retrace her steps in the dark corridors; her guide was nowhere to be found.

As she made her way through the Merchants' Quarter back to the palace she asked herself if the Holy Father's parting words had been a blessing or a warning. She found no sleep that night as she searched for an answer.

5

Parion Glasswright took his time choosing the robes that he would wear to greet the Traitor. He had long ago grown familiar with the layers of cloth, accepting that the majesty and power he commanded as guildmaster meant that he was constrained by his garments. He paused in front of a polished mirror and studied the visage that looked back at him.

There were deep lines in that face, furrows etched by age and fatigue and a craving for revenge. Parion had once been considered a handsome man—he knew that much from gossip and from the whispers of women he could trust. He was a feared man, as well; people hesitated to excite his wrath, to summon the famous fury that hovered beneath the surface of his calm guildish demeanor.

His parents had not been glasswrights. His father had been an armorer, spending more time in the Soldiers' Quarter than in the Guildsmans' Quarter of his youth. Parion's mother had been a master in the Embroiderers' Guild—eyes opened or closed, she could pick out designs more delicate than anyone could imagine.

Parion had learned craft from both of his parents. From his father, he had absorbed the importance of strong arms, of powerful muscles to manipulate heavy iron. Yet from his mother, he had mastered the value of delicacy. He knew that a single stitch taken in a particular way could change the way an entire tapestry appeared. He knew that fine work made the difference in a finished piece. Details mattered.

And as a glasswright, Parion applied those lessons. He needed to craft windows, design armatures heavy enough and secure enough to protect delicate panes of glass. He also needed to paint, to indicate expressions and thoughts, individual lines that could be read by thousands of viewers from the floor of a cathedral.

Parion had taken his parents' lessons and applied them well. He might have made mistakes. He might have taken missteps, but he had never made the same error twice.

Sighing, the glasswright straightened his garments. He had chosen deepest gold today—a topaz so rich that it shimmered in the light from the window. Let the Traitor be dazzled upon their meeting. Let her measure out the wealth that belonged to the guild, that had come to the glasswrights since they moved away from Morenia. Let her wonder if Parion sent a message of intimidation or one of greeting.

And if she could decipher the emotion behind his welcoming her back to the guild, then she was a better sleuth than he. For Parion himself did not know how he felt.

He knew that he was bound as guildmaster to protect all the glasswrights sworn to him. He knew that he was obliged to honor the apprentices and journeymen and masters who had passed their respective tests, who had joined the guild, free and clear of other obligations. He knew that he must stand strong against the priestly government of Brianta, stand firm to keep his guild a separate creature from the pilgrims' bureaucratic tangle.

But must he welcome a traitor? Must he open his arms to one who had literally cost the glasswrights lives and limbs? Would he not serve the glasswrights better—the true glasswrights, the ones who had committed to the guild with their hearts and souls and hands—would he not serve them better if he destroyed the Traitor? Without thinking, he moved his hands in the automatic signal of supplication, sending forth his thoughts to Clain, asking for the god's guidance and protection.

There was a knock at the door, and Parion turned abruptly. An apprentice entered and brushed the prayer bell before saying, "She has arrived, Master. Ranita Glasswright."

Parion heard the awe in the boy's voice, the amazement that a figure from the guild's rich past could walk among them. Well, he was every bit as much a part of that story. He was every bit a member of the guild. He flashed a sign of gratitude toward the apprentice, his fingers moving automatically through the Briantan custom. "Very well. I will attend her in the audience hall."

The audience hall, he thought, as the child responded to his gesture. That was a grand name for the guildhall's largest chamber. The Glasswrights' Guild in Morenia had boasted high walls and shimmering windows, the finest of the guild's handicraft displayed like a treasury. Here in Brianta, the guild had poached land from Jin, the god of bread, whose followers had finally collected enough gold to build themselves another hall, a grander symbol of their dedication.

The glasswrights had been too poor to raze Jin's old buildings. Instead, they had adapted the religious compound, turning one low structure into dormitories, another into workshops. The kitchen had become the meeting hall, a dusky, low-ceilinged room, with smoky rafters suspended across the roof.

The place still smelled of burned bread, of the darkened offerings that pilgrims had roasted to Jin. On a good day, the smell was a comforting one, an anchoring memory that reminded Parion that he was a person, that his belly must be filled. He remembered the nourishment of day-to-day struggles, the pale sustenance of revenge.

And on bad days, the smell of burned bread reminded

him of ashes. The ashes of the Morenian guildhall pulled down and destroyed. The ashes of his ruined life. The ashes of funeral pyres, like the one denied Morada.

This was a bad day.

Parion ran a hand through his hair and followed the apprentice out of his study. Almost as an afterthought, he brushed his hand across the bell beside the door. It couldn't hurt to invoke Clain's blessing on this venture. Couldn't hurt at all.

Arriving at the audience hall, Parion took in the scene with a quick eye. The guild's handful of masters stood at the front of the room, outlined against the wall of ovens that had once served Jin. They spoke among themselves in low tones, clearly concerned about this new development, obviously wondering at Parion's intention in bringing the Traitor into their midst.

Parion reached back into his memories. How many of them had actually known the girl when she was an apprentice? Not Delion; he was from Brianta originally, and Framia and Cordio, as well. Yalinta had come from Zarithia, bringing two young masters with her. The other ranking guildsmen, though, were Morenian. Some had already achieved their rank when the Traitor worked among them. Seven had been journeymen, and thus had been spared the worst of the king's revenge. Five had been apprentices, though, now raised to master status. Raised despite the tools they must use to complete their work, the Hands that they employed to function in their craft. . . .

Thirteen who had known the Traitor and six who had not. Thirteen as likely to stab the girl as elevate her to the rank of master—and that did not even count the journeymen who had labored under a difficult system, who had struggled with their own milestones and markers rather than relying on some wayward player troop to validate their work.

That would be another element to make this meeting more challenging. The Traitor was bringing her accomplice—the player man who had set up his own system of glasswork.

Parion shook his head, wondering if he had chosen correctly in receiving the Traitor here, in public. He had no choice, truly. The guild was already in an uproar about her arrival. The day before, the journeymen had sent a formal letter to him, all twenty complaining that he had agreed even to entertain the notion of advancing the Traitor to master. Larinda had started that, he supposed. She had a way about her, a way of getting others to follow her will. The journeymen were right, though. The Traitor claimed a status that had never been officially sanctioned by the guild.

All but eight of the journeymen had been Morenian apprentices. All but eight worked without their thumbs.

Parion's quick count showed that the majority of his apprentices were present, as well—nearly three dozen of them. They huddled at the far end of the hall, eager to witness their guild's grand events, but afraid to call too much attention to themselves. To an apprentice, *attention* meant obligations. Duties. Jobs delegated from the rest of the guild. He could remember when he had served as an apprentice—long ago, in happier times. Times when the guild had not needed to negotiate with religious fanatics, had not needed to pay off priests at every turn of the road. Times when it did not need to deal with traitors . . .

Well, the *guild* did not need to deal with this one. He did. Parion alone. He was the guildmaster, he had written the letter on behalf of the Fellowship, and he had brought about this confrontation.

As if he needed to remind himself of the reasons behind his decision, he looked again at the journeymen, at the masters who wore the new Liantine Hands. Each wounded glasswright had been equipped with the machinery; each now possessed the latest tools to ease a maimed craftsman's burdens. The Fellowship had been truthful at least—it seemed that they had waited only long enough to be certain that Parion had sent his letter, and then they had released the Hands.

That was not the Fellowship's only interest in the guild, however. Parion glanced into the hall's shadowy alcoves, in the corners where doors had once stood, passages to the dark pantries that had fueled Jin's bakeries. By squinting, he could make out two shadowy figures lurking in the darkness, nearly obscured by their dark robes and high hoods. Their faces were entirely hidden by black masks.

The Fellowship had informed him that it was stationing members in the guildhall. The visitors could be ignored— the glasswrights did not need to feed them or speak to them, to acknowledge them in any way. Parion had agreed readily enough. The intrusion had seemed like a small thing once the silk-wrapped Hands had arrived. If any guildsman questioned the shadowy watchers, Parion could explain that they visited from the priesthood. They were watchers looking for witches, looking for people who twisted the blessings of the Thousand Gods to evil. That would not even be a lie. At least not much of one.

And Parion was relatively certain that the Fellowship would not discern his true plan. Not now. Not when he planted the seeds that would take long weeks to blossom. The robed figures could watch, they could listen, and they would discern nothing to make them suspicious.

Nevertheless, Parion *did* wonder what the Fellowship wanted. What could they gain by lurking in the guild's hallways? They had cleverly arrived before the Traitor; if she even noticed them when she entered the hall, she would think that they were part of the guild's composition, some form of loyal glasswright membership here in the religious tangle of Brianta.

But why was Parion wasting two heartbeats speculating on what the Traitor might think, about how she would view a few robed figures? Had he already forgotten that the Traitor was—at most—a journeyman? She had no right to question the guild. She had no right to challenge the guildmaster. She would not inquire about the hooded figures. Not if she valued her future as a glasswright. Not if she hoped to advance to master.

Parion nodded tightly as he took in the Fellowship's two obscure watchers. If they took his gesture as a greeting, neither replied.

Parion turned to a wizened master, a woman who had made the journey from Morenia with him years before. "Sister Gatekeeper," he said, and the two words settled silence over the hall, "I believe that we have guests here at the guildhall."

"Yes, Guildmaster."

"Please invite them into our hall, Sister. Ask them to join us."

"Yes, Guildmaster." The old woman raised a hand to her chest, fingers moving in a Briantan symbol of submission. Parion accepted the gesture with a curt wave of his own. He stifled his impatience as the elderly master walked the length of the hall; he swallowed hard as she threw open the doors.

Of course, the Traitor was taller than he remembered. And shapelier, too—she had grown from a child to a woman. Her hair was still blond, but it swept off her face in an elaborate braid, a far cry from the tangle she had sported as an apprentice. Her eyes were the same—blue-green as ocean water, and piercing as shards of glass.

She pinned him with that gaze as she walked into the room. Her gait was steady, slow, and she looked to neither the left nor the right. She carried herself erect, as if an iron embrasure encased her body. She had to be aware of the four score glasswrights around her—masters she had known before, journeymen who had served with her as apprentices, children who knew her name only as a curse.

Carefully, with the exact touch of a new convert, she reached out a hand to the prayer bell that stood inside the doorway. She barely touched it, moving the clapper just enough to elicit a jangle. She had studied the customs of her adopted home, then. At least she knew some of what was expected of her in Brianta. At least she was prepared to offer up some semblance of submission to her new home.

Parion was so intent on studying her that he nearly overlooked the companions who followed behind her. The first was a tall man, a bold creature who walked with a nobleman's confidence as he darted his copper gaze about the hall. The second was a woman of medium height, dark hair, dark eyes. He might have overlooked her entirely if she had not carried an infant swaddled across her chest. The child appeared to be sleeping; at least, it did not cry out in the death-still chamber. Parion resisted the urge to glance at the Fellows. Had they known that the Traitor would bring an entourage? Had they expected these others to arrive?

She took her time crossing the hall. She must be aware that all eyes rested on her. She must know that everyone in the chamber blamed her for loss, some counting death and dismemberment in the balance. She must know that she came as a supplicant.

And yet she looked as if she were a queen.

She paused as she came to stand before him, and for a long moment she took his measure. Parion remembered her as a child, the rebel who had complained about grinding colors, about stirring pots of paint. He remembered the shock and horror of the day that Prince Tuvashanoran died, the day that changed his life forever. *Morada* . . . he thought, and he could picture the bold instructor standing beside him. *Grant me the wisdom to speak to this one. Grant me the courage to do what must be done.*

Even as he voiced the thought inside his own mind, the Traitor sank to her knees before him. Her plain grey cloak billowed behind her, as simple as a pilgrim's garment. She had already learned that the Briantan street preachers expected modesty in dress. Parion would see if she extended that lesson to his guild.

She inclined her head as if she knelt before an altar, but when she spoke, her voice was pitched to carry through the room. "Guildmaster Parion."

He forced himself to speak her name, twisting his lips around the bitter syllables. "Ranita Glasswright."

"I am grateful that you summoned me here. I am pleased to be within the hall of my fellow glasswrights once again, after all the intervening years."

A Briantan would have added a hand gesture, emphasizing her humility. Parion caught his own fingers twitching, automatically moving into the sign that accepted a humble offering. At least the girl's words were spoken with an appropriate tone; he could not voice anger at her phrasing. Grudgingly, he settled for vague truths. "Much may change over the course of years." *Traitor.* He could not bring himself to repeat her name. "Your guild welcomes you."

He felt her eyes on his face, and he knew that she was measuring him, counting up his anger, calculating her risk in coming here. She settled on an earnest response. "That pleases me, Guildmaster. More than I can say, that pleases me." He heard the catch in her voice, saw the moment that her lower lip began to tremble. She stifled the emotion quickly and said, "I would introduce my companions to you, Guildmaster."

Again, he resisted the urge to glance at the Fellows, to gauge their acceptance of the additional intruders. Why should he worry, though? It wasn't as if the Fellowship could take back its Hands. He had done his part. He had gotten the Traitor to Brianta. His voice frosted, though, as he thought of how the others might ruin his own plans. "Please do."

She cleared her throat and raised a hand. "Guildmaster, I present to you a man who claims mastery of our craft in his own right. Tovin Player of Liantine."

At least the man wasn't staking claim to a guild name. But what sort of station was *player?* Had the man been a true Morenian, his name would have identified him as a merchant. Parion had certainly heard of the Liantine players, though. They did more than sell wares. They worked all sorts of witchery in their land, playing with men's perceptions, tricking them into seeing things that were not there.

Parion raised his chin, making his challenge unmistakable. What would the upstart glassworker do? Would he submit to the guild's power here in Brianta?

Tovin Player met Parion's gaze without hesitation. The man nodded once, as if he were deciphering some mystery, calculating the true meaning of an important tale. As all the glasswrights watched, Tovin Player swept into an elegant bow, bringing his chestnut curls to rest against one well-turned knee, and he flung one arm up behind him.

The effect was to look grand and important and at the same time to acknowledge the guildsman's power. Parion had to admit that he was impressed—the glassworker was certainly not submitting to him, but he *was* acknowledging Parion's position. In fact, he was recognizing Parion as an equal, conveying the information effectively without the constant Briantan coded gestures.

"Welcome, Player." Parion tested the words in his own mind before he spoke them aloud. He was not quite disdainful—that might be construed as an insult. Nevertheless, he was skeptical. He was wary. He was protecting his guild from a potential invader.

"Many thanks, Glasswright." The player's response was cool, and his voice filled the kitchen. He had pitched his few words carefully, so that everyone present could hear what he said, so that each listener thought that he or she was being spoken to directly.

And, of course, he refused to acknowledge Parion's title.

Parion took a moment to glance at the newcomer's hands, to see if he bore the scars of a true glass craftsman.

He was annoyed when he realized that the intruder wore soft leather gloves. Then he caught Tovin's gaze and realized that the player had known he would be measured by such a standard. Annoyance turned to slow-burning anger.

"Aye," the player said softly, and now his voice was pitched for Parion alone. "I have worked glass. I have mastered the ways of silver stain and flashing, of carving sheets of Zarithian cobalt."

The player flicked his eyes toward the bare walls of the chamber, toward the ash-blackened ovens. Parion felt an unreasoning anger rise in his throat. Of course there was no glass here! Of course he had not displayed his ability and the skill of his guildsmen in this hall. That would be a foolish waste in this home of exile!

The player's gaze intensified as he peered into the shadowed corners. He had found the Fellows. Nevertheless, he did not remark on those black-robed observers. In fact, he said nothing at all. Parion had to remind himself not to be goaded into starting a fight. He gritted his teeth and nodded once, flicking his eyes back to the Traitor, intending to dismiss the player.

He was surprised by the look he found on the girl's face. She was attuned to the player man, soldered to him with invisible bonds. Parion watched as she measured the anger flickering behind the player's eyes, as she calculated the aggression coiled in his arms.

But beneath that watchful gaze, Parion saw more. He saw devotion. He saw dedication. He saw a glasswright who had foresworn her guild and taken up the cause of another.

Very well, then. Parion had already worked out a plan to break the Traitor. He could factor in the player man. He would even enjoy the new challenge. He stored away a sudden surge of glee and said to the Traitor, "And who else do you bring into our hall? Who else have you brought here, all uninvited?"

If the so-called journeyman were ashamed of her actions,

she gave no sign. Instead, she raised an imperious hand toward her dark-haired colleague, taking in the child that was swaddled at the other's breast. "This is Lady Mair, Guildmaster. Lady Mair of Moren. She carries her son, Laranifarso, the heir of Baron Farsobalinti."

Parion's eyes narrowed as he turned to the young mother. A Touched girl, by her name, but bred to a nobleman. What business did a rebellious glasswright have, bringing a noble's paramour to Liantine?

No, Parion corrected himself. Not a paramour. He recognized the band about Mair's wrist. She was bound to the nobleman in the eyes of the church. The Thousand Gods had looked upon her wedding and blessed her nuptials.

That was even more curious, then. A Touched girl wed to a nobleman. What else had changed in Moren since Parion had decamped? What other rules must he learn, if he were to work his vengeance, if he were to regain all that was his by right?

He forced himself to craft a civil greeting for the wench. "Welcome to the glasswrights' hall." He started to call her "lady" and stopped short, far enough into the appellation to be insulting. Why give her the honor in his guildhall? Why recognize any potential power that she could harness against him?

The Touched girl started to speak, pursing her lips to deliver some tart retort. She glanced at her companion for permission, though, and the Traitor shook her head, one tiny motion of denial. Transparent as the finest clear glass, the Touched girl at first rebelled against the instruction, but the Traitor shifted her weight.

Nothing was said. No words were exchanged. Nevertheless, the Touched wench backed down, forfeiting the argument she clearly longed to make. She inclined her head gravely, as if she were accepting a polite greeting from Parion. He did not force the point by saying anything more; rather, he returned his attention to the Traitor.

"So. You've come to the Glasswright Guild in exile."

"I report to my guildmaster." There was a curious long-ing behind her words, and Parion could almost believe that she did desire to submit to him, to submit to the guild that she had so nearly destroyed. "You summoned me, and I re-sponded to that summons."

"My call did not ask you to bring accomplices."

She swallowed audibly. Parion caught a murmur among the other glasswrights—they were pleased that he was being curt with her. Well, they would be more pleased before he was done. They would be more impressed when they saw just how broken one traitor could be.

She finally found words to reply. "Your word *accomplice* connotes that my companions intend to work some evil upon our guild. They do not, I assure you."

Argument. She was always arguing. She was always parsing words and making excuses. Morada had complained of that years ago. He thundered: "And you can know that? You can know the inner workings of their minds?"

"They have sworn devotion to me, Master. I am dedi-cated to our guild, and so they are likewise dedicated to the betterment of glasswrights the world over."

Pretty words, Parion thought. Pretty words that sparked obvious rebellion in the player, at least. The guildmaster watched a sudden pulse beat strong in the other man's throat. That one did not like his loyalties proclaimed by an-other. He did not like being committed to any particular path in the battles that were brewing here. Parion swallowed a smile. Like it or not, the player was bound by the wench he claimed to serve. Bound, but he would be helpless to assist her in the final accounting.

Before the guildmaster could craft a suitable reply, he caught a flicker of movement from the corner of his eye. There, in the darkest shadows beside the ovens. One of the Fellowship had moved.

Likely, the hooded figure had only shifted from foot to

foot. After all, it *was* warm in the former kitchen; the air was still and heavy with the scent of ancient bread. Nevertheless, Parion suspected that the Fellow could have stayed still if he—or she—had chosen to do so. No, Parion was being sent a message. He was being ordered to move forward with this charade, to bind the Traitor back to the guild, to guarantee her presence for long enough that the Fellowship could have its way with her.

Very well, then. Parion was more than willing to play at that game.

"So," he said, facing the Traitor squarely, "you call yourself a glasswright."

"I *am* a glasswright, Master."

"That is for the guild to determine. In this time of testing, we will set aside quarters for you here in the guildhall. You will report to one of our journeymen each morning for the next ten days. That guildsman will test your mastery of the basic concepts of working with glass. If you can demonstrate journeyman skills, you will be allowed to begin preparing for the test."

"If it pleases you, Master, I cannot live at the guildhall."

Parion let his voice freeze. "Cannot? What sort of disobedience is this?"

"Not disobedience, Master." She answered immediately, but he saw how she swallowed hard, how she cast a quick glance toward her companions. She was not as composed as she would like him to think she was. "I am bound to others here in Brianta. I am not free to act entirely on my own."

"And yet you come to us as a petitioner? A petitioner who is not prepared to follow through on her petition?"

"I come to you as a guildsman, Master. But I also come as a subject of Morenia. King Halaravilli ben-Jair himself has charged me with responsibilities here in Brianta. I must stay with Princess Berylina in our pilgrims' accommodations. Nevertheless, I shall submit to all else that my guild requires of me."

Halaravilli ben-Jair. The cursed king, whose own father had brought Parion to these bitter straits. The house of ben-Jair would not issue commands here in the Briantan guild-hall! Morenia had forfeited that right when it destroyed the innocent guild, when it ordered the glorious old hall torn stone from stone. Parion would die before he would yield to ben-Jair. He would do whatever must be done to see the king crumple in defeat!

Patience, Parion reminded himself. He had waited for all these years; he could wait for a few more. Patience was all that he required . . . . Eventually he would return to Morenia. Eventually he would be back in the land of his birth, with access and power to destroy the king.

"Very well, then," he said, and he realized that only a few heartbeats had passed, despite the fire of his thoughts, despite the flash of fury that had pumped through his veins. "You shall stay with your princess, stay with the pilgrims. But each morning you shall report to the guildhall by no later than sunrise. You shall report to Journeyman Larinda, that she might test your skills."

"Larinda!" He heard the raw surprise in the Traitor's voice, and he resisted the urge to smile against it.

"Aye, Larinda. You knew her well when you once worked with us. Who better to gauge your fitness to return to our midst?"

He saw the knowledge flit across the Traitor's face. He watched her swallow hard and curl her hands into tight fists, folding her glass-scarred fingers protectively over her thumbs. She was no fool. She knew what fare Larinda had paid. She knew how harshly the former apprentice was likely to deal with the instrument of her maiming.

Before the Traitor could fashion a response, Parion looked to Larinda. Even he was surprised by the expression on the girl's pinched face, by the open flame of hatred there. He was reminded of the look in Morada's eyes when she first learned that the guild would not permit her to travel about the land, to present her skills to all who wished to hire a glasswright. Morada, who had given her life in service to her guild, who had struggled as an instructor to raise up the Traitor, to teach the girl who had brought only brutal, bloody death to her sisters, her brothers . . .

Parion closed his eyes for just a moment, resisting the temptation to breathe a prayer to Gar, the god of vengeance. Gar would have his due, after all, no matter what Parion did at this juncture, no matter how he acted. Gar would make all right for Parion here in Brianta, and for Morada, wherever she walked in the Heavenly Fields.

Swallowing his thoughts as if they were a bitter draft, Parion raised one hand to summon Larinda forward. The guildmaster made certain that his sleeve fell back as he did so; he guaranteed that all who stood in the meeting hall could see the ragged scars across his own forearm. The Traitor blanched at the inflamed reminder of his blood sacrifice.

In response to the gesture, Larinda stepped away from the other journeymen. As if inspired by Clain himself, she crossed her arms over her chest, taking care not to jostle her silk and metal Hands unduly. Parion could not have crafted a finer gesture if he were sketching out a design on parchment—the girl managed to capture her loss and her power, her anger and her sorrow, all in one smooth motion. He nodded once, again regretting that Morada could not be here to witness the child that she had trained, the shrewd guildsman that she had set upon the path toward success.

He turned back to the Traitor. "Do you accept that term?" He nearly stumbled and called her by his private epithet. That he could not do. Not yet. Not publicly. "Will you report to Larinda Glasswright?"

The Traitor glanced toward her Touched companion, clearly seeking counsel. The dark-haired girl took advantage of the infant that she held, shifting the child from one arm to the other and using the motion to soften the shake of her head. So, the Touched girl thought the guild's requirement was overly harsh. She thought that her precious friend should not submit to Larinda's oversight.

The Traitor was not content with that advice, though. Instead, she also looked to the player, settling her gaze on the man's face for a long moment.

The player was more aware than the Touched girl. He knew that Parion was watching him. With all the composure of a man accustomed to performing in crowds, the rogue glassworker took a step backwards, settling his gloved hands on his hips. The motion let him shrug his shoulders eloquently, disclaiming any certainty, any knowledge, any belief in what would happen if the Traitor acted or if she did not. Tacitly, he indicated that she should submit.

The Traitor was clearly displeased with such counsel; she started to protest. Before the words could rise from her throat, though, Larinda spoke.

"Ranita." The journeyman's words were low, whispered as if she were only just awakening from deepest sleep. "Welcome to our guildhall, Sister. I look forward to sharing with you once again, as we shared the secrets of our youth."

The Traitor had the grace to look ashamed as she turned to face Larinda. When she answered the gentle words, Parion could hear emotion behind her voice. "I think of you often, Larinda. I remember our working as sisters, in furtherance of our guild."

"Side by side, we labored. And now, we may do so again."

The Traitor swallowed audibly and stepped toward Larinda, extending her hand in a time-honored gesture of peace. She said, "We may do so now. I look forward to the opportunity."

Parion saw the instant that Larinda grasped the Traitor's hand. He saw the way the maimed journeyman flexed her wrist, the way that she closed her Hand more tightly. He knew enough about the mechanical contraption to understand the pain Larinda was causing, but the Traitor did not register the hurt.

Instead, she merely shifted her own wrist, tightening her own grip. She set her jaw and raised her chin, as if she were once again the defiant glasswrights' apprentice, once again the girl who had spent untold hours on her knees before the altar to Sorn, the god of obedience, and to Plad, the god of patience.

"Be welcome in our house, Sister," Larinda said.

"Many thanks for your kindness. I will do everything in my power to make you pleased with the decision you have made."

Parion wondered if he was the only person who heard the shuffle of the Fellows in the shadows. He must complete this exercise now, before they chose to show themselves, before they elected to tear down the fragile edifice that he was constructing.

"That is settled, then. You will submit to Larinda Glasswright during all the time you visit our guildhall. That is not our only requirement, however. There is more that we expect of you."

"More?"

Parion heard the challenge in her throat, saw the uncertainty that flashed across her eyes. He raised one hand, pointing sternly to count off the second of his rules. "You shall eat no food in Brianta but what we serve in this guildhall. I will allocate for you a plate, a bowl, and a cup for your exclusive use."

He saw the arguments she thought to present, imagined the protests she would make—all about political obligation and duty and other excuses. He locked eyes with her, bringing to bear all the power of his position with the guild. She must agree to this. She must submit. Otherwise, all his plans would come to naught. He smothered a smile as she lowered her head and nodded once. "I agree."

And yet he narrowed his eyes, discovering that a part of

him truly did not want her submission. He wanted her to fight him; he wanted her to misstep so that he would have an excuse for banishing her. No. She had accepted his proviso. She had opened the door to the heart of his revenge.

Setting aside the liquid thrill of that discovery, he continued, "You shall not correspond with your king while you reside in Brianta. You shall not send him any letter, by any messenger."

"Master," she started to protest, but she must have read the certainty in his gaze, his determination to remain inflexible on these points. She settled for casting a glance toward her colleagues, a plea, and he imagined that she would beg them to write her correspondence for her.

"*Any* letter," he underscored. "One written by your own hand, or one dictated to another."

"But if the king should write to me, I must respond, Master. He is my sovereign lord."

"You seek reinstatement with your guild. Do you think it wrong to swear to the basic precepts that any apprentice promises? Do you think that you should be granted special exemption from your guildish oaths of loyalty?"

"But ordinary apprentices would have no reason to contact their king!" She must have heard the stridency in her tone, for she swallowed hard and lowered her voice. "Master." She took a deep breath, and her exhalation was loud in the still room. "Might I write to the king once to tell him the reason for my future silence?"

Bargaining. Always bargaining. The Traitor had started her life as a merchant, as a calculating thief, measuring out how much she could steal from hardworking souls in the marketplace. He gritted his teeth, but he said, "One letter. One sheet of parchment, with nothing enclosed. Deliver it to me by midnight tonight, and I will send it on for you."

"I agree." Her voice quavered on the two words, but she spoke them—aloud and before witnesses.

Parion nodded and continued with his rules. "You shall

remain pure in body and in mind. Each morning, you shall complete a ritual bath in dedication to Clain, washing away the filth of your flesh and of your thoughts. Each evening, you shall complete a cycle of prayers to Clain and to the other gods whom you have offended throughout the day. You shall refrain from all unclean touch, but especially from the touch of any man."

He was not surprised to see her gaze flicker toward the player. Parion had already read the silent story of corruption between the two of them; he understood that she had sought refuge in the unholy circle of that rebel's arms. Parion had lived in Brianta for long enough that he was scandalized by such libertine acts.

Nevertheless, the guildmaster was surprised by the player's response to his demand. In the midst of the audience chamber, surrounded by all the members of the glasswrights' guild, the man laughed aloud. He threw back his head, letting his chestnut hair catch the glimmer of the smoky torches. His throat rippled, and his guffaw was so rich that it brought smiles to the other glasswrights' faces before they remembered themselves.

As if the man suddenly recalled that he was a guest in the hall, he straightened, and he ran his gloved fingers down the front of his tunic. He gave every appearance of a creature abashed, of a man who regretted having disturbed the solemnity of an event. Parion glared, but his fury was nothing compared to the Traitor's. The girl stepped forward, deliberately turning her back on the player. "I agree, Master."

Well. That had been more successful than Parion had hoped. Perhaps he had even driven a true wedge between the Traitor and her strongest supporter. He must remember the trick.

"One last promise, and then we will be done here. You must agree to submit to me in all things. I am the master of the guild you wish to join, and I am the final arbiter of your fate here. I am the one who says, ultimately, whether you join our ranks or not. I am the one who says what you must do and when you must do it. I am the law within the walls of the guildhall. Do you agree to submit to me?"

He saw the arguments move across her face. He saw that she wanted to carve out exemptions from the absolutes. She wanted to submit on some points and not on others. She wanted to claim independence. She wanted to declare herself superior to him in a thousand niggling ways.

He would have none of that, though. She must yield now, from the beginning. She must understand that she would have no rights here in the guildhall; she would have no ability to destroy the fragile structure that he had built here in Brianta.

"I may not submit to you if that would require me to forswear other oaths that I have made."

Parion's anger was immediate—a red poker that flashed through his gut. "Then you do not wish to go forward with this! Your presence here has been a game."

"I *do,* Master! I do!" Without his bidding, she crossed the few steps that separated them, and she collapsed onto the floor, ignoring the grime between the bricks. "Please, Master. Understand that I cannot change the past. I will submit to you on all matters in the future, but I cannot take back other oaths that I have spoken."

He met her eyes, the green-blue eyes that seemed so much older than the young woman who knelt before him. Those eyes had witnessed death. They had witnessed destruction. They had witnessed treachery and all its costs. They had witnessed his beloved Morada's head, severed and thrust on a post, carried about the Morenian marketplace.

Unflinching, the Traitor met his gaze. "I will submit to you, Master, but only from today forward. Only in our new endeavors. Only in the future. You cannot ask more of me— more than that no glasswright could agree."

He heard the pleading in her voice, understood the desperation that sparked her words. For just an instant, he contemplated refusing her, imagined her devastation as all her hopes crumpled at his feet.

Before he could indulge the fantasy, though, there was a shuffle in one of the shadowed alcoves, a shift of fabric as the watching Fellows made their presence known. Parion must accept the Traitor. He must welcome her into the fold. Whatever reasons he might have for wanting her gone, wanting her destroyed, wanting her utterly ruined, the Fellowship wanted more.

The Fellowship of Jair controlled him. After all, this was Brianta, birthplace of the First Pilgrim. The Traitor might think that Parion held all the strings; however, he knew that he was manipulated by other, greater forces.

He would accept her for now. But he would make her pay for all that she had done, for all that she had cost him, past and present and future. He had plotted out the course of his revenge, and it would prove sweeter for the delay. She would suffer more for thinking that she held the upper hand now.

"Very well, then," he said. "I agree to your limitation. Rise, Ranita Glasswright, and be welcomed into your guild, until Clain's feast day when your skill and dedication will be tested by your fellow guildsmen."

She kissed his hand as he extended it to her, and he wondered if she realized that she did not first look back toward her companions, toward the player and the Touched girl. Parion saw them, though. He saw them, and he realized that both were worried for her. Both resented that she did not look to them for guidance. Both recognized that the Traitor was in danger in the guildhall.

Parion withdrew his hand, moving his fingers in the complicated Briantan gesture of paternity. "Welcome, Ranita Glasswright. Welcome to the Glasswrights' Guild."

6

Berylina stood in the street, trying to remember to breathe, to breathe, to look up at the sheer stone walls in front of her. The birthplace of First Pilgrim Jair. Here.

A smile tweaked the corners of her lips. She had done it. She had journeyed to Brianta. Despite a father who believed that she was possessed, despite a new sovereign who was mystified by her, despite a priest who was in awe of her, she had traveled all the way over the Great Eastern Road, arriving at last at Jair's home.

Poor Father Siritalanu. Setting aside his oft-voiced misgivings and his fears for a sixteen-year-old girl, he had completed the journey with her. He had spoken with innkeepers, making sure that Berylina had a private chamber each time they stopped. He had knelt with her in the corners of strange inns, held her hands between his, helped her to call upon the various gods to bless their days. He had spoken with Berylina long into the lonely nights, keeping her company as they listened to the Touched girl, Mair, comfort her crying child. He had cleared his throat and raised his voice to cover the noise of Ranita Glasswright and Tovin Player as they settled into their own private chambers. . . .

A flush painted Berylina's cheeks. Ranita and her lover had tried to be discreet. They had tried to keep their actions from the other travelers, tried not to let anyone know about the moments that they stole.

But how foolish did they think she was? How many times could any two reasonable people forget valuable items in their saddlebags after the horses had been stabled? How many times could doors creak in the night, even in the least-maintained country inn? And how many times could Mair's crying baby be an excuse for changing rooms, for bleary eyes and soft smiles in the morning?

Berylina shook her head. She did not care about Ranita and Tovin. She did not care what they said or thought or did. After all, the Thousand Gods blessed the bodies of men and women. Berylina cared only because poor Father Siritalanu had been embarrassed. He had looked at the princess with concern, as if she might expect him to protect her from the indelicacy of the situation.

She was no child. She was a princess of Liantine, the youngest girl in a family with four brothers. She knew the ways of men and women.

And she knew that she would have none of them.

Berylina smoothed her fingers down her green caloya robes, and the silk warmed against her flesh. The Thousand Gods did not call upon all of their servants to be chaste. Men and women were permitted to marry and remain in service to the gods. Nevertheless, the purest of the worshipers, the inner circle of those who remained true to the Thousand, proved their dedication by remaining pure in body and in heart. They remained devoted. They remained strong. Berylina was determined to be one of their number, to dedicate her chastity to the Thousand Gods and First Pilgrim Jair.

And she might as well start here at Jair's very birthplace. She raised her chin. "Very well, Father. Let us enter."

Siritalanu smiled upon her, and she was warmed by the kindness on his face. He understood. He appreciated her. He knew what she meant by bringing her pilgrimage here to Brianta. He nodded once and pushed open the door.

Berylina blinked and stepped over the threshold.

Darkness. As Siritalanu let the door close behind him, Berylina caught her lower lip between her teeth. Who cared if the movement emphasized her heavy jaw? The First Pilgrim knew her and loved her even in her stunted, broken body. He would watch over her, no matter the appearance of her teeth.

Making a holy sign across her chest, Berylina took a single step into the room. A post stood by her right hand, and she reached out to caress the prayer bell that hung there. The jangle was sharp in the chamber, alive, tinkling with power, and Berylina had to smother the urge to wrap her fingers around the bell. She did not want to disturb the other pilgrims. She did not want to summon them from their worship.

No one even looked up, though. No one acknowledged the princess's presence. Thousands of pilgrims touched the bell every day; thousands of worshipers offered up their anonymous prayers in this temple, in the birthplace of the First Pilgrim.

When Berylina blinked hard, she could make out people in the shadows, men and women who knelt at the low altars that lined the walls. She knew all about this holy place; she had heard tales from other travelers and read accounts in Morenia's great library. Each of the altars was dedicated to Jair; each contained a relic of his life, something that the First Pilgrim had touched, had used, had blessed.

Legend said that there were one thousand relics of the First Pilgrim, one for each of the gods. Certainly there were not that many objects in the temple. The counting was a mystery, a token of faith among Liantine pilgrims.

Berylina's knees ached to kneel before the holy objects. Her fingers twitched. She had not had a chance to draw during her long journey to Brianta—her crayons and chalk had been carefully packed away. She had needed to set aside the gods as they came to her, promised to capture the images later.

Those promises had borne fruit, though. With her visions of the gods held at bay, her other sensory impressions had waxed. Every step through the Briantan streets had been a titillation, a stimulation of her nose, her mouth, her ears, her flesh.

As she took another step into the chamber, her eyes began to adjust to the dim light. A single candle burned in the center of the room, thick as her arm and fashioned from plain white wax. The light was suspended from a wrought-iron chain that wound its way to the ceiling. One altar huddled beneath the candle, but it was surrounded by a thick knot of worshipers.

Berylina knew why they gathered there. The central altar was built on the precise spot where Jair had been born more than one thousand years before. His holy mother had crouched before her midwife, delivering the child who would change the world, the child who would open the hearts and eyes of mankind to all the Thousand Gods.

Berylina closed her eyes and breathed deeply, filling her lungs with the room's holiness. Her fingers tingled, and the roof of her mouth thrummed with power. The power of the Pilgrim. The power of the Thousand Gods.

Worshipers moved about the room, crawling from altar to altar upon their knees. Women sobbed; men grunted their devotions as they crouched before the holiest of relics. Berylina wanted to join them; she wanted to be filled with the glory that was Jair. She turned to Siritalanu and half whispered, "Father . . ."

"Aye, child," the priest breathed. "I feel the power."

Siritalanu guided her to one of the altars, his hand trembling against the small of her back. He knelt beside her and leaned close to whisper in her ear. "Hail, Holy Pilgrim Jair. Look upon this penitent with grace and compassion and bless the journey that she undertakes in your name. Keep her and protect her from harm, that she might continue to offer up praises in your name to all the Thousand Gods. Blessed Jair, we thank you for your guidance and your wisdom in all things."

Berylina's heart expanded with the words; her chest rose, and her breath came faster. Jair *would* watch over her. He *would* protect her. He *would* keep her safe from harm. Exhaling slowly, Berylina opened up her heart to Jair, expecting to feel the Pilgrim's presence fill her with his unique essence, with whatever sight or sound or touch or taste or smell heralded the First Pilgrim.

Nothing.

Berylina took another deep breath, and the room's close air rushed across her rabbit teeth. She closed her eyes, cutting out all distractions, limiting the warped vision from her twisted gaze. She told herself to ignore the whispers of prayer from the other pilgrims, to ignore the flicker of light from the single candle at the center of the room. She told herself not to hear the prayer bell as a newcomer brushed against it. She told herself not to smell the stifled air, not to think about the press of close bodies.

Focus on the Pilgrim. Feel his grace. Feel his protective mantle settle about her shoulders. Know that he stood with her, beside her, before her, and above her, that he was ready to guide her on her mission through Brianta, through the city of the Thousand Gods.

Nothing.

Berylina's eyes popped open, and she fought the urge to reach for Siritalanu's hand, to fumble for comfort like a child seeking a nurse in the night. After all, what did the priest *really* understand of the ways that she knew the gods? How much could he really know of the sights and the sounds, the tastes and the touches of the gods? How could he comprehend that she could *smell* the very deities, that she could *taste* them? And what would he make of her feeling nothing now?

Staying on her knees, Berylina crawled to the next altar. She squinted in the dim candlelight, and she could just make out an ivory comb centered on a golden cloth. Its teeth had been weathered by the years, most of them splintering, so that only four long prongs remained. Berylina imagined Jair's mother combing his hair, teasing his unruly locks into some semblance of submission.

She imagined the touch of ivory beneath her fingertips, the way the comb would warm beneath her hand. She thought about working the four sad teeth through her own hair, manipulating the instrument to untangle her wiry snarls. "Hail, Holy Pilgrim Jair," she repeated with Sirita-lanu. "Look upon this penitent with grace and compassion and bless the journey that she undertakes in your name. Keep her and protect her from harm, that she might continue to offer up praises in your name to all the Thousand Gods. Blessed Jair, we thank you for your guidance and your wisdom in all things."

She forced herself to focus on each word, to feel each element of the prayer. Surely Jair would come to her when she had proven her persistence. Once he knew that she was not going to give up, that she was not going to be swayed by an instant of invisible silence inside her mind, he *must* reveal his distinctive pattern.

When the First Pilgrim remained distant, Berylina dragged herself to the next altar. Another worshiper knelt there, an old woman who raised one wrinkled hand toward the spoon that rested in the place of honor. Berylina focused on the glint of candlelight that reflected off the bowl of the utensil—she could see that the tiny flame was upside down against the pewter. The princess tried to use the image to concentrate, to bring her attention to bear. She was certain that she could break through to Jair, certain that she could prove her worthiness by staying on her knees, by opening up her heart and soul.

After all, some of the other gods had proven elusive when she first met them. When Berylina first tried to listen, first tried to hear above the chaos that Liantine's Horned Hind had sown in her mind, she had scarcely been able to make out the voices of any of the Thousand.

Berylina was being tested here. Well, she had been tested in her father's house, and in her new home of Morenia. She was tested every time that she—a sixteen-year-old girl born with cast eyes and rabbit teeth—proclaimed some special knowledge of the Thousand. She had risen to such challenges before, and there was no reason to think that she would not succeed this time. "Hail, Holy Pilgrim Jair," she began again. She schooled her voice to patience. "Look upon this penitent with grace and compassion. . . ." She finished the trope mechanically, trailing off on the word *wisdom,* trying not to let her fears carry her away.

Maybe she had approached Jair incorrectly from the very beginning. Maybe she should have waited until a place had cleared at the central altar, at the platform that marked his birthplace. Maybe she should have purified herself before coming to this holy house—she should have bathed another time, or fasted another day.

But Jair should not be so demanding. He should not be that difficult, that aloof. After all, he was not actually a god himself. He was a man, a human man who had found the truth of the Thousand Gods within himself. He was a signpost, a guide, a starting point for all those who thought to worship strong and true. He was a guiding light for Berylina.

Another pilgrim entered the sanctuary and jangled the prayer bell. Berylina looked about the room, trying to see it with fresh eyes. Once again, she was struck by the realization that there were far from a thousand relics. There were only two score altars against the walls. Each held one item precious to the First Pilgrim, something from his life, his journey through all the castes. Each relic, then, must be counted in a special way if the symbolism were to work, if the counting were to reach one thousand.

The comb, for example. Perhaps each tine should be considered separately. Four teeth, and the total of the comb— five was the counting for that relic. The spoon should be one. But perhaps it was two. Perhaps the top of the bowl and the bottom of the bowl counted separately. For that matter, the handle might be an item unto itself. Or the top of the bowl, the bottom of the bowl, the handle, and the spoon as an entire entity. One god, two gods, three gods, four . . .

What was Berylina doing here? She was no mystic. She was no scholar. How was she to tell when she had measured out true faith? How was she to know when her worship was acceptable to the gods? In the past, she had always been instructed, first by her nurses, then by Father Siritalanu. She had always prayed and reached the point when the gods came to her, when they opened up within her mind, expanded inside her senses. Jair did not seem inclined to appear.

But he *must* come to her. She must start her pilgrimage by honoring the First Pilgrim. She must begin at the beginning, here in the house where Jair had entered the world, where he began his mystical journey. She dared not proceed with her true mission, with the initialization of her cavalcade and her journey to the shrines of several gods, until she had received the First Pilgrim's blessing.

Trembling, she crawled to the next altar.

A young man's tunic, narrow in the chest, flared across the hips, a style so ancient that it had not been worn for centuries. Laces ran down the sleeves, crossing themselves over and over. Berylina started to count the eyelets for each lace—was each symbolic of a god? What if she miscounted? What if the tunic were to be taken as a whole, but something else, another relic was to be broken down into nine hundred ninety-nine pieces? "Hail, Holy Pilgrim Jair," she started to say, but she could not bring herself to complete the prayer. Instead, she lowered her head to her fists and fought back tears.

Here she was in Brianta, traveled all the way across the land, and she was too weak to make her worship meaningful. As the tears came, hot and pulsing behind her eyes, she felt Father Siritalanu's touch upon her shoulder.

"My lady," he whispered. "Do not fret so."

"I can't feel him," Berylina said, horrified that other pilgrims would hear her in the close, dark chamber. "All the gods I can feel or smell, taste or hear or see, but the Pilgrim is invisible to me."

"For now," Father Siritalanu chided. "For now. Come, child. Come kneel here, in the center of the room. Forget the relics. Forget the signs. Kneel beneath the candle and say your prayers with me."

Berylina let the priest help her to her feet. She let him guide her to the raised altar in the center of the room. Beneath the candle was a child's plaything, a ball that had been carved from a single piece of wood, as white as the candle above.

Berylina caught her breath as she stared at the toy. It was perfectly smooth, completely even. There were no marks on the surface, nothing to distract a watcher, nothing to disturb the counting of the object. It was *one*. One undivided piece. One single entity.

"There, my lady," Father Siritalanu whispered. "There is Jair's first relic. Meditate on it and find peace. Find power."

Berylina turned her head to the side so that she could look at Siritalanu with her good eye. Did he understand? Did he think that she was mad, trying to establish some sort of rapport?

No. He believed in her. He always had.

Berylina took a deep breath and lowered her head. When she exhaled, she heard a slight whistle, the sound of air passing over her jutting teeth. She set aside her embarrassment, though, set aside her anger and frustration about her differentness. "Hail, Holy Pilgrim Jair," she started.

This time, the words were different. This time, they were loaded with power, with potential, even as they formed at the back of her throat. "Hail, Holy Pilgrim Jair," she repeated. Her vision grew within her. No, not vision. Jair was not a shape. He was not a color, not an odor, not a taste. He was a solid, complete wholeness, an impenetrable sphere. He was the power and the essence and the solidity of the ball that stood on the platform, of the child's toy that graced the very center of the temple.

Berylina felt the wholeness with her entire mind; she understood it with every fiber of her body. She reached toward the sphere, stretching her fingers toward its infinite completeness. "Look upon this penitent with grace and compassion," she said, and she *understood* the words; she knew that they were true. She gathered in the power that she recognized as uniquely Jair, that came from the holiness of this place, and she raised her voice, "And bless the journey that she undertakes in your name."

In one tiny part of her mind, Berylina knew that other pilgrims must be staring at her; they must be focused on her. They could hardly ignore her as they struggled to pay attention to their own worship, their own recognition of the power and glory of Jair.

Nevertheless, Berylina could not quench the certainty inside her, the absolute knowledge that she was right, that she was strong, that she was revealing the true core of First Pilgrim Jair, or having it revealed to her. Her voice rang out: "Keep her and protect her from harm, that she might continue to offer up praises in your name to all the Thousand Gods." Tears streamed down her face, and she stretched her arms, held them toward the child's toy as if she were summoning the very core of the universe. "Blessed Jair, we thank you for your guidance and your wisdom."

The ball moved.

It rolled from the center of the altar, from the center of the room, from the precise place where Jair had crowned between his mother's knees more than a millennium ago. Gathering force from somewhere, summoning power from some secret well, the smooth white ball rolled across the altar and into Berylina's waiting hands.

She could feel the power there. She could feel the energy of First Pilgrim Jair beating beneath the smooth surface. She recognized more colors than she had ever known, scents more delicate than the entire universe could hold, sounds and tastes and touches that she had barely imagined.

All were contained inside the sphere. All were encompassed by First Pilgrim Jair. All pulsed against her palms as she caught the ancient relic, as she cradled it against her chest.

And then she remembered to breathe again. She remembered that she was a mortal woman. She was standing in the center of a temple, beneath the light of a candle that had flared high, had burned bright enough to attract the attention of all the surrounding pilgrims.

"Father," she croaked, and she extended her hands to Sir-italanu, offering him the relic.

"My lady," he said, and for a moment she thought he would be too afraid to take it, too awed to accept the gift she had to give. Then he seemed to understand. He took the ball from her, and he set it back in the center of the altar. Seeing the toy in his hand, she shuddered, like a dog casting off a coat of morning dew. The motion brought her back to full awareness, back to the temple, back to Liantine.

Back to the crowd of pilgrims around her.

"Behold!" one man exclaimed.

"She touched the ball," a woman cried.

"The candle! It burned brighter for her!"

And then there was a whisper, very faint, from the edges of the crowd. "Witch."

Berylina started to offer up explanations. She started to tell them that she had not intended to move the ball, that she had not tried to disrupt the altar. The crowd would not listen, though. They did not care what she had to say, what she believed.

Even as she struggled to explain, she felt the Jair-shape within her mind, the perfect sphere, and she knew that it was not a complete vision. It was a symbol, a sign, a promise. It stood in her thoughts as a potential, as a glimpse of the true Pilgrim's power.

The crowd cared only about what they had seen, what they had witnessed.

"Stand back!" Father Siritalanu said. "Give Princess Berylina some room!"

Her title caused another swirl of whispers to curl among the pilgrims. A princess! In their midst! Communing with First Pilgrim Jair!

Father Siritalanu set his jaw. His boyish face matured in an instant, creased into lines of concern and determination. He placed a protective hand under Berylina's elbow, guiding her away from the central altar.

"Father," she whispered, leaning heavily on him. Her breath caught in her throat as his fingers closed around her arm, and she used his solid flesh to anchor herself back in Jair's temple, back in Brianta, back in the corporeal world.

"Child," Siritalanu said. He cleared his throat and repeated the word. "Child. It is time that you initiated your cavalcade. It is time that you officially began your pilgrimage."

She saw that the other worshipers continued to look at her in awe. Grown men knuckled their foreheads; women wept as she moved by. Even children, the sort who had stared at her, who had pointed and laughed and mocked her deformities, even children gazed at her in amazement.

"Bless us, in the name of Jair," one woman pleaded as she passed.

Berylina stumbled on the uneven floor, and the praying woman caught her hand, accepted the touch as a blessing. "Yes!" a man cried. "Bless us! In the name of Jair!"

She was surrounded by hands, by grasping fingers, by clutching fists. She touched as many of the people as she could, desperate for a path to the door, to the outside, to escape and air and sunlight. Father Siritalanu moved in front of her, clearing the way, and she kept her eyes focused on his shimmering robes.

She felt eyes upon the caloya green of her own gown, and several people fell to their knees, reaching out for the hem of the garment, raising it to their lips. *No!* Berylina tried to cry. *Do not honor me! Find the strength of the First Pilgrim for yourself! Find Jair in your hearts!*

Father Siritalanu finally reached the door. Berylina felt, rather than heard, his hand brush against the prayer bell. She breathed the instant that his fingers closed upon the latch; she absorbed the power of his fist encircling the iron.

When the door opened, it brought in light and air and clear, free-flowing thought. Berylina gasped at the freedom. She had thought of Brianta as a dusty town, sere in its summer drought, but now the streets gleamed in clarity. She staggered out of the temple and into the road in front of the temple.

"Come, Berylina. Come with me." Father Siritalanu was using a tone she had heard long ago, an urgent phrasing that she remembered from the days when they had first met in Liantine. He had pulled her then, urging her forward. He had given her the strength to flee the Horned Hind, to embrace the Thousand. He had paved a solid path beneath her lost and wandering feet.

Now Berylina followed the sound of his voice, marveling at the crystal tones. She turned his presence around and around in her mind, enchanted by the solidity of it. "Here, Berylina," he said. "Follow me. We'll walk around the temple. We'll speak with the priests. Follow me. There you go."

She stumbled beside him, only vaguely aware of the people, the buildings, the things that they passed. Her fingers trembled as if she still cradled the white ball, and she felt the warmth, the power, the protective energy of Jair grow and spread within her.

Berylina knew the process for beginning her pilgrimage. She was supposed to speak to a priest. She was supposed to state her name and her homeland, to outline why she had come to Brianta and who she hoped to honor especially among the Thousand Gods. Before she was ready to begin her official journey, though, she found herself standing in front of an ancient priest.

A young boy stood beside the old man, stretching up to whisper something in one of his hairy ears. The child wore the short green tunic of an acolyte; he clearly served the Thousand Gods in some temple. In the House of Jair, Berylina realized, as she made out the small badge on the child's shoulder, a woven emblem of a perfect white sphere.

The child stepped back, and the old priest took in her caloya robes and frowned. Lines were carved so deeply into his jowls that she thought his face might split. His voice was dark as mahogany as he asked, "Who comes before the Thousand Gods making a mockery of First Pilgrim Jair?"

Already? How could he know? That boy! The child must have been inside the temple. He must have seen her touch Jair's holy relic. He must have seen the ball roll toward her, the candle flare high.

Berylina knew that she must answer the priest. Father Siritalanu could not speak for her here. For just an instant, though, she felt as if she were a child herself, as if she were huddled in her father's court. She longed for the nurses she had known then, the loyal women who had guided her along the dark and confusing paths of a princess.

Those women were gone, though. One had been slain when Berylina fled her ill-fated nuptials; the others had long been left behind, when Berylina abandoned her homeland in pursuit of all the gods.

She was alone here. She must stand before the Thousand and their earthly representative, the priest.

She stepped up to the old man and made a holy sign across her chest, swallowing hard before she summoned the courage to speak. "Father, it is I, Berylina Pilgrim, who stands before you, but I never meant to mock First Pilgrim Jair."

"You touched his holy relics, did you not?"

"I prayed before the First Pilgrim's altar, if it may please Your Grace." Berylina felt the solid wholeness that she had sensed as the ball touched her fingers—she remembered the feeling of all colors, all sounds, all tastes, all touches commingled in her mind. She gathered up the power of that wholeness, and she said, "First Pilgrim Jair came to me, Father. He offered up his relic."

Before the priest could respond, Berylina heard more words that she should speak; she felt them in the marrow of her bones. Jair was delivering a message. She was afraid. She wanted to deny the Pilgrim; she wanted to refuse. But there was no declining to embrace the word, the power, the glory of Jair.

"The First Pilgrim says that his house is ill-tended, Father. He says that the priests have . . ." Berylina struggled for a moment, trying to think of a softer word, trying to think of a gentler blow. Jair stirred within her, though, glowing, pulsing, *being* within her, and she abandoned all attempts at editing his holy words. "He says that the priests have hoarded coins that should have gone toward his worship. He is meant to be worshiped in the light. There should be tapers at every one of his altars, at every corner of his house. The priesthood should not prosper on the coins they save by leaving the house of First Pilgrim Jair in darkness."

"What!" The priest's lined face flushed crimson, and Berylina stepped back from the fury in his eyes. He sucked in breath, as if he would extinguish every candle in Brianta, and when he howled at her again, spittle flicked from his lips. "What blasphemy do you speak here, false caloya?"

Berylina might have cowered at making demands in a foreign land. She might have doubted the new voice that whispered in her thoughts, that spoke to her in shades of white, that brushed against her mind with utter stillness.

She knew, though, that she was no false caloya. She knew that the Thousand Gods spoke to her, that they came to her because she was good and true and faithful. She knew that the priest before her might criticize her for her physical failings; he might call her ugly or twisted or flawed, but he could make no claim about her fidelity, about her faith, about her true, true power.

She pulled herself to her full height and ran her hands down her green robes. The gesture stilled her pounding heart, lent strength and power to her spine. "I say again, Father, that I am Berylina Pilgrim. I speak the words that First Pilgrim Jair bids me say. He wants candles in his sanctuary. He wants light to mark the place of his birth."

Berylina became aware of the crowd that had gathered behind her, aware of the people who pressed into the tiny courtyard. There were all the pilgrims who had prayed in the house of Jair, and others who had been passing in the street when this commotion began. Even now, rumors whipped through their ranks, and she wished that she could silence the speakers, could restrain them and remind them that she did not desire their thoughts, their speculations, their surprising conclusions based upon her prayer. Her desire to silence the crowd grew sharper as she heard someone exlaim, "She speaks against the priests!" Another voice rumbled, "Witch!"

Nevertheless, the believers hushed the skeptics. People who had witnessed Berylina's prayers whispered about what they had seen. The voices of dissent flickered into silence.

The old priest was no fool. He read the crowd with

bulging eyes, and then he clambered to his feet behind his oaken table. He, too, wore robes of green, but his gown was embroidered with leaves, with reminders of richness and power and blooming springtime beauty. He moved his fingers in a complicated gesture, a symbol that was aped by half the crowd. Berylina could not decipher the meaning behind the motion.

"Pilgrim, if you would complain about the keeping of a church, then you must speak to the Keeper of the Temples. We have no power to respond to the complaints of every weary wanderer here. The Keeper sits at dawn on every third day, in the center of the market. Plague him with your demands."

"I will, Father," Berylina said, and a part of her was grateful that she could address someone other than this angry priest. She had not meant to condemn the man, only to question the practice, only to clarify the words that Jair spoke within her mind.

"Be gone, then." The priest glared at her as if he would roast her caloya gown with his eyes. His hands moved in another sullen pattern, one that she could recognize this time—it was clearly a dismissal. She started to gather up her skirts in her fists, using the old gesture of her childhood.

No, she reminded herself. She was no longer an awkward Liantine princess. She was a pilgrim, beginning her long journey in service to the Thousand Gods.

"In a moment, Father, I will be gone."

"In a moment!"

"Yes, Father. If it pleases you, if it pleases all the keepers of the Pilgrim's paths, I would start my cavalcade today."

"Your cavalcade!" The man might never have heard of the instrument of faith.

"Yes, Father. I mean to journey in service to the Thousand Gods, if it pleases Your Grace."

"It would *please*," the priest started to grumble, but then he caught himself before he could utter more harsh words.

He glared at Berylina, and she knew that he was wishing her far away.

The crowd, though, pressed forward. Four pilgrims fought to stand behind Berylina, as if they waited for their own cavalcades. These men defied tradition, for each was a burly soldier, and each set a hammy fist upon the hilt of his dagger. Pilgrims were not supposed to carry steel. Well, pilgrims were not supposed to bandy about accusations of witchery, either.

One man said, "We watched the girl in Jair's Temple. She prayed on her knees like everyone else." The crowd murmured.

Another man added, "The Temple *is* dark. There *should* be more candles."

The other two men only nodded, but they shifted their hands on their weapons, managing to convey their ominous displeasure. The choleric priest paled.

He glared at Berylina, and she whispered, "If you please, Father. Just sign my cavalcade, and I'll be on my way."

Swallowing hard and eyeing the men, the priest started to say something else to Berylina, started some further protest. "In the name of Jair and all that is holy," she said, falling to her knees, "allow me to redeem myself, Father. Allow me to speak glory in the name of all the Thousand Gods. Allow me to find the paths that First Pilgrim Jair has made for me; permit me to walk in his grace and his safety and his shadow for all the days of my existence."

The words were part of an ancient formula, a prayer that Berylina had learned from her nurses long ago. She had known that they were part of the timeless power of religion in Brianta, that the priests here had taught schoolchildren decades past, before Berylina had ever been imagined by the royal house of Liantine.

Something about the words worked magic. The formula soothed the priest, made him recognize the exuberance of the pilgrim before him. Berylina might have frightened him.

She might have inspired the warrish men who glared at the assembled masses. She might have disrupted the order in the old man's life. But she spoke the words of the faithful. She embraced religious truth as he knew it.

She watched his fury melt away, and she knew the precise moment that he decided to assist her. She started to breathe a prayer of gratitude, but she was not certain which of the Thousand Gods had interceded for her, which had broken through to the cornered man. Lest she offend one of the Thousand, she settled for thinking a prayer toward Jair, toward the First Pilgrim who had guided her steps along this shaky path. Clumsily, she wove her fingers into a Briantan symbol of gratitude.

The priest reached down to the ground beside his throne-like chair. An ornate box rested on a cloth-of-gold pillow nestled between four extravagant tassels. The sides of the box were covered with pounded gold, and intricate enamel designs twisted across the gleaming metal. In a flash, Berylina took in the paintings that showed the life of Jair, a fitting start to Berylina's own official pilgrimage.

The priest raised the lid of the golden casket, and he produced a piece of parchment. Flourishing the document before the assembled crowd, the holy man dug in the box for a fine quill pen and a pot of blackest ink. He took his time settling the writing implements on his table, making certain that every symbol was neatly lined up, that all was in its proper place.

He cleared his throat once, and then he dipped his pen, letting the excess ink drip back into the pot. "Your name, then, Pilgrim?"

"B-berylina." She stuttered as she voiced her answer; never before had her name carried so much import.

"And your home, Pilgrim?"

She paused. She could not name Liantine, not the place of her birth that had abandoned her, that had thrust her forward on a bloody path to faith. Morenia, then. That was her home. She had sworn fealty to Halaravilli ben-Jair, after all. She felt Father Siritalanu stir behind her, and she knew that she could answer truthfully. "Morenia."

"Very well, Berylina Pilgrim of Morenia. There will be five specific gods that you honor with your pilgrimage, five special deities among all the Thousand. They will watch over your steps; they will guide your words and worship. They will protect you and keep you for all the rest of your days, if you please them here in Brianta. Who is the first god that you would honor in this fashion?"

Berylina had thought about this matter, of course. She had pondered the meaning of her pilgrimage, the special gods who had spoken to her in her life. She had held some of her favorites close to her heart, knowing that they already recognized her faith, that they already knew she cared for them, that she spoke to them, that she acknowledged them as sovereign in all things. Thus, she did not need to honor Nome on this cavalcade. She did not need to reach out to Kel, or Par, or Glat.

She had spoken with Father Siritalanu many times, exploring possibilities. Gently, he had suggested that she dedicate herself to some of the more basic gods. After all, he had pointed out, she was only sixteen years old. She had demonstrated her vocation; she had proven her dedication to all the Thousand. There would surely be other pilgrimages in her future, other opportunities to show that she was devoted to the more challenging gods.

Berylina had rebelled against such thought, though. There was nothing that she was going to accomplish when she was older that she could not do now, nothing involving The Thousand Gods, at least. They had spoken to her since she was a child, since her first nurse opened her eyes and ears and heart to their majestic presences. She *knew* them already.

She had listened to Father Siritalanu, and she had nodded, creasing her brow in the way that they had agreed long ago meant that she was serious, that she was contemplating the importance of his words. She told him that she would consider the matter further, continue evaluating possibilities.

And she had made her own choices.

Change. That was what she wanted to master. That was what she wanted to explore. This pilgrimage was going to change her life, change her faith, change the world around her. Therefore, she would focus on gods of change.

She had been surprised to learn that there was no single god of change. She had thought that the concept was so basic, so inherent in the building up and tearing down of the world that there must be a deity dedicated to it and to nothing else.

But she had examined the scrolls in Morenia, the long listings of all the gods. She had read books written by great philosophers; she had struggled through words and concepts well beyond her training. Finally, she had brought herself to ask Siritalanu.

He had shrugged as he answered. There were many concepts not recognized among the gods. One thousand was an awesome number; however, it could not encompass all things in men's experience. There was no god of change. Berylina had accepted that verdict with goodwill. Who was she to question the wisdom of First God Ait? Who was she to renumber the pantheon?

She would just have to focus on other gods. On gods who captured the notion of change, gods who would convey the essence that she craved.

The old priest glared at her and asked again, "Who is the first god that you would honor?"

Berylina clenched her fists and announced, "Ile." The god of the moon. The god that endlessly changed his face in the sky, that presided over the ebbing and flowing of the tide, over the courses of her woman's body.

"Ile," the priest said, and if he thought her choice was

strange, he did not say so. Instead, he dipped his great pen back into his inkpot, and he inscribed the god's name onto her cavalcade.

As the priest wrote out the word, Berylina felt her nose fill with the smell of new-mown hay. Ile's aroma flooded the back of her throat as if she were drowning in a sea of green-gold grass. The priest intoned, "Go forth in the name of Ile, and learn the ways of that god. Learn to honor him and do right by him, and may he bless you for all the rest of your days." The grassy scent grew even stronger, and Berylina longed to hold her breath forever, but she forced herself to exhale evenly, folding her fingers into a holy sign.

The priest seemed not to notice. He scarcely paused before he asked, "And your second god?"

"Mip, the god of water." Berylina had studied the ocean on her crossing from Liantine to Morenia. She had studied the stone that sat beneath the eaves of her palace chamber; she had seen the smooth hole bored by the persistent dripping of rainwater. She had seen the banks of rivers and bluffs that rose high above meandering streams. Water had great power to modify the world around it, to shape even the hardest ground.

This time, the priest did look at her oddly. Berylina merely turned her head to the side, pinning him with one eye, making it easier for him to study her, to grant her desire. "Mip," the priest said, and he shook his head. What child would offer up a pilgrimage in the name of Mip?

Still, the priest wrote out the name and added his holy seal. The scratching of the pen released the sound of bird-song, the delicate trilling of a nightingale that spread across the courtyard. The sound was so clear, so perfect, that Berylina looked up, glancing at Father Siritalanu, at all the assembled pilgrims, to see if they could hear the bird.

Nothing. Mip spoke to her alone. As all the gods, he presented a private face for her to worship. The priest spoke his formula quickly: "Go forth in the name of Mip and learn the ways of that god. Learn to honor him and do right by him, and may he bless you for all the rest of your days." Berylina eagerly curled her fingers into the gesture of devotion.

The nightingale trilled once more and then fell silent. As if the priest feared another odd response, he took a deep breath before he said, "Your third god?"

"Nim, the god of wind." The crowd murmured.

Berylina had questioned herself about this choice. After all, did wind change the world as much as water? For a long while, Berylina had feared that she was choosing Nim only because of Queen Mareka, because of the power that the peach-flavored god had spread across her tongue at the funeral of the two little princes.

But then she had thought about changes she had seen, wrought by wind in the world around her. Once, when she was a child, a waterspout had come up out of the sea. Spinning and spinning, it had roared over her father's palace, plucking up all the rosebushes from the garden and shattering a wall of glass in the royal receiving hall. Teheboth Thunderspear had decided not to replace the glasswork; instead, he had ordered a wooden screen. That screen was the first touch of the Horned Hind in the house of Thunderspear, the first hint that the Thousand Gods were losing their grip in Liantine. All because of Nim . . . All because the god of wind had thrown a tantrum one morning.

The old priest cocked his head to one side, but he scrawled the name onto her cavalcade. Berylina scarcely heard him as he repeated his formula. Her mouth filled with the essence of peach, with the perfect taste of summer fruit as she signaled her gratitude. She nearly missed the priest's demand: "And your fourth god?"

Berylina hesitated. She had debated long hours before she had settled on her fourth choice. She knew that Father Siritalanu disapproved; he thought her decision inappropriate for a child. Well, she was hardly a child. And her choice made sense in the context of her goals. She wanted gods of

transition, and there was hardly any god who presided over
more transition than this one. She forced herself to raise her
voice, to speak loudly enough to be heard. "Zil. The god of
gamblers."

The priest slammed his fist against the table. "Zil! You
mock me, girl!" The crowd exclaimed, and one of Berylina's
four armed supporters flushed, looking as if he wished he'd
never come forward.

She hastened to say, "No! I am drawn to the god of gambling, Father. He speaks to me in ways that I do not yet understand. I undertake this journey to understand him better,
to know the truthfulness of his ways."

"You make this journey to mock us here in Brianta."

"Father, you must not believe that! I have meditated on
my choices for all the long days and nights of my journey to
this holy land."

"You're a slip of a girl. Why waste your time meditating
on gambling? What evil thoughts do you work inside your
head?"

Berylina's response ran cold through her belly. How dare
the priest—a man dedicated to *all* the Thousand Gods—insult one of them in such an offhanded manner? Certainly Zil
was not reliable. Certainly he played games with those who
came to him for guidance. Certainly he brought great men to
ruin and raised up others who scarcely seemed worthy of the
honor.

But for a priest to speak against one of the Thousand? For
a man to reject a god?

Berylina clutched the green fabric of her robe, trying to
remember that priests were fallible, like all men. Priests
were subject to mistakes, just as caloyas were, as princesses
were, as ordinary sixteen-year-old girls were. Berylina
would not be perfect even when she had completed her pilgrimage and studied the gods and offered up her heart of
hearts.

"Please, Father," she tried again. "At first I thought to

dedicate my pilgrimage to Wain, the god of fate. Surely he would be pleasing to you. I realized, though, that another god has walked beside me, another god has shaped the strange days of my life. I chose Zil because I have felt his force molding me, creating me. My father gambled with his faith and other things. I have tried to learn the folly of his ways, that I might avoid them and stay true to the Thousand for all the days of my life."

She saw the lines in the priest's face relaxing, saw that he was going to yield to her. Well, she hadn't lied. Her father *had* gambled—gambled on the saving grace of a woodland goddess. Berylina's dedicating her pilgrimage to Zil might teach her a little more of what her father had hoped to gain, of how he had planned to build a kingdom on a hope and a prayer and a shaky, false foundation.

"Very well," the priest grumbled, as he jabbed his pen back into his inkpot. "Zil." The old man scratched away at Berylina's cavalcade. Immediately, her skin was embraced by ermine—soft, soft fur brushing against her arms, her legs, her face.

For just an instant, she was distracted by Zil's presence, lost in wondering why he would choose ermine as his worldly presence. Why did any of the gods choose their presentations, though? What made any of them think that a particular sight or sound or touch was characteristic of their essential self?

Before she could divine an answer, the priest recited the formula invoking the god. He rushed through the words, and then Berylina signaled her acceptance. She was released from the ermine touch. "And your last choice, Pilgrim?"

"Tarn." Berylina whispered the name.

"You are a child!" the priest bellowed. The crowd exploded.

"I am acquainted with Tarn's work, Father! I know him now, as all of us must come to know him. He greeted me at my birth when he took away my mother, and I know that he will wait for me until all the end of my days."

"Can't you choose a single child's god? Can't you honor Shir, the god of song? Or Purn or Shul?"

"The god of dance does not come easily to me, Father, and the god of mirth abandons me altogether." Berylina stepped closer to the table, certain that she could convince this priest, as she had at last convinced Father Siritalanu. "Father, a pilgrimage is not meant to be easy. It is not meant to let one frolic and play. I must test myself, and so testing build my faith in all the Thousand Gods. I have prayed about this for long, long days, and even longer nights. Do not keep me from my labor, Father. Do not force me to change my cavalcade."

As she spoke, the priest's eyes became hooded, and she wondered what memories she evoked for him, what history she spun inside his mind. His face softened; he was no longer an irate gatekeeper. Instead, he was a young man, a passionate man, a man who had found his faith and his profession among all the Thousand Gods.

"Tarn," he said, and he dipped his pen back into his pot of ink. "Very well, child. If you think that the god of death is appropriate for you, I can only give you my blessing."

"That is all that I would ask, Father. That is all that any living man can give me." Berylina watched him complete the cavalcade. The lines of the pen summoned the familiar green-black of Tarn's cloak, the shimmer of a beetle's carapace in the corners of her mind. She moved her fingers in grateful acceptance.

Then she smelled the crimson wax that the priest dripped onto the parchment. She heard the faint crack as he lifted free his golden seal, and when she swallowed, she tasted tears at the back of her throat. She shivered and ran her hands along her arms, trying to remember the feel of Zil's soft robes, the touch of ermine comfort.

When the priest presented the cavalcade, Berylina drew

herself straight inside her caloya gown. "I dedicate my pilgrimage to all the Thousand Gods, but most particularly to Ile and Mip. To Nim and Zil. And to Tarn."

The priest's tone was relieved as he handed her the parchment. "Go forward, Pilgrim. Go forward and find your fate within the holy precincts of Brianta, and in all the wide, wide world. Go forward in the name of Ile and in the name of Mip, in the name of Nim and in the name of Zil. Go forward, Pilgrim, in the name of Tarn."

Berylina took the parchment with a bow. She stepped back and gazed at the four soldiers who had supported her—the two who had most pressured the priest, the one who had stood fast, the one who had wavered. She nodded, and each man's hands flew in some Briantan signal. Berylina did not know the proper response, and so she only nodded.

Then she walked through the murmuring crowd, trying to ignore the strange combination of awe and fear and wrath. She gained strength from Father Siritalanu behind her, strength to stand tall as the heat shimmered up from the stones beneath her feet. She tried to ignore the victorious flutter of Tarn's green-black wings as she left the holy courtyard.

7

Rani watched as Mair looked up from Laranifarso, who had fallen asleep at her breast. The Touched woman pitched her voice low, obviously trying not to disturb her son, but there was an urgency behind her words. "You have to sleep sometime, Rai."

"I'm not tired."

"You were bathing before the sun came up, and I heard you grinding those colors until late into the night."

"I'm sorry. I never meant to disturb you with my work. I'll try to be more quiet tonight."

"You weren't *disturbing* me!" Mair lowered her voice when Laranifarso fussed. "You weren't disturbing me. It's just that you worry me. You need to sleep. You can't serve the guild and the princess and yourself, if you can't even keep your eyes open."

Rani stifled a yawn as she set down the glass pestle she had been using. She stretched her fingers and tried not to grimace as the tendons and ligaments eased back into place. She could not remember how long she had been gripping the tool, how long she had scraped the glass over her smooth stone tray. Lapis, cinnabar, ochre—she had ground the colors for hours, processing each from stone to powder to dust.

She had not started, though, until after sunset. She had finished the day's labors at the guildhall and washed the

grime from her face and her arms at the ritual glasswrights'
bath. She had choked down a few bites of the dry bread that
Master Parion permitted her, swallowed two glasses of
murky water from the plain glazed mug that he had given
her.

On the way back to the hostelry, she had stopped at the
temple of Hern, the god of merchants. She had not been surprised by the gold and ivory and enamel trappings of the
place. Any merchant able to make a pilgrimage would have
donated handsomely to the place.

Bardo would have offered up riches. Rani purchased a
candle as thick as her wrist and lit it from another. She sank
to her knees and tried to form words appropriate to Hern.
She gave up after a few tries, though, deciding to offer cherished memories instead.

Bardo flashing a grin at their mother and father as he carried new stock into the shop. Bardo laughing as he presented
her with a sweet roll. Bardo insisting that he could do better
than the Merchants' Council, that he could set market policies that would foster greater profits.

Bardo arguing with their father. Bardo slamming the
shop door in rage over a stolen buckle. Bardo begging her in
Morenia's House of the Thousand Gods, pleading with her
to join his subversive Brotherhood. Bardo looking up from
the executioner's block, alone and afraid.

Rani reduced her prayer to Hern to a few repeated words:
"Watch over the lost. Watch over the fallen."

She'd slipped a handful of gold coins into a slatted
wooden box as she left the temple. Her pilgrim's cloak had
stifled her as she made her way through the dusty streets,
past a preacher who demanded that the immodest be cast out
from Brianta. She nearly ran past a wild-haired woman who
shouted that witches stalked the city.

Mair sighed, bringing her mind back to their shared
room. "I don't understand, Rai. You can't use lapis to paint
on glass. You told me that yourself."

Rani shook her head and caught another yawn against the back of her teeth. "It's the same skill. We glasswrights grind lampblack and lead white for our colors. The painting guild uses the other colors. Here in Brianta, there's trade between the guilds, much more than in Morenia. Master Parion has structured an arrangement with the painters. We grind colors for them. The labor teaches us what we need to know about grinding and pigments, and it puts them in our debt."

"Puts them in *your* debt," Mair repeated. "Why should the guild profit from your labor like that?"

"I'm a member of the guild." Rani's voice heated in warning, but Mair did not seem to recognize the dangerous ground that she trod.

"*If* they choose to let you in. Why are you doing this, Rai? Why are you letting them force you back into jobs that you should have been shed of years ago? You said yourself that grinding colors was an apprentice's job. You're a journeyman, ready to rise to master. They should at least let you do a journeyman's work."

"They must learn to trust me," Rani said. Her voice was soft as she spoke, as she said all the things that she'd been thinking for so long. "We're like a family, Mair. A family that knows it must stay together, must stand against the rest of the outside world. And yet we do not truly trust each other. Love each other, yes, because we must. But *like* each other, no. Not at all." She pictured Bardo smiling and shaking his head as he left her at the guildhall gates, years ago, in Moren.

"Well, Rai, I couldn't work with a group of people who all despise me."

"They don't all despise me." Mair merely cocked her head. "They don't! I've already become friendly with two of the journeymen—Belita and Cosino. They come from Zarithia; they've worked in the great glass workshops there. They were the ones who showed me how to grind the ochre fine enough."

"Well, then. Two friends out of four score. All hail Belita and Cosino!"

"Why are you being so stubborn?"

"I don't like to see you hurt yourself for these people. I don't like to see you working for them when they don't appreciate you."

Rani managed a smile. "It was all well and good when I worked for your Touched troop years ago."

Mair snorted, and the sound was enough to wake her son. Laranifarso opened his pink mouth to wail, and the Touched mother shifted him to her other arm, taking the opportunity to suckle him at her other breast. He quickly settled down, filling the room with his greedy sucking noises.

Before Mair could fashion a reply, there was a sharp rap at the door. "Come," Rani called, reluctant to set aside the fine ochre dust that she was working. It was close to finished. So close . . .

But it would not be done for some time, she realized as the door swung open and Tovin stalked in. The player declined to brush his fingers against the prayer bell just inside the door. In fact, he glared at it for a moment before making a transparent decision not to comply with Briantan tradition. Already, Rani missed the jangle—she had been in Jair's homeland for long enough that she expected the chimes; she expected such tangible dedication to the gods. "Where have you been?" she asked, noting that he was carrying his pilgrim's cloak.

"Downstairs. Eating a meat pie and enjoying what passes for ale in these parts. I tired of waiting for you, and I was hungry. I knew you would not join me." He swallowed, then said, "At the table."

Rani felt a blush rise on her cheeks, and she flashed a look to Mair. The Touched girl became engrossed with her son's blankets, but a smile twitched her lips.

Tovin said, "While I sat belowstairs, a messenger arrived."

"A messenger?" Rani kept her voice neutral, but acid fear leached into her empty belly. A dull ache pounded behind her eyes.

Tovin glanced about the chamber as if he expected spies to lurk in the shadowy corners. "From the Fellowship." He managed to hiss the sentence, delivering it as a secret, a true whisper, not the sort that he would utter on the stage.

Mair looked up from Laranifarso. "I wondered how long it would take for them to demand our presence."

"Too long," Tovin said, his copper eyes narrowed. "They've known we were here for nearly ten days. They've been planning something."

Rani forced her voice to an even register, fighting down irritation with the man. He could at least look happy to see her. Even if she was forbidden to touch him, forbidden by the oaths she had taken to Master Parion . . . the player could at least pretend he'd missed her. "They can't be planning anything against us. We're *members.*"

"A lot of good that did your king on the Amanthian plain."

"That's an old story, Tovin. You players spend too much time dwelling on the past." She had thought that she might at least harvest a smile from him, an acknowledgment that the troop did collect old stories, used them in new ways. Instead, the player merely glared at her as if she had insulted him. Consciously setting aside her own anger, she asked, "When are we to meet them?"

"Tonight. When the bells ring for Mern."

The bells. That had taken some getting used to in this strange city. Each god had his own time of worship, his own exclusive hour of the day or night. Bells rang out across Brianta, cascading in complicated patterns, summoning the faithful to one shrine or another. It was quite common for pilgrims to drop to their knees in the middle of the road, dirtying their robes and lowering their heads to the dusty street in dedication to their particular god. One mark of a truly dedicated pilgrim was a sooty stain upon the brow, dirt ingrained from constant lowering to the ground.

"And where?" Rani asked.

"They will come for us here."

"Come for us?" She did not like the sound of that; the words bore too many memories of the King's Guard run amok, invading private homes to carry off traitors.

"Aye. They say they must keep their location secret. We will be escorted to the meeting place."

"What about Berylina? What if the princess needs us?"

"She has Siritalanu," Tovin said, shrugging. "And she's not likely to go wandering about at night. Even *her* devotion must have its limits."

"Very well." Rani worked hard to keep her voice even. "I should finish grinding these colors, then. I would not want to be in the middle of the task when they arrive." Tovin's eyes narrowed at her humble answer, and she knew that he wanted to protest, that he wanted to complain about her easy acceptance.

This was the *Fellowship,* she wanted to exclaim. This was the shadow force that could have destroyed her at any time it chose in the past five years. She had schooled herself not to fear them in Morenia. She must not let her resolve falter here in Brianta. Even if she were leagues from home. Even if she were separated from her king, from her liege lord, from all the modes of power that she knew and understood. Even if she were hungry and thirsty and ordered to stay apart from the man she loved. She swallowed hard.

Mair rose to her feet. "I'll leave the baby with Chalita, then."

The serving woman Chalita had come to them on their first day in Brianta. The landlord had recommended her as someone who was experienced with children; he had said that she could tend to Laranifarso if Mair needed to pray. The Touched woman had not taken the opportunity to visit temples, but she had let Chalita watch over Laranifarso each day while she caught a few hours of treasured sleep. Rani kept her eye on Tovin as she said, "Mair, you needn't come with us."

"I'm a member of the Fellowship. I'll come."

"Laranifarso needs you."

"Laranifarso is a babe. He needs someone to hold him and nurse him and keep him safe from harm. Chalita can do that for an hour or two. Better that I meet this Briantan Fellowship and know their number."

Rani shivered, for it sounded as if Mair wanted to identify an enemy, quantify an opposing force. Rani would not argue, though. She wanted Mair by her side. She wanted known companions as she met the powerful cabal on their home soil.

Mair closed the door behind her, and Rani was left alone in the chamber with Tovin. He came to stand at her side. "Ochre?" he asked, glancing down at the powder.

"Yes." She took a deep breath, mustering her arguments, preparing to explain yet again why the task was a good one, why Master Parion had been wise to set it for her.

"Not a bad notion." Tovin shrugged. "You get a feel for handling their equipment. They can barter your wares with the painting guild."

Rani flashed a grateful smile. "Exactly."

"But you're still leaving the particles too coarse. Painters require work far more fine than we glasswrights." All of her relief turned to anger as he said, "Here. Let me show you."

She knew that he did not have to reach across her to get the pestle. He did not need to fold his fingers around hers. He did not need to take the half-step toward her, to edge around the small table where her stone palette rested. He could have offered her instruction from across the room, in fact.

Her breath caught in her throat, and she felt herself lean closer to him, felt the heat radiating from his body through his rich players' silks and velvets. Without realizing it, she had closed her eyes, and she opened them to see him more clearly.

He had taken a step back, settling his fists on his hips and measuring her with narrowed eyes. "Tovin!" she gasped.

"You would be forsworn so quickly, Ranita Glass-wright?" She heard his dire tone, and she hoped that he was using one of his players' skills, that he was exaggerating his words for effect.

"Forsworn?"

"I was present in those kitchens that your glasswrights call a guildhall. I heard you agree to abandon me."

"I agreed to refrain from unclean touch."

"And from the touch of any man. You may think your oaths a jest, Ranita, but I can assure you that Parion did not."

"And how would he know what we do in the privacy of my chamber?"

Tovin glanced toward the window. He lowered his voice just enough that she needed to step closer to him. "Are you willing to wager that there are not eyes in that tower across the courtyard? Are you willing to stake a bet that there are no ears about this place? If not in the hallway outside this door, then in the room above us, or below." Tovin raised his voice. "You forget, Ranita. You forget the power of the guild you joined as a child. You forget how that guild knew your comings and your goings, every one of your thoughts, just as well as it knew your deeds."

For an instant, Tovin's words catapulted Rani back to a time when she had believed that the guild was invincible. Her instructors could read her very mind, could sense rebellion in her unspoken thoughts.

Of course, she had learned much since those naive days. She had learned the suspicious look of a guilty child, the furtive curve of a sneaking person's back. She had learned to parse half-truths and partial tales. She knew the ways of the world around her.

And yet she could not shake the belief that the Glass-

wrights' Guild could control her, could know the heart of
what she thought and what she said and what she made be
true. She had sworn an oath to Parion Glasswright, and she
must stand by that promise. At least until she was declared
a master in her guild.

Silently, she bowed her head over the ochre, working the
pestle with a tight wrist. The grains squeaked between the
glass surfaces, and she bore down harder, spun faster. Only
when her breath pressed tight against her throat did she look
up at Tovin defiantly. "There. Is that texture right?"

He quirked an eyebrow at her, and she knew that he was
commenting on more than her grinding. "Aye," he said at
last. "It seems fine enough."

She set the work aside, trying to ignore the trembling in
her forearms. She should not exert herself so much this early
in the game. She had a long course to play; she would fail in
her quest if she pushed too hard now.

All of this would be easier, she sulked, if she weren't so
hungry. If her head did not ache.

She tried not to think of the long tables in the Pilgrims'
Hall, the communal feasts shared by all who came to Brianta
to honor the Thousand Gods. At least she had been spared
that temptation tonight. At least she had not needed to sit beside Berylina and hear about Ile's temple as the princess
filled her belly with mutton stew and wine. Praying to Hern
had spared Rani the pilgrims' feast.

The feast, and Berylina's growing distance. The
princess's conversation had become saturated with the
gods—it seemed that she was determined to visit the shrines
of each of the Thousand in addition to her cavalcade
choices. Night after night, sitting at the table, she chattered
with Father Siritalanu as if they were the only pilgrims ever
to grace Brianta. They recounted symbols and omens, coin-
cidences and facts that tested Rani's credulity. They spoke
about the rabid street preachers as if they could make out
some secret message in the crazed babbling.

And all of those tales were relayed over boards that groaned with fresh-baked bread, with new-churned butter, with rich, wholesome fare. Repeatedly, Rani was catapulted back to her apprenticeship in the guild. Then, too, she had been hungry. Then, too, she had longed to belong to a community, to a group of worshipers. . . .

Her belly growled loud enough that Tovin looked up from across the room. She fought against a blush. "Ranita," he said. "Starving yourself again?"

"I eat," she answered too quickly. "I'll eat tonight. At the guildhall."

"A grand feast, I'm sure."

She started to reply, but the door glided open. Mair entered, matter-of-factly running her fingers over the prayer bell. "Lar's sleeping now," she said. "Chalita said she could keep him until dawn."

Without her son, the Touched girl looked her old rebellious self. She still wore her hair short, cropped unevenly, as if she had taken her own dagger to it. Her smile was crooked, and she posed nonchalantly, with one hand on a jutting hip. "We'd best get our cloaks and hoods, then. There's no telling when the Fellowship will come a-calling."

Mair did not fall back into her Touched patois, not quite. Her words were loose, though; they flowed more easily than any noble's. Rani took comfort in the easy drawl, gathering strength in the things that were not said. Even in a strange land, Mair did not hesitate to take the lead. She did not pause before moving forward. All would be well in Brianta. No matter what the Fellowship had in store for them.

And Rani did not have long to wait before the Fellowship asserted its presence. She had scarcely shaken out her midnight cloak and fingered the folds of its shadowy hood, when there came a knock at the door. Tovin stepped forward to open it, his hand displayed broadly on the hilt of the dagger at his waist. Tovin Player was no pilgrim. He walked the streets of Brianta armed.

The hooded creature who waited in the corridor might have noticed the bellicose display, but it gave no hint. Instead, the Fellow bowed slightly, taking in all of them with the gesture of one black-swathed arm. "Come," the person whispered.

"Where?" Tovin grunted the word, but the messenger did not deign to answer. Rani saw the player start to tense; she watched anger spread across Tovin's face like a painted design. She took a step forward and raised her hand as if she would smooth away his ill temper.

Tovin pulled back, glaring at her. He would remember her glasswright's oath even now; he would keep her from touching him. She had wounded him in the guildhall, although he had laughed out loud. She knew that he'd been hurt when she accepted the guild's edict so readily, when she agreed to avoid his solace and support.

There would be time enough to repair that bridge later. Time when the Fellowship was not watching their every move. Time when she did not need to fear spying eyes and ears and tongues.

Rani pulled on her own cloak, taking only a moment to settle the hood carefully. The motion reminded her of her midnight meeting with Holy Father Dartulamino. She must make a choice, he had said. She must decide between loyalties. Was the matter to fall before her now? Was she to learn more of the Royal Pilgrim now that she was ensconced in Brianta?

She pulled her hood forward, reaping comfort from the familiar gesture, and she caught a whiff of incense on the silk. She remembered the last full meeting of the Morenian Fellowship when she had worn the heavy cloak.

She had known who led her cell then. She was accustomed to receiving cryptic orders from Glair, the twisted Touched woman who commanded the Morenian contingent. Rani was accustomed to the castes of her world being turned upside down by the Fellowship.

The Briantan branch could hardly be more surprising, more unsettling. Or so Rani hoped.

Her hopes, though, turned to queasy fear as the hooded Fellow produced three scraps of cloth from a hidden pocket. "Here," the creature whispered. "For your eyes."

For just an instant, Rani thought that she would refuse. She had been blindfolded before, brought before another enclave, another group united with evil in their hearts. Standing here in Brianta, she could remember those early days in Morenia. She could remember the feeling of walls pressing close around her, the dread that had filled her belly when she realized the blood oath that the evil Brotherhood had expected of her.

"We can't," she said. "We can't wander through Brianta blinded, in the middle of the night. We'll lose our way."

The hooded figure waited for a moment, and Rani wondered what type of eyes glared at her, what sort of anger waited inside the other's hood. Then the Fellow whispered, "Pilgrims are blindfolded every day. As a test of their faith. Their dedication."

Rani had to admit that she had seen such worshipers in the street. They came alone or in pairs, with a guide to bring them around to shrines. They wore elaborate Thousand-Pointed Stars, as if they hoped to announce to all the world the depth and breadth of their faith.

Rani believed in the Thousand Gods, like any good merchant girl from Morenia. She had even donned a Star for this journey. It had never occurred to her, though, to announce her faith so broadly, to place her trust in the pantheon quite so blatantly. "I—we can't," she extemporized, looking frantically at Mair and Tovin, wishing for their support. "We can't go with you tonight. If you've found us here, you know why we have journeyed to Brianta. You know that we came with Princess Berylina, and we cannot abandon her to go with you."

"The princess is safe enough with her priest." The

hooded figure stood straighter, and Rani felt an aura of menace emanate from its dark cloak. She still could not determine if she spoke to a tall woman or a short man, and the confusion was disorienting. The hissed voice did nothing to ease her distrust. "The Fellowship commands your presence. You may choose to obey, or you may pay the penalty later. I will argue with you no more."

Rani swallowed hard, and she glanced at Tovin. His eyes were narrowed in the way that meant that he was weighing options, calculating costs. She knew that he produced such mannerisms as carefully as he crafted a performance on the players' stage, but his aggressive stance did nothing to ease her mind. Did he truly feel threatened?

What should she do? Where did the true danger lie? And what might the Fellowship teach her?

Rani shrugged and reached for the blindfold.

It was more substantial than she had expected. The black cloth was tightly woven, and it covered a broad pad of some soft stuffing. As Rani settled the device about her brow, she lost all of the light in the chamber, even the glints of vision at the corners of her eyes. She started to rethink her decision, began to change her mind, but then the Fellow was standing beside her.

She felt wiry fingers through black gloves tightening her baffle, and then a rope was slipped around her wrist. Even though her thinking mind knew that the rope was intended to help her, intended to give her something to grasp as she was guided through the streets, she felt as if she were a prisoner, a condemned woman being marched toward a scaffold. Before she could speak, she was tugged toward the doorway.

Rani thought that she was first in the strange line of blinded pilgrims. The rope played out in front of her, strong and steady, and she believed that the seeing Fellow must move before her. She wanted to stretch out her hand behind her, to see if Tovin or Mair were next, but she did not have the time. She needed to devote all of her attention to walking through the city streets.

As always, Brianta was full of pilgrims. The chatter of their collective voices reminded Rani of the great market days of her childhood, when merchants and customers would come to Moren from all the corners of the world.

This was no Moren, though. Heat radiated up from the ground even though the sun had set hours before. Rani could smell the press of hot bodies, and she tasted dust at the back of her throat.

As they maneuvered through the streets, she forced herself to walk steadily, to set her feet upon the cobblestones with confidence. She attempted to ignore the sharp odor of rotting food, the stench of thrown slops. In between the unpleasant smells there were softer scents—a flower garden nestled beside some woodland god's shrine, the whiff of fresh-baked bread, even at this late hour.

It was difficult to keep track of time and space. When Rani had left her rooms, she had told herself to count footsteps, to measure the turns that they took. She hoped that Tovin and Mair would do the same; they could compare their results later.

Such naive plans, though, were dashed as their mysterious guide drove the pilgrims deeper and deeper into the city. Brianta seemed to have no organization, nothing of the order in Rani's home. There were no distinct quarters for the castes of the world—such division was not meet in the birthplace of the First Pilgrim, who had traveled through all the castes.

Instead, streets were jumbled together, a row of fine noble houses fronted onto the marketplace, a sturdy barracks for soldiers hulked beside a chapel. And there were chapels everywhere—tiny huts dedicated to obscure gods, grand churches like Hern's, devoted to the most popular of the Thousand.

Rani knew that she was marched past many of these tumbled buildings. She suspected that her guide twisted the path, bringing them to some places two, three, even four times. The scent of roses was heavy in Rani's nose at the beginning of their trip, and in the middle, and as they neared— she hoped—the end.

And, at last, they *did* approach the end of their wandering. They arrived at a stone threshold; Rani felt the surface beneath her feet. The walls of the building that they entered must be thick, for the interior was blessedly cool.

Cool and silent and tinged with a hint of dankness, as if water seeped through the stone walls. Rani breathed deeply, wishing that her hands were free so that she could mop at the perspiration that trickled down her face, that crept along her spine and made her want to shudder.

There was no time, though, no respite. The guide moved them across a long room, a chamber that seemed to be empty, for they did not need to dodge furniture or altars or any other clutter. At the far end, Rani heard a door scrape open, and then the Fellow tugged on the rope, indicating that she should step down. Stairs. One. Two. Three. Rani counted forty before she hit level ground, jamming her knee a little with the unexpected solidity of the floor. Another few steps, another door, another large chamber, from the feel of the air.

A large chamber, with many people present. They stood quietly, but Rani could hear them breathe. She could make out the tiny rustles as they shifted from foot to foot, as they watched Rani and her companions.

How many people stood inside the chamber? A dozen? More than that. Two dozen? Three? Rani longed to tear away her blindfold, to see the forces arrayed against her.

"Hail, Fellows. Well met." Rani started at the volume of the voice. Female. Young. Confident. The sounds well formed and schooled.

No Touched girl, then. Probably not a soldier, either. A

merchant? A noble? A guildsman? Who led the Briantan Fellowship?

Rani suppressed a shudder as another drop of sweat traced her spine. She did not want the speaker to be a guildsman, at least not a glasswright. She had enough problems with Master Parion without adding another tangle of loyalties, another hierarchy.

The girl continued. "We welcome you to Brianta, to the home of First Pilgrim Jair. All blessings flow from the Thousand Gods through Jair."

"All blessings flow from the Thousand Gods through Jair." The benediction was repeated by the assembled Fellowship, and Rani barely restrained herself from jumping at the voices around her. There were more people gathered together than she had thought; their prayerful worship was much louder than she had expected. In Morenia there were several dozen Fellows, maybe fifty. Here, there were several *hundred*.

Several hundred people joined in a cause, bonded together by their faith and worship and belief in a higher order. An order higher than their king, their nobles, even their priests.

Rani had seen the havoc that the Fellowship could wreak in Morenia; she had witnessed the orders they could issue, the demands they could make. What might the organization do if they were five times as powerful, ten times?

In a rush, Rani realized that she could not afford to think about the Briantan Fellowship as an entity distinct from the Morenian one. These people stood against all the world. They were a force to be reckoned with, across lands, across kingdoms. Like the stone foundations that supported an entire row of merchant buildings, the Fellowship underlaid Hal's kingdom and Jair's homeland and more besides.

The Fellowship was like an onion, with layer sealed around layer. Each time that Rani thought she had discovered the core of its power, she learned that there was another

level waiting beneath. And each level was stronger than the
one before. More virulent. More dangerous. Rani ordered
herself to focus, to pay attention to what was being said.

She must learn the full extent of the Fellowship, of its
power, its plans. After all, she *was* a member. She acted of
her own free will. She could choose the direction she wanted
the Fellowship's powerful river to flow around her, and she
could control her pace within that current.

"In the name of Jair," the girl leader said, and something
about her voice made clear to Rani that she should repeat the
incantation.

"In the name of Jair," Rani said.

"Now then. We have among us three of our number, three
of our members from Morenia. They are sworn to our Fellowship, but they are not familiar with our ways. Unbind
their eyes that they might see. Untie their hands that they
might feel. Bring them into the world of our Fellowship, like
children brought into the world from their mothers'
wombs."

Rani did not care for the imagery of birth, for the pain
and blood and hard labor those terms implied. Nevertheless,
she was grateful when she felt another Fellow behind her,
and she blinked hard when the cloth was taken from her
eyes, when her hood was pushed back.

The chamber was even larger than she had expected—
long and low. Clearly, they stood beneath some great hall.
Torches smoked along the edges of the room, but their light
did not reach the center of the gloomy chamber. The dark
room seemed more close because of the bodies that filled it.

Making a quick tally, Rani found that the number was
even higher than she had first expected. There were nearly
four hundred people in the room. Four hundred conspirators.
Four hundred robed, masked Fellows.

Four hundred potential allies, Rani reminded herself.
Four hundred brethren.

She looked at Mair and Tovin, who stood beside her, and

she saw awe on their faces, awe that must be echoed on her own. Even though she could count the Fellows who stood in the room, Rani was no closer to determining who they actually were. Each Briantan wore a dark, heavy cloak with a hood that swept up. Rani felt oddly naked as she looked about the chamber with her hood cast back. She craned her neck to look at the Fellows closest to her, and she saw that they wore other devices—misty black veils that were suspended inside their midnight cowls. The effect was utterly unnerving, for it looked as if the people had no faces. Each appeared to have a ghostly body, a spiritual essence that bore no relation to life in the physical world.

One of them, though, stood on a platform, a raised dais at the center of the room. She—for Rani was certain that figure was the one who had spoken—seemed to be of middling height, of average build, and older than Rani had first thought. There was nothing that would enable Rani to recognize her outside the limits of this chamber.

The woman spoke again. "We gather in the name of the Thousand Gods, here in the city of Jair. May the Thousand look upon us and watch over us in their wisdom. May they lend us strength and wisdom and courage to do all that we must do in furtherance of their name. In the name of all the Thousand, so be it."

"In the name of all the Thousand, so be it."

"And we bind ourselves together in the name of the First Pilgrim, in the name of Jair who first recognized the power of the Thousand. We bind ourselves together in the name of Jair, so be it."

"In the name of Jair, so be it." Rani felt the power rising within the group, the harmony and thrumming energy of people united in a cause. She whispered the last three words simultaneously with Tovin and Mair.

"And we pledge our bodies to the cause of our Fellowship, to the service of the truths and ideals and potentials that we might bring into being through our community of believers. In the name of the Fellowship, so be it."

"In the name of the Fellowship, so be it." Rani repeated the line, making her voice firm.

The woman on the platform raised one commanding, gloved hand, and her masked face turned toward the corners of the chamber. Rani followed her line of sight, looking past Mair and Tovin to a cluster of Fellows who stood between the torches. Those shadowed figures moved forward, spreading through the crowd.

Where they passed, a ripple of commotion followed. Rani saw Fellows turning, one to the next, touching gloved fingertips to gloved fingertips. Whispers passed between people as well, some muttered formula so soft that Rani could not quite make it out.

Then the person closest to Rani took a half-step forward. It must have been the Fellow who had claimed her from her chamber, Rani realized, the man or woman who had conducted her through the city streets. That person reached toward Rani, pressing a partial loaf of bread into her hands.

"In the name of the Fellowship," the Fellow whispered, and Rani realized that she was supposed to tear a bit of bread from the loaf. Her fingers slipped over the smooth surface. The dough had been braided into an even link, and the link had been twisted upon itself, twined into an intricate form. Rani could feel flour on the bottom of the loaf, and a yeasty smell filled her nose.

She was pledged to the Glasswrights' Guild. She had promised Master Parion that she would not eat or drink away from the confines of the guildhall. She had sworn to follow her guild's precepts, taken a vow when she was a twelve-year-old child.

She could not turn her back on that pledge now. Not for a single bite of bread. Not for the Briantan branch of the Fellowship. Not for new loyalties, conflicting obligations.

Nevertheless, Rani knew that the Fellows were staring at

her. She tore at the ornate loaf, ripping off a small bite. She passed the loaf to Mair, taking care to whisper, "In the name of the Fellowship."

Mair took the bread quickly, ripping off a sizable chunk before passing it on to Tovin. When it seemed that every person in the room had a piece of the loaves, the woman on the dais raised her own morsel. "With this feast, we bind ourselves each to the other. We declare our love and honor and respect for our Fellows, our dedication to serve our cause with the fervor that Jair first served the Thousand Gods. In the name of Jair, so be it."

"In the name of Jair, so be it." Rani repeated the vow with the hooded figures around her.

Something about the solemn vow called to mind another ritual, and Rani cast about in her mind for the connection. Bread. Shared in the name of the church.

Her belly tightened as she realized she was remembering the funeral service. She blinked, and she could picture the small loaves that Hal and Mareka had shared as they honored their lost sons.

Shivering, she palmed her bread rather than eating it. The maneuver caused her to wave the fresh-baked morsel in front of her face, and her belly clenched at the savory scent. Nevertheless, promises were promises. She folded her hands into her sleeves and then made as if to brush crumbs from the front of her robe. She used the swift gestures to secrete the scrap of bread in a pocket of her robe, offering up a silent prayer to the First Pilgrim that he forgive her for her duplicity.

"Very well," the woman said, as each Fellow swallowed. "The word of the Thousand Gods has traveled far and wide, moving beyond even those paths trod by First Pilgrim Jair. Our Fellowship stretches to the north and the south, to the east and the west. Our brothers and sisters from distant lands come to us to report their successes, to note their failures. Today we begin the season of the Counting."

The Counting. Rani did not know what the Fellow meant;
however, the announcement was obviously important. Fellows around her leaned forward; tension in the room ratcheted a little higher. The woman said, "Let us hear, first, from
our Fellow newly arrived from Zarithia."

The crowd shifted, and a cloaked figure moved toward
the dais. Rani knew before the Fellow spoke that he must be
male; no woman could boast such height, such girth. Even
so, Rani was surprised at the man's deep tones. His voice
rumbled like thunder across a valley.

"Greetings from distant Zarithia, where the Fellows number six and twenty in all the land. Although we are the smallest outpost of the Fellowship, we are pleased to report on
our progress. In the past year, we saw a third member raised
to the Merchants' Council, so that we have even greater influence over that body. We have used some of that power to
deflect our city's plans to record all merchants' sales in the
Grand Ledger, for we concluded that tracking shipments
might prove dangerous to hidden Fellows and would have
no benefit for us. Under the Council's own rules, the matter
cannot be raised for another two years."

There were murmurs of approval from the crowd, even as
Rani caught her breath. She was familiar with the Merchants' Council in Moren. She even knew that the Fellowship had manipulated it in the past, to her own benefit,
contriving to send Rani on errands of their own making, to
keep her safe from the dark cabal that would have seen her
executed in the market square.

Nevertheless, the notion of outside Fellows controlling a
Merchants' Council beat against her caste-born blood. Merchants had a hard enough time carving out their livings between the guildsmen and the nobles. They should not need
to fight hidden influences such as the Fellowship. Not without some compensation. Not without some knowing negotiation.

The burly man continued his report. "Unfortunately, our

attempts to control the nobles have not been as successful. We had thought that one of our noble members might be named to the King's Council upon the passing of old Baron Semblay, but the king granted the favor to one of his border lords instead. In the ordinary course of things, we do not anticipate another opening on the King's Council for several years. We do not currently advise that any change be made, for there are no policies we need to enforce that require noble participation at this time."

Any change.

Two short words, two common words, words that any person might use in any speech. And yet Rani's breath came short as she realized their import. The Zarithian spoke of removing a member of the King's Council, manipulating the very core of the noble caste in his homeland. At best, such manipulation might be done by spreading lies and innuendo. At worst, the man spoke of murder.

Rani's head shot up, and she sought out her colleagues' eyes, finding Mair's first. The Touched women seemed to have reached the same conclusion that Rani had, for her lips pressed together tightly. She returned Rani's gaze steadily, but she swallowed hard. Rani looked to Tovin as well, but the player's attention was directed solely at the dais. He seemed to be absorbing the speaker's words, incorporating them into his very being.

Rani had seen that intensity before—when the players created a new performance, when they mastered new roles. She had watched the men and women of the troop focus so intently that they would not hear a building crash around them. And she had seen the creations that rose from such awesome concentration.

Her heart beat faster, and she told herself to focus on what Tovin must be gathering from the report.

The burly man concluded: "And so Zarithia completes its report, with our six and twenty members submitting to the Fellowship, offering up our lives in service to our cause."

The woman nodded once, stepping forward to stand beside the giant. "Thank you for your report, Zarithia, and for offering up your service to the Fellowship." She raised her hand to gesture toward his head. "In service to the north"—she pointed toward his feet—"and to the south"—she moved her hand toward his right and then followed through to his left   "to the east, and to the west, you offer up your report in furtherance of the Fellowship. May First Pilgrim Jair and all the Thousand Gods watch over you as you move our plans ahead."

The woman crossed her arms over her chest and bowed, and the man repeated her gesture. Then he stepped down from the dais and disappeared into the crowd.

Rani's mind reeled at all that she had witnessed. The Fellowship was far stronger than she had imagined, than Hal had ever dreamed. What did Glair have planned for the kingdom's future, back in Moren? What would her emissary report to this Council? Who lurked in unexpected positions of power in Morenia? Rani looked around the room, wondering who would report from her homeland.

She felt strangely exposed without a silken mask, with only her hood to hide her from her Fellows. At the same time, she resented the masking robes, the invisibility of her Fellows. If only she could find a Morenian in the crowd, she might know if Hal were in some immediate danger. Was this why Dartulamino had warned her? Was this why the Holy Father had told her that she must make a choice? And where did the Royal Pilgrim fit into all of this?

Even if she deciphered a threat here, she fretted, she would have trouble reporting it. She had sworn to Master Parion that she would not correspond with her liege lord. She could not even dictate a letter to Mair or to Tovin; she could not communicate with Hal in any way. In frustration, she caught her lip with her lower teeth. Before she could catch Mair's eye, another figure was summoned to the dais.

"Next in the counting, we have our newest member. Step forward, Liantine, and report upon your findings."

The crowd shifted again, and someone else was allowed to move toward the dais. Rani saw that this Fellow moved with a tremendous limp, as if his left leg refused to obey the commands of the rest of his body. How could the Fellowship exist in Liantine? she wondered. The land had fallen away from faith in First Pilgrim Jair, from belief in all the Thousand Gods. Liantine was given over to the Horned Hind almost entirely. And yet the woman's words had been perfectly clear—she had said that the Liantine chapter of the secret organization was the newest.

Rani understood as soon as she heard the messenger speak. "Greetings from distant Liantine, where the Fellows number two and forty in all the land."

Crestman.

His voice was ragged, breathy in a way that suggested he spoke through great pain. Rani was so surprised that her throat tightened; she could not help but make a noise, like a woman surprised by a sudden cramp, like a child beset by a stinging insect. Tovin glanced at her sharply, and she swallowed hard, trying not to betray any further emotion. The other Fellows closed in around her, as if they expected her to take some action against the Liantine messenger.

But the woman who led the convocation continued as if there had been no interruption. "Greetings, Liantine. We gratefully count your two and forty with the twenty-six members we've already noted. How fares the Fellowship in your land?"

"We struggle," Crestman said, his voice scarcely more than a whisper spread across gravel. "My Fellows and I are gathered from outside the castes of Liantine, from outside the royal household, the Merchants' Quarter. The guildhalls."

Rani heard an entire story behind those words. When she had last seen Crestman, he had been carried off as a slave within the spiderguild's twisting corridors. He had thought that she'd abandoned him, that she'd forsaken him and his Little Army in favor of precious riberry trees. Even as she had heard his bitter accusations spat across a shadowy hall, she had longed to tell him her ultimate plan, longed to assure him that she had not forgotten his cause.

She had not had the chance, though. He had lost all faith. He had gone to his slavery with the bitter conviction that he was alone in all the world, that she had bartered him and his army of children for a handful of trees.

Rani started to step forward in the guildhall chamber, but she was restrained by Mair's hand upon her wrist. She tried to wrench her arm free, but the Touched girl only tightened her grip. Didn't Mair understand? Didn't she realize that Crestman needed to be helped?

As if he were confirming Rani's thoughts, the wounded soldier said, "I have gathered my people in a series of caves on the edge of the Liantine highlands. Each of us has a reason for leaving our birth caste. We have been together only since winter, and we have not yet measured out a way to gain true power in Liantine. I have come to this conclave so that you might know my loyalty to your cause, but I do not yet have any great success to report."

Loyalty. Couldn't the Fellows hear the bitter sarcasm behind his words? Didn't they realize that Crestman would not bow to them? Crestman had one goal, had always had one goal—to redeem the children who had served with him in Amanthia's cursed Little Army.

Rani remembered the first time she had ever spoken with the boy-soldier, when he himself still fought in that cursed force. Even then, he had rebelled against authority; he had battled orders issued by his supposed superiors. His voice had been younger and stronger, but it had held the same bitter twist.

The woman on the dais seemed unaware of the danger in the man who stood before her. Instead, she leaned closer to him as he spoke. Rani felt an old scorn rise within her. She swallowed a metallic tang at the back of her throat as Crestman concluded his report.

"I will return from this convocation and spend the summer strengthening my forces. We will be ready, come winter, to make our first bid on behalf of the Fellowship. I am considering a handful of targets, with varying goals. Some will consolidate our power in Liantine. Others will reach beyond our borders, will bring more glory to the Fellowship in other lands."

Crestman looked out over the assembled Fellows as he spoke. Rani could not make out his features behind his silk mask, but she knew his lips would be twisted by bitterness and spite. "Come summer next," he said to all the assembly, "we definitely will be prepared to make our move."

The woman nodded slowly, and her voice was pleased as she accepted his report. Her hands moved in the same way that they had with the Zarithian man, but Rani could see that she leaned a little closer to Crestman, that her hand hovered just above his brow, swept toward his feet with a peculiar grace. Her fingertips nearly brushed against his palms as she gestured east and west. "Thank you for your report, Liantine, and for offering up your service to the Fellowship. In service to the north and to the south, to the east, and to the west, you offer up your report in furtherance of the Fellowship. May First Pilgrim Jair and all the Thousand Gods watch over you as you move our plans ahead."

Crestman inclined his head slightly, and then he turned away. He needed to steel himself visibly as he stepped down from the dais, and Rani wondered what havoc could have been wrought upon his soldier's body, what damage could have made him move so painfully. Once again, she started to take a step forward, to raise a hand, as if she would aid him.

This time, however, Tovin caught her wrist. The player's touch blazed against her flesh, and she almost thought that he was forcing words into her mind, a crystal warning on the deepest levels that they had shared while Speaking. The pinch of his fingers hurt her, and she started to pull away. His grip was too tight, though, and she hissed, "My lord, I have sworn an oath!"

Tovin dropped her wrist immediately, and she could imagine the bitter twist of his hidden lips as he stepped back.

Her whisper was enough that Crestman looked across the assembly; his face was turned directly to her. She *knew* that he was staring at her. She *knew* that there was a message in his masked eyes. He needed no words, though, to convey his scorn as he pulled himself straight. She could only imagine the pain that shot up his damaged leg, that ricocheted along his twisted spine as he stepped away and disappeared inside the crowd.

Rani turned back to Tovin, ready to make amends, ready to explain. He had already moved away from her, though, his broad shoulders set in denial. She knew that he was angry. She knew that he would have nothing of her excuses, her explanations. She knew that he would leave her to complete her glasswrights' test alone, whatever the demands of the Fellowship, whatever the demands of the hooded masses that even now could be well ranged against Morenia. She settled down to await the Fellowship's counting and report on her homeland.

8

Berylina bent her head over the prie-dieu in the corner of her room. She needed to concentrate on her prayers. She was going to Mip's temple that afternoon, to make her first pilgrim's offering to the god of water. She had waited nearly four weeks to go to Mip—four weeks of focusing on other gods, more familiar gods. Easier gods.

She could wait no longer, though. Not if she wanted to remain true to her cavalcade.

"Hail, Mip," she prayed silently. "Carve my life and make it yours. Cut through me, like the river cuts through the earth. Make me yours. Make me holy."

Berylina concentrated, trying to hear the nightingale song that was the god's special signature. She had discovered it the night before—heard a real bird, that was. She had listened to the delicate trill, and she had known that Mip held great things for her, that the god intended for her to work magic on his behalf.

The sound had inspired her to set up her easel, to dig out her parchment and colored chalks. She had sketched for long hours, squinting at the drawing first through one eye, then the other.

Initially, her lines were strong. She saw Mip as clearly as she saw any of the gods when she was a child in Liantine. The more she drew, though, the more she realized that her

depiction was incomplete. Surely, any worshiper could see
Mip's soft jowls; anyone could make out his tangled hair.

She must convey more. She must represent the nightingale song that filled her ears. She struggled with red chalk
and a black crayon, sketching in firm lines, blurring them
with her fingers.

By the time that she was finished, Mip's face had disappeared; it was lost beneath a symphony of cross-hatched
lines. Berylina was pleased, though. *She* could hear the
nightingale. Mip was there with her.

Now, in the middle of the day, Mip seemed distant and
vague.

Perhaps he was offended that she prayed here in her
apartments instead of at his shrine. Perhaps he was angered
that she had drunk a glass of pale wine the night before instead of simple water. Perhaps he was hurt that Berylina had
waited so long to visit him.

Or maybe he was staying away because of the racket in
the outer room. Berylina tried to close her ears to the conversation, but she could not block out entirely the fight between Ranita Glasswright and Mair. Their debate had
escalated since the last bells had rung; they were nearly
shouting at each other.

Ranita said, "How many times do I have to tell you? I
don't *know* why they summoned us that night!" They?
Who? Beyrlina caught her breath to better hear Mair's response. "Maybe they wanted the others to see us. Maybe
they wanted our faces known."

"That's never been their way before." Mair's voice was
stubborn. "*Think.* It makes no sense."

Berylina crept closer to the door so that she could hear
Ranita's reply. "I *have* thought. I think they meant us to see
Crestman. I think they meant him as a warning."

"A warning? Or a threat?"

"He hasn't done anything!" Ranita's words were hurried,
desperate.

"But ye 'ave no way t' say wha' 'e might do, Rai. Ye 'avena seen 'im since ye left 'im a' th' spiderguild." Mair had slipped into her Touched brogue. Berylina eased the door open a bit to hear even more clearly.

"You know that I did not just leave him! I had a plan!"

"'N' well it served ye."

"I'm not going to fight this battle with you again. I did what I had to do. I bargained for the riberry trees. If I had not made the choices that I did, Moren would have suffered even more than it already had. We needed the trees. We needed the octolaris. We needed the silk trade to redeem the city."

"I'm only sayin' that yer choices 'ave consequences."

"But *Crestman!* In the Fellowship! Do you really think they'll use him to topple Hal?"

"*They* use *'im?* I warrant 'e'll be th' one usin'. Th' boy is 'urt, Rai, 'n' 'e's angry. 'E's a danger t' you, 'n' t' Moren besides, 'n' maybe t' King 'Alaravilli most o' all."

"So what would you have me do? I need to speak with Crestman, Mair. I need to remind him that he is a subject of Morenia. I need to—"

"Ye can stop that plan right there, Rai. 'E'll not be list'n'n' t' ye. 'E'll not be trustin' ye anymore. 'E tried that twice before, 'n' ye failed him both times."

"I did not!"

"Ach, sit down. Ye know I speak th' truth. 'E counted on ye in Amanthia, thought ye'd be 'is lady. 'N' 'e counted on ye in Liantine as well, built up a story i' 'is own mind about i'."

"I never gave him reason—"

"Rai, it's *me* ye're talkin' t'. No need t' spread yer tales o' fancy 'ere."

"They aren't tales! They're the truth!"

Berylina heard the frustrated sound that Ranita Glasswright made, the growl in the back of her throat. She almost opened the door, almost stepped in to tell the women that they should forget the soldier. When Berylina had knelt at her prie-dieu, she had seen Tarn following the man, enveloping him in the god's green-black cape. She recognized Crestman easily enough, even though she had only seen him briefly in her father's court. If she told Ranita and Mair of her vision, maybe they would realize what was important. They would stop bickering and they would start to pray—to Tarn, or to any one of the other Thousand Gods.

And that's what Berylina should be doing herself, praying, preferably in a temple. That was why she had come to Brianta, after all. Not to hide in some sheltered room. Not to become embroiled in Morenian politics. She had undertaken this pilgrimage to test her dedication. A fine job she'd done of it so far. . . .

She glanced at the prie-dieu's kneeler, at the Thousand-Pointed Star that she had set there. She sighed and gathered up the symbol of her pilgrimage, fastening it to her caloya robes. The brooch had made its mark upon her knees, digging deep into the bruises from the day before and the day before that.

Pilgrims were meant to bear the Star. That was how their holiness could be known. That was how they announced their presence at the Heavenly Gates. Berylina must not hesitate now just because her journey was becoming difficult. What was a little pain in the face of the glory of all the Thousand Gods?

Unbidden, she pictured her kindly nurse, the woman who had first taught her of the power of the Thousand. Nurse had paid for Berylina's instruction, had paid with her life when the princess's father discovered what he called betrayal.

Closing her eyes, Berylina felt her father's spear thrust through her own chest, felt her own heart rend at the bloody wooden tip. Her green robes rustled in the still room, and she knew the pain of a wound opening across her own flesh. "Tarn keep her and protect her," Berylina whispered, forcing the words past the agonizing pain.

They worked, as they had dozens of times in the past.

Tarn rustled his green-black wings above her, retreating to the very edge of her vision. She could feel the wound close upon her chest. She knew, though, that if she peered inside her spring-green robe, she would see a line of vivid red. She would see the results of her father's spear, the visible reminder of the force of his anger. She would see the blood that had been shed to set her on the path of the Thousand Gods.

With a fee such as Nurse had paid, how dare she waste her time locked inside a chamber? Forcing her bruised knees to unlock and move, she opened the door.

"I'm going to find him!" Ranita said. "You can't stop me!"

Berylina cleared her throat, and the two women looked up at her in surprise. They had clearly forgotten that she was in the inner chamber. A blush spread over Ranita Glasswright's face, but the Touched woman merely lowered her gaze and muttered something beneath her breath.

Ranita recovered first, and she sketched a bow toward Berylina. "Your Highness."

"My lady."

"I hope that we did not disturb your prayer." She sounded embarrassed. Berylina tilted her head to focus her skewed vision. Ranita squirmed beneath the gaze, and she knew that the glasswright wanted to step to the side, to center Berylina in her own gaze. The princess was used to that reaction, had witnessed it for her entire life.

When she was younger, she would have glanced away. She would have clasped her hands in her robes, gazing at her interlocked fingers as if they held the secret of all the Thousand Gods, attempting to ease their exposure to her blighted body.

Now, though, Berylina felt no such obligation. She knew that the Thousand Gods had made her as she was for some reason. She was not yet certain if she was meant to be a warning to the hale and hearty, or if she was to serve as a reminder, to summon all the faithful to pity and to caring. She knew, though, that she would never serve the Thousand by hiding her true form.

She stared at Ranita Glasswright, her twisted gaze unblinking. As if to emphasize her deformities, she darted a tongue over her lips, across her rabbit teeth.

To Ranita's credit, the glasswright did not react. Instead, she swallowed hard and said, "I'm sorry, Your Highness. Lady Mair and I were discussing matters important to our king. I fear that we let ourselves get carried away with the force of our arguments."

"The gods are not distracted by our puny human fights." Berylina felt the words rise within her, steady, certain. She wished that she could always feel that quiet confidence, always know when the gods spoke truth through her. "The Thousand do not care about your dispute."

Berylina cared, of course. Berylina cared enough that she would write to King Halaravilli. That night, before she went to bed. She would relay the words that Ranita and Mair had spoken, let him know the danger that they perceived from the soldier Crestman. After all, the Thousand Gods had seen fit to set King Halaravilli upon the throne of Morenia. Berylina must be one of their instruments to keep him there.

She would have plenty of time later to write. For now, Mip had waited long enough.

Berylina settled her caloya robes more comfortably across her frame and tensed her legs beneath her long skirts. Yes. Her knees were steadier now. They would carry her through the streets. She would not embarrass herself, or Father Siritalanu, or any of the Thousand Gods.

She smiled at Ranita and Mair. "I'll leave you to your debates, then."

"But we'll come with you, my lady!" Ranita protested. "We're here to see that you are safe in Brianta."

"I'll be safe enough. Father Siritalanu will accompany

me, and my Thousand-Pointed Star will protect me. I am only going to Mip's temple."

Berylina watched conflict play out across the glasswright's face. Clearly, Ranita felt obligated to accompany her. Just as clearly, though, the glasswright had her own desires, her own goals. Something to do with her broken guild, Berylina supposed. Or the secret that she shared with Mair, the secret that involved the soldier Crestman. Of course, the private obligations won out—Berylina *was* safe with Father Siritalanu.

The princess raised her hand over the prayer bell at the door before she said to the two women, "May all the Thousand Gods watch over you. In the name of Hin, I hope that you resolve your dispute." She left before the look of protest faded from Ranita's face. The god of rhetoric filled Berylina's nose with the essence of lilac.

Father Siritalanu was waiting for her outside. He gazed down the street as she descended the stairs. His face was creased with fine lines, and his lips were pulled into a frown. Here in Brianta, he always seemed to fear for her safety, for her well-being. As soon as Berylina stepped out of the hostel, he leaped toward her. "You were supposed to be here after Jin's bells."

"I needed to finish my prayers, Father. I'm sorry that I worried you."

"You didn't worry me, Your Highness." His protest was automatic, and his fingers moved in the peculiarly Briantan gesture that resolved disputes. She wanted to tell him that no one should lie—not even priests. "I merely feared that we would be late arriving at Mip's temple."

She inclined her head as if she were accepting his chastisement, and her own fingers wove in an additional Briantan suggestion of humility. After all, Siritalanu meant only to help her. He meant only to serve her and guide her worship. Poor man.

As always, the Briantan streets were crowded. Berylina

eased her way through a knot of pilgrims who were vying
for a merchant's wares. It took her a moment to realize that
the old man was selling gold-washed leather representations
of the Thousand-Pointed Star. Each symbol could be per-
sonalized with a tiny medallion, a twist of leather that was
stamped with the sign of a particular god. The trinkets
looked gaudy, and Berylina wondered who would dishonor
a god with such a thing. Even as she asked herself the question, though, she realized that many pilgrims would leap at
the chance to return home with such a tangible reminder of
a trip to Brianta.

People wanted to remember their travels. They wanted to
hold treasures in their hands, concrete images to help them
recall the time that they had spent upon the road. The city
teemed with trinkets—carved wood emblems unique to each
of the Thousand, clay figurines, colored ribbons. What was
next? Berylina scoffed. Was every Briantan set on earning
gold in the name of the Thousand?

Berylina needed no such physical reminders, of course.
She had the images in her head. She had the twisted paths
that the gods revealed inside her own mind, the chambers
that they excavated inside her senses. She sighed and hurried past the busy merchant.

Father Siritalanu guided her to Mip's temple with a di-
rectness and care that showed he had already scouted out the
path. Only once did he take her down a side street. When she
looked at him curiously, he flushed and walked a little faster.
"Father?" she asked, in a tone that hinted at her royal line-
age. She used that voice rarely, because it made guilt prick
at the back of her throat. This time, however, the commanding voice worked to her advantage. The priest turned toward
her but refused to meet her eye. "Father? What is it? Why
are you taking me this way?"

"I wanted to avoid the crowds in that street," he said at
last.

"What crowds? What is in there?" She stopped and

planted her hands on her hips. She was determined not to miss out on any aspect of her pilgrimage, on any worship that she might make to complete her journey.

"A temple, Your Highness. Nothing more. No need for you to worry."

"I'm not worried, Father. I'm curious. What god?"

"Perhaps I was mistaken, Your Highness. Perhaps we could have continued without mishap."

"Father!"

"Your Highness . . ." Father Siritalanu actually produced a kerchief from beneath his robe and began to mop at his brow. Berylina wondered at the priest's discomfort. After all, he was pledged to honor all of the Thousand—to recognize and exalt each of the gods for what that deity could bring into the world.

Berylina hardened her voice, strengthening it with the snap of command that she had learned at her father's knee. "Who is it?"

"Quan, Your Highness."

The god of harlots. Berylina's belly flipped, and she stifled an uneasy laugh as her nose was filled with the sharp odor of boxwood. She had not met the god of harlots personally; he had never come to her as she stood ready with her crayons and parchment. Nevertheless, she had heard men whisper of him, and a few of the gods spoke to her about their colleague. She knew that Quan was a wastrel, a spendthrift. She could imagine what form worship took in his temple.

Or perhaps she couldn't.

"Never mind, Father. You were right in choosing this path for me. I appreciate your guiding me to Mip." She strengthened her approval with a hand gesture.

The look of relief on Father Siritalanu's face was almost comical. Berylina wondered just what she *was* missing by not forcing her way into Quan's temple. Poor Father Siritalanu. He would probably never recover if she demanded passage. Instead, Berylina turned away from the sharp box-wood scent. "The afternoon escapes us. Let us go to Mip."

Berylina followed Father Siritalanu through the streets, trying to ignore the maelstrom of sensations as she walked. As she passed minor shrines, the gods beckoned to her, sending out their particular signatures. Her nose filled with scents, and she narrowed her eyes to slits in an attempt to cut down on the spinning, flickering visions. Never before had she been surrounded by so much godhood; never before had she sensed herself to be among so many holy beings.

She knew that they were nearing Mip's sanctuary when the trill of a nightingale rose above the chorus. The birdsong was still soft, delicate, but it resonated louder as she turned one last bend in the street. She could feel the notes in her ears, but they traveled down her nerves, into her body, into her bones.

Berylina fell to her knees on the threshold of the temple. "Hail, Mip, holy god of water. Welcome this pilgrim into your sanctuary and look upon her with blessings. Recognize her dedication to you and accept her prayer as the blessing that she means it to be."

The god heard her. She felt his attentions turn her way, sensed them as an intensification of the nightingale song. Berylina glanced at Father Siritalanu, to where the priest patiently knelt beside her, but he did not seem to recognize the power that rose before them. Nevertheless, the birdsong grew louder, and Berylina raised her eyes, amazed that none of the other pilgrims seemed to hear it, to feel it.

The crescendo continued to build, the notes gliding ever sweeter, ever closer to their true, eternal meaning. Berylina could see into the temple's courtyard; she could make out pilgrims kneeling and praying. An altar stood in the precise center of the space, raised as high as Berylina's waist. A delicate metal framework stood behind the block of polished stone, and Berylina could make out a pair of artisans who worked at something.

What were they doing? What had they brought to honor Mip?

Berylina turned her head, letting her better eye focus on the workers. Ah! They were glasswrights! They were installing a frame, a panel that saluted the god of water.

The green-clad princess stepped closer to the construction, angling to one side.

There . . . Without the sunlight shining directly on the glasswork, she could see the craftsmanship, recognize it for the beauty that it was. The panel was a medley of cool blues and greens, soft colors that swirled into each other like all the shades of a river. They caught the sky and reflected it back, breaking it into its component planes. They snared the stone of the courtyard as well, softened it, smoothed it. They captured the essence of Mip.

Berylina realized that her eyes had filled with tears. She had never seen guildwork like this. She had never imagined that an artisan could create such a true work of art, such a strong sense of rightness. The nightingale trill pounded through her limbs as she looked about the rest of the courtyard, checking to see which of the pilgrims had recognized the beauty, the *rightness* of the glasswrights' labors.

No one paid attention to the guildsmen, though. Pilgrims made their offerings, prayed before priests, spoke to each other. Families gathered together, sharing common meals as the sun climbed toward noon. The glasswrights might have been invisible for all the attention that was paid to them.

Berylina watched the worshipers kneeling before Mip's fountains. There were three watery displays inside the temple walls. In the first, a single great spray of water arced toward the sky, pushed to glory by arcane engines beneath the ground. In the second, a pool of water spread in a perfect circle, the water welling up slowly and mysteriously, cascading over the sides of its stonework ramparts like a sheet of liquid silver, only to be caught in a larger, placid pond.

The third fountain, though, was the one that cried out to

her most clearly, speaking in a voice almost as perfect as the glasswrights' panel. Great blocks of stone were arranged in tiered layers, rising up like the stairs in a god's castle. Water splashed from the top of the rocks, cascading down in leaps and arcs, hitting new surfaces and sparkling as it fractured in the air. Everywhere that Berylina turned, rainbows glinted, prisms arced as they caught each other and bent and glimmered. The patterns were always glorious, always holy, and yet they changed eternally. The fountain cycled through different patterns, and water crashed down on different planes of stone.

Mip. Mip was present in every droplet of that water. He was there in the arcs, in the jets. He was there in the mist that framed the rainbows. He was there in the pool at the bottom of the stone steps, in the slick paving stones.

Berylina caught her breath and opened up her mind to the great god's presence, feeling him fill her, expand within her. His song pulsed inside her body, beat inside her brain. She caught a breath against the nightingale's tremor, exhaled it with the sheer beauty of Mip's presence. Unable to bear the perfection of the rainbows, she closed her eyes and let the god fill her from within.

And then, when she thought her entire attention was given over to Mip, she heard the scream.

At first she forced it from her thoughts, believing that some pilgrim child was playing in the fountains. The first shriek sounded like one of joy. Berylina registered it, but she did not permit it to distract her.

The cry was repeated, though, sharper, more desperate. Berylina could not tell herself that the sound was part of her prayer; she could not believe that it was related to Mip's delicate nightingale song. She opened her eyes as if she were awakening from the deepest dream.

She could not place the sound, could not find the direction of the cry. Perhaps she *had* imagined it. No one else was disturbed in the courtyard. The glasswrights continued to affix their offering to its metal stand. A cluster of pilgrims knelt by the still pool, watching the water cascade over the sides. An elderly priest stood by the tall jet, speaking to a crowd of eager worshipers, explaining to them that the stream of water hit upon the Heavenly Gates, knocking for entrance on behalf of all believers.

Even Father Siritalanu seemed unaware of the voice, oblivious to the desperate cry. He knelt beside Berylina, his head still bowed in his own quiet prayer. From this angle, she could see the growing bald spot on the top of his head; he was a young man, but his head would be smooth within a decade. The thought made Berylina start to smile, but then she heard the cry again.

"Help!" This time, there was no mistaking the word. She turned toward the rocky fountain, to the great blocks of stone. There, jumbled toward the center, was a particularly tall boulder. Water plummeted from the highest part of the fountain, crashing down onto the rock with all the force of cascading falls. Berylina turned her head to one side, and she could make out a small child trapped behind the curtain of water, crying out in terror.

She scarcely had time to wonder how the boy—for she could see his flimsy tunic plastered to his flesh—had arrived at such a perilous place. He must have been playing in the fountain; he had likely circled around to the far side, escaping the watchful eyes of his parents and all the priests and pilgrims.

He tried to step through the curtain of water, but it was falling too rapidly, sheeting down too hard. Berylina could see that the child was only a few steps from freedom; he just needed to be braver as he moved through the falls.

The fountain, though, chose that moment to cycle to another of its phases. The heavy sheets of water that had blocked the boy's escape slowed to a trickle, stopped. In their place, rivers gouted up between the stones. The water poured forward, as if the very core of the world had been penetrated. The crowd exclaimed at the change, crying out as if Mip himself had strode into the temple compound.

The changing water caught the boy off guard, and he slipped on the stones. Berylina saw his head crack against the rocks, and then the water pushed him forward, forced him across the slippery surface. Mercilessly, the rainbows arced in the air above the boy, dancing as if there were no danger.

Berylina heard Mip's nightingale, the sweet song sharpened by a sudden urgency. Without conscious thought, she sprang to her feet, leaping toward the fountain. She wrenched up the hem of her caloya gown as she stepped over the ring of mortared stones that contained the fountain's flow.

The water was cold. Shockingly, bitterly cold, even on such a sunny afternoon. It seemed to carry a cavern's bitter chill, like the frozen blood of the earth. It sucked away Berylina's breath, even as she tried to tell herself to move forward, to move to where the boy had slipped beneath the sparkling surface.

Her robes tangled between her legs, caught by the swirls and eddies of the pool. Her feet slipped in their pilgrim's sandals, wrenching both of her ankles as she fought to remain upright. Despite her best efforts, she lost her footing, and she caught herself hard on her right wrist. Pain shot up her arm, a red-hot poker that burned against the freezing water.

She forced herself back to her feet, refusing to concede to the fountain. Mip sang to her, encouraging her. His notes rose in urgency, growing louder, louder, and she turned to face the source of those desperate tones. "Here!" the god seemed to cry. "You'll find the boy here!"

The direction made no sense—the child had slipped in at the top of the pool. There was no reason for him to be to Berylina's right, in the relatively placid pond that spread out beyond the stones. She edged forward, ignoring the pain in her arm, twisting to stay upright in her sandals. Her caloya robes ballooned behind her, but then she fell, and they were drenched completely. They dragged her toward the bottom of the fountain.

When she fought toward the spot where she had seen the boy fall, Mip's song grew fainter, as if he were chiding her poor choice. She turned back to his original direction, and the nightingale grew more spirited. She took one tentative step, and he encouraged her, his song becoming so sweet that she could taste it at the back of her throat.

Mip commanded her. She must set aside her human logic, must ignore her thoughts and expectations. Mip knew right and wrong. He knew good and evil. He told her to move across the fountain, and she did.

She fell once, twice, three times. A priest distracted her, bellowing from the edge of the holy pool. She made out Father Siritalanu's face, saw his fear that she had taken leave of her senses.

The currents proved stronger than she ever would have expected, sweeping deep beneath the surface of the water. Her ankles were frozen into blocks of stone, and a fan of icy water pulled her to one side. This time when she fell, her Thousand-Pointed Star dug into her side, and its spikes were wicked talons, forcing in the penetrating cold.

She gasped and struggled to regain her feet, but Mip's song rose even higher. She could not help but cover her ears, try to protect them from the assaulting music. That motion, though, caused her to lose her grasp on a rocky outcropping, and she splashed beneath the surface of the water, submerging her head entirely.

And then she saw the boy. He was trapped beneath the surface, his body wedged into a stony niche. His mouth was open, as if he were screaming for help, and his fingers floated in the water like widow's weeds. Berylina pushed herself to the surface and gasped a breath of air, and then she fought her way across the pond.

Her arm ached where she had fallen wrong. Her side burned with the mark of her Thousand-Pointed Star. Her ankles throbbed where her sandal straps had dug in. And yet she forced her way forward, drove her reluctant flesh to the paired stones that trapped the child.

Pausing only to offer up a wordless prayer to Mip, she dove beneath the surface.

The child was a dead weight in her arms. He was not pinned by the stones; he had only been pushed against them by the force of the water that rushed from the top of the fountain.

As Berylina's fingers worked to pull him free, to break the water's hold, a part of her mind continued to analyze the problem. The fountain worked with massive pumps, she realized. Mighty engines sucked water through holes between the stones. The water was collected in some subterranean chamber and then pushed—by what energy she could not name—to the surface.

Mip required great offerings to his glory. He demanded a literal outpouring of respect, of faith. He demanded that water rush to the top of the fountain, all the water that trapped the boy. That trapped Berylina.

She gathered her remaining strength and pushed to the surface, snatching another breath of air. As the water broke around her face, she cried out to the great god, "Mip! We came to honor you! Do not crush the pilgrims who would do you glory!"

And then she fought her way back beneath the surface. She was tiring now. Her bones ached. Her heart pounded. The nightingale music was lost behind the speech of her own body, behind the agony of her exhausted flesh. *Mip,* she managed to think. *Mip. Mip. Mip.*

She reached the paired stones. She grasped the boy's hand, taking it in both of hers. She closed her fingers around his wrist, felt how limp it was. *Mip,* she thought, and her feet found the pond's stony floor. *Mip*. And she pushed upward, fighting for air and light and peace and life. *Mip*.

The boy came with her. She broke the surface of the pond, and she raised her hands, fighting to bring her face up, struggling to breathe. Her hands were full, burdened, and it took a moment before her frozen mind realized that she had succeeded; she had brought the child with her.

The realization lent her strength that she had not known she could command. She fought to the side of the pool, dragging the boy along. She clambered out of the water, ignoring the staring pilgrims, ignoring the goggle-eyed priests.

Father Siritalanu waited for her, and his hands were confident, calm. He steadied her as she struggled to stand. He reached for the boy, taking up the child's tremendous weight. Only after her arms were empty did she feel the ache in her shoulders, did she recognize the sharp burn of muscles pushed beyond their endurance.

"Mip," she whispered, and Father Siritalanu seemed to understand, for he nodded and eased the child to the ground.

A woman keened, her voice penetrating the crimson haze in Berylina's mind. She broke off long enough to speak, to form words, words that the princess could not translate, could not parse. The woman snatched up the child, letting his limp neck fall back with a startling crack. Her cries grew even louder, and she pointed a shaking finger at Berylina, furious, accusing.

A man stepped out of the crowd, the weight of his Thousand-Pointed Star pulling his cloak askew. Roughly, he took the child from the woman, pushing aside her trembling hands. He laid the child out on the misty stone, and he pressed his fist against the boy's belly. He hollered as he worked, swearing obscenities at the priests, at the woman— his own wife, Berylina somehow realized. He swore at the boy—at his son—cursing the child's stubbornness, ordering him to respond, to open his eyes, to come back to life.

The nightingale song came back to Berylina's ears. She understood it as clearly as she understood human speech.

She drew herself to her full height, twitching her shoulders to shake free of Father Siritalanu's hands. She crossed the few paving stones that separated her from the child, stepping around his body as if it were a great fish on the beach. She knelt beside him, ignoring the protest in her knees, her side, her arm.

The nightingale sang to her, and she knew what she must do. She clutched the father's hands, tightening her fingers into steely ropes. He drew back in startlement, as if no one had ever brooked his authority before. Then, before he could bellow for reinforcements, before he could make new demands, before he could guarantee the death of his son, Berylina leaned over the boy.

The nightingale told her what to do. It sang to her of placing her lips on the child's. It trilled about delivering the kiss of peace, the kiss of strength and love and everlasting worship. It told her that she would taste water with the kiss, that she would taste the fountain, that she would drink the very glory of Mip.

She kissed the boy soundly, deeper than she had ever kissed another being.

And then she sat back on her heels.

For a moment, nothing happened. The pilgrims were startled into silence. The father was gathering his anger, collecting it in his hard fists. The mother was still keening—she had never stopped. Father Siritalanu looked upon Berylina with consternation, clearly worried about her own safety.

And then the child coughed. One sputter at first, and then another, and another. His body curled about itself as he collapsed into spasms, deep convulsions that brought up water where his father's fists had done no good.

The nightingale song crested in the courtyard, resonating so loudly against the stone and water that Berylina was certain all the pilgrims must hear it. She threw her head back in sheer joy at the music, in pure exultation at the unbridled sound.

"The child is saved!" Father Siritalanu exclaimed.

"Thanks be to all the Thousand Gods!" cried another pilgrim.

"Thanks be to Mip," Berylina said, forcing her voice past the nightingale's perfect beauty.

"Mip tried to kill my son!" the mother cried.

"Mip saved him," Berylina said.

"The god of water drew him beneath the surface—"

"He slipped!"

"Mip wanted to take my son! He wanted to murder my child!"

"Your boy brought this on himself. He got to the center of the fountain, but he slipped on the way back."

"And I suppose Mip himself told you these lies!"

Berylina was shocked by the anger in the mother's face, by the unalloyed rage that burned within her. The princess looked around the courtyard, sought out the priests, the glasswrights, anyone who would understand. "Didn't you see? Didn't you hear him cry for help?"

Silence, and then one old woman stepped forward. "I saw you," she said. Berylina recognized the voice. The old woman from Jair's birthplace. The woman who had shaken with rage that the First Pilgrim's plaything had come to Berylina. "I saw you. You pushed the boy beneath the surface of the pool."

The crowd exploded. "No!" Berylina protested. "He fell! I helped him to safety! Mip sang to me, and I saved the child!"

The father stepped up to his son before anyone else could speak. "Tell me, Chavit. Does this woman speak the truth? Did you cross to the center of the fountain?"

Berylina could see the man's fingers curl back into a fist. She heard the anger in his voice, the scarcely suppressed fear and fury. Chavit was no fool—he heard the emotions, as well. "I— I don't know what happened." He paused to cough, and the crowd's suspicions tightened while the child's narrow shoulders shook.

"Did you go into the water?" The father towered over the boy, his voice as sharp as the stones in the fountain.

"No! Papa, no! I waited for you and Mama to finish making your offerings to Mip! I waited by the fountain, just like you told me to."

"How did you get in the water, then, boy?"

"I don't know!" The child started to cry, and his sobs brought on another fit of coughing. When he could speak again, he repeated, "I don't know!"

"Don't lie to me, boy! Not here. Not in Brianta, before the Thousand Gods!"

"I'm not lying! I don't . . . I—" Chavit looked about the courtyard desperately, cringing as if his father had already landed a heavy fist.

The boy's eyes fell on Berylina. She saw him register her roaming eye, saw him take in her rabbit teeth. All her life, she had watched people measure her differences, watched them recoil at her flaws. She had seen cruelty blossom on some faces and impotent rage on others.

She recognized Chavit's craftiness as the boy's eyes narrowed. She was familiar with the shaking line of his finger as he pointed to her face. She knew the heat of the blush that reflexively stole across her features, of the shame that she was different, she was damaged, she was wrong, wrong, wrong.

"She did it!" Chavit cried. "She pushed me! She pushed me into the pool!"

The father snapped his head around to look at Berylina, and she struggled to meet his eyes, fought to overcome the wave of shyness, of shame, of terror as disabling as any she had ever suffered in her own father's court. She barely heard the man say, "Don't lie to me, boy. She jumped into the water to save you."

"Only after I cried for help!" The crowd murmured and stepped closer, and Chavit's story firmed up. "Only after other people saw her. She held me under at first, before she realized that others would see." The boy put his hand to his chest, as if he were swearing an adult's vow. His fingers scrabbled across his Thousand-Pointed Star, and the emblem seemed to give him some new inspiration. "By Mip," he said, and his voice was steady. "That woman meant to kill me. I swear she did! In the name of Mip!"

Berylina wanted to explain. She wanted to tell them that they were wrong. The boy was frightened. Exhausted. Terrified.

But the words were not there. Instead, she felt herself surrounded by the demons of her childhood, by the bloody Horned Hind that had haunted her dreams, by the lonely certainty that she was damaged, she was marked, she was wrong . . .

A priest stepped forward, his ancient face grave. "Speak, child," he said to Berylina. "Tell us whether this boy says the truth."

Berylina's throat worked, but she could say no words.

"Speak," the priest said again. "In the name of Mip, tell us what happened here."

The nightingale song rose loud and clear, and Berylina cast her head about, seeking out the source of the music. Surely the crowd must hear it! Surely they must know that Mip was in their midst! She tried to form words, tried to push speech past the nightingale song, but there was nothing she could say, nothing she could do.

"The god's name freezes her," Berylina heard, and she knew it was the old woman speaking again. "Mip protects us from her evil! Mip protects the faithful!"

As Berylina's throat worked, the crowd began to murmur. Other pilgrims joined the old woman, calling upon the god of water. Many covered their Thousand-Pointed Stars, as if her broken gaze would pollute their badges.

"Mip save us!"

"Mip keep us safe from harm!"

"Mip wash away the evil!"

"She's a witch!" The old woman's voice rose high above the crowd. "The girl's a witch!"

Father Siritalanu loomed above Berylina, as if he would enfold her in his robes, as if he would keep her safe from harm. "Nonsense, woman. She is a penitent, like all of you. She is a pilgrim who has offered up her very soul to Mip. She *saved* that boy."

"She's a witch, I tell you! She is marked as a witch. She cannot speak the god's name! I accuse her in the name of all the holy pilgrims in Brianta! I demand that she be brought before the Curia and judged as the witch that she is! I demand justice for all the pilgrims in Brianta, for all the faithful who pray to the Thousand Gods!"

Brianta heard Father Siritalanu's protests. She heard the older priest ask for clarifications, for justifications. She heard the crowd exclaim. She heard the old woman tell the story of Jair's House.

And then she felt a rope slip around her wrists. She felt her Thousand-Pointed Star ripped from her clothes. She felt the wind rise, cutting through her soaked robes, as if she stood naked in the courtyard.

She saw Father Siritalanu speaking to her. His lips moved. He must be telling her that she would be taken to the prisons, that she would be locked inside a cell. He would come to her, he said. He would explain to the priests. He would prove that she was a woman of faith. He would save her.

But she had no words. She could not speak. She could not make herself heard above the trilling notes of a nightingale song. She could not move beyond Mip's music, even when she was escorted from his temple, even when she looked back at the angry old woman who had accused her. Even when she looked back at the frightened boy, at Chavit, who shivered on the edge of the fountain that would have brought him death . . .

Berylina was silent as she was led away, as she was labeled a witch, as she submitted to the will of the angry, frightened crowd.

9

Rani caught her tongue between her teeth as she leaned over the whitewashed table. Her argument with Mair had made her late returning to the guildhall for her afternoon session. Despite her vow to her Touched friend, Rani had not dared to seek out Crestman that day—she had work that she must complete.

She had sketched out her drawing of Lor the night before, but she found that she was more critical of the god of silk by daylight. Somehow, his face now seemed too fat, too prosperous, as if he did not need to work for his wealth. She should make him more slender, more bony. Cutting the glass pieces would be easy enough with the diamond knife that she had mastered under Tovin's tutelage.

Sighing, she started to rub out part of the drawing. She leaned far over the table—she wanted to preserve her carefully sketched background. It had taken her hours to draw the octolaris, and she was pleased that she had managed to hint at the spiders rather than mandate any actual depiction. After all, there were other sources of silk in the world—curious worms from distant Pelia, for example. Just because Morenia had built *its* silk empire on spiders' handiwork didn't mean that Lor relied only on octolaris for his glory.

Rani's fingers trembled as she rubbed out the god's face. They had taken to tingling lately. She supposed that was a reminder of the food she was missing, the meals that she forsook when she was not at the guildhall.

Even those meals, when she got them, were plain, served on glazed pottery that Master Parion had mandated just for her use. Her mornings were brightened with only a dollop of porridge. Lunch was likely a heel of bread spread with thin butter. Dinner was a bowl of broth with an occasional stub of turnip. Everything tasted odd—dull, metallic—and the warm water she was permitted did nothing to wash away the aftertaste.

What did that matter? she tried to remind herself. She was here for the test, after all.

Once she had rubbed out the god's face, his shoulders seemed the wrong proportion. Then, when she corrected the shoulders, the figure's sleeves draped too dramatically. She fixed the sleeves, but then was forced to redraft the hands. She started to reposition the fingers, and then she found that she had, in fact, leaned on the whitewashed table, obliterating the carefully drawn octolaris.

"Burn it all!" she swore.

"My lady!"

Rani jumped and whirled about, even as she identified Father Siritalanu's shocked tone. "I'm sorry, Father. I didn't mean to offend you. It's just that—"

The priest interrupted her. "I wasn't offended!"

Rani set down her charcoal and brushed an errant lock of hair from her face. A few strands came away against her fingers, but she did not have time to worry about them. The young priest before her was anxious, wound so tightly that he seemed about to weep. "What is it, Father?"

"Her Highness. Princess Berylina." The man was panting hard, and Rani could barely make out his words. His face was crimson against his bright green robe, and his chest heaved as if he had run all the way from Morenia.

Rani felt the blood drain from her own cheeks, and she forced herself to swallow hard before she said, "Calm yourself, Father." She wished that she had wine to offer him, something of sustenance, but she could not provide anything, bound as she was by her glasswright's vows. "Sit down, Father. No, I won't hear another word. You're useless, if you collapse here on the floor."

The man grimaced, but he complied, throwing himself into a low chair. When he looked up at Rani, there was something petulant in his expression. He looked like a little boy.

No little boy, though, would deliver such a grave message: "It's Princess Berylina," he said, his words ratcheted down to a tone that approximated normalcy. "She's been taken as a witch."

"A what?" Rani might never have heard the word, she was so astonished. A pilgrim, certainly. A self-righteous girl. A pompous religious fanatic. But a *witch?* Like the herb-witches of Sarmonia? Who would bother to take a woman who dried herbs and brewed tisanes? And why would anyone mistake Berylina—Berylina!—for an herb-witch? "There must be some mistake."

"Of course there's a mistake!" The priest's voice broke on the last word. "They accuse her of harnessing magic because they cannot see that the gods actually speak to her! They did not realize the rescue was Mip's doing. He was truly there!"

"Mip?" Rani could not piece together what the priest was saying. What rescue? When?

"Aye, Mip. The god of water. We were at his temple this morning."

The priest explained something about the princess's cavalcade, and fountains, and a child, and an old woman, and a ball. Rani did not actually understand everything he said—his words had become fast again, and he stood to pace the chamber, twining his fingers as if he would mold his joints into a weapon. Her head began to ache, a slow steady

pounding that beat behind her eyes like the Pilgrims' Bell
back home.

"Father," Rani finally interrupted, "where is she now?
Where is Princess Berylina?"

He blinked as if he had only just remembered that Rani
was in the room. "She's in jail. In the Gods' Midden."

Rani caught her breath, momentarily overwhelmed by
her own memories of being cast into a dungeon. Even now,
in the Briantan sunlight, Rani could remember the stench of
soaked straw, the foul odor of too many bodies in too little
space. She could see other prisoners eyeing her with distrust, with hatred. She could feel the filth on her own flesh,
the disgusting slime of another person's spit.

Berylina could never last in prison. She was a princess.
She was more than a bit daft. She was utterly unprepared for
the brutal reality of prosecution. "We have to go to her!"

Even as Rani shut her workshop door, she knew that she
should find Journeyman Larinda. She should explain why
she was leaving her work undone. After all, Rani had sworn
to follow the guild's orders in all things. She was supposed
to complete her drawing by nightfall; she was destined to
practice cutting the glass the very next day. Time was running short for her to prepare for the guild's test.

"There are obligations, and there are obligations," Rani
groused to herself. It was easier to ignore the guild's restrictions now and see to the princess. She could explain herself
to Larinda later, to Master Parion if necessary. Rani was
bound to Berylina—Hal had ordered her to see the princess
safe on this journey.

She started to mutter as she threw her dark pilgrim's
cloak over her shoulders. Where was Tovin? If he had stayed
close at hand, she could rely on him now. She could send
him to straighten out this ridiculous confusion with
Berylina. He would likely enjoy the challenge—a chance to
speak to soldiers and make them seem like fools.

She had been arguing with Tovin, though, almost con-

stantly. He had taken to sulking at the inn, complaining
about her vow to the guild. If she so much as smiled at him,
he chided her, asking if Master Parion would approve. The
night before, she had come back from the guild well after
dark, her belly aching, barely eased by the watery broth that
had been her supper. Tovin had complained about the heat in
the rooms, even so long after the sun had set, and she had
growled at him, telling him that she'd give anything to warm
her bones, chilled by her hours in the guild's dark workrooms.

Tovin had snapped at her and slammed the door, leaving
behind a mystified Mair and a squalling Laranifarso. Rani
had declined the implicit obligation to follow him belowstairs to the tavern, to apologize for her words. Why should
she beg Tovin to come back upstairs? Why should she stand
there and breathe in the smell of fine ale and hearty grilled
meat? Why, indeed?

And yet she wished that Tovin were beside her as she
abandoned her glasswork. He would be a comfort in the
crowds on the streets. He would make her feel more secure
as she passed the vagabond preachers, the bearded men who
cried out at women who walked in daylight, even women
who wore the Thousand-Pointed Star.

But Tovin was not there, and Rani was left to help Father
Siritalanu, to assist Berylina. On the way to the prison, Rani
made the priest repeat his tale. She slowed his torrent of
words this time, forcing him to reiterate bits of the story.
Rani realized that Berylina had actually saved a boy's life,
that she had somehow called upon the Thousand to rescue a
child. If the princess had that sort of power at her disposal,
then what help could Rani possibly be?

Arriving at the Midden, she repeated the question to herself. The prison was located against one dark edge of a city
square. Dust puffed up in the street, swirling into vicious
devils that clutched at Rani's cloak and dried her throat. The
dark blocks of stone that formed the Midden walls were red

tinged, as if they had been shaped from the blood of the prisoners inside.

Rani shook her head. Surely she was being overly dramatic. The prison was a prison, like any other. Less dangerous than most. After all, the vast majority of the inhabitants were pilgrims who had proffered too many coins to the gods to pay their hostelry bills. Or they were worshipers who had grown drunk on wine and the words of their special gods.

The Midden was not the worst prison that Rani had ever seen.

Nevertheless, as she looked up at its brooding silhouette against the afternoon sky, she realized that she had rushed here headlong. Tovin would be furious to learn that she had not summoned him. Even if she had not dragged the player along, she should at least have called Mair.

But Mair was sleeping with Laranifarso, recovering after a night made sleepless by the babe's teething. And Tovin . . . Tovin would merely tell her that she had no place in this dusty square. He might laugh and say that the princess's problems would be resolved by daylight. He might offer to solve the problem for her, to clarify the mistake on his own. He might make light of Berylina's plight, even as he had jested about Rani's own problems, even as he had laughed when she told him that she was finally through with grinding colors and had at last been permitted to sharpen a grozing iron.

She did not need Tovin to set things right, after all. She did not need him to look after Berylina, to fulfill Rani's own promise to Hal. Setting her lips into a firm line, she said to Father Siritalanu, "Very well. Let's speak to the guards. Let's explain their error."

Rani knew that she was in no true danger as she approached the Midden walls. She was not the prisoner. She was not the accused, not the one trapped behind dank stone. And yet her heart beat faster and her breathing came sharp. Her headache reclaimed the pounding space behind her eyes. She wiped suddenly clammy palms against her skirts, wished again that she could warm herself in the sultry summer streets.

"My lady," Father Siritalanu said, but Rani shook her head. She could hear the despairing concern in his voice, and the emotion angered her. She was fine. She could confront some upstart guards in a city prison where the people did not even accord true respect to their king.

"Halt!"

Rani's heart clenched so tightly, she thought that she must cry out. Instead, she swallowed hard and ordered herself to remember the lessons that she had learned with Tovin, the players' tricks for performing power. She stood up straight, and she swallowed once, reminding herself to pitch her words low. "I am here to see Berylina, Princess of Liantine and ward of King Halaravilli ben-Jair of Morenia."

Out of the corner of her eye, Rani could see Father Siritalanu's nervous glance of surprise, and he took one step away, clearly trying to separate himself from her strident tone. The guard continued to stare straight ahead, as if she had said nothing. "No prisoners may receive visitors after the hour of Charn."

Charn. Rani ran through a quick recitation of the gods. The god of knives. When did his bells ring in the city? Some time in the morning, most likely. At least that was what the guard's attitude suggested.

"The princess was only just brought here to the Mid—" Rani stopped herself in time. No reason to insult the guard. No reason to imply that he was merely a fly buzzing about a dung heap. "To the Thousand Gods' Hall of Justice. I could not see her before Charn's bells, because she was not here then."

"Then you will see her before Charn on the morrow."

"She is a princess, man!" Rani's voice was suddenly shrill, and she swallowed again, forcing her tone back toward the players' rich register.

She might have been reciting children's tales for all the impact her words had on the guard. "Princess or pauper, we make no distinction here. All men and women are equal in the eyes of the Thousand Gods."

The matter-of-fact tone pricked Rani's anger, even as she wondered what it meant for Berylina in practical terms. If all prisoners were equal, then the princess would be sleeping on straw. She'd be filling her belly with greasy water and cold gruel, if she even got that.

Hal was going to be furious with Rani. He would look at her with condemnation, and then he would sigh that sigh that made him sound as if he were a hundred years old. . . .

A crimson curtain fell across Rani's eyes, and she stepped toward the guard with a new determination. "You don't understand, you miserable dust-sucking dog. You've got a woman in there by mistake. She doesn't belong in your stinking Midden, and when she is released, you are going to be held personally responsible. King Halaravilli will see that you spend the rest of your days mucking out garderobes in his own castle walls! He'll see—"

Father Siritalanu closed his fingers around Rani's arm, his grip betraying more strength than Rani ever expected the man to possess. He cleared his throat and said, "I am the princess's spiritual guide, good soldier. I would like to pray with her, to help her find the path of right and wrong through all that she is accused of."

The guard stared at the priest suspiciously, his eyes as shrewd as a hawk's. Rani caught her breath and waited, belatedly realizing that she and Father Siritalanu were entirely at the man's mercy. The Thousand Gods, however, must have smiled upon their mission, because the bells in a nearby temple began to ring. The clamor was picked up by bells across the courtyard, and by a more distant, deeper claxon. Rani resisted the temptation to cover her ears against the noise.

Instead, she watched the Briantan soldier relax into the

sound. It seemed as if he gathered confidence from the bells, breathing in their peace as easily as Rani breathed air. His angry glare faded, and Rani was reminded of the old Holy Father of her youth, of the ancient man who had recited his words of prayer with a passion and a confidence that even now echoed across the years.

"Very well," the soldier said, as the bells started to fade away. "You may pray with the prisoner. But we must search you first, to ascertain that you do not bring any contraband into the cells."

"By all means," Father Siritalanu said, bowing his head in a humility that Rani could not imitate. Nevertheless, she submitted to the guard's brisk touch, allowing him to verify that she did not carry weapon or tool, no means of liberating Berylina from her unjust cell.

The soldier's touch reminded Rani of other times that she had been searched—nearly a decade ago in Morenia, when she was cast into the old king's dungeons, two years ago in Liantine, when she'd approached the spiderguild at their desert stronghold. She had emerged alive—if not unscathed—from each of those encounters, and she tried to comfort herself that this soldier's impersonal touch would result in no lasting harm.

She was grateful that she had followed the precepts of pilgrimage and walked the streets of Brianta with no weapon on her person.

At last, the guard was satisfied, and he summoned a fellow who stood inside the prison gates. That soldier looked Father Siritalanu and Rani up and down with bright-eyed skepticism, but he complied with a direct order from his fellow and led the pair through a small antechamber, into a warren of hallways.

Rani had trouble catching her breath inside the prison. Each time that she filled her lungs, she was tempted to cough, to force out the evil aura that pressed upon her. Her heart pounded fast beneath her hastily donned robe, and the tips of her fingers tingled. Her belly clenched with hunger, but she wondered if she could have kept food down in her nervous state.

She wanted to turn about and run; she wanted to go back to her workroom at the guild, to the chamber that she shared with Mair. How had she been foolish enough to come here without even letting her Touched friend know her destination? Without telling Tovin, without bringing him along for protection and for his wry wisdom? What fool choice had she made? How could she go on?

Father Siritalanu must have sensed the panic that was growing inside her. He glanced at her as she held back at one particularly shadowy juncture, and a ghost of compassion haunted his eyes. Rani thought that he was about to speak, that he was about to offer her some words of solace, but then the guard drew up sharply in front of an iron-barred cell.

"My lady!" Father Siritalanu exclaimed, and Rani's attention was dragged to the tiny chamber.

Berylina sat on a stone bench against the far side of the cell, stark beneath a single slit of a window. Her back was pushed up against the wall, and it seemed that the stone was the only force that kept her upright. Her knees were tucked beneath her chin, and her fingers clasped about her shins as if she were trying to lock in some boundless passion.

Or as if she were freezing.

Even in the dim light of the soldier's flickering torch, Rani could see that the princess was shivering. Her lips were tinged blue, and her face was ashen against the green of her caloya robes. The dark green of her caloya robes. The sodden green—the robes were clearly soaked through.

"You did not even let her dry herself before you cast her in here?" Father Siritalanu's voice echoed off the low ceiling, and his face flushed purple with rage. "She worked Mip's own mission, and yet you leave her to catch a chill and die?"

"She's a prisoner, Father." The guard answered immediately, but then he swallowed uneasily. He was clearly accustomed to yielding to religious men, to giving way before the power of the Thousand Gods and all their earthly representatives. "She is accused of witchcraft, Father. Surely if she were uncomfortable in her cell, she would call upon her ungodly powers to warm her."

"If she *were* a witch, she might do just such a thing," Rani snapped.

Father Siritalanu said, "She's a child! A blessed, far-seeing child, who saved the life of another child this morning." The priest sighed, as if he realized further argument would be fruitless. "Let me go in there."

The guard shook his head. "You may speak with her. You may not enter the cell."

Rani argued, remembering to move her arm in an expansive gesture, as if she were performing on the players' stage. "Look at her! She can't even come to the door! Let us go in!"

The guard merely shook his head, one curt motion, and then he crossed his arms on his chest and looked away. Rani glanced at Berylina, saw that she was not even following the guard's refusal. The girl was looking off to her right, not trying to see with her good eye, not trying to crane her neck to bring the trio of free people into focus.

"Do you realize what you're doing, Soldier?" Rani forgot any semblance of players' art as anger overtook her. Her voice rang shrilly against the stone walls. "That girl is a princess of the land of Liantine, heir to the house of Thunderspear. She is a protected member of the court of Halaravilli ben-Jair. When her father ... When my king ... When they find out that you have treated Princess Berylina Thunderspear like a common harlot, armies will be raised! The princess is a pilgrim, in the name of all the Thousand Gods! She came to Brianta as a worshiper! She has a cavalcade and a Thousand-Pointed Star!"

Rani stopped her tirade only because she needed to draw

breath, because she needed to fill her lungs and think of some argument that could persuade this soldier, this stupid, mind-closed guard, this idiot—

Father Siritalanu stepped forward and clapped his hand on the man's shoulder. The priest leaned close and said, "I understand, my man. I understand your predicament." And when the father stepped back, the guard moved to the door, opening it with a quick jerk of one of the keys that jangled at his waist.

Rani stared in amazement as Father Siritalanu stepped over the threshold. It was not until the guard eased to the side for her to pass that she saw the glint of gold in his palm, the edge of a coin that he tucked into a pouch beside the ring of keys. He turned slowly and walked down the corridor with apparent nonchalance. Rani shook her head and stifled an oath before she stepped into the cell and crossed to Berylina in two quick strides.

"My lady," Father Siritalanu was saying as he eased an arm around his charge. "You must be freezing! Don't worry, now. We're with you."

"I do not worry, Father." The princess's breath was high and wispy, like clouds on the hottest summer day. Rani could see tiny drops of blood on her lips, where her teeth had pierced her flesh as she shivered.

"We're here now, my lady," the priest continued to say, filling the deadly silence with soothing chatter. He swept his cloak off his shoulders, eased it behind the princess. The ends of her hair were still wet, but the roots had dried so that her wiry strands stood out from her head. "You're not alone any longer," the priest crooned.

"I was never alone, Father." The princess had to pause to muster more breath, to form more words. "I have not been alone here."

"Your Highness," Rani said, swallowing the coppery flavor of fear at Berylina's strange words. "We will get you out by morning. We'll demand in King Halaravilli's name that you be released."

Berylina shook her head weakly, finally turning her neck to pin Rani with one wandering eye. "I am not here as the king's woman. I am a pilgrim." For the first time since Rani and Father Siritalanu had entered the cell, Berylina showed a hint of emotion: Her lower lip trembled with more than a chill, and tears welled up in her eyes. "I am a pilgrim, seeking the guidance and the blessing of all the Thousand Gods."

"Yes, my lady," the priest muttered automatically, still trying to ease his cloak more closely about her. The operation was made more difficult by his apparent aversion to touching her.

"They speak lies against me," Berylina said, her voice filled with childlike surprise.

"They are frightened," Father Siritalanu said.

"They are fools," Rani snapped. "We'll do away with their accusations by dawn!"

"I am not a witch," Berylina whispered. "The gods would not speak to me if I were a witch. They would not come to me. They would not let me see them. Hear them. Taste them . . ."

"You are not a witch," Father Siritalanu said, but his forehead wrinkled. He continued to speak, but his words were so soft that Rani could scarcely hear him. "My lady, you should not speak of the gods coming to you. Not here. Not now."

"You know they do, Father."

"I know that your prayers are strong, my lady."

The princess laughed, and Rani's skin crawled at the high, eerie sound. She thought of a midnight storm and the wind trying to pry thatch from the roof. She thought of old Glair, the Touched woman who led the Fellowship back in Moren, who pretended to be mad as she huddled in freezing doorways.

"Do not fear me," Berylina said, when she could catch

her breath after her laughter died. The princess looked past Father Siritalanu, pleading her case directly to Rani. "I *do* see the gods, and smell them, as well. Taste them and touch them and hear them. Why should they hide from all my senses? They are omnipotent, no? They can do all things? Why should they be limited to appearing before my eyes?"

"My lady," Father Siritalanu said, "we'll speak of this tomorrow, once you are out of this cell. We'll address your spiritual questions then. For now, you should stay quiet—"

"Quiet!" Berylina gasped. "Quiet! Ask instead that I sit here without stinking of water, without smelling of Mip's fountain. Ask that I not taste the blood on my lips! Ask that I not hear my own heart beating against my rags!"

"Please, my lady!" Father Siritalanu cast a look of despair toward Rani. "Please. Let us help you. Let us wrap you in a clean gown, in a dry one. Let Lady Ranita serve you in this, at least."

The princess thrashed her head, as if she were a horse trying to fight free of a bridle. She stopped herself, though, and turned toward Father Siritalanu, pinning him with one glittering eye. "If Ranita would serve me, there is one thing that she might do."

"Yes, my lady?" Rani asked, wanting to help the poor creature before her even as she was frightened by the princess's vehemence.

Berylina whispered, "Speak with me."

"I *am* speaking with you."

"No! *Speak* with me!"

Rani realized the princess's intention even as Father Siritalanu sucked in his breath. "My lady," he protested, loud enough that Rani feared the guard would return. Berylina ignored him, though, clutching at Rani's cloak as if it were a rope tossed to save her from drowning.

"Please, Ranita Glasswright. I would Speak with you. I would plumb the depths of my worship of the Thousand. You have told me tales of the players, about how you learned your glasswright skills. I would apply the same lessons to myself, to my worship."

"My lady," Rani protested, "This is hardly the place! Besides, I have never guided anyone in the ways of Speaking."

"But you have been guided yourself, many times."

"Let me send for Tovin Player, my lady. He is far more skilled than I."

"And you think the guards would let him pass? You think that he would guide me better than you? He is a player, Ranita Glasswright, a man who makes his living masquerading as something that he is not. He was raised in godless Liantine. He does not know my heart; he does not understand my worship. You do. You can help me."

Rani wanted to protest. She wanted to explain that she did not understand the princess. She did not understand the fire of religious passion that clearly burned behind Berylina's fevered brow. Besides, Rani had not been lying when she protested. She was not schooled in all the players' ways, and she had never tried to guide another in Speaking.

Nevertheless, a prideful whisper taunted, she *did* know a great deal about the practice. Tovin had guided her for years now, taking her through her memories, helping her to explore her thoughts and reasoning and beliefs.

She turned to Father Siritalanu. "Father, if you could watch in the hallway, make sure that we are not interrupted by the guards."

"You aren't actually going to *feed* this madness, are you?"

"I am going to help the princess, Father. She has asked with a clear conscience and with a good heart. I am going to guide her so that she might serve the gods."

"The Thousand care nothing for your Speaking!"

"Then it will work no harm for us to try. The gods will only ignore us." Rani saw the smile grow on Berylina's lips, realized that the princess was pleased with her argument.

"Please, Father. We don't know how much time we have before the guards return."

Father Siritalanu took one lingering look at his charge, and he seemed about to cast another argument. He caught himself instead and waved his hand in a religious gesture. "May First God Ait watch over you, and may Jair himself guide all your steps."

"Amen," Princess Berylina whispered, the word slipping over her blue-tinged lips.

Rani waited until Father Siritalanu had stepped into the corridor before she knelt beside the princess. "Please, my lady. I will guide you in this thing to the best that I am able. But first you must take my gown. You must be warm and comfortable to do your work. Your mind must be free of your body's needs, if you are to make the journey of Speaking."

This time, Berylina acceded. She gathered herself slowly from her stone bench, moving as if she were awakening from a very deep sleep. She struggled with her clinging garments, and her teeth began to chatter as she peeled away the heavy layers. First her cloak, then her gown, then her clinging undergarments, shed from her body with all the naive certainty of a child.

Rani looked away, embarrassed by the naked body in front of her. Berylina was a *princess,* after all. How could Rani look upon her this way? Pulling at the laces of her own garment, Rani rapidly cast down her cloak. She lifted her dress over her head and passed it to the princess, taking care not to touch the chilled royal fingers, not to focus on the girl's blue-tinged limbs.

In fact, Rani looked at Berylina only after the princess had pulled her wiry hair free of the garment's neck, after she had smoothed the lines of the gown down her body. The fabric was snug across the princess's curves, but Rani thought that the tight cloth might warm Berylina faster, might speed away some of her deadly pallor.

"Very well," Berylina said, and her teeth had stopped clattering. "I have acceded to your demands. Now you must yield to mine."

Rani inclined her head in silent acceptance of their bargain. Berylina must focus on something, some instrument to bring her deeper into the Speaking. Rani glanced about the cell, but she found nothing for the duty, nothing that would work except for the glittering Thousand-Pointed Star that was puddled in her cloak. She retrieved the worked gold and balanced it in her palm.

"Very well, my lady," she said, as she contemplated what she was about to do. What would Tovin say? How would he criticize Rani when he found that she had appropriated the players' tool? "You must make yourself as comfortable as possible. Put my cloak around your shoulders. No. No protest. I'll take it back when I leave, to cover my shift, but you must be freed from thinking of your body now."

Much to Rani's surprise, Berylina complied. The princess settled the wool about her shoulders, and then Rani opened the fist that she had made around her Thousand-Pointed Star. She tilted it toward the weak sliver of sun from the room's window, turning it to reflect more of that light. "Look upon the Star, my lady."

Rani tried to remember how Tovin had first introduced her to Speaking, how he had initially brought her to the altered state where she could see her past, where she could excavate all the energy and passion and knowledge that she'd ever gained. "Look into the light, my lady, and let it become a part of you. Let it be your guide and your path. Let it be your eyes and your sight. Let it take you into your heart and through your mind. Let it guide you into your thoughts, farther and farther, so that you are beyond this room, beyond Brianta."

Berylina had focused on the Star as soon as Rani extended the symbol. Her breathing deepened with every phrase that Rani uttered. The princess's lips stopped their trembling, and her face smoothed, cleared of worry. Rani felt a surge of power build beneath her own breastbone. She was guiding this Speaking!

"Berylina, I'm going to ask you to count for me. After each number that you say, take a deep breath. As you breathe out, you will travel deeper into the Star, deeper into your thoughts, deeper into the Speaking. Each breath will bring you greater peace. Each number will bring you closer to your self, to your thoughts, to your true inner being. If you'd like, you may close your eyes as you count. Now, say the first number with me. One."

"One." Berylina whispered the word, and then she filled her lungs, breathing deeply, as if she were preparing for some sublime pronouncement. She held the air for a long moment, and then she exhaled. Rani could feel the breath driving the princess deeper, closer to her core, closer to the depth of Speaking. "Two." Berylina repeated the process, and when she exhaled for the second time, she closed her eyes. "Three." Rani felt her surge deeper, farther, more distant.

Rani waited for Berylina to voice the next number, but the princess remained silent. She continued to fill her lungs, breathing in so deeply that Rani wondered if the seams of her stressed gown might split. But then the princess exhaled, pulling herself to an ever more distant place.

"Very well," Rani said, after the princess had taken another half-dozen breaths. "You can feel the power of the Star. You can count all the Thousand Points. You can wind between them, finding your way, guiding yourself, moving, moving, moving. Follow the Star back to one specific day, Berylina. Find the most important memory in your heart, in your mind. Follow the Star to that day."

Rani waited while Berylina thought. Emotions flitted across the princess's face—fear and hurt and anger. "Be easy, Berylina," Rani said. "You can choose the memory. You can choose a place that is safe. A place where you learned, where you grew. None of your memories can hurt you. Not here. Not now."

Berylina's breathing smoothed, and her face became placid. The deep breathing—or perhaps Rani's warm shift and cloak—had brought a touch of color back into her cheeks, a hint of rose beneath the alabaster. "When you are ready, Berylina, I want you to tell me where you are. Tell me what you see."

The princess was silent for a long minute, as if summoning words were a task worthy of a warrior. "Liantine," she whispered at last.

"You are in Liantine?" Rani was not surprised. The princess had lived thirteen of her sixteen years in Liantine. "Tell me where, Berylina. Tell me what you see."

"I'm in my nursery. The old nursery. Before they took down the spidersilk hangings. Before they brought in the Horned Hind." Rani heard the wonder in the princess's voice, the child's softer forming of the words.

"How old are you, Berylina?"

"Nine. Today is my birthday. We had almond cake, and my father gave me a kitten." The whisper of a smile crept onto the princess's lips. "I had other gifts, as well. A gilded mirror and a gown the color of the sky. And no one laughed at me today. No one at all."

The princess's lips trembled, and her forehead creased into a frown. "No one will laugh at you now," Rani assured her.

"But my eyes are not right. And my teeth stick out."

"No one will laugh at you," Rani repeated. "Not now. Your Speaking is in your memory, my lady. You have power over it. You can end it whenever you desire." The words soothed the woman-child, and Rani waited for her to draw a few more deep breaths. "Tell me more about the day, my lady. Why have you chosen to Speak this story?"

"I've come from the dining hall. I still have crumbs on my hands." Berylina's fingers were curled into fists, managing to echo the chubby knots that she must have known in her childhood. "My nurse greets me, and she takes the kitten. She says the kitten must go to sleep, and so must I."

Berylina raised her hands as if she were offering up a small, furry comfort. Rani feared that the animal would meet some dire fate, that some disaster that would make this day important in Berylina's memories. But no, the kitten seemed to be carried away without trauma.

"Nurse says that I should pray with her before I take my nap. She's a new one, this nurse, new to me, because my brothers have teased all the other nurses into leaving. She's young. She comes from Amanthia, from far away."

Amanthia. Rani's mind flashed to her own memories of that land, to its wild forests and ragged coastline. To the Little Army. To Crestman. But Berylina had never traveled to Amanthia. She did not hold those visions.

"Nurse makes me kneel beside her on the prie-dieu. The bench is still too high for me. I can't rest my head on the cross bar. I bow my head, though, trying to be like Nurse." Berylina suited action to words. In the washed-out light of the cell, she looked as if she were a child, as if her arched neck were a humble, vulnerable offering.

"Nurse prays to her gods, to the Thousand, who make their home in Amanthia. She prays in the name of Pit and Dol and Roat. She asks Nome to watch over me."

Berylina bowed her head even farther, and her lips began to move in a silent incantation. Rani waited for a moment, expecting the story to continue. When the princess remained silent, Rani prompted, "What are the words of her prayer, Berylina?"

" 'Hail Nome, god of children, guide of Jair the Pilgrim. Look upon this pilgrim with mercy in your heart and justice in your soul. Guide the feet of this pilgrim on righteous paths of glory that all may be done to honor you and yours among the Thousand Gods. This pilgrim asks for the grace of your blessing, Nome, god of children.' "

The words cut through Rani, icing across her heart. Those were the words her mother had said every morning and every evening. The prayer was traditionally spoken over the dead, but Rani's mother had made it one of protection for the living, for her children. Those words had guided Rani every day of her childhood, before she knew that she was destined for the Glasswrights' Guild, before she knew that she would betray her family and her friends. Before her life changed forever.

"Nurse tells me that I must pray, as well," Berylina said, and Rani was forced to remember where she was now, who she was, that she was responsible for guiding this Speaking.

She took a breath that was shakier than it should have been, and she asked, "What words do you pray?"

"I pray for Nome to bless me. I pray, 'May Nome look upon me with his grace and goodness. May Nome protect me. May Nome guide me.'" Berylina's words were still softened with the speech of childhood, but her tone was brilliant, fierce. As Rani watched, a light bloomed within the princess's face, a burning power that expanded like a candle catching in the night.

"What?" Rani whispered. "What do you see?"

"Not see!" Berylina said. "Not see!"

"What is it? What happens, Berylina?"

"Nome comes to me!"

"What does he say?"

"Nome does not use words! Nome brings the sound of music! He pipes, like the players at my birthday feast! He speaks in music!" Joy spread over Berylina's face, and she turned her head as if she were listening to the most beautiful notes in the world.

Rani watched the transformation, watched the princess's rabbit teeth disappear, watched her strange otherness melt away. When Nome played for her, she was a different girl, a blessed girl, a child who was perfect in the hearts of the gods, in every way that mattered. She was safe. Loved. Free.

Rani wanted to let the princess stay inside the memory, wanted her to live within the beauty of the past. She could not, though. The guard would check on them shortly, bribe or no bribe. Rani must bring the princess back to normal wakefulness.

"My lady, it's time for you to come back to me, back to Brianta." Rani saw Berylina's brow start to wrinkle, a protest start to blossom in her throat. "I'm going to count from ten to one. When I say *one,* you will awaken, refreshed and unafraid. You will remember everything we've spoken about, everything you've told me. You will not worry, though. You will not fear. You will be warm and safe and secure."

Rani glanced about her at the walls of the prison, wondering how she could even offer up such a suggestion with seriousness. No sane woman would feel secure inside this cell. Nevertheless, Rani pushed confidence into her voice and counted. "Ten. Nine. Eight." She watched Berylina's face change, watched her move from her memories toward the present. "Seven. Six." The princess's jaw seemed to jut more; her teeth protruded above her lower lip. "Five. Four." Berylina turned her head to the right, her habitual stance for viewing people standing close to her. "Three. Two. One!"

Berylina gasped as if she were surfacing from under water. Her eyes burst open, and she heaved forward. Her breath was strangled, frantic, a wheezing clatter that echoed in the cell, louder than any of the words she had spoken.

Suddenly, Father Siritalanu was standing on the threshold, his face whey pale beneath his tonsure. "What have you done to her? What did you do to the princess?" Berylina's eyes were rolled up into her head, and Rani caught her as she slumped to the ground, limp as a bolt of raw silk. "What did you do to my mistress?"

"Hush!" Rani said, looking meaningfully toward the door. "The guard will hear you!"

Father Siritalanu started to bark out something, but then

he swallowed the words, as if they were too angry even for
a prison cell, in this land of Jair's birth. Instead, he settled
for crossing to Berylina. He lifted her right hand between
both of his and he chafed it, raising it up to his heart as if he
would transfuse his life force merely by the power of his
prayer. "My lady," he whispered, urgency sharpening the
words. "My lady, come back to us! We need you here, my
lady."

Berylina's eyes flew open. The cast one floated wildly, as
if she could not focus, but the direct one pinned itself on
Rani. "Please!" Berylina croaked, the one word sounding
like the flood of water from the mouth of a near-drowned
man. She reached forward with both her hands, thrusting Father Siritalanu away.

Rani felt the princess's fingers close about her own;
Berylina clutched at her with more strength than she had
ever imagined the girl might have. Just as Rani was about to
cry out, she felt a surge of energy—hot cold black white
sharp sharp sharp.

Rani's hand throbbed with the pulse, and then her arm,
her neck, her entire head. She had felt a force like that once
before, years back, in Morenia, when Hal had tested her before the old king. Then, she had been forced to place her
hand upon the Inquisitor's Orb; she had been required to
hold it there as it burned hot with the power of all her
thoughts, all her beliefs, all her dreams and expectations.
Now, Rani opened her mouth to cry out, but she could make
no sound, form no words.

Inside the void, she heard Berylina's whisper, heard the
words that the princess had shared only a moment ago.
"Nome does not use words! Nome brings the sound of
music! He pipes, like the players at my birthday! He speaks
in music!"

And Rani's head was filled with music—the most perfect
jig ever piped, the most perfect reel ever played. Her heart
raced with the music, pulsed with the notes. She heard the

music in her core; she felt it in her being. She *became* the music. She became Nome.

And then, when her heart could beat on its own again, she sensed the other gods standing in the shadows, ones that she knew were especially sacred to Berylina. There was Mip and Nim. Ile and Zil. And there, in a corner of Rani's mind, tucked away where she would rather ignore him forever, was Tarn, the god of death. He was wrapped in green-black swirls, iridescent as a beetle's back.

So this was how Berylina saw the world. This was how her mind worked behind her cast eyes. This was what she worshiped when she journeyed on her pilgrimage, when she declared her faith beyond the world of common men.

For just an instant, Rani was catapulted back to her youth in Moren. When she had been only thirteen years old, she had stood on the steps of the House of the Thousand Gods, been greeted by the old Holy Father himself. The ancient man had named her the First Pilgrim of the year; he had elevated her to a symbolic station, thrust her into the life she now led.

Then, Rani had thought that she should hear the gods, feel them move about her daily life. She had been ashamed that she felt nothing. She had known that she was masquerading, staking claim to a holiness that was not hers by any right.

This was different, though. This was real. This was true.

Rani wondered how Berylina had come to convey this beauty. She wondered what power the princess had used, what magic she had worked, what reverse Speaking she had fashioned. Perhaps Berylina truly *was* a witch.

Even as the fearful thought crossed Rani's mind, she discarded it. Berylina had worked no evil here. She had not used her powers to harm any other. Instead, she had reached out to share beauty and power and light. She had reached out to share her knowledge of all the Thousand Gods.

"My lady," Rani said, bowing her head.

"This is how I know the gods, Ranita Glasswright. This is how I know them in my heart of hearts."

"I understand, my lady."

"Some say that I am evil for this knowledge."

"They speak in ignorance, then."

"They'll fight me, Ranita Glasswright. They'll fight to have me buried as a witch because they do not understand. They'll smother me with earth."

"I'll keep you from that." Rani raised her head to the single narrow window, blinking her eyes in the light that suddenly seemed too bright. "I promise that I will do all in my power to keep you from that." A thousand visions and smells, tastes and sounds and touches rose up in joyous cacophony, affirming Rani's vow. "I'll protect you, Berylina Thunderspear, or die in the trying."

10

Rani blinked as she stepped outside the prison. How could the sun still hang in the sky, the dust still billow in the courtyard? How could pilgrims still walk back and forth, tugging their robes into place, fingering their Thousand-Pointed Stars? How could everything be the same?

She glanced at Father Siritalanu, but the priest refused to meet her eyes. The man had called upon his personal gods in Berylina's chambers, demanding that the princess explain what had happened, what forces she had summoned. Berylina had only smiled wanly, pulling Rani's gown closer about her still-pale body. Then the princess had dismissed both of them, claiming that she needed to meditate on what had happened, study the message from the gods and the lessons she had learned from Speaking. No amount of protest from the priest would change her mind.

Rani shivered on the prison steps. She had left her gown with Berylina, although she had reclaimed her cloak, draping it over her shift. She should not be cold in Brianta. She should not be chilled beneath the desert sun.

Her belly twisted, and she remembered that she had not eaten since the spoonful of lumpy gruel that Larinda had permitted her upon her arrival at the guildhall that morning. Larinda was reveling in the power that Master Parion had given her, seeking out ways to torture Rani with their sorry past. Each morning, the journeyman required Rani to mix the gruel as she had years ago, when Cook controlled the kitchen.

Rani had contemplated refusing, but she knew that her disobedience would be reported back to Master Parion. She could not afford to brook the guildmaster now. Not when her test was so close. Not when his orders had been so explicit. Not when she had voluntarily agreed to eat only at the hall and to be bound in all guildish things by Larinda Glasswright.

Rani sighed. She was a fool. The gods were stirring in Brianta, and she was letting herself be distracted by a rivalry more than a decade old.

Her dissatisfaction turned to true concern, though, as she contemplated what Tovin would say about the afternoon's development. He had never told her explicitly that she must not lead a Speaking, but surely he would expect her not to act without his permission. What would he say when he learned of Berylina's demand? How angry would he be with Rani when he learned that she had given in?

She hesitated even longer on the steps, and bells started tolling. The carillon was distinctive—trios of high-pitched tones, which were picked up by only a handful of other temples. Father Siritalanu cocked his head and then he said, "Bern."

Bern. The god of rain. The name summoned up an immediate sensation for Rani—her skin was brushed with the rough rasp of sand, as if she were rolling on a distant beach.

"Father!" she gasped, even as her mind rebelled against the illogic of the touch. Rain? Sand? Why should the two be joined in sensation? Was this the madness that had driven Berylina to be so different all her life, that had set the princess apart in Liantine and in Morenia and now here in Brianta?

"I do not wish to speak of this," Father Siritalanu said. "Not here. Not now." He glanced at the Midden behind them, his scowl seeming to state that the very walls had ears. He hurried around the corner of the building, away from the door, away from the guards.

Rani followed after, determined to ask for guidance. What was happening to her? Bern's touch was as clear as a voice, as certain as rain in Zarithia. What had Berylina done to her? What madness was taking over her mind, her skin, her ears, her eyes? *What happened inside that cell?*

As if to echo her fears, a pilgrim detached himself from the shadows at the foot of the building, limping toward them as if he were ancient or terribly scarred. "Alms," the man whispered. "Alms in the name of all the Thousand Gods."

Rani started to shake her head and continue on her way. She was hungry and tired and worried about her oaths to guildhall and lover. There were too many beggars in Brianta, too many supposed innocents preying on the devotion of the faithful. And she was not willing to open up her cloak to get at the pouch where she kept her coins. The Briantans would be scandalized to see a woman on the street wearing only her shift.

Apparently, Father Siritalanu was also willing to ignore the pauper; he glanced at the creature and picked up his pace, striding down the street beside the prison.

"Mercy!" the beggar whispered. "Have mercy on a poor soul!"

Rani refused to look at the man; she hastened after the priest.

"Hold!" the beggar urged, his raspy voice becoming harsher. "If you would call yourself holy, stop in this place of sorrow and of wrath!"

"Father!" Rani called, anxious to be rid of the man. If the priest would just give the beggar a coin, they could be gone from here. They could return to their rooms and begin the serious work of figuring out how to help Berylina, what to do for her now.

She feared that Father Siritalanu would ignore her. She

could see the angry set of his shoulders, measure his high emotion in the pounding of his booted feet against the cobblestones. Rani wanted to tell him that he wasn't being fair—*she* had nothing to do with whatever strange force had come into Berylina's cell.

Rani was not to blame. She was not at fault, no matter what the priest would have her believe. *She* was the victim here, not some robed, sanctimonious man who was young enough to be her brother. She was the one who was hungry. And cold. And weary.

"Father, stop!" Rani's command, though, was lost against the stone. Even as she spoke, a trio of dark shapes rose up in front of her, hooded figures that flowed from the shadows at the base of the prison wall as if they were living images of its horrors. "Father!" she cried again, but this time the single word was filled with terror, with warning, and with rage.

The priest whirled toward her, but he could take only one step before he was overpowered. The three shadows closed around him like well-trained soldiers. Rani saw glints of steel, soon hidden in the darkening streets. She turned to run, but two more shadows coalesced at the end of the lane, where the street debouched in front of the prison. Tossing her head, she could make out another two creatures at the far end of the passage, beyond Father Siritalanu, beyond the armed attackers.

"In the name of Jair, be still!" the beggar barked, dropping his pretense of a whisper.

Crestman.

Rani knew the voice at once. She had dreamed that voice, had hoped for some sort of reunion, reconciliation. But when she had nestled safe and secure in Morenia, she had never imagined that she would speak with him in Brianta, in a twilit street, with a knife sparkling between them. In the name of Jair . . . Her belly twisted with more than hunger. This was Fellowship business, then.

"Crestman," she said.

"Ranita." He betrayed no emotion in the single word.

"Do not hurt the priest. He has done nothing."

"So long as he does not fight my men, he will not be harmed."

Crestman stepped closer to her, and his cloak slipped to the side. Even beneath his garments, she could see his twisted leg, his deformed arm. "What happened to you?"

"I was a slave in the spiderguild." She heard the grim statement, knew that he accused her, although there was no open condemnation in the specific words he chose.

Rani's fingers longed to reach out to him, to pull his cloak closed, to cover him and protect him. Instead, she asked, "What did they do to you?"

"I tended their octolaris. The spiders' poison is strong, but for some it is not deadly."

For some. Rani listened to the untold stories behind the statement. *Some,* the poison had killed. Some—the Amanthian soldiers that Crestman had bartered for. Some—the children that he had hoped to save.

"I'm sorry, Crestman." Her words came in a rush, tumbling as if she had not rehearsed them night after night after night, only that afternoon. "I did not have a chance to explain to you. I did not have a chance to share my plans. I was going to negotiate for the Little Army in the spring, after we had the riberry trees, after we had the spiders. I was going to—"

"You were going to trade us so that your king could be safe."

"He is my sovereign lord, Crestman. You know that. You used to value loyalty above all else."

"I value loyalty when people are worthy of my devotion." Volumes were written behind his dark eyes. Rani remembered the battles that he had fought, the way that he had struggled to dedicate himself to others. Crestman had told her of his induction in the Little Army and the horrors that he had been forced to commit in that body's name. He had told her of deeds he had done so that he could be devoted, so that he could be loyal, so that he could be true. But that loyalty had been offered to those who were not worthy, to those who would enslave an army of children for profit.

She forced her voice to be steady as she nodded toward his hooded black cloak. "So you are loyal to the Fellowship now?"

"Aye."

"Without knowing their goals? Without knowing their designs?"

"I know enough to see that we can walk together for some time. Our paths might diverge farther down the road, but for now, I think that they want precisely what I do."

"What is that, Crestman?"

She saw ghosts behind his eyes, shadows of all he longed for. She saw a desire so sharp that her heart clenched and a rage so hot that she took a step back. He recovered quickly, and when he spoke his voice was steady, level, a commander's on a battlefield. "We want Queen Mareka dead."

"What!" Rani's exclamation echoed off the stone walls. Even in her amazement, she glanced at Father Siritalanu as if to see whether the priest had heard the absurd demand, as if to measure whether she were dreaming.

"Dead. By the feast day of Dol." Dol. The god of good health. Rani heard the sound of rustling parchment.

"But what has Mareka ever done to the Fellowship?"

"We have plans, Ranita, and she is not in them. We have goals, and she stands in our way."

"Plans. Goals. The Fellowship always whispers so. I think that our leaders change the rules of this game whenever the wind shifts."

"Then you admit you are one of us? You admit that you are bound by the Fellowship and all that it works toward?"

Rani gaped, openmouthed. Never, in all her years of association with the shadowy cabal, had she been asked so openly to affirm her dedication. At least not in a darkened alley with a blade glinting in failing daylight. "How can I, Crestman? I know nothing of those ultimate goals. I am kept in the dark."

"We're all of us in the dark sometimes." His response immediately made her think of the time he had spent in the spiderguild, the time that he had lived as a slave. She wondered what darkness had surrounded him then—physically, spiritually. What torment had he suffered?

He closed his fingers about her wrist, grinding the fine bones as if his grip were iron. She was embarrassed to hear her belly growl, as if it were unaware of the importance of this exchange. "You say that you're a Fellow, and now you're asked to prove it. You are to slay Queen Mareka by no later than Dol's day. The queen must die if the Fellowship is to survive."

"But Hal is one of us!"

"King Halaravilli ben-Jair is not to know of the Fellowship's plans, not until they have transpired." Rani heard Crestman's hatred, heard the unspoken vow of vengeance behind his bitter words. She knew that the soldier believed Hal to be the source of all his pain, the root of his imprisonment.

"Crestman, do you realize what you're asking? Even if I chose to betray my liege lord, even if I chose to harm Morenia, I would be covering my hands with royal blood!"

"As if you haven't killed before!"

The exclamation turned Rani's stomach. Suddenly, she was thirteen years old again. She was kneeling in a soldier's barrack room, watching wine-dark blood pool upon the floor. She was looking into the eyes of a good man, an honest man, a soldier who had given up his life to her suspicions. Dalarati. The man had forfeited his blood when Rani was led astray by dark conspirators. Dalarati had been

young and faithful and strong and true, and she had slain
him because someone had told her lies.

Crestman nodded. "You've held a knife. You're no
blushing virgin there."

Rani heard his rampant jealousy. Dalarati might have
been the first man that Rani had killed, but Crestman was
the first she had kissed. Even then, years ago, she had felt
the passion on his lips, she had known the heat that burned
for her. She had known, and yet she had ignored—she had
chosen Hal over him, chosen her king over a soldier.

And then Hal had chosen Mareka.

Rani could still remember her dismay when she learned
of Hal's impending marriage. She had returned from the
spiderguild, flush with her success in negotiating for the
rare riberry trees. She had mourned the loss of Crestman,
feared the damage that she had worked with the solider, but
she had gloried in the success of her mission. She had acquired the trade goods that her king demanded.

And yet she learned that Hal would wed Mareka. Not
Berylina, who at least would carry the wealth of the house
of Thunderspear. Not some other princess, with the weight
and authority of royalty. Mareka Octolaris. Like herself, a
mere journeyman in a guild. A manipulative, scheming
woman who had gotten herself with child in order to extort
the king of Morenia.

And now Rani was being offered the chance for revenge.
She was being handed a knife and told to use it. She was
being ordered by the Fellowship—by the very forces that
had saved her life when she was only thirteen years old.
How could she not obey?

She pictured herself sneaking into Mareka's chambers.
The night dark, the shutters closed, the curtains drawn
about the royal bed. Rani entered, wearing a shift of coal
black, carrying an iron dagger. . . .

Rani swallowed. Of course she pictured the murderer in
a black shift. Of course she envisioned that particular dag-

ger. The players had a character in their pieces, the Assassin. Rani had repaired the glass symbol for the role only a few months past, setting the dark pieces in a new lead framework. She was casting herself in a players' piece, applying the knowledge of a troop of pretenders.

Like Tovin. Rani had joined with Tovin before she learned of Hal's betrayal. She had been with the player even before the king had taken Mareka.

She might believe herself wronged. She might believe Hal foolish. She might believe Mareka shrewish and manipulative. But she had made her choices as well. She could not punish Hal for the same decisions she had made.

"I can't, Crestman. Tell the Fellowship that this is more than I can do."

"Ah, Ranita . . . This is precisely why you could never be a soldier."

"Why? Because I listen to my heart? Because I have a conscience?"

She saw him flinch, and she realized that her words bit even deeper than she intended. His voice was tight as he shook his head. "Because you make decisions without learning all the facts." She started to protest, but he cut her off. "No. Listen. You have access to the queen. You will work for the Fellowship. You will poison Mareka before Dol's day. And if you do not, then others whom you love will pay the price."

Rani felt the threat slide down her spine like the edge of a dagger. "What have you done, Crestman?"

"Me? I've done nothing but convey your orders to you. Our colleagues, though, are quite taken with children. Even though Laranifarso is a difficult babe. Even though he cries when he's away from his mother. Even though the Fellowship dares not grow too close to him, too attached, in case they need to . . . manage him. In case they need to prick your memory of your vows to the Fellowship."

"You wouldn't!"

"We already have. Hurry home, Ranita. Mair needs you. Her child has gone missing, and there is nothing that she can do. Nothing at all that *she* can do."

"You're a monster!"

"I'm a soldier, Ranita. You understood that once."

"But what can the Fellowship gain by this?"

"What can the Fellowship gain by having Mareka out of the way? What can the Fellowship gain by placing another queen beside Halaravilli ben-Jair, a woman who can bear a living heir?" Rani heard the threat that even Crestman did not dare to speak aloud. If Hal had an heir, a biddable child, then he himself would become unnecessary. By breeding a son, Hal would sign his own death warrant. The Fellowship would gain control of Morenia once and for all.

Rani argued. "Laranifarso is a child, Crestman. He's a helpless pawn in this game."

"We all are, Ranita Glasswright. We all are." Rani saw memories shift behind Crestman's eyes, crazed sorrows and angers and loves. He lowered his voice so that she was forced to step closer to him. "How naive can you be?"

"What do you mean?"

"Do you think it mere coincidence that you are in Brianta at the precise moment that the Fellowship needs you here?"

"I am in Brianta because the glasswrights came here. I am in Brianta to take my guildsmans' test."

"You are in Brianta because the Fellowship told your precious guildmaster to summon you."

"What? Why?" Rani's shock bit off her words into short exclamations.

Crestman laughed bitterly. "You've heard the tales before. A Royal Pilgrim will lead the Fellowship, will unite all the lands."

A Royal Pilgrim. Rani's thoughts flashed to Berylina, to the blooded princess who sat confined in her cell. Was she the one? Rani's skin tingled as she thought of the raw power that has passed between them, the energy that had sparked from the Speaking.

Crestman shook his head, as if he were rejecting what had transpired in the cell. "The Fellowship called you to Brianta. It wanted you to know that the wait for the Royal Pilgrim grows short. It wanted you to see the forces that are gathered in dedication to Jair. It wanted you to hear the counting, to know our strength, to see—once and for all— just where you and Halaravilli and Morenia stand within our plans. The Fellowship wanted to give you one final chance to cast your lot with us forever."

"You want me to murder."

"We want you to show your loyalty. We want you to join us as we mount our final bid for power."

"Mareka is my *queen.*"

"And the Fellowship is your family. We summoned you, Ranita, to remind you of that. To remind you of all that we have to offer you. Of all that we have to achieve."

"And if I refuse?" She dared to look him in the eye.

"If Laranifarso proves not sharp enough a spur, look to your glasswrights' test, Ranita. Look to your guildwork. Accept your mission with the Fellowship, or you will see your precious Glasswrights' Guild turn against you as well."

He stepped forward, and for one insane instant she thought he meant to kiss her. He lurched as he moved, shifting his weight from his damaged leg to his good one, clenching his teeth as if he felt pain. Then his hand flashed inside his cloak, and Rani thought that he would pull out another weapon, a second knife to balance the one already in his hand.

He must have read her fears, because he laughed as he extracted something from the shadows beneath his cloak. As the grating amusement rose inside his chest, Rani thought about the boy she had known in Amanthia, the youth that she had abandoned in the spiderguild. He was lost now, banished from the world, poisoned by the octo-laris and more.

In his place was this man who had seen terrible things, done terrible things, caused terrible things to happen. This man who could kill a harmless puppy, who could sacrifice a soldier in his command without the hesitation of a blink. This man who could torture or maim or kill, all in the serv-ice of some great cause.

Crestman held up a glass vial, turning it so that it caught the last of the dying sunlight. "For Mareka, Ranita Glass-wright. Poison her by Dol's day, or Laranifarso will die. Poison the queen, or you'll never call yourself a master in any guild."

Rani reached for the vial in reflex, and Crestman barked a command. The shadowed figures in the street melted away, hiding their metal blades, seeping into the gloaming night. Rani fell to her knees beside the prison wall and sobbed.

Parion Glasswright turned away from the looming figure that stood beside his worktable. He forced his voice to stay even as he said, "Must I remind you that I am the master of this guild? Glasswrights throughout the city look up to me."

"We are aware of that," the visitor whispered.

Parion resisted the urge to clench his fists, and he swal-lowed hard so that he would not snatch at the midnight hood. These damned Fellows were getting closer and closer to the business of the guild. It was one thing for them to provide the Hands—provide them for a goodly amount of gold. It was another, though, when they came to dictate his daily decisions, his daily actions as guildmaster.

After all, it wasn't as if Parion had ever been invited, had ever agreed to join the Fellowship. Once he learned of its existence, he had purposely kept his distance. He wanted to run his guild. He wanted to determine the fate of the glasswrights in Brianta. He did not want to be beholden to anyone else.

He gritted his teeth and said, "We will test Ranita Glasswright in the same way that we test each of our members."

The Fellow laughed softly, a chortle that was almost lost inside the folds of black cloth. The sound was distinctly masculine; this was one Fellow who did not fear to reveal his gender. "Oh, aye. You'll test her. You'll put her through her paces as if she were a mare in the royal stables. But then you'll decide her fate based on what we say."

Parion could taste the easy fruit the Fellow offered him. The guildmaster need not balance his emotions and the truth. He need not ask if he were acting fairly or unfairly, if he were judging the Traitor based upon her true abilities. He need not think about the glazed pottery, the special flask of water. He could sit back like a child, and merely do what he was told.

If the Fellowship dictated that the Traitor must fail, then she would be banished from the guild. Her life ambitions would be crushed. She would never plague Parion again, never remind him of all the glory the guild once had, of all the beauty and the power and the prestige. He would be free to move forward, to work as best he could in memory of Morada, in memory of the past that he could not change.

And if the Fellowship required the cursed Traitor to pass, then Parion would manage to stomach that event. After all, he *had* trained her. He had taught her the basics of her glasswright skills.

Even as he recognized the easy path beneath his feet, he saw the folly of giving in. After all, the Fellowship was responsible for all the pain that poor Morada had suffered. The Fellowship had fanned the flames of its conflict with Morada's faction; it had fed the secret battles that had threatened to split Morenia in two.

If the Fellowship had not existed, then Morada would not have been caught up in secret battles. If the Fellowship had not existed, then Morada would still be alive, would still stand at his side. Parion and Morada together . . . They would have led the wealthiest guild in all Morenia by now. They would have been in their homeland, in power, in control of their destinies.

Without glancing at the cloaked messenger, Parion reached toward his table, toward the flawed swirl of black and clear glass that Morada had made. The surface was smooth beneath his fingertips, as smooth as her remembered flesh. He spread his palm upon the surface, and he could feel the contrast within the worked piece, the heat of absorbed sunlight from the black, black glass, the cool peace of the clear.

The Fellow interrupted Parion's memories with the guttural growl of a cleared throat. A harsh whisper cut through the room. "You will test her, then. But you will wait for us to dictate whether she passes the test. You will wait for us to determine her fate before you pronounce her future."

"And if I do not?"

Parion should have been prepared for the Fellow to move. He should have known that any hint of rebellion would anger the cloaked figure. He should have expected that the Fellowship had ways to enforce its demands.

Nevertheless, he was surprised by the speed with which the Fellow's knife appeared. The blade flashed in the sun, blinding white as the light glinted off a sharpened edge. Parion did not have a chance to step back, a chance to reach for his own weapon, even a chance to protect his own flesh. The Fellow settled the flashing blade with perfect precision, pressing the keen edge into the taut skin of Parion's wrist. "You'll listen to the Fellowship, Glasswright. You'll listen, or you'll find that not even a Liantine Hand will be enough for you. You'll listen, or you'll pay the price."

Before Parion could protest, the Fellow drew his blade across the glasswright's wrist, leaving behind a stripe of bloody red. The wound was so startling that Parion could only see it at first; he could not feel the injury. Then the cut began to sting as if someone had salted the very edges of his skin.

Parion sucked in his breath, catching his lower lip between his teeth. He swore at the Fellow and grabbed at a cloth, any cloth, the snowy binding that had protected Morada's medallion. The old glasswork slipped from the table, falling against the wooden floorboards and breaking along its flaw. Parion registered the two pieces and his heart contracted, seizing in his chest as if he were clamped in a glasswright's lead vise.

Even as he realized that the medallion was ruined, even as he knew that he had lost the last treasure that Morada had ever made, Parion wrapped the pure white linen around his wound. The cloth stung his cut, burning like the sudden hatred that melted across his vision. He was transported back to Morenia, back to the days before he was guildmaster. He remembered being questioned by the old king's men, commanded to give up the Traitor. He had been cut then, daily, bled out while he pledged the truthfulness of his answers.

Now he pressed hard, trying to force the blood to stop. The fingers of his good hand grew moist, and he needed to fold the linen once again, needed to add another layer to staunch the wound. Against the stinging pain, he managed to flex his injured hand. The Fellow might be wickedly fast with a blade, he might have struck out of nowhere, but he seemed to know his business. He had worked no lasting damage.

Parion looked up from the crimson-stained linen. "We'll test her," he hissed through clenched teeth. "We'll test Ranita Glasswright, and we'll determine if she passes."

"Just remember, Guildmaster. Just remember what hangs in the balance as you make your determination." The Fellow paused on the threshold for one long moment, and Parion longed to rip away the mask, longed to see the identity of his tormentor. The figure whispered, "If you are wise, you'll wait to make your decision. If you are wise, you'll wait for us to tell you how Ranita Glasswright fares."

And then the threat was gone. The Fellow bowed slightly and ducked through the door. Parion's eyes narrowed as he saw the figure catch against the doorframe as if he were in pain, as if he needed support. Parion could hear the Fellow's steps disappearing down the hallway, one leg dragging like a heavy weight, an untold loss.

Parion swore as he turned back to the worktable. In a moment of choking rage, he swept his uninjured arm across the work surface, sending his original offering to the Thousand Gods flying. Scores of glass pebbles rattled across the desk, against the windowsill, onto the floor. Parion swore again and kicked at the rubble, cursing a dozen gods.

Morada's medallion had broken cleanly, he reminded himself. Perhaps he could fuse the pieces. Perhaps he could meld them into a single round without the original flaw. He could anneal the fragments in a kiln, join them together into a new whole, a perfect whole. . . .

Ah, Morada, he thought. *If only you were here. If only you could tell me what I should do. . . .*

It would be so easy to fail the Traitor on her test regardless of any instructions from the Fellowship. He could watch her face, see the eager expectation in her eyes. He could witness her excitement as she presented her masterpiece, as she set forth the culmination of all her labors. He had observed other apprentices over the years; he knew the power of their hope, their dreams.

She would suffer when she was rejected. She would collapse in self-doubt, in fear, in sorrow. She would be alone and lost. He had that power over her. He could make her pay. He could make her sacrifice, as he had sacrificed. She would lose the love of the guild, as he had lost his own love. She would ache, ache, ache. . . .

But what if the Fellowship demanded that the Traitor pass? Could Parion do that? Could he forfeit his own

power? Could he yield the force of guildmaster, concede to
the Fellowship the greatest achievement of his life? And
what about the taste of revenge that he had already con-
cocted? Could he forfeit it? Could he change what he had
already wrought?

What would the Fellowship require?

*Morada . . . What should I do? Should I yield to them?
Should I let them decide?*

The broken medallion stared up at him like the empty
eyes of an idiot.

What did Parion truly know of the Traitor's ability, of
the likelihood of her passing the guild's test without interference? He'd had precious few hours to watch any of the
journeymen in the past several days. He had relied almost
entirely on other glasswrights, on Larinda in particular, to
tell him how they fared.

Well that, at least, he could change. He could collect
more accurate information. He could learn where all the
competing journeymen stood.

He hesitated only a moment before digging a scrap of
linen from a drawer. He collected the two pieces of
Morada's medallion, wrapping the broken glass carefully.
When he placed it next to his chest, he could feel it slowing
his heartbeat, calming his mind.

The guildhall was strangely silent as he walked through
its corridors. There should have been apprentices scurrying
about, journeymen intent on their labors. Instructors should
have been barking out commands in the workrooms, young
masters debating the rules of their craft.

Instead, the hallways seemed as deserted as a winter
beach at sunset. "Just as well," Parion muttered to himself,
tugging on the rough bandage around his wrist. He was in
no mood to chat with his fellow glasswrights. No mood to
talk politely about the way the world should work, the
proper manner for the guild to function.

Parion had lived in Brianta for long enough that his footsteps automatically pounded out a prayer. *Clain, bring me peace,* he thought as he walked. *Let me see the path beneath my feet. Let me know the way of truth and of justice. Guide me, Clain. Bring me peace.*

Repeating his petition to the god of glasswrights, Parion turned a corner, and he found himself in the long, low hallway where the journeyman labored at their masterpieces. He took a moment to brush his fingers against the prayer bell, speaking only Clain's name as a form of petition.

At least this chamber was not deserted. Five journeymen hunched over their tables, intent on their labor in the short time remaining before their test. Belita. Wario. Sharlithi. Cosino. Larinda.

No Traitor.

Larinda's table was closest to the door, and Parion approached it without preamble. He watched the girl take in his countenance. Her eyes moved from his face to his wrist and back again. She paled when she saw the stained cloth wrapped around his flesh; he could only imagine the memories that blood-soaked linen must summon up in her mind. He ignored his heart's momentary clench of pity. "Larinda Glasswright."

"Guildmaster." Her words were as steady as ever—calm, calculated. Parion resisted the urge to touch the broken medallion against his chest, to send his thoughts toward his lost Morada.

"The glasswrights' test begins two weeks hence. Are you prepared?"

She hesitated only a moment; she clearly had not anticipated such a mundane question. "Yes, Master."

"I would like to see your drawings. I would like to see what you intend to craft before the test commences."

Again she hesitated, but this time her response managed to convey a dozen questions. "Yes, Master."

Well she might wonder what he intended. The journeymen were expressly forbidden from speaking to masters as they planned their test pieces. The journeymen's ideas should reflect their own abilities at solving problems, their own thoughts at creating designs. By asking to see Larinda's work, Parion was toppling the entire process.

Well, other things were toppling, in every direction that Parion looked. He would see Larinda's work. It would give him an idea of what to expect from the Traitor. For now he forbade himself from looking at that one's empty table, from questioning where she had gone and why.

Larinda interrupted his thoughts with a careful question, pitching her voice so that the other glasswrights would not hear her. "Are you well, Master? Would you like assistance dressing that wound?"

Would he like assistance? . . . Would he like someone to stand beside him, to aid him? . . . Would he like to set aside the burden of the Glasswrights' Guild—just once, for just a day? . . .

But no. He could not proffer that responsibility to Larinda. Not now. Not yet. Not until she had proven herself with the test.

"I am fine, Journeyman. Let me see your work."

Parion suspected that Larinda's masterpiece was part of the massive project of bringing glass panels to the shrine of each of the Thousand Gods. Thinking of that goal, Parion's heart quickened, clearing his mind for the first time since the Fellow had interrupted his morning labors. Parion *would* be remembered as an expert guildmaster. He *would* be spoken of for generations to come. Even strangers would honor his name when they journeyed to Brianta, when they saw the glory and the power that the glasswrights brought to all the Thousand Gods.

And then the guild would be free of petty Briantan politics. No more Fellowship to guide things. No more alms to proffer to the daily priest-collectors. Parion could sit back and watch his empire grow. . . . His empire of glasswrights. His guild restored.

And when he chose, when he desired, when he deemed that Morenia had suffered enough, *then* he would approach the house of ben-Jair. Then he would offer up his services, and the services of all the glasswrights beneath him. Then he would collect more gold than any guildmaster had ever dreamed of; he would make the glasswrights the wealthiest guildsmen in all Morenia, in all Brianta, in all the world. . . .

Parion blinked, surprised to find himself still in the journeymen's workshop. He watched as Larinda brought a lamp closer, and for once he did not look away from her Hands. She manipulated the spidersilk and leather with expert twists of her fingers and bends of her wrists. If a god were to descend from the Heavenly Fields at that very instant, without any knowledge of how a human's hands should work, he would not believe that there was anything amiss. He would not think that Larinda was flawed in any way.

"Let me see your drawings, Larinda Glasswright," Parion said as the girl stepped back.

"Here, Master." She hesitated only a moment before she lifted a linen covering from her whitewashed table, revealing the heavy charcoal lines beneath.

Parion sucked in his breath. Larinda was more daring than he had ever expected. She had selected Clain as the subject of her test. The god of the glasswrights. Larinda Glasswright had re-created the guildhall of her youth, each flawless line illuminating the home that she had known before she lost her thumbs, before her life was ruined.

Her drawing was perfect. It captured every line, every upright, every arch, window frame, and door. "How could you? . . ." he started to say, but he let his words trail off. He moved to the end of the table and stared at the drawing from the opposite side. Perfection. "You were only a child when the guildhall fell. How could you capture it so completely?"

"I see it every night, Master. Every night when I sleep." Larinda's arm twitched as she spoke, and she frowned at her Hand as she brought it under submission. Something about the motion made Parion return his attention to the table, made him study the design more closely.

Now Parion could see the anger in the memory. He could see the awesomely heavy lead joins that Larinda had sketched. He could see the thick glass that she had designated, unflashed crimson so dark that it would appear black. The panel was not a thing of beauty; it was a landscape of torture, of sorrow.

Parion forced his voice to a steady tone, ignoring his own pang of loss. "Tell me, Journeyman. How do you rank yourself in comparison with the others who compete for the title of master?"

"Rank?" She might never have heard the word. She held her eyes steady on him, not looking at her four fellow guildsmen, who watched the exchange from across the room with frank interest.

"Aye. Are you the best of my journeymen? Are you the best the guild has to offer?"

He could see her struggle with the question, balancing pride and modesty in her blatant, calculating mind. Her eyes fixed on her drawing, and her face transformed as she studied its lines, absorbing the anger and sorrow and pain of the Glasswrights' Guild that had been. "I am better than Sharlithi and Cosino and Tomuru. I work in a different style entirely from Wario and Cordio and Belita. As you know, they learned their craft in the north."

And the Traitor, he wanted to ask. "And Ranita Glasswright?"

Larinda's lips pursed, as if she had bitten an unripe plum. "She is good, Master."

"Are you better?"

Larinda met his eyes, and he read her fierce determination, as grim as his own when he had spoken with the Fellow. "She is better, when she is permitted to use her rogue tools and her outland ways. But if you test her guild knowledge, Master, if you test what we have taught her, she is not better. She is prideful of her methods, but those methods are flawed. They cheapen our work, Master. They sell us to her players' troop, like a bolt of silk or a leather strap."

There. Parion had his answer.

He would let the Traitor work her own demise. He would let her use her diamond knife and her other players' tricks. He would let her bring her eastern toys into the guild's workshop. And if the other masters chose to elevate her, if the Fellowship approved her advancement, fine. Parion would wait. He would ruin her in the future, casting aspersions on her skill. He would note that she had entered the guild only with cheap imitations of true workmanship, that she had succeeded only because she had been permitted to use her players' ploys.

Parion had waited for vengeance all this time; he could spend another few years crafting the Traitor's fall, even if the Fellowship decreed otherwise. If he practiced patience, he could do as he desired. He could reap the harvest he had sown with his glazed bowl and goblet with the growing power he already exercised over the Traitor's body.

And if the other guildmasters decided wisely, if the Fellowship decided she must be cast out from the guild immediately, better.

Larinda brushed her hair back from her face, using her Hand with accomplished nonchalance. "Are you well, Master? Does your wrist pain you?"

Parion glanced from the whitewashed table to her fretful face, and for just a moment, he thought that he saw a streak of white in her hair. *Morada* . . . his heart whispered, but then she took a step closer, and the light shifted. "I am well, Larinda Glasswright. Your words have eased my heart."

She might have said something more then. She might have taken a step closer to him. She might have raised her cool fingertips to his wound, brushed against it with the spidersilk and metal of her Hand.

Before anything could change, though, the door to the chamber crashed back against the wall. An apprentice stumbled into the room, gasping for breath, even as he glanced, wild-eyed, for the prayer bell. Jamming his fingers against the metal trappings, the boy stumbled toward Parion and Larinda. "Come quick, Guildmaster! To the Middens! The Morenian princess is called out as a witch! And Ranita Glasswright stands as her defender!"

11

Berylina sighed, lost in the haze between wakefulness and sleep. She had been dreaming again. She'd seen herself condemned to dig her own grave, sentenced to hollow out a pit in the earth where her body would be cast, to rot for eternity. Her punishment was even crueler because she could see a purifying funeral pyre as she dug. She could see the iron crossbars, the bracing that should have been prepared to receive her wrapped body. She could smell the ladanum that should have sanctified her corpse. She could feel Nim whipping up the flames that waited to receive others, taste the peach essence of the god of wind who waited to gather in the wandering souls of the pure.

As she labored, she felt her flesh pierced again and again, shattered by her father's spear. He tested her faith, tested her devotion. He challenged her with thrust after bloody thrust.

She was pure, wasn't she? She had opened up her heart and her mind and her soul to all the Thousand Gods. Why should her father condemn her? Shouldn't she be blessed with a pyre? Why should she be forced into a filthy grave?

Berylina forced her eyes open, relieved to find that she was still in her cell. With shaking fingers, she lifted her gown—Ranita's gown. She could make out the bloody image of the spear on her breast, the jagged measurement of her faith. The wound was already closed, though, already converted to an angry crimson scar.

She had only dreamed her condemnation. She had only dreamed that she was brought before the tribunal, that she had been sentenced to death.

Soon, though. Soon she would be asked to prove her faith.

The notion frightened her more than she was willing to admit. If only Siritalanu had come to pray with her. Then she would be more comforted. Then she would feel more hope. But the priest had come back to the Midden only one time. He had still been angry with her for Speaking with Ranita. His lips had been stretched tight in an odd white line, as if he were being forced to cross a rope bridge over a chasm.

Poor Siritalanu. He did not understand. He was wholly devoted to her—of that she was certain. But he did not begin to comprehend how the gods spoke to her, how they manifested themselves inside her mind. If he did learn, if he did come to believe her, would the Briantans even let him stay at her side? Wouldn't he be forced to denounce her for her strangeness? Wouldn't he be forced to declare her a witch?

The thought made Berylina's heart beat faster, and the skin beside her roving eye started to twitch. She forced herself to take deep breaths, to find the calm place inside herself where the gods came to her. The place that Ranita had opened by guiding her in the Speaking.

She was not a witch.

Of that she was certain. The gods spoke to her in mysterious ways. They carried messages that she could barely comprehend, but she did not use her godly powers for evil. She did not corrupt herself or others.

Even as Berylina completed the calming litany in her mind, she heard the guard clank down the hallway. This was the leader of the day watch, the one who breathed heavily and whose body always stank. She imagined him sitting at the entrance to the prison cells, carving off hunks of bread and swallowing them whole, with blocks of cheese and wedges of onion to complete his constant meal.

As if she were spurred by the unclean guard's habits, Berylina sat up straighter. She ran her fingers through her wiry hair, hoping that she was taming it rather than making it stand out even more. She pushed her hands against her skirts, trying to smooth out the wrinkles. Only three days had passed since the glasswright had visited, but the dress seemed to fit Berylina better than it had before. Perhaps she had lost weight on the miserable prison rations. Or maybe the fabric had stretched.

Or maybe the gods had provided for her. Berylina cast a quick word of thanks toward Jol, the god of cloth. He might have added to the garment. He might have kept an eye on her in her solitude. Jol responded with his expected sound of a cow lowing. Berylina smiled. How could she be condemned for her familiarity with the gods? How could it be wrong to let a deity speak to her?

"On your feet!"

Berylina had nearly forgotten about the guard. She truly must focus. Today was likely to be her test, her trial. If she failed, her nightmares might spin into reality. If she failed, she might die.

"May all the Thousand bless you," she said to the guard.

"And you, as well," he said, automatically completing the familiar greeting and weaving his fingers into the appropriate gesture. Then he seemed to remember that she was a corrupt prisoner. "On your feet!" he repeated.

She stood, taking a deep breath against the sudden wave of dizziness that swept over her. She was light-headed, as if she had a fever. She'd been seriously ill only once, when she was still a child. Then, her Amanthian nurse had stood over her, laying cold compresses on her brow. The woman had called on all sorts of gods—Zake, the god of chirurgeons, and Nome, and others whom Berylina could not remember through the fog of her illness.

She still associated her occasional light-headedness with the gods the nurse had invoked. Nome's piping always left Berylina feeling like a silk banner drifting in an easy wind. Zake's astringent mint flavor on her tongue always summoned the feel of cool, damp cloths, of a nurse's compassionate hands.

"Let's go," the guard said, clearly unaware of Berylina's thoughts.

"Where are you taking me?" Her voice sounded strange in her ears; too high, too breathy.

"To the Gods' Court. The Curia is called to judge you today."

"The Curia?" She knew the term of course, but she had no idea how such bodies worked in Brianta. She had no idea of the forces that would be arrayed against her.

"Aye. And they'll be more disposed against you if you keep them waiting." The guard's lips twisted into a frown that might have been tinged with pity. "No reason to start off any worse than you already are."

Nevertheless, Berylina took the time to pause on the threshold of her cell. She looked back at the narrow window, and she whispered a quick prayer of gratitude to Par, the god of the sun. He had kept her company when everyone else seemed to have abandoned her. He had visited through the tiny, unglazed slash. As if in reply to her grateful words, she felt the warm wash of water that was Par's signature.

The guard caught his breath in an impatient sigh as Berylina bowed her head. She took special care in phrasing her prayer. She wanted the gods to know that she did not bear them any ill will. After all, they were not responsible for how the Briantan priests interpreted—or misinterpreted—their words. To the contrary, the gods suffered when humans failed, suffered even more than Berylina might at the hands of the Curia.

"Please," she said, just before leaving the cell, "I'd like my Thousand-Pointed Star."

"You are to have no weapon before the Curia."

"It's a Star!" Her voice broke, surprising her. She had not realized how desperately she missed the outward trappings of her faith.

"It's a brooch, with a spike of metal as long as your thumb. You're a prisoner, and you'll be treated like the criminal you're accused of being, especially when you stand before your betters."

Berylina wanted to argue. She wanted to say that she had offered no resistance so far. She had done nothing to make the guards suspect her. With her wandering eye, she was scarcely able to focus on another person, how was she supposed to threaten great lords? Especially when there were eager soldiers standing nearby, anxious protectors who would sacrifice her as soon as help her toward a greater faith.

But then Berylina realized that she did not need her Star. She was secure without it. The gods understood her faith. They knew that she honored them, that she saluted their power in all her daily life. She settled for making another holy sign across her chest, and then she followed the guard down the hallway.

He signaled to seven of his fellows as they approached the Midden's double door. The men fell in beside her, their armor bristling like the plates on an octolaris's legs. She had only a moment to wonder at the symbolism, to question whether the soldiers had purposely numbered themselves to honor her past, her homeland, the land of the great silk spiders.

And then the lead guard cast open the door, and she realized that the men meant no honor. They merely hoped to spare her life.

A crowd had gathered in the courtyard in front of the Midden. Men, women, children—hundreds of pilgrims filled the square. Sunlight flashed off of Thousand-Pointed Stars, glinting as if fires burned on every breast.

A rotten cabbage sailed over the first of the guards and caught Berylina squarely on the chest. The impact was strong enough to knock the air from her lungs. She made a squeaking sound as she tried to pull back, but the guards forced her forward, four of them grabbing her arms, two poking her from behind with their short swords. Two of the men began to cut their way through the throng.

The cabbage was only the first of many missiles. Berylina soon found herself pelted by all variety of filth. It seemed as if every rotten vegetable, every stinking fish head, every chamber pot in the city had been saved for her disgrace. The guards carried rectangular shields that they used to keep the worst of the offal from themselves, but Berylina was left exposed to all the crowd had to throw.

Ranita Glasswright's dress would be ruined, she thought to herself. The sturdy gown had served Berylina well inside her cell. It was a shame to destroy it here, in the open air, in the middle of a courtyard filled with pilgrims.

The garbage was bad. The words the crowd threw were worse, though.

"Witch!"

"Filthy whore!"

"Lying strumpet!"

Berylina's eyes filled at the shouts. She was none of those things. She had never given anyone reason to believe that she was evil, that she was less than chaste. One phrase was repeated the most often, and it grew to a chant throughout the crowd. "Bury the witch! Bury the witch!"

Berylina slipped in a patch of slime, and her guards barely kept her from crashing to her knees. Their fingers dug sharply into her flesh, and she imagined the bruises she would have the next morning. When she regained her footing, she found herself face to face with a furious woman, a wrinkled old alewife who thrust something toward her.

For one moment, she thought that she was being offered a present, a gift, something to comfort her in the midst of the

horror. She could see that the item in the old woman's hand
was long and thin—it appeared to be a walking staff that
Berylina might use to keep her balance across the filthy
square. Even as the princess reached for it, though, she recognized the thing, and she pulled back in revulsion.

A leg bone. A human leg bone. Long and lean and mealy
white. The hideous thing had been dug up from the earth;
clearly it belonged to a body that had not been consigned to
purifying, blackening flames.

Berylina was grateful that she had eaten nothing of her
prison meal that morning, for she knew that she would have
emptied her belly on the stones before her.

And yet that filth would have been cleaner than much
that was hurled at her. The guards were swearing at the
crowd now, cursing them roundly, and the angry words
heightened the mob's anger. Berylina saw children shouting
so loudly that spittle flew from their mouths. One man
raised an earth-crusted spade high above his head, shaking it
at her as if it were a weapon itself. "Bury the witch! Bury the
witch! Bury the witch! Bury the witch!"

The man looked familiar; Berylina knew she had seen his
face before. Where? Where? And then she knew—he was
one of the burly soldiers who had supported her as she began
her pilgrimage; he had forced the stubborn priest to initiate
her cavalcade.

The guards wrestled open a door on the far end of the
courtyard, pushing Berylina, pulling her, dragging her into
quiet darkness. She heard the ironclad wood slam shut, but
the crowd's rage did not diminish. The chanters battered the
door, stomping their feet, clapping their hands.

One of the guards hawked and spat at Berylina's feet, as
if he were clearing the evil experience from the depths of his
lungs. Another cursed her openly, and two made a great
show of wiping their hands clean on their filthy garments.
The first guard, the one who had come to her cell, said,

"This way. Things will go worse for you if you keep the Curia waiting."

Berylina started to argue that she had not intended to keep anyone waiting, but she gave up the protest. After all, these men did not care to hear her. They did not care to listen to what she had to say. She could share with them everything she knew about the gods; she could tell them about how each of the Thousand came to her, and they would ignore her. Some people were not prepared for the reality of the Thousand. Some people wanted to insist on the comfortable and the familiar; they supposed they knew the truth.

The guards made short work of bustling Berylina into an audience chamber. A part of her mind analyzed her surroundings with a princess's critical eye. There. The woodwork was quite fine on that door. Servants had oiled the hinges. The room had been constructed by a master; air currents kept it from becoming too hot, even on this scorching summer day.

Berylina gave free rein to those analytical whispers; they kept her from focusing on other things, more dangerous things. She could pretend that she did not see the five judges who sat before her or the throng that filled the room. She could pretend that she did not see the raised dais, the balustrade stained dark with the grip of nervous witnesses' hands, or the holy altar in the very center of the chamber. She could pretend that she did not see the brazier that glowed in the corner of the room or the stones that nestled in the coals or the heavy iron sheet that leaned against them.

She could pretend that Ranita Glasswright was not standing at the front of the chamber, pale and grim, anger fighting with fear across the battleground of her face.

But Berylina could not pretend that she did not see Father Siritalanu. She had spent too many years attuned to messages on his broad, placid face. The priest had been her guide, after all. He had led her from the dark places of her father's court; she was accustomed to following him, accus-

tomed to turning herself over to his capable hands for safe-
keeping.

Those hands were trembling now. Every line of Father
Siritalanu's body was drawn tight, as if he were the one
being tortured with the Curia's strange implements.

Berylina smiled gently as she approached her mentor.
"Father," she said, as if she might comfort him.

"Silence!" The priest in the center of the Curia thundered
the command. He was a young man, given over to fat. His
lips pursed as if he were forced to drink sour wine, and a
sheen of sweat stood out on his brow. His dark hair had
begun to recede, even though he could not have seen more
than thirty summers. When he spoke again, his voice trembled with authority. His words were oddly pitched—too
high for a man of his girth. "You will not speak until the
Curia has spoken to you!"

Berylina started to agree, but she caught her words
against the roof of her mouth. Suddenly she was not a
princess surrounded by the power, beauty, and glory of all
the Thousand Gods. Instead, she was a child, a lost and wandering soul attempting to find her way in her father's court.
She was standing in the Great Hall of Liantine, surrounded
by dead wooden tokens of the false goddess, the Horned
Hind. She was ungainly and awkward, and her tongue
cleaved to the roof of her mouth.

Berylina swallowed hard, forcing herself to look at Father Siritalanu. Those days were past, she chided silently.
She had grown beyond her childhood. She was a woman
now. She was not the child who had stumbled in front of her
father, who had been forced to appear at his feasts and his
convocations.

The familiar blush of shame began to steal up her neck,
and Berylina knew that her skin would mottle. Her cheeks
would flush with an unbecoming color, and her eyes would
start to water. Without being conscious of any movement,
Berylina started to clasp the fabric of her skirt—of Ranita

Glasswright's skirt—opening and closing her fists as if she were a cat kneading a lap.

The gesture brought her some shadow of comfort, some edge of familiarity. She could hear her nurse's soothing voice, she could remember unfortunate public appearances as a child. She had survived those encounters. She had out-lived the embarrassment and shame. She would do just fine here in Brianta. All would be well. She clenched the fabric again, barely noting the unsightly wrinkles that she caused. All would be well. All would be well.

"Stand forward," the central priest commanded. Berylina complied with his command, stepping away from her guards. She dared a look at the Chief Inquisitor, and she re-alized that he wore a priest's green robes. Those robes were shadowed, though, covered with a dull brown overgarment. A quick glance confirmed that each member of the Curia wore the same ominous combination—green declaration of faith overlaid with the earthy threat of punishment.

Berylina argued for her life before this panel. The ulti-mate punishment that the Curia could assess was death. Death beneath the earth. Death apart from the purification of flame. Death eternal.

"I am Torio, prelate of this Curia. I will guide my broth-ers in their judgment of you today, in this grave matter where you are named witch. State your name, that our clerk may inscribe it in the book of this proceeding."

Berylina swallowed hard. Torio, then. He would be her judge. He would decide whether her nightmare became re-ality. She had lived in Morenia long enough that it seemed odd for a priest to have so short a name. *Five syllables,* she thought. *His name should twist for five syllables.*

She knew that she should not worry about such foolish concerns. She should look directly at the Curia. She should face them down with the same grim acceptance that she had mastered in the Morenian court. She should conduct herself like a princess; like the poised young woman she had become.

But all of those lessons were cast out of her soul, squeezed from her body with the short, panting breaths that had taken over her lungs. She could not look directly at Torio; she was reduced to the sidelong glances that had filled her childhood. Her tongue was thick in her mouth, and her protruding teeth seemed to take so much space that she could never hope to push words around them. "Berylina Thunderspear," she managed at last, forcing out the words as if they were poisoned fruits.

"You are called before this Curia on the most serious charge that can be brought against a pilgrim, the most serious accusation in all of Brianta. You are called a witch, and you are asked to account for the purity of your body and your soul."

No! Berylina wanted to cry. *I am not a witch! That's a lie!*

She could say nothing, though. She could only look around the chamber, at Torio and his henchmen, at the guards ranged to either side, at the people who watched with eager curiosity. She could only look at Ranita Glasswright and Father Siritalanu, standing helpless at the front of the room.

Torio waited until she had returned her attention to him and his brethren. "How do you plead, Berylina Thunderspear? Are you a witch?"

Protests pounded through her head, arguments and scholarly rebuttals. Of course she was not a witch. Could a witch speak the names of the Thousand? Could a witch describe the appearance of each of the gods? Could a witch travel to every shrine in Brianta, making offerings, studying altars, dedicating her very soul to the Thousand Gods?

"Do not waste our time, Berylina Thunderspear! You must plead. Are you a witch?"

Her father had berated her like this. He had taken her before his court in Liantine and forced her to speak in front of his nobles. His face had twisted with shame of her, with hatred that her birth had cost him his beloved wife. Berylina had shrunk from those appearances, longed to disappear, to fade away before the Liantine court.

"I ask you one last time, Berylina Thunderspear! Do you claim the name of witch?"

"No!" cried Father Siritalanu. "She is not a witch! She is the holiest pilgrim I have ever laid eyes upon, the most faithful woman I have ever met."

"Silence, Priest!"

"No," Berylina finally managed to answer, but her word was lost in the crowd's uproar over Torio's rebuke of a robed priest. "No," she whispered into the melee.

Torio pointed a fleshy finger at Siritalanu. "You will stay silent, Priest, or you will be cast out from these proceedings. We need not call you as a witness. We have enough to speak against your ward, and all here know that you are biased."

Nevertheless, poor Siritalanu looked as if he would protest further, as if he would tell Torio that such rules were patently unfair. No, Berylina wanted to say to her protector. There was no use in argument. Torio had made up his mind already, without the difficulty of a Curia. Without the need for his implements of torture.

Like Berylina, Ranita Glasswright seemed to understand the play that they were acting. The guildswoman shook her head slowly and stepped toward Siritalanu, laying one hand upon his arm. When the priest did not acknowledge her, she leaned toward him with greater urgency. Berylina could see that the gesture had two purposes—Ranita was pulling the priest closer to whisper in his ear, but she was also leaning heavily upon him.

Poor Ranita. Even from across the room, Berylina could see that she was exhausted. She must have been so frightened when Berylina Spoke with her. She must have been terrified when Berylina unleashed the power of the gods within her. Even now, Berylina wondered how she had found that strength, how she had guided that force. She was no priest, after all—not even truly a caloya.

And yet the gods had come to her during the Speaking. She had felt them deep inside her mind, rank upon rank. She could see the ones with colors, smell the ones with scents. Flavors and sounds and sensations—all were laid out inside her mind like volumes on the shelves in King Halaravilli's most treasured library.

She had known that if she touched Ranita just *so,* that she could pass on the secret of those ranks. Berylina had felt them flow out of her, surging across space like a flame jumping toward a fine beeswax candle. The moment of that connection had frozen Berylina, paralyzed her body and her mind. She had felt power leap out of her, but then circle back a hundredfold, burgeoning and blossoming. . . .

"I said, is it true that you stole a holy relic from the altar of First Pilgrim Jair?"

Berylina was shocked back to the Curia, to the grand chamber, to Siritalanu's and Ranita's fearful gazes and Torio's furious bellow. She blinked and clenched her hands in her robes, trying to remember what the priest had just asked her, what he wanted to know.

"Please," she said, and the sound of the one word slipping past her jutting teeth was an embarrassment. "The ball came to me. It rolled into my hands. I was only counting the thousand relics, offering up my prayers."

Berylina managed to raise her eyes from her clasped hands, and she was surprised to see an old woman standing on the dais, gripping the balustrade. That was the angry woman, the one who had taken such a dislike to Berylina in Jair's House. The one who had called her a witch at Mip's temple.

Now the creature was dressed in the darkest of pilgrim's robes, and she seemed to have borrowed a larger, more ponderous Thousand-Pointed Star. The old woman pointed a bony finger at Berylina and said, "She lies, that one does.

She pretends to listen to the gods, to steal the attention of the priests. She acts as if the Thousand speak to her, as if they come to her, special that she is. She uses her power as an excuse. She touched the sacred relic of Jair. She laid her hand upon the First Pilgrim's plaything, upon the ball that sat in the middle of his altar."

The crowd gasped in horror, and Berylina was forced to cry out, "No! I did not reach out for it. It came to me! It rolled across the altar into my hands!"

"She's a witch, I tell you," the old woman shouted. "A witch! How else could the relic move? How else could it be summoned to roll across a perfectly flat altar? She claimed to speak for Jair, to criticize the priests who keep his temple!"

Torio thanked the woman for her testimony, and she was guided from the dais. When she walked past Berylina, she wove her fingers into a warding sign, and she spat at the princess's feet.

Berylina tried to plot her rebuttal, but other witnesses were called. An attendant at Ile's shrine who had seen Berylina light a dozen tapers to the god of the moon without visibly kindling the first one. A child who had walked behind Berylina in the streets and who said that she cast no shadow. The sour man who served beer at the alehouse beneath their rooms, who said that he had never seen Berylina take a bite of bread or a sip of ale, nor her companions, either.

She wanted to explain. She wanted to tell them that they were exaggerating; they were making up stories. They were missing the truth in their haste to find a path to the Thousand Gods.

Torio glowered and called one last witness, Thurda of Zarithia. Berylina did not recognize the name, but she knew the face—the mother of the boy who had nearly drowned in Mip's fountain. Berylina started to relax. Here, at least, was a good tale. Here was a truthful story of how the gods had watched out for the princess, of how they had enabled her to save a child.

"She took my son, she did." Thurda stood on the dais, as tall as her rotund body would let her. She peered over the balustrade, leaning urgently toward the Curia. Setting her hands on her hips, she jutted her chin forward as if she would battle the entire room with such a weapon. "He's a good boy, my son. He wanted to see Mip's temple. He'd heard about the fountains, heard about them all the way back in Zarithia. It was a hot day, and we told the poor bairn that he could cool himself there. He could praise Mip and cool his feet all in the same day."

Torio frowned, clearly displeased that Mip's temple was considered little more than a child's bath. Thurda sensed the Curia's disapproval. She drew herself up even straighter, and she pointed a quavering finger toward Berylina. "And then *that one* got involved! She wanted to prove her faith. She wanted to prove her worship. She took my poor boy and held him under the water, held him there until he started to drown. And then, when she knew that we were desperate, she pretended to rescue him. She pretended to bring him up. She pretended to call on the Thousand to save him. She lied and used our little boy in her filthy games!"

Berylina wanted to laugh. She wanted to point out the folly of the woman's words. If Berylina were a witch, why would she have staged a miracle with a child? Why would she introduce another person into her rituals? Why would she call attention to her dark means of worship?

Torio shook his head, his jowls quivering. He glared at Berylina. "And you? What defense do you have to this charge of witchcraft?"

Before Berylina could speak, Siritalanu interrupted. "That woman made no charge of witchcraft!"

The Curia exploded into competing bursts of agreement and disagreement, and Torio had to fight to be heard above his fellows. "What say you?" he berated Thurda, who still stood on the dais. "Do you accuse Berylina Thunderspear of witchcraft? Or of mere chicanery?"

Gol, the god of liars, came to stand beside Berylina, bathing her flesh in the sensation of summer sun.

She has listened well to all my lessons. She wants their attention; she's a lonely one. She'll do anything to keep their gaze on her.

Berylina nodded, wanting to turn her face to Gol's rays. Suddenly she understood. With a handful of words, the god of liars had shown her the truth. There was nothing she could do before the Curia, nothing that would change her path. She *would* be found a witch; the gods planned it so. There were patterns, designs, reasons that she could not hope to understand. The gods meant for her to be a martyr. They meant for her to die.

Berylina understood the meaning of her pilgrimage. She had embraced gods of change; she had dedicated her cavalcade to shifting deities. She'd had the time to make her offerings to Ile and Nim, to the moon and the wind; she had thought to dedicate herself to Mip.

But she had not had a chance to honor Zil, the god of gambling. This Curia was the final stage of her worship. She was casting dice, with her life in the balance. She was playing out her final game. And even as she realized that Zil was watching over her, she knew that her luck was spent. Change. It happened too slowly at some times, too fast at others.

"She's a witch, sure enough," Thurda said. "I heard her call upon the gods as she bent over my son. She spoke Mip's name backwards. She reversed her prayers to work her magic."

Berylina felt Gol's rays flicker hotter; he was feeding off the woman's lying tales. The crowd in the chamber exclaimed, and many made holy signs to protect themselves.

"May I be heard, Your Honor?" Ranita Glasswright's voice cut through the room.

Torio ignored her, asking instead, "Are there others who would speak against Berylina Thunderspear?"

Berylina thought that someone would step onto the dais, that another spectator would take the opportunity to claim fame before the court. There were no others to speak against her, though. No other liars to build their own accounts. Torio shook his head as if he were disappointed, and then he turned to Ranita. He licked his fleshy lips before he said, "Aye. You may speak."

Ranita crossed the room, staring directly at Berylina. There was pride in that look, but fear as well. Berylina remembered Ranita's calm voice, the way that the glasswright had guided her in the Speaking. She remembered how she had followed those words, how she had moved deeper into her heart, her thoughts, her memories, her soul. She remembered how the gods had gathered around her, how they had nurtured her and lifted her, as if they were an ocean and she a cradled ship.

And yet Ranita did not seem to have that strength within her now. She gripped the balustrade with shaking hands. Her face was pale and drawn, pinched as if she had not eaten in many days. There were hollows beneath her eyes, grim circles that called to mind the ashes of long-extinguished fires. Ranita looked about the room as if she counted allies, as if she sought out friends. Berylina could have told her not to waste her time, not to squander her breath.

Torio knew his decision already. He knew the Curia's judgment, and nothing would change his mind. He knew what Brianta desired, what the city needed. What the gods decreed.

"The princess of Liantine is a good woman," Ranita began. Clain, the glasswrights' god, came to the surface of Berylina's mind, conveying disappointment in his protégé, even as his cobalt light flashed brighter. Berylina wanted to explain that the god should not judge his guildsman harshly. Ranita was fighting a battle that could not be won. She was

arguing a case that was already decided. Berylina closed her
eyes and took comfort from the cool brilliance of Clain's
cobalt core. She contemplated the beauty and the purity of
his essence, ignoring the string of words that Ranita laid out
before the Curia.

"And so," the glasswright concluded, "Berylina might
seem different, but her faith is strong. Pure. She has a power
that the rest of us can only dream of. She has a connection
to the gods, a link to them. She is no witch. In fact, she is the
farthest thing from a witch that any of us can imagine. She
is a new type of worshiper; she brings a new type of faith."

"A new faith?" Torio asked his question, and Berylina
could hear the rolling thunder of Shad, the god of truth. It
seemed that the god arose to contest Gol's supremacy, to
carve away the power of the god of lies. Alas, Shad came too
late to save Berylina.

"Yes!" Ranita was eager to continue, pleased that she had
finally evoked a response from the Curia.

"What sort of faith? How does Berylina differ from the
other pilgrims in Brianta?" Berylina heard Shad roll nearer.

"The gods come to her, Your Honor. They present themselves to her without the intermediary of priests. She sees
the gods, and she hears them. She can reach out and touch
them, smell them, taste them!"

A crack of thunder echoed inside Berylina's skull as
Torio bellowed, "I will not listen to this blasphemy!" At the
same time, Siritalanu leaped toward the dais, stretching out
his fingers as if he would strangle Ranita Glasswright.

"I speak the truth!" Ranita cried, and Berylina wondered
if she protested against Torio or against Siritalanu. "Ask the
princess, if you do not believe me. She is closer to the gods
than any of us in this room. She knows them better than we
can ever hope to."

Berylina felt the moment that Torio fully hated her, felt it
as if a ray of light leaped forth from a shuttered lantern. His

voice shook with fury as he said, "Is this true, then? Do you claim this nonsense to be the truth?"

Once again, thunder crashed in Berylina's ears. She tried to hold herself a little taller, tried to make her spine a little straighter. She brought her good eye to bear on her prosecutor. "Aye, Your Grace. The gods come to me in many forms. I've come to know them through my eyes and through my ears, through my nose and tongue and skin."

Men cried out as if Berylina were an enemy on a battlefield. Women shrieked as if she had admitted torturing small children. Ranita's face paled, and Berylina knew that she only now recognized the wrongness of her defense. Siritalanu moaned softly, a faint sound somehow audible across the room.

Berylina wanted to speak to them all. She wanted to tell them that she would be safe, that the gods would watch over her. She wanted to say that she understood, she knew, she believed.

As she watched Ranita, she realized that the glasswright was not yet through. The other woman gripped the balustrade with wiry fingers, with hands that were newly scarred from cutting glass. Berylina suddenly understood that Ranita was going to tell what had happened in the prison; she was going to share news of the Speaking, of the power that had flowed from Berylina into Ranita.

That must not happen.

With Shad whispering thunder in her ear, Berylina knew the truth. It came to her as a singular wholeness, a smooth perfection, the white ball that she had first seen in Jair's shrine. As if the First Pilgrim spoke to her himself, Berylina knew that Ranita must not be allowed to condemn herself. She must not be permitted to share the strange way that she could now commune with the gods—not yet, not now, not here in mad Brianta.

Berylina took a single step forward. She raised her hands above her head as if she were summoning down all the power of the Thousand. She threw back her head like the priestess in Liantine had done long ago, the woman who had dedicated herself to the old goddess, to the Horned Hind. Berylina filled her lungs with one deep, shuddering breath, letting the air pour into her, letting it fill every space in her body.

As she breathed, she gathered in the power of the room. The thunder of Shad filled her veins, and the sunlight of Gol. She tasted the honey of Sorn, god of obedience. Even though she stood straighter, taller, her limbs were cradled in a down comforter, in the touch of Pelt, god of order. She heard the soft sound of a child's greedy suckling, and she knew that Arn stood beside her, the god of courage shielding her with his confidence. She smelled lilac, soft and sweet, and she knew that Hin, the god of rhetoric, agreed to walk beside her.

"Behold!" she cried. All eyes turned toward her, consumed her, but for once in her life she did not feel the cringing terror, the hateful certainty that she was not worthy of the attention. Her hands stretched above her head, drawing, strengthening, summoning. She knew that her hair must be wild; her jaw must be distorted, but she was speaking now, she was commanding the attention of all within the room. "Behold the power that is mine! I speak with the gods! I know them! They come to me to work their good upon the earth!"

The room was filled with the silence of a graveyard, the eerie still that filled the places where murderers and suicides were forced to rot. "You condemn me for my power, but your words are only jealousy. You wish that the gods spoke to you as they do to me. You wish that you knew the gods with your own eyes, your own ears, your own flesh."

The words worked magic on her body. As she filled her lungs, she felt the thrust of her father's spear, knew again the driving pain as he had executed her nurse, her first guide in the ways of the Thousand Gods. Her flesh split at the impact; she saw a crimson rose bloom across her bodice.

A flurry of hands moved in pitiful holy signs. Fools. She now knew that the Thousand ignored such symbols. She now knew that the gods listened to prayers formed inside human hearts, to words whispered inside human minds. The gods cared about their worshipers' good works; they cared about dedicated missions accomplished by the faithful. They would not be moved by superstitious trappings, by silly twisting fingers.

"You try me here because I saved a child. You question me because I called on Mip, because I asked the god of water to give back one who was too young to be taken. You say that I'm a witch!"

Berylina heard the gasps of horror, as if she called down the power of evil by claiming the accusation for herself. She stretched her arms higher, felt her new wound gape wider. She could make out muttered prayers, frantic exhortations to this god or that. The name of each deity swarmed across her body, filling her with dozens of sensations.

All of the Thousand were here now, present with their myriad sensations. Berylina raised her eyes from the horde of terrified humans, and she saw that the room was filled with gods.

Nome, piping in his corner, pleased that his young charge was acting nothing like a child. Kel, who had brought King Halaravilli to Berylina, across the sea, so many years ago. Feen, the god of marriage, who had given up his hold on her when the house of ben-Jair joined with the spiderguild.

Berylina spun about, gathering all of them to her. She glimpsed horror on Siritalanu's face, and she knew that he could not see the gods, that he did not know what she envisioned. The poor man must think her mad; he must think her truly possessed. She wanted to explain to him. She wanted him to know that he was mistaken, but when she opened her mouth, she could only laugh.

The gods were so beautiful! Even the ones who were terrifying, even the ones who were dark and grim and sad. Berylina stretched toward the ceiling, willing her body to expand, to flow, to encompass all the power and beauty and glory in the room.

"Stand still!" Torio bellowed. "I order you to stand still!" Berylina could not obey him. She could not make her body stop; she could not still the energy that beat inside her veins. "The woman is possessed!" Torio cried. "We must drive the demons out of her! We must free the witch!"

A part of Berylina's mind listened. She knew that Torio ordered his guards forward. She knew that two of the bravest men caught her arms. Another pair clung to her kicking legs. Torio issued more orders, and additional guards appeared. They grabbed at her, clung to her, weighting her down like boulders.

She knew that she was carried to the stone table in the center of the chamber. Her back was forced upon the altar. She laughed as her spine kissed the rock, giggled like a maiden greeting her young lover. The soldiers bore down on her arms and legs even harder, trying to suppress her writhing, trying to make her submit.

Torio barked another command, and four guards went to the heavy sheet of iron in the corner of the room. They wrestled it to the altar, lifting it with difficulty. Berylina felt the weight settle on her chest, on her belly, on her thighs. San, the god of iron, filled her mouth with the taste of sweet wine, and she swallowed as rapidly as she could, drinking him down, filling her belly, filling her soul.

More shouts, more hasty actions. Some of the guards stoked the fire in the corner. The faithful among the onlookers surged forward, ready to help, desperate to save the witch's soul.

Yot, the god of stones, cried in Berylina's ears, shrieking his heart-stopping hawk's wail. Berylina heard him count

out the stones that the priests dragged from the fire; he cried
for each of his creations.

Gir, the god of fire, measured the heat of his flames, filling Berylina's eyes with gold-flecked waves of white. The
god of fire's earnestness almost smothered Torio's commands, almost covered the priest's bellow for more wood.

Yot came closer then. His hawk cry filled Berylina's ears,
poured into her body. She felt the first of Torio's stones settle on the iron plate.

Fire. Crushing. Pain.

Berylina reached out to Gir, gathered in Yot. The gods
swaddled her in their being, collected her in their hearts,
greeted her like lovers.

"Will you admit that you are a witch?" Torio's voice rang
above the shrieking hawk, beyond the golden white curtain.
Berylina could not speak. She could not summon the words
to deny the gods beside her; she would not ignore the deities
who filled the room. "Another stone!" Torio cried.

Weight. Heat. Agony.

"Admit that you're a witch!" Berylina tossed her head,
turning so that Gir's gold-white curtains settled over her. Yot
screamed in her ear once again. "Another stone!"

Blistering. Smothering. White hot jagged ripping pain.

"Say that you're a witch! Admit that you forsook the
gods, and you'll be free!"

One part of Berylina's mind could smell her scorched
robe. She realized that she had soiled her gown—Ranita's
gown—and a part of her was ashamed. She tried to fill her
lungs, tried to gather together the words that seemed so far
away, so long forgotten. . . . But what was it that she must
say? What must she do?

Collecting all the power of the gods around her, she
opened her eyes. She could see the edge of the metal sheet
digging into her chest. She could make out the lumps of the
heated stones even now searing through the iron. She could

see the terrified guards, standing back now, making their silly religious signs across their chests.

"Confess, Witch! Confess, and you'll be free!"

Slowly, slowly, Berylina turned her head. Torio stood upon his dais, terror and anger and shame mixing on his fat face. She wanted to talk to him, wanted to tell him to open his heart, to open his soul, to receive the gods around him, but she could not draw the breath.

"Witch!" he cried. "Do not curse me with your wandering eye! Confess! Repent!"

She summoned more of her waning strength and turned to Siritalanu. The priest was stretching toward her, reaching with fingers that seemed like claws. She saw the guards restraining him, remarked in a distant part of her brain that it took four men to hold him back. Four men! She would not have thought that Siritalanu had the strength. His lips were twisted as he cursed the guards, and his face shone with spit and sweat and tears.

"One more stone!" Torio called.

There was little time, then. Berylina craned her neck, gently pushing aside Gir's gold-white curtains. She must find one other. She must look at one other. She must . . .

There. Standing on the dais. Still stranded on the platform where she had testified, where she had spoken the words that had provoked Berylina's demise. Ranita Glasswright.

Look at me, Berylina wanted to cry. She fought to fill her lungs, but she could find no air. She struggled to shape the words, but her mouth was pulled into a different shape, a horrific shape, a tortured stretch of flesh. *Look at me!*

Torio's men struggled forward with another stone, the largest yet. They swayed the burden between them, rocking forward like workmen in a quarry, manipulating the shimmering stone with massive iron tongs. It took them three counts to heft the weight, to lift it onto the others, atop the metal plate, on Berylina's chest.

Look at me!

And somehow, past the hawk cry, beyond the white-gold curtain, Ranita heard. The glasswright locked eyes with the princess, held her gaze across the frantic, scurrying room. *You see the Thousand,* Berylina thought, and Ranita nodded. *You hear them and taste them and smell them. You feel them with your flesh and blood.*

The glasswright took a step closer, reaching out to Berylina with both hands.

"Confess that you're a witch!" Torio's scream echoed in the chamber, bouncing off the ceiling like rays of heat off stones.

Berylina fought for one last breath. *Don't abandon them, Ranita Glasswright. Don't forget what they would have you do. Remember the gods in all your life.*

The stones were beyond heavy now. The heat had charred her flesh. She could not resist much longer, could not stay with the shrieking hawk, could not linger behind the white-gold cloth.

She cast her thoughts down to the deepest parts of her mind, to the depths that she had plumbed with Ranita during her Speaking. *Say that you will walk with the gods,* she thought to Ranita. *Say that you will work their labors. Say that you will be their pilgrim. Say it, Ranita. Say it now.*

"Yes!" Ranita cried. "By all the Thousand Gods, yes!"

Berylina heard the words like the creaking of the Heavenly Gates. All the gods around her exploded in their joy. The Thousand danced and sang and laughed and cried, accepting Berylina's transfer, blessing the bargain she had made.

"Confess!" Torio cried again, but Berylina scarcely heard him.

Instead, she closed her eyes and threw back her head, letting her clenched fists relax. She settled into the depths of her memory, the core of her being, sank down the pathways that Ranita Glasswright had shown her only three days before.

Then she was beyond the iron plate, beyond the stones, beyond the frenzy and the panic of the Curia. She was alone and not alone, alive and not alive. She found the last gate in her mind, the final barrier that stood between her body and the Heavenly Fields. She set her thoughts against it, spread out the very core of her being in acceptance, in glory, in joy. She unfurled the last turn of her cavalcade, took the final step of her pilgrimage. This was the power Jair had promised her when she first prayed in his house. This was the wholeness, the oneness, the glory that he had pledged.

She recognized Tarn's familiar rustle before his green-black wings filled her soul.

12

Rani listened to the bells toll across Brianta, each metallic clang echoing like the ache behind her eyes. She twisted her hands as she looked out the window, ignoring the whisper of her dry, powdery flesh. "Let me get my cloak, Mair. We can go back to Nome's shrine, see if the priests there can offer us any further guidance."

Tovin answered before Mair could respond. "You were supposed to be at the guildhall by sunrise."

"I cannot take the test. Laranifarso is more important."

"That's absurd." Tovin said, and Mair gasped.

Rani rounded on him, anger sparking her words like the pinpricks that tormented her palms. "Laranifarso is a helpless child! Besides, the test is beyond me now. How could I think of going through with it after what I saw two weeks ago? Berylina was murdered in front of me, murdered by the fanatics in this city!"

She had broken a vow. She had promised that she would free Berylina or die trying, and she had done neither. Rather than fighting free of the Curia, rather than testifying about truth and power, Rani had watched helplessly as the breath was crushed from the princess.

Tovin seemed unaware of her failure, though. "I know that. But Laranifarso has been gone for those same two weeks. You've said that the Fellowship has no reason to harm him—yet. You cannot bring back Berylina by refusing to submit to your guild. You are trying to find excuses not to complete the glasswrights' test."

"Now who is being absurd?" Rani settled her hands on her hips, applying an old players' trick to seem more commanding. "Tovin, you have no idea what it was like in that chamber with Berylina! You were off somewhere in the streets."

"Off somewhere—" He bit off a furious retort, and when he started again, his voice was frighteningly calm, smooth like a pool of oil waiting to burn in a lantern. "Ranita, you have made it clear from the day that we arrived in Brianta that you have no use for me. You swore publicly to avoid me. You have ignored my advice with every step you've taken. If I was 'off somewhere,' it was because the man who pours ale at the Star and Horse provides better company than you."

"Aye," Rani snapped. "The man who pours the ale, and the woman who tends the chambers abovestairs!"

"You have no business accusing me—"

"Stop!" Mair's voice cut between them, sawing apart their arguments like a forester downing trees. "Yer fightin' 'll get ye nowhere!"

Rani raised the heels of her palms to her eyes, pressing hard. She felt stretched, pulled, as if she were ready to sob for days, and yet she had no tears. This cursed Briantan heat . . . She'd been parched since the first day she arrived. She could see a flagon of water on the mantel, but she had not yet broken her vow to eat and drink only at the guildhall. She would not fail at that at least. She could keep that promise. She swallowed hard as Mair continued: "Rani, ye'll go to yer guild'all 'n' ye'll complete yer cursed test. Ye've wasted enow time trippin' about th' city wi' me."

"But Mair—"

"I willna 'ear more fro' ye. Laranifarso 'as been missin' fer near a for'night now. Either th' Fellowship is good t' its

word, or it isna. Our 'opes mean nowt. Yer takin' yer test
means nowt. Finish yer business wi' th' guild so we can all
return t' Moren 'n' plan our response."

"I—"

"Finish!" Mair's shout was so loud that Rani took a step
back. "Finish wha' ye came fer! Finish!" The door slammed
behind her so hard that the floor shook.

Rani started to follow her friend down the stairs and out
into the city streets, but Tovin's voice pulled her back.
"She's right. The world doesn't stop because the child is
taken."

But Mair does not know why, Rani wanted to say. Mair
could not understand. A note had been left in the hired
nurse's chamber, a single line saying that Laranifarso was
joining the Fellowship. Mair did not know that her infant
was being held hostage for Rani's behavior, that Laranifarso was being kept safe until Rani murdered Queen
Mareka.

Tovin did, though. In a mad fit, Rani had told the player
when she and Father Siritalanu had returned to their room-
ing house, shaken and desperate. She had found Tovin in
the tavern room, already deep in his cups, and she had
dragged him abovestairs, trying to ignore the sharp smell of
the ale, the pungent aroma of the grilled meats and the savory pies and the fresh-baked bread.

If she had wanted the player to spring to her defense, she
was disappointed. If she had expected him to strap on his
sword and stride through the Briantan streets, demanding
mercy and justice, she was crushed. Instead, he had nodded
slowly, folding himself into the chair by the cold hearth,
placing his boots on the stone edge. He'd narrowed his eyes
as Rani continued to speak, as if he were counting out her
words. When she paused for breath, he said, *"The Hapless
Assassin."*

"What?"

"A players' piece. We haven't performed it in years, but

you've seen the glass for it. A farmer is recruited by a prince to murder the king. The farmer's scythes are held captive—the man can kill, or he can starve."

"Laranifarso is not a tool!"

Tovin had only looked at her, his copper eyes dark. Rani knew better. She swallowed hard and asked, "What happens to the farmer?"

"He is slain trying to kill the king."

Even now, as Rani remembered Tovin's offhanded summary, a chill crept down her spine, sliding between the rivulets of sweat. Two weeks since she had learned the players' story. Two weeks that she had spent trying to comfort Mair, helping her friend comb the marketplace, the shrines, any place she could think that might hide a child. Two weeks that she had avoided writing to Hal, avoided dragging in the house of ben-Jair. Avoided violating her oath to Master Parion.

"This is all my fault," she said.

"It will be as much your fault when you're a glasswright master as it is right now."

"You expect me to walk into that guildhall and pretend that nothing has changed? You expect me to act as if Berylina isn't dead? As if Laranifarso is not held hostage?"

"What else do you intend to do, Ranita? Do you really believe that you can find one small child in an entire city— if the Fellowship has even *kept* him here? Do you truly think that you can bring back Berylina?"

You weren't there, she wanted to say again. *You did not see the princess die. You did not watch her face contort across the room, begging, pleading. You did not promise something, anything, scream out a vow to try to ease her passing.*

And now Rani was haunted by her failure. Had her promise done any good? Berylina would never know that Rani did not understand the commitment she had undertaken, that Rani had merely agreed in order to ease the princess's death. Berylina would never breathe again. The princess lay in a dirt-bound grave, an unmarked horror on the edges of Brianta.

Tovin reacted as if she had protested aloud. "Ranita, for two full months you have made your life a misery here in Brianta, yours and the lives of those around you. You've kept your foolish oaths, eating and drinking only with your guild, forbearing letters to your king, avoiding me as if I bore the plague. End it now. Complete your test. Stop acting like a spoiled child and finish your commitments in this cursed land."

"I'm not acting like a spoiled child!"

He merely stared at her, one eyebrow quirked in a silent challenge. It irritated her that he could cast his face in such a perfect expression. He was using his players' tricks against her, trying to manipulate her as easily as he worked a crowd in the king's feasting hall. She said, "Mair needs me." There. Let him argue with that.

Tovin slid his boots from the stone hearth and planted them firmly on the floor. "I'll go find her. We'll try Nome's shrine again. We'll try to find the meeting place where the Fellowship does its business in this cursed town. Now go to the guildhall before you lose any more time."

She knew that he was right. She must act; she must move forward. Nevertheless, she wanted to reach out for him, draw him to her bed, apologize for all the grief that she had caused him, caused both of them, in the past two months. She hung her head and whispered so softly that she thought he would not hear, "I'm afraid."

"Go."

She heard his implacable tone, and she knew that he would offer her no more comfort. His anger ran deep, a crystalline fury that had taken two months to turn to stone. Two months of living by promises, by oaths, by words that had been forced from her. As if to emphasize the matter of her vows, her belly clenched, demanding food and drink.

She ran a hand down the front of her gown, barely touching the pocket where she had hidden Crestman's bottle of poison. It was still there, hard as a tumor. She would not think about it yet, though. She would not think about Mareka, about Moren, about what Hal would say and do. She would face her glasswrights' test first.

"Come with me," she pleaded to Tovin. "Walk with me through the streets."

"Go, Ranita. You've wasted enough time."

She forced her trembling fingers to adjust her Thousand-Pointed Star, and then she remembered to brush her palm across the prayer bell. She resisted the urge to slam the door even harder than Mair had.

An old woman guarded the guildhall gates. Rani greeted her with as much respect as she could muster, even though she realized that the woman glanced at the sun to gauge the time, smiling broadly as she calculated that Rani was late enough to endanger her test. Hurrying through the hallways, Rani wished that the passages were more familiar, more comfortable, more like the guildhall of her youth.

That was the whole point, of course. The Briantan guildhall was nothing like the Morenian structure. The dark corridors, once sacred to the god of bread, had nothing to do with the soaring spaces Rani associated with Clain.

Cobalt blue flashed behind Rani's eyes, and she froze in the hallway. No. She was not going to think of Berylina. She was not going to think of the princess, of the dead girl's special relationship to all the gods.

Whatever had passed between herself and Berylina, whatever silent communication had poured from the princess during their Speaking, it must be imaginary. Rani must have wished it into being, convincing herself that something more powerful had transpired. After all, she had been conducting her first Speaking. She had been violating the rules of the man she loved. Surely she would imagine things under such circumstances. Surely she would concoct stories to justify her actions, to make her risks worthwhile.

She set aside her vision of the cobalt light, but then she felt guilty, vulnerable. "Clain watch over me," she muttered as she reached the door to the journeyman's hall. She coupled the prayer with a holy sign.

As soon as she stepped over the threshold, she became the center of attention. Even the other journeymen, intent on their work, looked up from their benches. The other glasswrights—masters and apprentices and instructors— stared at her as if she had shouted out in the middle of a prayer service.

"Ranita, we are grateful that you chose to honor us with your presence," Parion said dryly, stepping out from behind a table where he had been studying a journeyman's design. "Perhaps you misunderstood, though. The master's test began at sunrise."

"I'm sorry, Guildmaster. An urgent matter kept me from arriving earlier."

"Urgent? Something more important than your master's test?"

A stolen child, she wanted to say. *A dead princess. A fight with the man I love, the man who no longer loves me. A Fellowship intent on spinning me about like a child's plaything.* She swallowed hard. "I am sorry, Master. I have no satisfactory excuse."

The technique was an old one, a method that she had not applied for years. She had perfected it when she was a child, when she was charged with displaying her family's goods in their market stall back in Moren. Occasionally, she would forget that it was her turn to set out the silver pieces, or she would purposefully wander away from her obligations, taking her poppet to play with Varna Tinker.

And when Rani's mother called her to task or—worse— her father demanded to know what she had been thinking, she would confess. Openly. Without guile. Admitting fully to her failings and submitting herself to their mercy.

The trick worked this time, as it had so often in her childhood. Certainly Parion narrowed his eyes—he knew that he was being taken, being manipulated. And yet he chose to submit to that manipulation rather than call her out. After all, what more could he hope to get from her than a confession? What better response could he desire than an abject admission?

Parion nodded slowly, and then he pointed toward the empty table beside Larinda. "Very well. Get to work. You have until sunset, like all the other journeymen. You will receive no extra time."

Rani nodded. The punishment was fair. She had expected nothing better.

The glasswrights worked their test differently from other guildsmen. Other masters tested the accumulation of their journeymen's skills. They permitted their members to labor for days, for weeks, for months—all with the goal of creating one perfect work.

The glasswrights, though, understood that much could happen over time. Masters could assist journeymen beyond accepted limits. Finished works could be purchased from distant lands and disguised to look like test pieces. Journeymen could conspire among themselves to help with projects, help beyond the ordinary support of fellow guildsmen.

And so the glasswrights tested their journeymen in one day. From one sunrise to a single sunset. The guildsmen were watched, studied, scrutinized. No mistakes could be made. No lies could be told.

Rani felt every eye upon her as she crossed to her table. She took off her pilgrim's robe and folded it carefully, raising the Thousand-Pointed Star to her lips before she placed the garment on the floor. Around her, the other journeymen returned to their work, frantic to accomplish as much as they could before the test ended. Only Belita took a moment to flash her a smile, but even the Zarithian journeyman did not waste time on any further gesture of support.

Rani bowed her head and forced herself to take a deep breath. She must approach this test with a clear mind. No Berylina. No Laranifarso or Mair. No Tovin. Just Rani, her design, and her glass.

"May all the gods look upon my craft with favor, and may they take pleasure in the humble art created by my hands. May Jair himself be pleased with the humble offering I make, and may the least of my works bring glory to the world. May my works guide me to the Heavenly Fields in my proper time, as the gods do favor. All glory to the Thousand Gods."

The words came easily to her lips, for she had spoken them every morning in the old guildhall. Upon rising, upon beginning any project, upon sitting down to any meal or sleeping, Rani had said the prayer so often that she scarcely heard the individual phrases. Hoping that Clain had heard her, fearful to reach out and see if the cobalt god was in the chamber, Rani lifted the linen shroud that covered her whitewashed table.

White. Blinding new-washed wood.

The table was like Berylina's vision of Jair, like the princess's image of the First Pilgrim himself. *No,* Rani chided. *No Berylina.* She must concentrate on the table in front of her. She must ignore her pounding heart, ignore her chilled, dry flesh. She must forget about the prickles in her palms, the ache behind her brow. She must act like a glasswright master. She must complete her test.

Catching the tip of her tongue between her teeth, Rani picked up her charcoal crayon and began to draw.

At first she was aware of every sound in the chamber. She knew when Parion took a breath and when he exhaled. She knew when one of her fellow journeymen broke his charcoal crayon. She knew when an apprentice shifted from foot to foot, when a master padded out of the dim room.

Next to her, Larinda worked. Rani resisted the temptation to watch her fellow journeyman. Every day that Rani had labored in the old Glasswrights' Guild, she had compared herself to Larinda. She had measured out the sticks of wood that each carried to the kitchen; she had counted the pots of gruel that each stirred. She had calculated who received precisely which compliments, who was allowed to grind which colors. Now, in Brianta, Rani had watched Parion's support of Larinda with jealousy.

She wanted to know the design of Larinda's piece. However, when Rani took a step back to view her opponent's table, the flickering torchlight caught on Larinda's Hands. Rani could make out the dull glint of metal, the soft swirl of leather and silk.

Ashamed, Rani returned her attention to her own work. She reminded herself to focus on her own drawings, on the studies that she had completed of Lor. She thought about how she had made the god too fat the first time she drew him. She remembered to leave adequate space for the leading, a narrow margin for the diamond knife.

She worked without making any errors. A part of her mind remarked that she was moving as if she were deep in a Speaking—her fingers had a confidence, a sureness, a certainty that she had never known before. The charcoal was smooth beneath her fingertips, but she knew its hidden shape, its structure. She knew there was a weak point in the side, just beneath her index finger. If she applied too much pressure, the stick would snap and she would lose her concentration, lose control. She relaxed her fingers slightly, shaking her hand, avoiding the problem.

It seemed that no time had passed, and yet she was staring at a completed drawing of Lor. His eyes looked out at her, simple and direct. A bolt of cloth leaned against his legs, a rich symbol of his wealth.

Rani straightened, and she was surprised to feel that her muscles were tight across her back. She had not realized how long she had crouched over the table. She set down her charcoal crayon and shook her fingers, longing full sensation to return, wishing that she could be free of the prickling that had tormented her for weeks.

Of course, the other journeymen had already completed their drawings. As Rani looked around, she saw that several of her peers stood at the far end of the chamber, helping themselves to a platter of fresh-baked bread. Cosino glanced up and met her eyes; he held up a chunk of bread, as if to offer her some of the feast.

Rani's belly clenched. When had she last eaten? Not that morning, certainly, and not the night before—she had been roaming the streets with Mair. The morning before then? No, she had thought to come to the guildhall, thought to eat something where her vows could be observed, but she had let Mair drag her out before the sun rose.

Now she stared at the bread longingly, but she realized that she could not waste her time. There would be time enough for food after the test. She would have a lifetime for bread once she became a master. *If* she became a master. She shook her head at Cosino, making herself add a smile to the resigned gesture.

Rani crossed the chamber to the great bins of glass. The guild made this concession to its one-day test. Journeymen were not required to pour their own glass, to wait for it to cool. They did not need to treat the panes with silver stain, with other pigments. Instead, they could use colored sheets from the guild's storehouse.

All of the journeymen had combed through those sheets in the days preceding the test. Rani could recite everything available, the colors and the textures. She had taken great care to study her options with nonchalance, so that none of the other glasswrights might notice what she preferred. Rani would not be surprised if some of her fellows purposefully took prized sheets early in the day, if they appropriated the crimson that was perfect for Lor's robes, the flawless white panes that she intended to cut into a bolt of silk.

Now, behind her fellows, Rani needed to choose with care. She needed to select her most treasured pieces first, then return for less valuable shades, more common sheets. There. She had captured the grey for Lor's eyes. She seized a serviceable piece for the deep crimson of his gown. She collected the brown for his fringe of hair.

Nevertheless, the white glass that she had hoped for was gone. The bolts of silk were central to her design; she had intended the creamy Zarithian white to set off the crimson perfectly. She would have to make do with a murkier shade, a sheet of glass that had impure streaks of yellow.

Only when she walked past Larinda's table did she realize who had taken the creamy white. The other journeyman was settling the sheet on top of her own charcoal drawing. Rani could not make out the shape of the heavy lines beneath.

That was just as well. No reason to compare how each would have used the treasured pane. Rani would work without it. That was right. That was fair. She tried not to wince as Larinda flexed her Hand and picked up a heavy grozing iron.

Rani settled at her table and thought her way through the Guildsman's Prayer once again. The words were hardly necessary, but they helped her to focus, to center. Then, when she believed that she might not be the object of *every* eye in the room, she reached beneath her table and took out her roll of tools.

The leather was smooth beneath her fingertips, well worn from years of service. Ordinarily, her family would have purchased her glasswright tools for her when she rose to the rank of journeyman. By the time Rani achieved that rank, though, her family was long gone, dead in Moren's rubble.

Tovin had given her her tools. He had tried to act casual when he presented them, as if he were not changing her life. He had shrugged off her effusive thanks, pointing out that he had not even had a new leather roll crafted for her; he had merely given her his spare.

And yet she knew that he had traded some of his tools to her. She had his good diamond knife, the blade that she had first used when she discovered the power of such a device. She let her fingers smooth the leather, as if she were smoothing Tovin's flesh. Soon, she told herself. By that very night. After she had finished her test. After she had completed the matter at hand. Then she would make her peace. Then all would be right.

Rani steeled herself, knowing that her diamond knife would attract much attention from the other guildsmen. When she picked up the tool, she half-expected Parion to bark a command, to forbid her from using the instrument. When the master remained silent, Rani raised her eyes, seeking out his explicit approval.

Parion was waiting for her question. His eyes locked on hers. Rani was startled by the line of his jaw, by the hard glint of his gaze. She had known that steely demeanor in her past; she had worked for an instructor who was as rigid, as unyielding, as stern.

Instructor Morada. Rani flashed back to the last time she had spoken to the woman, on an ill-fated scaffold outside Moren's House of the Thousand Gods. Rani had followed Morada in the marketplace, tracked the woman to an abandoned quadrant of the city. Morada had met with her own secret cabal, and then the instructor had paid for her collusion, paid with her life. Was that the fee that would be demanded of Rani? Was that the price for joining with shadowy others?

Rani shuddered and moved her hand away from the vial

hidden in her pocket. There was no time to question the Fellowship, to explore its demands, its goals. She must complete her test.

Slowly, she raised the diamond knife, twisting it in her hand so that it caught the gleam from torches on the wall. She made certain that Parion could distinguish it from the guild's traditional grozing irons; she wanted him to know precisely what she intended to do.

The guildmaster's eyes were drawn to the dark metal as if he were enchanted. She saw him scrutinize the narrow blade, study the device until Rani thought that he would never breathe again. Then he raised his eyes, snaring hers and nodding once. Master and journeyman sighed at the same time, and then Rani set to work cutting her glass.

The diamond knife flowed beneath her fingertips. She had perfected her technique in the years since Tovin had first shown her the tool. Now her fingers bore down with a precise weight. Her wrist made minute adjustments as she traced the lines of her drawing. She sensed a small air bubble in the glass, and she automatically relaxed her fingers, letting the knife ride through the weakened space.

Her work was not flawless. The first time that she cut Lor's eyes, she pressed too hard, trying to make the orbits perfect. The grey glass crumbled to dust beneath her heavy hand, and she bit back an oath. The crimson for the god's robes was flashed; a piece of deep crimson glass was melded to clear, so that the color was not overwhelming. Rani forgot that the melding might be flawed, and she was rewarded with shattered fragments on her first attempt. Her initial cut for the bolt of silk left a broad orange streak down the center of the piece; it looked as if the cloth were stained.

Nevertheless, she worked quickly, efficiently. She stacked the good pieces on her whitewashed table, layering them carefully. Twice, edges of glass nicked her fingers, leaving tiny trails of blood. Once, Rani's prickling fingers slipped on the iron handle of the diamond knife, and she was rewarded with a stinging cut. She scarcely noticed the wounds, though—they were part of the glasswright life, part of the guild that Rani ached to join. She wiped her hands against her robes and went back to her labor.

At last, she was through with the cutting. By long custom within the guild, she must return her unused glass to the bin—there were always other glasswrights who might need her remnants. She collected the pieces quickly, ferrying them across the room with careful hands.

Her fingers tingled as she placed the partial sheets back in their bins. She felt as if she had been panting for hours; she needed to remind herself to fill her lungs with one complete breath. When she turned back to her table, it seemed that her head followed too late after her body.

She saw that the other journeymen were through cutting their glass. Several gathered at the far end of the hall. The tray of bread had been replaced by bowls of fruit. Belita and Cosino were actually chatting with each other; Belita coasted her hand over Cosino's arm, and the pair laughed. The sound of amusement wafted across the room, carrying with it the aroma of the peaches in the bowl between the journeymen. Rani's mouth started to water.

Nim, the god of wind—he tasted of peach.

No, she remonstrated with herself. Not yet. She would worry about Berylina's demise after her test.

She ignored the food and returned to her table. Parion was standing over her cut pieces, examining them with a master's eye. Her first reaction was to cry out, to order him away. She remembered herself in time, though, and she settled for hovering anxiously as he fingered the glass.

He lifted the diamond knife as well, tested it with a well-scarred thumb. Then, as she watched balefully, he reached toward her, letting his sleeve fall back along his arm. The crossing scars were plain in the torchlight; the raised flesh was livid, as if it had only just been carved by the Morenian King's Men. Parion set the diamond knife against his own dead flesh, as if he could measure the blade more exactly that way.

Rani held his gaze, refusing to remember how he had acquired those scars, refusing to admit how she had contributed to them. At last, Parion nodded and returned the diamond knife to the table.

Her hands moved as if they were guided by another. It was time to wrap metal foil about the edges of her pieces, pressing it smooth with one of Tovin's tools. In the interest of the timed test, she was not required to create the foil herself, pounding it thin between felt-wrapped blocks of iron. Each of the journeymen was permitted to take completed foil from the guild's stock.

Rani arrived at the table just after Larinda. She had to remind herself that the test was not a race; Rani was not trying to complete her work faster than any other journeyman. Rather, she needed only to compete against the sun, to finish before the end of the day.

Larinda was fumbling with the fine foil, trying to pry away a single sheet of the clinging stuff. Her Hands did not readily give her the dexterity to lift the foil, and on her first attempt, she came away with three. Her second try netted no metal at all. Rani watched the other woman set her jaw; she imagined the muttered curses that she could not hear.

When Larinda's third attempt resulted in thin sheets splayed across the table, Rani stepped forward. "May I help you?"

"I don't need your help!" Larinda snapped. As if in reflex, she curved her wrist, and the Hand's thumb snapped close to her forefinger. Rani was reminded of a brutal crab, and she leaped back, looking away until she heard Larinda stalk back to her worktable.

By the time Rani returned to her own table, her headache pulsed inside her skull, sending shafts of nausea down her throat, into her belly. More bells started tolling outside, and

she whipped her head toward the doorway, fearing that the
sound marked sunset. Of course, it did not. The other journeymen were still hard at work; every guildsman watched
in eager anticipation.

She blinked hard to clear a swarm of black spots from
her vision, and then she forced herself to move slowly,
carefully. If the foil buckled after it was applied, it would
take the lead with it, rendering the finished panel unstable.

The long pieces of Lor's robe were simple to prepare,
but the round sections caused more trouble. Twice, she
needed to rework the god's eyes, and the bolt of silk required four attempts before it passed her critical inspection.

By the time she wrapped the edges of the last piece of
glass, her eyes stung, dry as the Briantan streets. She did
not have time to rest, though, did not have time to ease her
aching head by rubbing at the nape of her neck. Instead, she
collected her lead stripping from across the room, hefting
its simple weight on her palm. The metal was coiled tight,
and Rani needed to coax it into a straight line back at her
worktable. She heated it over her brazier, taking care not to
breathe too much of the acrid fumes. Nevertheless, the stink
of the molten metal made her belly clench.

She turned her head to one side, swallowing hard, and
she saw that Larinda was just finishing the foil on her own
creation. Several of the pieces were large—understandable,
since they had been cut with a standard grozing iron. Larger
pieces were easier to cut, easier to foil, easier to solder.
They required less dexterity.

Rani started to gloat over her fellow's inferior effort, but
she stopped herself before she could complete the thought.
If Larinda simplified her design, it was only because of her
past in the guildhall. It was only because of the past that she
and Rani shared, the injuries that Larinda had suffered
when Rani called down the wrath of the King's Men.

Rani's lungs hurt as she bent over her lead stripping. She
was exhausted now, and she had to blink her eyes rapidly to

make herself focus. She wondered if she should take a moment to close her eyes, let them rest. She could not afford to ruin her piece now. She could not afford to drop the work from clumsy fingers.

How much time remained? How long before Parion snapped out a command? Were other journeymen finished already? Had other guildsmen left for afternoon prayers?

Concentrate. Forget about the others.

Rani heard Tovin's voice, smooth, calm. She let his words flow over her like water, like the river that he had guided her down years ago, when she first Spoke with him. He had taught her the secrets of glass then, on the Liantine plain and in her workshop in Morenia. He had told her all she needed to know.

And she had abandoned him here in Brianta. She had set him aside at the guild's first order. She had thrown him into the arms of the tavern wench.

Tovin must understand, though. He knew what the glass meant to her; he knew how she longed to advance within the guild. That was why he had come to Brianta with her, after all. That was why he had accompanied her. He wanted her to succeed. He wanted her to become a master.

Rani turned away from her brazier and filled her lungs, breathing as deeply as she was able. When she exhaled, she did so slowly, edging her chin toward her chest, emptying her body.

Berylina had been emptied. Berylina had been crushed.

No. Concentrate.

She remembered the flowing river, remembered the power of Speaking. Tovin had given her that. It was a tool, like the diamond knife, like the fine jeweler's tongs that he used to fashion lead chain. She needed to find her core. She needed to find her strength. She needed to reach into her Speaking and find the power of her past.

She inhaled again, remembering all the lessons that Tovin had ever taught her. She exhaled, and she released her guilt, her fear, her memories of Tovin and Berylina and Mair and Laranifarso. She breathed in again, filling her lungs, raising her chest, breathing, breathing, breathing.

When she opened her eyes, the black spots were gone. The ache behind her brow had receded to an echo. She picked up her tongs, and she soldered the lead joins for the god of silk, using the foil to anchor the joining compound.

Each seam was unique. Each required her attention as she discovered imperfections in the foil, limits in the glass. Each demanded that she check her work, that she smooth it completely, that she let it cool, hoping, praying that nothing went wrong. She completed the first join, and the second. The third, the fourth, the fifth.

She stopped counting, reaching for the glass as if she were one of Davin's machines back in Moren. She understood what she was creating; she knew what she must do next. She dropped a piece of glass and retrieved it unbroken, settled back immediately into her rhythm. She ran out of lead stripping, and she retrieved more from across the room, gliding past her colleagues as if she were invisible.

Then the leading was done, and she had completed the body of the window. One more step remained—painting on the design. She ground the lead-black pigment with instinctive fingers. Gone were the days when she needed to test the powder, to sample its fineness. She knew when she had ground enough, when the particles were small enough to soak up water. She mixed the paint on a jagged pane of extra glass, and then she selected a brush.

Her wrist was steady as she filled the bristles, rolling them about on the glass so that they absorbed an even amount of pigment. She squeezed out the extra, pressing the bristles between fingers that were beyond aching, beyond exhaustion.

She did the fine work first, the lines of Lor's face, the ray of wrinkles beside his eyes. She drew in gullies on either side of his mouth, deep troughs carved from his habit-

ual frown. She added texture to the bolt of cloth, making it
clear to any viewer that the fabric curved about its wooden
form.

And then she drew the octolaris. She remembered the
great glasswork spider that she had seen in Liantine, the
delicate design that had taken her breath away in the spiderguild. Crestman had stood beside her then, before she
had approached the master of the guildhall, before she had
bartered for Morenia's salvation.

Crestman had stood beside her before she betrayed him.

Even that thought was not enough to shake her hand.
She knew the design that she must complete, she knew it
with the certainty of all the Speaking she had ever done.
One line there, another, another. The silk web stood out
against the clear glass, called into being by the steady pigment.

And still Rani was not through. One last thing . . . She
turned her head to the side, catching the panel at an angle.
What was wrong? What was missing? She had not drawn
anything else in all her preparatory sketches.

And then she knew. She dipped the brush, filled the bristles, squeezed them almost dry. She levered her wrist
against the table, steadying her hand. She stretched the
brush toward the pane of glass, barely touching. There. In
the distance. Beyond Lor's vision, over his shoulder, away
from his conscious thought.

A single riberry tree.

Rani hinted at the smooth silver bark, at the intricate
branches. She ghosted in the leaves. She imagined the
markin grubs that would feed the octolaris, that would fuel
the growth of silk.

And then Parion called, "Time, Journeymen!"

Rani was pushed back to the guildhall, tugged from the
depths of her trance. She had not intended to use her Speaking powers; after Berylina, she had vowed that she would
never harness that strange art again. Nevertheless, in the

heat of the contest, she had drawn on Tovin's lessons, relied on the player's strength.

Several journeymen protested Parion's announcement, and instructors moved through their ranks, seizing brushes, taking away coils of lead stripping. Rani realized that one of her peers had abandoned his work quite early in the day, leaving shattered glass in the center of his whitewashed table. Belita and Cosino had apparently finished before the sun had set; their tables stood empty with some completed work centered, presented. Three other journeymen had also finished and left.

Parion said, "Thank you, Journeymen, for your attempts. You may leave the hall now. We masters will collect your projects, and we will confer upon their merits. Go forth, and eat and drink and sleep. We will tell you in the coming days if you have passed the test."

That was all. There was no fanfare. There was no slam of an executioner's axe. Nothing more.

Rani knew that she was beyond exhaustion. She was half starved. She was parched like a traveler who had ranged for days in a desert.

She was also freed from her vows to the guild. She could eat what she chose, drink what she desired. She could be with Tovin.

She set her hands against her table, using the sturdy wooden edge to help her rise. Her legs refused to hold her; her knees wobbled as if she were a newborn foal. She acted as if she planned to turn around, as if she actually meant to look at Larinda's table next to her.

The Morenian guildhall.

Rani cried out when she saw it—tall, airy. She remembered the awe that had blinded her when her brother first took her past its gates, when she had first entered the building that was to be her home for far too short a time. Larinda had captured it perfectly, adding just the right amount of delicate tracery on her glass panel.

"It's beautiful," Rani breathed. "Larinda, it's perfect!"

Larinda, though, ignored Rani completely, as if she had not heard a word. Instead, the other journeyman rested her head against her table. She splayed her Hands to either side, as if she lacked the knowledge to remove them.

Rani saw the creamy white glass, the pane that she had thought to use for silk. It was better in Larinda's work. Better as a stone wall. Better as a reminder of a building that had been leveled, destroyed, so that it now existed only in a handful of tortured memories. "Larinda . . ." she said again, but this time she did not expect a response.

She did not realize that she was sobbing until she felt strong hands on her shoulders. She turned about, yielding to the pressure. Tovin's arms folded around her, gathering her in, collecting her as if she was a little child.

"I'm sorry!" she gasped, forcing the words through her tears. She was apologizing to Larinda, to Parion, to all of the glasswrights. She was apologizing to Mair and Laranifarso, to Berylina. "I'm sorry!"

"Hush," Tovin said. He pulled her away from her table, away from her fragile masterpiece.

I should not have called out to Tuvashanoran, she wanted to say. *Long ago, I should have come forward in the guildhall and protected my fellow guild members. I should have spared poor Dalarati. I should have stood up for Berylina before the Curia. I should have bartered with Crestman for Laranifarso. I should not have accepted the Fellowship's charge; I should not have taken the poison for Mareka.* "I'm sorry. . . ."

And then Tovin guided her from the guildhall. He walked her past Larinda, past Parion, past all the apprentices and journeymen and masters. She felt his firm touch direct her through the streets, back to her room, back to her bed. His hands shone in the lamplight as he placed cheese on bread; his knuckles caught the light as he poured wine into a goblet, mixed it with water. He smoothed her hair as he urged her to swallow. His fingers were deft with her Thousand-Pointed Star; he set aside her pilgrim's robe.

She clutched at him then, pulling him toward her, down to the mattress, down to her side. "Sleep, Ranita," he said, and she started to apologize again. "Close your eyes and sleep. We've work enough in the morning."

"I'm sorry."

"Sleep."

And she did.

13

Halaravilli ben-Jair paced his tower room, staring at the parchment in his hand. He had read the words a dozen times, and they refused to change, refused to become any safer, any gentler, any more bearable. *Beware the serpent in your midst. She let the princess die, and she seeks to harm you further. She once slew your protector; do not let her act again. Look to your wife, the queen.*

The message was absurd. It clearly implicated Rani, but Hal knew that Rani would never harm Mareka. Throughout all of his struggle for peace and prosperity in Morenia, Rani had been the one person he could count on. She could be trusted amid all of the shaky alliances that he had forged. She was dedicated to him. She was devoted.

She had gone to Brianta to beg admission to a guild that his father had destroyed.

Hal had feared that Rani's journey would test her loyalty, but he had never imagined that she would reach her breaking point. What poison had the Glasswrights' Guild harbored? What carefully nurtured resentments about being torn apart, all by a royal mistake?

In an attempt to keep Rani in the fold—and because he had missed her—Hal had sent Rani missives while she was away. He had taken time with the long letters, explaining how the kingdom fared, asking for her advice. He had asked what progress she made at the guild, questioned Berylina's pilgrimage. He had his correspondence delivered to the Glasswrights' Guild so that she would be certain to receive them, certain to know that he honored and respected her work.

And he had heard nothing. Not one letter. Not one single reply.

Even as he cursed the glasswrights' vengeful nature, he thought he could understand the longing that Rani felt for status in the guild. He knew that she ached to belong to a family, to a mother and father, to brothers and sisters. To all that Hal's father had stolen from her years before.

Had the guild offered her that? Had they set a price for their companionship and told her that the only thing she must do to fit in forever was to strike out at him?

He read the parchment again. *Beware the serpent in your midst.* Whoever had written the note knew of Rani's past. They knew that she had long ago joined up with the Brotherhood of Justice, with the traitors who had plotted to overthrow the house of ben-Jair, to replace its lion sigil with the emblem of a twisted snake.

And they knew that Rani had slain Dalarati, Hal's own guard, in her mistaken zeal. In a moment of crashing self-pity, Hal felt keen regret for that lost soldier. Dalarati had been a good man, and true. He had been slain too early, sacrificing his life before he even knew that the battle was engaged.

Dalarati had brought Hal into the Fellowship, into the cabal, with its endless secrets and disguises, its intricate whorls of power. What would the soldier make of the Fellowship today? What would he make of the ongoing struggles for power? For money? What would he make of the warning that Rani intended to harm Mareka?

Compulsively, Hal read the parchment again, and he swore. Somehow it all made cruel sense. Even before she fell silent in Brianta, Rani had been distant. She had been cool to him ever since returning from Liantine, ever since he took Mareka to be his wife. . . . She said that she was kept busy by her responsibilities with the players' troop, by serving as their patron. But she had avoided him, avoided Mareka.

He was no fool. He had watched her swallow her pride and bow before her queen, bow before an elevated guildswoman from a distant land. He had seen the hurt behind Rani's eyes. There was no other way, he had wanted to explain. In a moment of passion he had played Mareka falsely, and now he must pay. He, and Rani, and all of Morenia.

The heavy summer air drifted into the tower window, cloying as guilt, and Hal caught a whiff of an acrid funeral pyre in the nearby cathedral close. He tensed. Funerals. More bodies committed to the flames, transferred through those gates to the Heavenly Fields. But he must not mourn. Those were not his sons who burned today. Other people, other losses. Other fathers cursing the gods.

Hal's eyes were dragged back to the parchment. *She let the princess die.*

Word had reached Hal five days before about Berylina's death. An unsigned message, from an anonymous Briantan religious tribunal. A bald statement about witchcraft and execution, about a pilgrim who did not repent before her soul was cast out forever from the Heavenly Fields. About a body thrown into a grave, denied ritual purification.

Nothing from Rani, though, even then. Nothing at all.

Had she even been there? Or had her jealousy driven her from Berylina's side? Could she have stood by and watched the princess tried and executed and yet said nothing, so that Hal would suffer? Could Rani hate him that much?

She seeks to harm you further.

When he had returned from Liantine with Mareka as his bride, he had hurt Rani. He knew that. He had been a new husband then, careful and afraid of his pregnant wife. He had watched Rani Trader going about the business of building his silk industry, delivering riberry trees to deserving nobles, counting out precious octolaris spiders. He had seen her command her players' troop, construct a tour for them, send them on their way about the countryside. As always, she worked with fierce independence, with desperate devotion. He had spoken to her only of financial things, only of the money that flowed in and out of his treasury.

But to his shame, he had dreamed of her. He had dreamed that she came into his throne room, that she sat beside him. She had worn the simple golden crown that he'd had fashioned for Mareka. She had folded her fingers across her flat belly, laughing at his unvoiced question, at his silent concern, and then she had pointed an accusing finger at the queen. The guards had carried Mareka out of the palace, out of Moren, out of all the kingdom.

Even now Hal flushed in embarrassment. He was a devoted man, a faithful husband. He had never touched Rani. He had never yielded to the secret message of his dreams.

And so he was left staring at a scrap of parchment and wondering if his honor had cost him a loyal subject. Had he driven Rani to her silence in Brianta? Had he forced her back to her old angers, thrust her into the midst of the guild's carefully nurtured hatred?

Look to your wife, the queen.

A sharp knock sounded at the study door, and Hal swore, reflexively crumpling the parchment. "Come!" he called, but the fierceness of the single syllable fed his wrath. He tossed the cursed message onto the table, letting it fall amid the miserable documents that he had been studying that morning.

For even before he discovered the secret warning on his writing desk, he had been in a foul mood. The other scrolls told a dismal story, a hopeless tale. Disheartened by their content, he had given explicit orders that he was not to be disturbed. Who would be foolish enough to violate that command? Was it so much for a king to ask for a few simple moments of privacy? Was it truly so difficult to comprehend a direct order to leave him alone?

Hal whirled to face his intruder, but the door remained closed. There was the muffled whisper of many voices. "Come, I said!" His voice shook.

Damned secret message. Damned spidersilk. Damned drought.

Another payment was due to the Fellowship within a fortnight, and he was still short one hundred bars of gold. He had taxed his nobles as much as he dared, *more* than he could do safely without risking open rebellion. While the silk auction at the beginning of the summer had filled his coffers nicely, he could not make all his payments on those funds alone. He had counted on income from the various summer fairs, taxes taken in from the various marketplaces. He had not reckoned on the drought that had tightened across most of Morenia, on the crops that had shriveled under the merciless summer heat.

Even now he tugged at the neck of his own garment, at the light silk that he had donned when the morning came— hot and muggy and hazy like all the rest. Davin could build a dam; he could construct a flying machine. Why couldn't the old man create something to cool the palace hallways during this beast of a summer?

The voices outside rose in pitch, but still no one opened the door. "By all the Thousand, come!"

The latch lifted slowly. Hal caught his breath in irritation and, when the door was still not opened, he crossed the small room, yanking the oak back as if he could crush all of his problems beneath it.

"Your Majesty! I must—"

"Sire, I told my lady Mair to wait—"

"My lord, they told us we must wait to see you—"

Mair. Farso. Rani. And looming behind them all like a shadow, Tovin Player.

So now the travelers were returned, come directly from the stables, if the stink of them was any indication. What was he supposed to do? How was he supposed to act? And why was Rani staring at *him?*

"Silence!" Hal bellowed, and the newcomers stopped in mid-exclamation. "My lady Mair. Rani Trader. Tovin Player. Welcome home to Morenia." He spoke his greeting with icy precision, not bothering to pretend that he savored the interruption.

Finally taking their cue from his dour words, all four responded with reserve, the two women bobbing into serviceable curtsies. Tovin bowed from the waist with feline grace as Farso swept into a deeper obeisance. Hal narrowed his eyes, determined to drive home his point. Desperate to avoid looking again at Rani, he shifted his weight from right foot to left, letting his body block her line of sight to the crumpled warning on his desk.

"Farso," he said, turning to chide his loyal man, "surely these travelers would be better served by stopping in their private chambers. We would have understood if they did not pay their respects immediately upon returning home."

Mair answered before Farsobalinti could muster a reply. "Sire, we came directly from the road because our words are so urgent. You must know the affront to your crown. You must understand the insult tendered in Brianta."

"I've already learned about Princess Berylina."

"But not about Laranifarso!" The woman's voice broke as she named her own son, and Hal could not keep his eyes from flashing over to Farso. Now he could see that his retainer's face was drawn, that the stolid soldier looked as if he had taken a brutal beating.

"Laranifarso." He pictured the tiny child, the precious son, wrapped in swaddling clothes. What calamity had happened in Brianta? What disaster had befallen his subjects in that land?

Mair gasped: "He is taken, Sire."

"Taken?" That made no sense. Who took a child? An infant?

"Yes!" Her insistence was heightened by her wild eyes, by the dirt that streaked her wind-flushed face. "By Jair, my son has been stolen from me!"

Her words peaked until they broke, and Farso stepped up, as if he could somehow comfort his wife. By Jair . . . The Fellowship was involved in this, then? Could the journey to Brianta have been any more disastrous?

Farso closed his fingers around his wife's arm, restraining her even as he lent her visible support. "Please, Sire. Mair has tried to speak to the Briantan authorities, but they said they could do nothing. If you were to write to them, or better yet, send your soldiers . . ."

Poor man. He did not know about the Fellowship. He did not know the strength of the force against them.

"Just a moment, Farso," Hal said. He glanced at Rani then, overcoming his anger to take in her strangely calm demeanor. She was somehow resigned to Laranifarso's disappearance. She was not arguing for him to send in soldiers, for him to unveil the Fellowship.

Do not let her act again.

What had Rani done? How far would she reach in her vengeance against him? Could she hope to gain anything by offering up her friend's child to the Fellowship? Hal kept his eyes on her as he said, "We need more facts before we can act. We need to know precisely who took the child and what they expect to gain."

Farso insisted, "Your men can learn that with the points of their swords, Sire! I beg of you! If this were your own son, you would demand an immediate response!"

Hal's anger flashed hot through his chest. "You know that I love Laranifarso like my own heir."

Farso swallowed audibly, and the blood drained even further from his cheeks. "Sire, I did not mean . . ."

"Of course not." The nobleman stammered more apologies, and Hal wanted to strike out at him. *Don't treat me like I'm some delicate maiden! Don't look at me with sudden pity!* Hal forced himself to take a calming breath. "Farso, I know that you intended no insult. Nevertheless, I cannot do anything until I learn all of the facts. And I will not learn the facts until the ladies—and Tovin Player—have recovered from their journey."

"Yer Majesty," Mair growled, "I'm as recovered as I'm like t' be b'fore my bairn i' safe."

"You have been in a distant kingdom for nearly three months. You have ridden hard on a hot, dry road." Hal forced his voice to a gentler register. "Please, Lady Mair. Eat something. Drink. Wash the dust of the road from your face. I will be here when you have rested. We can calculate our response then."

Hal watched the Touched girl measure his words. There was something fierce about her, something taut and angry. She had always rebelled against authority—his, the church's, even the Fellowship's. Hal turned to Farso. "Take care of your wife."

It was Farso's turn to look affronted, as if Hal's dismissal were permanent. "Sire, you know that I did not mean—"

"I know, my lord. I understand. Take care of Lady Mair. We will speak more once all of us are rested."

Farso frowned, but he shifted his fingers on Mair's arms; his grasp became more assertive. The Touched girl blinked hard, as if she were surprised, but she let herself be led to the door of the study. She seemed to take some comfort when Farso stopped on the threshold. "Sire, I know you will not sit idly by."

Hal met his retainer's gaze evenly. "You know that I will not. Take Lady Mair. We'll talk later."

And they were gone.

But Rani and her player remained. One traitor? Two? None? How could Hal be sure? How could he measure the real danger in this chamber, in all of Morenia?

He glanced toward the crumpled parchment, wishing that he had never read its accusations, that he had never needed to doubt. He drew a deep breath before looking Rani in the eye. "And I suppose you're going to tell me what this is all about?"

She glanced at Tovin, a quick look that contained some silent command. Hal thought that she might be ordering the player from the room, but the man merely looked at her, shrugging his shoulders slightly. She set her jaw in exasperation, but Tovin responded by smiling openly, easily. Hal shifted his weight to regain her attention, letting some of his frustration flow into his own expression.

"My lord," Rani said, "I know little more in this matter than you've heard already. The Fellowship has taken Laranifarso."

"But why would they do that?" Hal's voice was harsher even than he had intended. "Did they make demands of you in Brianta? Of Lady Mair?"

Rani darted another glance toward Tovin. The player, then? Was the Fellowship trying to manipulate *Tovin?* Why would they want to lever *his* loyalty? Certainly the man had bullied his way into the Fellowship's secret ranks. . . . Perhaps the cabal's core had decided finally to expel him. Maybe they had ordered him from their meetings in Brianta, and he had refused, and the child was now held hostage to guarantee his good behavior. . . . But that made no sense. No sense at all. The player was here in Morenia. If Tovin were the reason, the Fellowship would have released Laranifarso by now.

The player opened his hand, bowing slightly as if he were inviting Rani to continue her tale. Hal had no problem reading the look of frustration that she flashed at Tovin, the open exasperation that meant she did not want to proceed with him in the room. "My lord," she said to the player through tight lips, "I've just remembered that I left my saddlebags in the stable. Could you look to them for me? They contain my

Thousand-Pointed Star, and other things that are dear to me."

Tovin's face shuttered. "Surely, Ranita, you trust the king's own grooms." The man was clever. Rani could not challenge Hal's servants in his very presence.

Her voice was level as she said, "Of course I trust them. It's just that I feel strange after having worn the Star for so long. I feel unclothed without it."

A silent battle was fought between them. Tovin glared his frustration, transparently demanding to know why he was being dismissed. Rani remained unmoved, as if she were utterly unaware of the questions that he asked, the action that he demanded.

When the player spoke again, his words were so clipped that he might have been reciting lines from one of his plays. "If you send me from this chamber now, I might be long delayed in my return."

Rani swallowed hard, but she kept her voice even as she said, "I am certain that will not be the case."

"Only a fool states that the future is certain."

"Please, Tovin." The player glared, and Rani reached out toward him with a trembling hand. "I would speak with my king and liege lord alone."

The player clearly considered and discarded multiple responses; Hal could see the words form in his throat, the emotions dance across his face. Ultimately, he settled for inclining his head. "As you would have it, Lady Ranita." The player left before Rani could say anything, before she could order him back into the room, beg him to return.

Hal watched in frank surprise. He had never seen Rani Trader speechless. She stared at the door mutely, jagged loss patent on her face.

"Rani," he said, despite himself, and she jumped at the sound of her name. Only then was he aware of how pale her skin had become. Dark circles bled beneath her eyes, as if she had not slept in all the weeks that she had been gone.

Her lips were parched, chapped, and he could see that they had been bleeding recently.

Perhaps the parchment lied. Perhaps there was some other explanation for her silence, for her ignoring his letters. He wanted to ask her why she had not written, but suddenly the question sounded plaintive and childish. Weak. Instead, he said, "Your journey was a hard one, then?"

She shook her head slowly, but the gesture lacked confidence. "I was taken ill in Brianta." She folded her fingers into tight fists, but not before he could see the network of tiny cuts. Glasswright wounds. The cost of the guild that she fought for, the guild that hated him.

"With what sort of illness?"

"I do not rightly know, my lord. When I was there, I thought that it was merely fatigue. I thought that I was so intent upon my guildwork that I was exhausted."

"And now?"

"Food tastes odd. Drink seems tainted. My mouth tastes of metal, and I cannot warm myself, even under the summer sun."

Despite himself, he was concerned. "Had you not been secure in your guildhall, you might fear that you'd been poisoned."

Her eyes flew to his, startled, and she clutched at her skirts in sudden unease. "Why would you say that, Sire? I think instead that I have a lingering fever."

"A fever that leaves the taste of metal in your mouth?"

She squirmed beneath his gaze, twisting her fingers in her pockets. When she spoke, she sounded as if she were speaking holy vows. "I took all my meals at the guildhall while I was in Morenia."

Hal refrained from stating the obvious; he was not certain that he could speak more of the glasswrights without tainting his words with bitter suspicion. Instead, he forced himself to say, "And your test? Are you now a master?"

"I do not know yet." He heard the desperation in her

voice, saw it in the cords that stood out in her neck when she swallowed. "The guild will measure my work and compare it to that of the other journeymen. They will let me know their decision."

"When?"

"Soon." The word was almost lost in the chamber. "I left them one of your pigeons. They will send word when they have decided."

Her statement sounded like a prayer, and Hal resisted the ridiculous temptation to make a holy sign across his chest. The foiled motion, though, called to mind Berylina. He schooled his gaze away from the crumpled parchment once again and asked sternly, "What happened in Brianta? Why did you not write to me?"

"I did!" Her protest was sharp, and then she swallowed and looked away. "I did. Once. But I swore an oath to Master Parion that I would not correspond with you."

"An oath? To ignore your king?"

"An oath to be true to my guild, Sire. An oath to live like any other glasswright."

"Then you also refused to read my letters?"

"I never saw them." Her protest was curiously flat, as if she were drained of passion.

"I wrote to you repeatedly. My riders left each message with your Parion Glasswright."

He watched the battleground of her face, saw that she did not know whether she should believe him. Her sovereign or her guildmaster—whom should she trust? Where did her true loyalties lie? He decided to push her. "How did you let Berylina die?"

"*Let* her die!" Rani might have looked exhausted, but she poured vitriol into her exclamation. "My lord, you might think that I stood idly by while all the forces of the Briantan church were set against us, but I assure you that I did not, for one moment, *let* Berylina Thunderspear die."

"You do realize that Teheboth will see the princess's

death as the perfect opportunity to attack Morenia? He can gather together an army now, strike by the middle of fall. He'll say that he wants to avenge his daughter, but his goal will be to take our octolaris."

Rani nodded, and he could see that she had figured out that pattern on her own. Her calm acceptance was damning. How long ago had she worked out Teheboth's revenge? How long had she known the war that Morenia would face if Berylina died under her protection? Who had urged her to set the calamity in motion or—worse—had she acted alone? "Aye, my lord. He might do that."

"Might! Wouldn't you, if you were in his place?"

"The entire world knows that Teheboth had little love for his rebel daughter. Other lands might not look kindly on Thunderspear doing battle in her name. They might recognize the fight as blatant opportunism."

"Do you truly believe that? Do you truly think that anyone will side with us in the battle to come?"

"They will if they understand the market reasons to do so." Rani sighed, and the sound was as deep as the ocean between Morenia and Liantine. "You must gather them to your side, Sire. You must make certain that they understand the cost of a silk monopoly. If they truly believe that Liantine will regain exclusivity in the cloth market, then they will support you." She raised her eyes as if her next words were the most important thing she had ever told him. "Let them know the value of the silk, my lord. Let them know that they fight for their own treasuries as well as yours. Let them know that Liantine is the enemy of us all."

Hal heard the wisdom in her words, but he was reluctant to listen. What if this were part of her plan? What if she thought to lure him into battle and then leave him vulnerable? He said, "We have no choice but to try. Our spidersilk is our only hope of repaying the Fellowship."

Something flickered across her face, some secret message or protest. *What?* he wanted to shout. *What do you have to tell me about the Fellowship?* Her throat worked, and she said, "We always knew that it would be difficult to satisfy that body."

He decided to accuse her directly. "What do they plan, Rani? What do they mean to do with me?"

"You know as much as I." She took a deep breath, and then she met his eyes, as if she would convince him with the power of her gaze alone.

"Rani, tell me what happened in Brianta."

"They took Laranifarso."

"But why? They've never been in the business of stealing children before! Was Mair troubling them? Did she speak out against them?"

"No!" Rani's voice was sharp, the word edgier than anyone else would have dared to utter in his presence. "Mair did nothing! This is not her fault!"

He shoved down his automatic disapproval at her vehemence. "What, then? Why has the Fellowship changed its ways? What can they think to gain with that child?"

"I cannot tell you that." She swallowed hard. "Who can ever know the full intention of the Fellowship of Jair?"

He heard the bitterness in her words, the despair that she did not completely enunciate. "But why Laranifarso?" he insisted. "Why would they hold him without making a single demand? That makes no sense!"

"Few things in this world make sense, Sire." Her words fell like stones. "Why should the Fellowship be logical? Why should they act reasonably?"

"What is it, Rani? What are you not telling me?"

For just a moment, she struggled. He saw the voices inside her, battling across her face. She closed her eyes and drew a deep breath, but her pallor remained. He wanted to pour her a glass of wine. He wanted to close his hands about her arms and shake her. As if she heard the debate inside his own skull, she nodded her head. Once. Twice. Three times. When she opened her eyes, her face was smooth.

"Grant me a boon, Sire."

"What are you asking of me?"

"Say that you will do this thing, before I tell you. Know that I would ask only for your health and for the health of all Morenia. I've earned that much from you in the past, I should think."

He tried but could not keep his eyes from the crumpled parchment. Is this how she would work her mission? Bind him by his own word, then strike?

Earned, she said. Of course he owed her. He never would have kept his throne without her. Not with Bashanorandi plotting against him so long ago. Not with the fire that had rampaged through Moren, with the church and the Fellowship battling to tie him up in debt. Rani Trader had brought riches to Morenia. She had brought hope.

And yet only a fool would offer up a pledge without more knowledge of the cost. The simplest child learned that lesson in tales told at his nurse's knee. Hal pictured himself back in his old nursery, crouching in the window embrasure, playing with tin soldiers. He had learned his lessons of strategy then. He had learned how to organize men, to order resources. He had learned how to win battles.

"I cannot do that, Rani."

"Sire, I have asked nothing else from you, ever!"

The desperation behind her words confirmed that he was making the right decision. If she longed for his blind pledge so badly, she must be certain that he would deny her once he had full knowledge. For the sake of their past, he tried to force his voice to be gentle, but his words froze as he said, "Tell me first, Rani, and I will decide what I will do."

She turned away from him, plunging her hands back into her pockets. Her eyes drifted toward the windows, and he wondered if she looked for wisdom, or courage, or confidence. Or something even more rare, something he could not divine. "Tell me, Rani. I command you."

She raised her chin and said, "Set aside Queen Mareka. Return her to the spiderguild."

"What?" He gaped in astonishment, but his shouted exclamation seemed only to stiffen her resolve.

"Send her back to Liantine. Or to the spiderguild itself. Or leave her here in Morenia, in one of your homes in the countryside. Just set her aside. Have the priests declare her not your wife."

"Have you gone mad?" What was she thinking? Was this their past come back to haunt them? Was this the power that he had felt between them before, the draw, the desire for something more than a king should offer any of his subjects? *Look to your wife, the queen.*

Hal had once been so certain that Rani understood, that she realized a king could not make his own decisions of the heart. Certainly things would be different if he had not possessed a kingdom, if he had not had a dynasty to establish. . . .

A dynasty; that was the catch.

Hal had bred no dynasty. How long had Rani counted out the days before she could make her move? Had she measured each tiny royal corpse, counting herself closer to her goal with every funeral pyre? He looked at her and realized that he had no idea what thoughts ran inside her mind.

Surely, she had flaunted her men before him in the past—first Crestman, now Tovin. She had brought them into his court, pretending that they would serve him as loyally as they seemed to serve her. Had she exploited those others ruthlessly, using them only to advance her own twisted cause?

It was no secret that Crestman had considered himself betrayed—the soldier had cursed Rani, cursed Hal, cursed all of Morenia as he committed himself to the spiderguild's shackles. Rani had always argued tearfully that she never intended for Crestman to be taken; she had never meant for his life to be forfeit.

But what if she had lied? What if she had worked out her revenge years before, a revenge for a family and a guild and a life all ruined?

After all, she had lived with the players gladly enough. Was she every bit the actor that they trained themselves to be? What else had she learned from Tovin Player when she mastered his witchy art of Speaking? What other mysterious powers had Rani Trader leveled against Hal, against his family, his court?

Mysterious power. Here in the tower. How late is the hour.

He edged behind his desk, pushing aside parchment scrolls until he could see his iron dagger. He took no comfort from its sharp edge, though; he breathed no easier with it in sight. "You too, then," he said. "You have turned against me."

"No, Sire! Not as you are thinking!"

"I took Mareka Octolaris as my wife, before all of my people, beneath the eyes of the Thousand Gods. Even if I chose to do so, I could not set her aside now."

"You could if the church supported you! You could if the Holy Father himself declared your vows null and void!"

"Holy Father Dartulamino! Why would you suggest that I turn to him? You've never trusted him before!" By Jair, she never had.

By Jair. In the lair. Have a care.

"Exactly, my lord! I would not suggest this lightly! I would not tell you to set aside Mareka if it were not absolutely necessary. Your kingdom needs you to act!" Her words were strangled, and a strange flame burned high on her cheekbones.

He closed his hand about the hilt of his knife, and he moved carefully to place the desk between them. "I can imagine taking on allies, Rani. I can imagine trusting others. But Dartulamino? When you know that the Fellowship has always had a greater plan for Morenia . . ."

A greater plan. They think they can. Another man.

"Sire, don't look at me that way! This is all part of their plot, all part of what they want to happen. They want you to mistrust me. They want you to move against me. Don't do that. Don't yield to them." She fell to her knees, collapsing as if the strength had been punched out of her.

"Them? Who are *they?* Are you saying that the Fellowship intends to move against me? Do you bring an explicit threat from our so-called brethren? Did they send you to kill me and be done with me?"

She cried out as if he had plunged his dagger into her chest, a single desperate denial. "No!" Tears streamed down her face, blotching her cheeks, reddening her eyes. Madness. Rani Trader had gone mad. "Please, Sire, you can't believe that! I am not a threat to you. I am not against you; I have *never* been against you."

"Then why would you ask me to set aside Mareka? Why would you ask me to abandon my lady, my queen?"

"I have no other choice!" Rani's voice broke on the words. "Sire, I have nothing else I *can* do!"

He stared at her, stared at the longing, the horror, the spite that twisted her face. All these years, then. All these years he had harbored her inside the palace. All these years, he had thought that she understood their alliance, that she understood what could and could not be. "You too, then," he said. "You too have turned against me. After this summer, I expected Puladarati to advise me to set aside my bride. Jerumalashi and Edpulaminbi, too. But you! You think that I have no more honor than a strumpet in the streets."

"No, Sire—"

"Say no more! I will not listen to the lies upon your tongue!"

"My—"

"I thought that you would understand the decisions that I made and why I made them! I thought that we knew that much about each other."

"Sire—"

But he did not stay to hear whatever arguments she would make. He did not stay to hear the lies that she would tell. He did not stay to hear her stories about why he was wrong, why she was right, why he must abandon his wife and his honor.

He looked back at her once before he slammed the door to the tower chamber. He looked back, and he saw Rani Trader still on her knees. He saw her hand stretched out toward him, grasping like a pilgrim after wisdom. He saw the tear streaks down her pale, pale cheeks, and he saw the bitter twist of her lips.

He saw, and he understood that he had invited the enemy into his house. He knew that Rani would stop at nothing to make Mareka leave. He knew that he would have to take action. He would have to stop Rani Trader from whatever evil she planned. He would have to stop her from destroying Mareka and Morenia and the house of ben-Jair.

14

Rani Trader stood in the doorway, shaking her head as she looked about the plain room. Her bedchamber seemed so large. It had been months since she had enjoyed the privacy of her apartments, a suite of rooms set aside solely for her, without interference from anyone else. In Brianta she had shared a room with Mair and Laranifarso; on the road back she had huddled in common tavern rooms. Now the simple space seemed clean and fresh and good.

And empty.

Rani swore and turned on her heel. Where could Tovin have gotten to? She had read the threat on his face, the knowledge that he would not gladly submit to her order and leave her alone with Hal. She'd had no choice, though. She had needed to speak to the king alone, needed to try, try, try to convince him to set Mareka aside.

Without conscious thought, Rani's hand moved back to her skirts, to the pocket where the glass vial of poison still lay undisturbed. She had thought that she had a perfect solution. If she could convince Hal to send Mareka away, then the Fellowship might free Rani from her obligation. After all, their goal would be accomplished. Mareka would be out of Hal's life. She would no longer be a factor in the secret organization's plans. Rani would worry about protecting Hal himself later.

The Fellowship's plans . . . Rani had carefully avoided letting herself think about those machinations. It was clear that the Fellowship wanted Hal gone; they wanted the end of the house of ben-Jair. Rani's belly twisted, and she dug out the piece of parchment that she had found on Hal's writing desk.

She had not been violating his privacy, she told herself for the hundredth time. He had left her in his study, left her with the papers. She had been obliged to determine what was happening in the kingdom, what crucial events she had missed while she was in Brianta. It was not her fault that she had set her hand directly on the crumpled parchment when she pulled herself to a standing position. It was not her fault that the message was more intriguing than any figures about the sale of spidersilk. It was not her fault that she had been drawn to lies and manipulations more than to an accounting of taxes from scarce-attended summer fairs.

Crestman. Rani had recognized the man's hand immediately; she had seen it often enough in the letters they had exchanged years ago, during the sweet years after the liberation of the Little Army. He had a curious way of slanting his writing, as if he held his parchment perpendicular to his body. His letters were always scratched into the surface with more force than any scribe would condone.

Force. That he had attempted to use against her, to ruin her life, to betray her to Hal.

Thinking back, Rani could almost understand Hal's vehemence that morning. He had seen her as a threat. Of course he had viewed her as a manipulator. Of course he had seen that she wanted to separate Mareka from the comfort and security of the court, draw her off from the royal herd as if she were a beast to be cut down by wolves.

Crestman had primed that pump.

How could he hate her so much? Even as she asked herself that question again, she pictured his twisted arm, his dragging leg. The octolaris poison had ruined him. Crest-

man was a soldier, a mercenary, a fighting man who had always lived by the strength of his body. With that body
maimed, he was destroyed. He was not the youth that she
had met in Amanthia years ago. He was not the man who
had chafed under obligation to the house of ben-Jair. He was
a new creature, a wilder being, a desperate animal who
would stop at nothing in his quest for vengeance.

Who *had* stopped at nothing. Crestman had lied to see
her cast into prison, or worse. He would have no delusions
about the penalties for traitors; he would know that he had
bargained for Rani's death.

Rani read the lies one last time, and then she folded the
parchment, shoving it deep into a pocket. There would be
time enough to deal with it later. Time enough for her to explain to Hal that Crestman had manipulated both of them.

After she did what she had to do. After Mareka was taken
care of. After she found Tovin.

A quick glance confirmed that the dust on the stairs to her
tower glasswright study was undisturbed. Tovin had not
gone up there. She had sent him to the stables, ostensibly to
retrieve her saddlebags. Could the player actually have followed her orders? Could he still be with the horses?

She ran down the stairs, ignoring the startled glances of
retainers and guards. The hallways were almost empty;
many nobles had returned home to supervise harvests in
their own lands. Hal would convene an autumn court, but
Moren was close to deserted during the sultry days at the
end of summer.

Thus it was easy for Rani to see that Tovin was not in the
stables. His great bay stallion stood in a stall, munching con-
tentedly on hay now that he had borne his owner back from
Brianta. Someone had curried the beast and tended to his
tack, but there was no indication that Tovin had done those
duties. It was unlikely, in fact. One of Hal's grooms would
routinely have tended to the beasts, or one of the young
players.

The players. Of course. That was where Tovin must be. Rani nearly flew across the courtyard.

The heat shimmered off the practice field as she entered the clutch of buildings that housed the players. In a series of darting glances, she noted that a pair of young acrobats were practicing their routines, falling onto hay-stuffed bolsters as they negotiated a series of handholds. Children sat in a semicircle around one half-blind woman, watching as the old dame showed them how to stitch colorful costumes. Another woman paced back and forth on a wooden stage, gesturing with her hands toward absent fellows, muttering lines beneath her breath.

Everyone looked up as Rani staggered into the courtyard, and a few of the players called out greetings. Those kind words were frozen on lips, though, as people glimpsed Rani's face. She must look a fright. She knew that her eyes grew puffy when she sobbed, and enough people had told her that she looked a mess after whatever illness had struck her down in Brianta.

Poison? Hal had seemed so confident of his diagnosis. It fit, she thought, swallowing a leaden taste. No. She would not think of that now. Would not dwell on the glasswrights, on Master Parion. She had completed her test, and now she must wait.

The players. That was what she must handle now. Tovin.

She realized that her shoulders were hunched close to her ears, and she forced herself to take a calming breath. Another. Another.

There. She was ready to see him now.

She crossed the courtyard to the storage hut, to the building that housed the costumes and glass panels and all the other riches of the troop. When she settled her hand on the iron latch, she heard a voice within. A low rumble, the certain tones that she knew were Tovin's. Her throat tightened, and she had to remind herself to breathe once again.

And then there was a higher voice. A woman's tones,

flowing gently and firmly. Flarissa, Tovin's mother. The woman who had welcomed Rani to the troop years before, who had Spoken with her first, long ago in Liantine. Offering up a quick prayer to Fell, the god of families, Rani opened the door and stepped into the hut. She ordered herself to ignore Fell's sound, the plaintive cry of a cat.

Tovin was standing in front of a trunk, folding a length of crimson spidersilk. He looked up when the door opened, and the sunlight fell directly on his copper curls, teasing out all the glints of red. It was Flarissa who spoke, though. "Ah, welcome home, Ranita. Perhaps you can talk some sense into this son of mine."

"Flarissa," Rani said by way of greeting. "Tovin."

"Leave us, Mother." His voice was harsh; it sounded as if he had run too far in too short a time.

"I think that that would not be wise," Flarissa said mildly. Rani could feel the woman's curious eyes on her face. She resisted the urge to push her hair back, to straighten her skirts.

"Mother," Tovin said, "do you fear that I would strike our generous patron? Surely you do not think so poorly of your only son."

"Hush, Tovin. I know that you would never hurt with weapons. I also know that you underestimate the power of your words. You might do injury where you least expect to."

Rani longed for Flarissa to stay, for the woman's cool logic to prevail. Nevertheless, she knew that she needed to speak to Tovin alone; there were things that no other player should hear about the Fellowship, about Brianta. "Thank you for your concern, Flarissa. I think that you should leave us, though."

The woman glanced at her sharply. "You are certain, Ranita?"

"Yes." She tried to place confidence in the word, but it whispered into the dark corners of the hut.

"Very well, then. Be careful, children." As Flarissa

crossed to the door of the hut, she raised her hand to Rani's cheek. "Be very careful." Rani turned her head so that she could absorb the full touch of Flarissa's fingers, the blood warmth that flowed from flesh to flesh. She closed her eyes against sudden tears that seemed to well up from the depth of her memories, and she drew a ragged breath. "Very careful," Flarissa whispered again, and then she was gone.

Rani turned to Tovin and drew a deep breath before she began. "What are you doing?"

"You made your choice. And I've made mine."

"I needed to speak with my king. You know that he is my liege lord."

"I know that you were in danger. I know that you ordered me away. I know that you have manipulated me since the first day you decided to travel to Brianta. Since earlier than that."

"Tovin, you sound like a child! I did not ask to be alone with Hal as a way of *manipulating* you. There were words that he needed to hear. Words that he needed to hear alone, so that he could react to them as a man. Not as a king, not as a noble lord, but as a man."

"I see. And did your private audience with Halaravilli the man get you what you wished? Did you work your wiles upon him as you planned?"

"Tovin Player, you have no reason to be jealous! I did not touch the king!"

"A man can be jealous of thought. More harm can be done by a wandering mind than by any wandering fingers."

"So that's what this is all about? You think that I still long for King Halaravilli ben-Jair?"

He faced her squarely for the first time since she'd entered the hut. "Can you stand there, Ranita, and tell me you do not?"

She wanted to tell him that he was being absurd, that he was manipulative himself. And yet the words froze in her mouth. Any feelings that she might have for Hal were meaningless. He was a king and she a glasswright—not even a glasswright master yet, Clain be willing. Hal was the overlord of all Morenia, and he had a wife that he refused to set aside. What difference did it make if Rani still recalled their past? What difference did it make if Rani dreamed of how things might have been?

"There," Tovin said. "You've taken too long to answer."

"Don't be ridiculous!"

"I won't be. Not any longer." He finished folding the crimson silk and set it into the trunk. Another length of cloth followed and a tight roll of leather. His glassworking tools. He was truly leaving.

"Where are you going?"

"I'm not certain. Perhaps I'll try my fortune on the southern road, in Sarmonia."

"What, as an herb-witch?"

He frowned at her sarcasm. "I hear they have players' troops there. Maybe one of them needs a glasswright."

"I'm your patron. You can't leave without my permission." She regretted the words as soon as she had said them, but there was no possible way to comb them out of the air.

"Would you do that, Ranita? Would you chain me to you like a dog in a stable?" The planes of his cheeks caught the light, sending the rest of his face into shadow. She remembered when she had first met him, high on the Liantine plain. He had frightened her then, terrified her with the secret power of glass. The secret power of his masculine strength. The secret power of him.

"Please, Tovin! I need you here!"

"So you think. You think that I will stay to help you out of yet another predicament. You can't do that, Ranita. You've chosen to send me away once too often."

"I had no choice!"

"Do not lie. You took your oath in Brianta, before a hall of glasswrights, before Mair, before the Thousand Gods. I had traveled all that way to stand beside you in your labors, to aid you in your quest, and you set me aside as if I were an inconvenient dog."

"I—"

"And when we returned here, you ordered me away again, so that you could talk to the man you love, talk in privacy."

"Tovin—"

"I know that you don't mean to. I know that you think you had no choice. But I cannot live here knowing that you will do the same again. Whenever I am not convenient, whenever you need others more . . . A man can't live with that."

He closed the trunk and fastened it with a heavy iron lock. Rani flinched as he snapped the hasp closed, and she took a step back as he tested it with two quick jerks. Searching for words, for any argument, she said, "Crestman is trying to manipulate Hal against me. He wants me dead."

"Oh, you're too inconvenient to die."

"Tovin!"

"You've been jousting with that solider boy as long as you have known him."

"He's lying to Hal."

"All part of the drama, Ranita. You're a better player than that by now. You should recognize the pattern."

Recognize the pattern. That was what she had done since she was a child. Found the shapes. Found the lines. Found the connections between things. Things and places and people.

She closed her eyes, and she could see a map laid out before her, a map of all that had transpired to bring her to this place. She could see Tovin Speaking with her, teaching her the ways to plumb the depths of her consciousness. She could see their first frantic fumblings in the spiderguild's Great Well. She could see how he had stood beside her as she watched over the riberry trees, over the octolaris.

She saw other patterns, though. She saw a son who rode

from his mother, early and often, trading on behalf of the players. She saw a man whose pride was wafer thin, whose sense of self-worth was wrapped up in delicate glasswork and fragile lead chains. She saw a man whose eyes darkened whenever she mentioned her feudal obligations, her past life at court.

Now she saw the pattern. She saw the pattern, and she knew that she could not change it. Not now. Not with the tools she had at hand. Not with the mission that still lay ahead of her, the goals she must accomplish.

"Good-bye, Tovin." She was surprised that her voice did not shake.

"Good-bye."

For a moment, she thought that he would kiss her. She thought that he would close the distance between them, that he would fold his arms around her, that he would bring her near enough that she could hear his heartbeat.

But then she saw the shutters fall across his eyes. His fingers tightened on the iron clasp of his trunk. He was already moving on, already saddling his horse, already fleeing Moren. He was already gone.

She turned on her heel and left the hut, ignoring the laughter of the children, ignoring the good-natured curses of the acrobats, ignoring the joyful bustling life of the players.

When Rani woke, the last fingers of sunset pried through her window. She lay on her bed, catching her breath from the nightmare that she'd dreamed: Messengers had arrived from the Glasswrights' Guild—endless messengers streaming into the center of the players' enclave. Each of them carried a crumpled parchment message. Each of them bowed before her, proffering up the guild's verdict. Rani had taken every scrap of parchment, unfolded it, smoothed it with trembling hands.

Upon most sad reflection, I, Parion Guildmaster, determine that the journeyman once known as Ranita Glasswright has not yet mastered the means of creating glasswork. Until such time as said Ranita shall perfect her skills, she shall not be known by her guildname, here in Brianta or anywhere in the wide world that honors the name of the Glasswrights' Guild.

Failure. Scrap after scrap, messenger after messenger, reporting on her absolute failure.

Rani had sobbed in the dream. She had sobbed like a fiend, like a madwoman, like she had sobbed in Hal's study earlier that day. Was it only that day? Had she lost so much since dawn? Her king? Her lover? Her respect for herself?

She managed to sit on the edge of the bed. Her room was hot, and the air was still, but her skin was cold and clammy. She dragged herself to the small table in the corner, fumbling for an ivory comb. As she worked through the tangles in her hair, she tried to calm herself, tried to push away the bitter memories of her dream.

She did not know that Master Parion would fail her. Not yet.

Her hair was damp, and it hung limp against the back of her neck. When she looked at the ivory comb, she saw several fine strands glinting in the last of the evening light. It seemed that she'd been losing her hair since she'd been in Brianta. If she ran her fingers along her scalp, they came away twisted with strands.

Perhaps she *had* been poisoned. Perhaps the gods had a cruel sense of irony. Crestman had set her on a path, given her a vial to kill a woman, even as someone had worked to kill her with poison. Maybe the gods were laughing, enjoying her plight from their seats in the Heavenly Fields.

Rani poured a glass of water, but she could only choke down a single swallow before the metallic taste closed her throat. She glanced at the window again. It was still too early to do what she must do. She needed darkness. Total darkness.

She crossed to the prie-dieu that was set beneath the window, strategically placed to capture any errant breeze. Tovin had moved the prayer bench for her before they left for Brianta, before the summer reached its fever pitch.

He'd be gone by now. Gone, and sleeping in some inn. Would he really ride south to Sarmonia? She would have thought him too tied to his troop. But it was hardly *his* troop any longer. It had become hers in the years that the players had spent in Morenia.

There would be time enough tomorrow to think on Tovin. For now she had best pray to the Thousand Gods. She would need their assistance in the work that she must complete that night.

As she knelt on the wooden prayer bench, her hands found their way back into her pockets. There was Crestman's note. Now she could finger it without feeling the gaping hole in her chest. She could picture the proud soldier, twisted and maimed. She could remember him as he had been, as he wanted to be once again.

And beside it was the vial of poison. Her belly clenched as she thought of the smell of it, sharp, acrid. That afternoon it had taken her a long time to work the stopper loose. A small amount had splashed on her hand, and she had recoiled. Crestman had been quite clear, though. Mareka must *drink* the poison for it to do any harm. Rani was not likely to be damaged by a drop on her flesh.

Now she set the vial on the prie-dieu's crossbar, folding her hands over it in a careful attitude of prayer. Which of the gods would note her appeal tonight? Which of the gods was assigned to listen to a reluctant assassin?

Tarn seemed too easy a choice, but Rani reached out for him nonetheless. "Hail Tarn. Listen to this poor pilgrim and grant her petition. Watch over her, and keep her in your grace. Hail, great Tarn."

The rush of green-black wings was immediate even though her words were stilted. The small vial seemed to grow beneath her fingers, to expand until she could feel each bump, each whorl in its imperfect construction. Dusty bits of cork still flecked the container's mouth, and she brushed them off hesitantly, mindful of the liquid within.

"Hail, Tarn," she started again, only to stop when the green-black shimmer threatened to overwhelm her.

What had happened in that Curia chamber? Rani remembered the ecstacy that had spread on the princess's face, her certainty as she spoke of the gods. Berylina had clearly known that they were in the room with her, that they surrounded her. The princess had seen them; she wasn't crafting tales for the Curia priests. She had not exaggerated for the religious body.

And in the middle of the trial Rani had thought that she, too, might actually be aware of the gods around her. She could remember the power that she had felt during her Speaking with Berylina, her certainty that the gods were present in her ears, in her mouth, in her nose and her flesh. She had sensed the gods precisely as Berylina had.

But was Rani only imagining those presences? Were they part of the illness that had dogged her since her arrival in Brianta? Were they an expression of hope, of desire, of desperate longing to share poor Berylina's faith?

Or—even more frightening—were they real? Had the gods come to Rani with the strange emanations that Berylina had known?

Rani bowed her head, reminding herself to concentrate on the prayer at hand. She tried to speak to Roat and Arn and Fen. But none of the gods seemed near to her; none appeared to listen. Justice, courage, and mercy were distant ideals. Rani's fingers grew slick upon the glass vial; the container seemed to send out its own rays of heat.

Under other circumstances, Rani would have been grateful. It had been so long since her bones had felt warm, so long since she had taken a breath without stilling the urge to shiver. So long since she had been well.

After tonight she would have time to heal. After tonight she would be removed from the Fellowship's threats. Laranifarso would be delivered, and she could return to the serious work of supporting Moren, of supporting Hal. He would need her, of course. He would rely on her more, once Mareka was gone.

Life in Moren might return to the old patterns, to the customs and traditions from before the fire. From before Berylina and Mareka. Life might be simple again.

Rani gave up on prayer. She used the prie-dieu to pull herself to her feet. Her knees ached as she straightened, and her thoughts flashed on memories eight years old. As a young glasswright she had spent a great deal of time praying to Sorn, the god of obedience, and to Plad, the god of patience. The glasswrights' prayer benches had been embossed with the symbols of their craft; Rani's knees had been gouged more times than she cared to remember.

Those prie-dieus had perished in the old guildhall. Perhaps Parion had ordered more constructed for the hall in Brianta. Odd that Rani had not seen one while she was in Jair's homeland. Odd that the guild seemed all out of keeping with the gods. Odd that the glasswrights held themselves so far apart even in their new home.

More mysteries. More thoughts. More riddles to be solved.

After tonight. She was letting her mind wander so that she could avoid the serious business at hand.

Rani leaned out of her window, noting that the guards had taken up their nighttime positions by the palace gates. Their torches burned high, and she knew that the men's faces would shine with sweat in the summer night. She craned her neck and tried to look up at the royal apartments, at the window where Mareka slept. The angle was too steep, though. She could not see the queen's balcony from her room. She could not see her destination.

The Pilgrims' Bell began to toll across the night, summoning the faithful from the surrounding countryside. The deep tones had saved lives in the middle of winter, gathering in pilgrims who would otherwise have succumbed to snow or wolves or worse. Now, in summer, the bell sounded weary, exhausted, as if it longed only for one single night of sleep.

Sleep. Rani would have that after she completed her mission. Long hours of sleep with no more cares.

For now, though, she must begin. She must complete her task. Otherwise the Fellowship would never be content. Laranifarso would never be free.

The torches in the corridor outside her apartments seemed too bright. Rani shielded her eyes, slitting her fingers so that her vision could adjust. The skin beyond her eyelashes felt tight, stretched, as if it had been turned to leather by her sobbing that afternoon.

She glided through the corridors without a challenge from a single guard. She crept down to the kitchen, confident that Cook would be asleep. These were the few dark hours, after scraps from the evening's dinner had been fed to the dogs, before it was time to mix yeast and flour, to knead the next day's dough.

Rani knew these passages well. She had discovered them with Hal when she was little more than a child, when she first came to the palace. In the dark days after she realized that her family was gone, after she knew that Bardo had truly betrayed her to his own secret band . . . If only she had known then that there was lightness in those days, that there was quiet and comfort. . . . Those were the times before Hal was called to wear the crown, before they had the weight of a kingdom between them.

Hal had led her from the nursery to the kitchens, taking midnight passages to liberate secret hoards of sweet cakes.

Now, with the wisdom of an adult, Rani knew that Cook must have expected their visits. The plates were always filled, always covered with a single linen kerchief, always kept close to the warm stove.

Rani swallowed, trying to ignore the taste of metal. Secret palace passages . . . She had long thought them a thing of the past.

Taking a deep breath, she stopped outside the kitchen's double doors. She hesitated in the darkness, resting her fingers in her pocket, against the glass vial. It was there. Returned to its normal size. Its normal weight. Its normal cool, glassy feel.

Rani's fingers found the low door beside the entrance to the pantry. Her fingers worked the latch from memory, remembering to press down completely before pulling the door toward her. She needed to double over to stoop beneath the lintel; she had needed to duck even before, when she was still a child.

The hidden passageway was tall enough, though. Hal had speculated years before that the secret stairs had been built for the convenience of the palace servants, so that they could carry trays of food and drink to the royal apartments.

Rani surprised herself on the climb. She remembered where the staircase twisted. She remembered where she needed to stretch over a crumbled step. She remembered where leaking rainwater had slicked the outside edge of four consecutive stairs.

And then, before she had a chance to recall more of her childhood, more of her carefree days, she had reached the top of the secret passage. One sniff confirmed that she was at her destination; the upper entrance to the steps was hidden in a garderobe.

As a child, she had been terrified of that closet. It was secreted in the queen's apartments, in the nest of rooms that had been corrupted by Queen Felicianda. Rani's imagination had always run rampant; she had imagined that the royal conspirator's wraith still haunted the chambers where she had lived in life. Hal had teased her once, pointing out that even if the Amanthian queen's spirit persisted, it was not likely to linger in a garderobe.

Rani shook her head. She had greater fears now than any imagined spirits. She was haunted by more frightening images, by more dangerous threats. She was plagued by the living.

As if she suffered from a nervous spasm, she reached again into her pocket. The vial was there, mocking her with its barely perceptible weight.

Rani had to catch her breath before she could hear the Pilgrims' Bell here. She was deeper in the palace, more sheltered behind stone walls that were intended to keep out the most determined intruder. But the men who had designed the fortress had not counted on betrayal in their own ranks. They had not worked to keep the queen safe from someone already free to roam the keep.

Standing with her hand on the door that led to Mareka's bedchamber, Rani hesitated. There would be guards in the outer corridor. If the queen heard her moving about, she could summon help with a single cry.

Rani had called those guards to herself a lifetime ago. When she was thirteen years old, when she arrived at the palace of the First Pilgrim. She had chafed under the watchful eye of a guardsman, a stolid soldier who had dogged her every step, keeping her from making contact with her brother. What was the man's name? Mercu—? Mardo—?

She sighed. She was making excuses. She was delaying the inevitable. The soldier was gone, along with the thirteen-year-old girl who had summoned all the household guards by wailing in frustration. The conspirator Larindolian, the old king, the old queen . . . all were gone.

Now Mareka was the queen. Now Mareka slept on the other side of the door. Now Mareka must meet her fate, meet

a future delivered by Rani's hands. Touching her fingertips
against the vial once again, Rani lifted the latch.

Mareka's sleeping chamber was as warm as the rest of
the palace, as stultified by the heavy summer air. The queen
had flung her windows wide in an obvious attempt to harvest whatever remnant breeze came her way. A shaft of
moonlight illuminated the steps to the window, to the narrow balcony. Rani shivered as she thought of the queen
falling, of the pregnant woman fetching up against the
sharp-legged table. She shuddered as she thought of two
more heirs lost to Morenia.

The floorboards were swept clean. The heavy oaken
planks lay smoothly. Not a joist creaked as Rani moved, not
a board complained as she glided to the curtained bed.

There. On the small table. A single goblet glimmered in
the moonlight, pale as the belly of a fish. A flagon sat beside
it.

Rani had worried about the effectiveness of her plan.
What if someone else drank from the goblet? What if someone else sampled the contents of the flagon? What if someone else found the stoppered vial?

She had convinced herself, though, that none of those
thoughts mattered. The nights were hot. The morning came
early. The queen would be thirsty. Mareka was a
guildswoman at heart, not a pampered noblewoman. She
would pour herself a drink and drain her goblet. Otherwise,
why would she keep the accouterments beside her bed? If
she expected to be served, she would have left them with her
maidservants.

Enough. It was time for Rani to move. Time to push the
last piece of her plan into place.

She reached into her pocket. She gathered up the vial.
She held it in her left hand, turning it so that she could catch
the silvery moonlight. She levered one fingernail under the
edge of the cork, working it toward her, working it away.
She caught her tongue between her teeth, held her breath.

And she took one step closer to the bed, closer to the table, closer to the flagon and the goblet and her destiny.

The curtained bed exploded in a flurry of linens and bolsters. Rani's ears were filled with a wordless roar, and then a lantern was unshuttered. Her night-primed eyes were blinded as she tried to look away, but strong fingers closed around her throat, forcing her head forward, forcing her toward the bed.

She raised her fingers to scratch at the hands that held her. The vial slipped from her grasp as she tried to free herself, as she tried to pry loose the stranglehold. She twisted her back, arching as if she were a cat, and she added her own frantic keen to the wordless bellow of the creature who held her.

Her attacker shifted, and Rani was suddenly held from behind, secured by a silk-clad arm across her throat. It was easier for her to breathe at least, easier for her to squirm about. Her eyes had adjusted to the lantern as well, and she could see the thick hairs on the forearm that secured her. She bucked and twisted and broke her way free, and then she was panting, gasping, and staring into a pair of too-familiar chestnut eyes.

"Halaravilli." She could barely shape his name.

"Rani." He spat hers, and she saw the jagged sorrow that etched his face, the impotent rage that even now made him tense his fingers.

"You have to understand," she started to say.

"Drink it."

"What?"

"Drink the poison."

She stared at him as if he were mad. "I—"

"Don't talk to me!" His words lashed out at her, sharper than a whip. "Drink the god-cursed poison."

She shook her head, trying to find the words to explain to him, to let him know that she had worked out the pattern, that she had recognized the truth. She had analyzed the Fellowship's command, their order, their extortion. She had found a way to save Laranifarso, to bring the child back home.

Hal bellowed in the face of her silence, bending to scoop up the vial from the floor. The cork still clung to the glass lip, and he tore it off like a madman. He hurled the stopper at her, aiming for her face, but it bounced harmlessly off her shoulder. "My lord," she said, but she stammered over the familiar phrase.

"Drink the poison! Drink the poison and die!"

He grabbed her then. He knotted his fingers in her hair and pulled her head back against his chest, moving his fingers around her face so that he covered her nose, cut off her ability to breathe through her flaring nostrils.

He ground the vial against her mouth and pressed her lower lip against her teeth. She tried to break free, tried to step back, tried to explain, but he was a man possessed. He slid the glass against her mouth, pushing until she thought that her jaw would shatter. He tilted his wrist, farther, farther.

She needed air. She needed to breathe. She needed to expand her lungs, to fill her chest.

She felt liquid touch her teeth, roll against her lips. She tried to toss her head, but he only clamped his fingers tighter across her nose. Against her will, beyond any conscious thought, she opened her mouth, gasping for air, frantic to fill her lungs.

And then she was coughing, choking, fighting to keep the contents of the vial from flowing into her lungs with the air she needed so desperately. She felt the liquid in her mouth, knew that some of it dribbled past her lips, onto her chin. She could taste the metal remnant, feel her entire body clench in rebellion.

She swallowed.

The water burned all the way down to her belly.

She swallowed again, trying to smooth away the leaden

flavor. Fleetingly, absurdly, she wondered if water would ever taste the same again, if she would ever be grateful for the sweet kiss from an unsullied well.

And then she was drawn back into the queen's apartments, to the man who stood before her, breathing like a horse that had run a thousand leagues. He stared at the vial in his hands, gaping at the glass as if it were a living thing.

"Rani," he said, and her name sounded like a sob.

"Sire." She swallowed again, and then she extended her hand for the container.

"It is a slow poison, then? One that will not take you straightaway?"

"It is no poison, my lord. I washed out the Fellowship's foul brew. I filled the glass with water from your own well."

She saw the questions fly across his face. "The Fellowship? What hand do they have in this? Why would you work for them? Why would you lose the poison, yet still come to my lady's chambers?"

She answered his last question first. "I hoped to leave a warning, Sire. I hoped that my lady the queen would see the vial beside her morning cup. She would see what might have happened in the night, and she would know how easily she might be targeted the next time. She would recognize her vulnerability, and she would leave."

Hal shook his head in amazement. "You hate your queen so much, then? You are so jealous that you would kill her or frighten her from her place at my side?"

"I harbor no such enmity for Queen Mareka," Rani said, and she was able to force the words into a semblance of truth. "The Fellowship, though . . . They feel differently."

"The Fellowship?"

"Aye. The same who hold Laranifarso. They keep the child as a safeguard against my conduct. They took him so that I would kill the queen."

"Kill the queen," he said, repeating her words as if he

were awakening from a dream. "And yet you chose to defy them?"

"They want Mareka gone. They want to control your heirs, my lord. They want a child on your throne, a king who is more biddable than you have proven to be." She saw him complete the pattern, saw him measure out the lines that she had left undrawn. If Hal's child were on the throne, then Hal himself would be gone. She continued before he had to voice that certainty himself. "I thought that if I could make the queen leave without killing her, the Fellowship would be content. They do not care if Mareka lives or dies, they merely want her out of your life, out of your bed. They merely want her gone."

"And so you asked me for a boon this afternoon. You hoped that I would send her away and free Laranifarso in the process."

"Aye."

"And when I fouled that, you thought to frighten her off yourself."

"Aye."

"But the message I received? The warning that you were going to kill Mareka?"

Rani did not pretend that she had not found the parchment, that she had not read the hateful words. "Crestman wrote that. He wanted to manipulate you."

"For the Fellowship?"

"I do not think so. That does not fit the pattern. I think that Crestman acted on his own in that. He uses the Fellowship so long as their motives run even with his own, but his ultimate goal is different from theirs. He does not care if they remove you from Morenia. He is after me. He wants to punish me."

"And he thought to make me the instrument of that punishment."

"Aye." Rani worked to keep her voice even on the single word.

"He thought to have me kill you." Hal's voice was tinged with wonder, as if only now he realized how close he had come to that action.

"Or throw me in your dungeons. Or take me before a tribunal on a charge of treason."

"His hatred runs deep."

Rani thought of the boy-soldier she had met so many years ago, the child who had sacrificed puppies and soldiers and bonds of love. "Aye, Sire. Very deep."

"So what happens now?"

"That all depends. Where is Queen Mareka?"

He hesitated. She saw the uncertainty tighten his throat, the debate flash across his eyes. He lowered his gaze to the vial, and then he made a decision. "I've sent her to the castle at Riverhead. I convinced her that she would be cooler there while this summer heat persists."

"And who knows that she has gone?"

"No one. I fitted out her horse myself. The castle there has all the supplies that she will need. She traveled with two of her ladies and six of my household guards."

Rani nodded. Eight people to account for, then. She could easily weave a story to cover them. She could craft a tale of devoted servants, carrying word back to the Liantine spider-guild, letting the distant masters know that their sometime journeyman had perished in a foreign land.

"Listen to me, my lord. We can make this work to our advantage." But first, before she spun out her stories, before she hatched her plans, she needed something. She needed Hal to trust her. She needed him to believe that she was loyal to him, that she worked to save him, to do what was best for him, and him alone. She offered up her greatest proof of trustworthiness. "Please, Sire. It's been a long day. I saw Tovin Player leave me at noon, and that seems like a lifetime ago."

"Tovin is gone?"

"Aye. He said that he would not stay with a woman

whose loyalties lay with another." She watched Hal measure her words, watched him weigh her devotion. She saw the moment that he recognized her truth, that he accepted her renewed pledge of fealty. She nodded once, and then she said, "Come, Sire. Bring the lantern closer to the hearth. Let us sit and work out the best response to the Fellowship, and Crestman, and all the forces that stand against us."

Hal did not hesitate as he followed her to the low wooden chairs.

15

Rani stared at the iron crossbar of the pyre, and she wondered if her lungs would ever be free of the stench of funeral wood smoke. The sharp aroma of ladanum laced the air.

Rani had sprinkled the herbs herself, wrapping winding cloths about Berylina Thunderspear's most sacred possessions. Typically, priests would have performed the duty. But typically, the ladanum would have been sprinkled on a body. They did not have Berylina's body.

Instead, Rani and Hal had decided that they would use the princess's worldly goods to honor her and send her to the Heavenly Fields. They had gathered up her green caloya gowns and her inspired drawings of the gods. They had collected her prayer book and her scrolls of religious texts. They had bound all of the treasures to the princess's small prie-dieu, wrapping the ensemble with lengths of undyed spidersilk. Rani herself had fastened a Thousand-Pointed Star onto the collection, binding together a life of faith and fanaticism.

Holy Father Dartulamino had been asked to bless the funeral bread and wine before lighting the pyre, but he had refused. Rani and Hal were left wondering if the highest priest in all the land had declined the honor because of its unorthodox nature, or because he stood by the actions of the

Briantan Curia, or—the darkest possibility—because the Fellowship somehow wanted Berylina to be dishonored. Neither Rani nor Hal could forget for long that the Holy Father was the second-highest member of the Fellowship in Morenia.

Even though Dartulamino had not agreed to participate, Father Siritalanu would not be put off. As he stepped toward the pyre, tears streamed down his face. His voice broke when he began the traditional prayers. "Greetings to all in the name of the Thousand Gods."

Rani's voice was fervent as she proclaimed, "May all the gods bless you." She might have had her differences with the priest, might have believed that he did not act strongly enough to save Berylina, act soon enough. Nevertheless, she mourned with him on this funeral day. She understood his sorrow, his guilt.

"I come before you with a heavy heart," the priest said, and the words were not merely formula. Instead, Siritalanu's voice broke over them, rasped as if each syllable were a separate file. He drew a shuddering breath and continued. "Throughout our lives, we all must witness the work of Tarn. We all must greet the god of death and recognize the dominion that he holds over us. Tarn is not the first god, and he is not the last, but Tarn will gather each of us beneath his cloak when our course is done."

Rani listened to the familiar words with new ears. She could clearly see the god of death's green-black wings in the high summer sun that flamed behind Siritalanu. Rani was certain, as the princess had been certain, as Berylina had proclaimed through years of witnessing her faith.

As she listened, Rani's deep breathing carried her into the Speaking place, into the deepest caverns of her mind. She had slipped there more and more often in the past two weeks, as she and Hal met long into the nights, plotting, planning, outlining how they could take back their lives from the Fellowship. She thought that maybe she relied on the Speaking strength because her own body was so tired, so drawn out from her trials in Brianta.

But perhaps she reached for the peace of Speaking because it reminded her of Tovin. She longed to hear from the player, if only to know that he was safely arrived in Sarmonia. After all, she knew that she was the one who had hurt him; she was the one who had driven him away with her harsh judgments.

She swallowed hard, trying to ignore the metallic taste as she lifted her chin and focused on the religious service. Tovin had chosen to leave. His own pride had dictated that he could not stay with her. He had acted, and there was nothing that she could do. Truth be told, she had never had the ability to control the man.

That had been part of the excitement of him.

That was the reason that she was better off. Here. Alone in Morenia. Alone but for Halaravilli, Mair, and Farso, and all the rest of the court that she had come to know over the past eleven years.

Rani forced her attention back to the funeral rites. Father Siritalanu raised his hands over the bound prie-dieu and said, "Hail Vir, god of martyrs, guide of Jair the Pilgrim. Look upon this pilgrim with mercy in your heart and justice in your soul. Guide the feet of this pilgrim on righteous paths of glory that all may be done to honor you and yours among the Thousand Gods. This pilgrim asks for the grace of your blessing, Vir, god of martyrs."

It was a courageous choice, dedicating the ceremony to Vir. Rani tasted the complex fire of cinnamon on her tongue, momentarily drowning out even the metal that she had become so accustomed to swallowing. The spice surprised her with its strength, and her eyes watered even as she struggled to catch her breath.

As she swallowed, Rani pictured Torio, the fat priest who had conducted the Briantan Curia. The vision sent a shiver through her, a shudder more powerful than any of the tremors she had come to expect from her besieged body. The man had committed murder in his drive to protect his church from visions such as Rani had just experienced. What would happen if he learned that she, too, could taste the gods? How far would he reach to purify the church? Could he stretch from holy Brianta to punish her here?

Rani raised her hand in a rapid religious gesture, flitting the sign across her chest. She looked about to see if her movement had been noted, but she was relieved to hear Siritalanu intone, "This pilgrim asks for the grace of your blessing, Tarn, god of death." The flicker of green-black wings was so familiar that Rani almost forgot to worry.

And then the hard work was done. Siritalanu thrust a torch into the oil-soaked wood at the base of the pyre. The flames caught rapidly, chewing their way into the afternoon sky. Despite their heat, they remained nearly invisible against the dying summer's light.

Rani leaned her head back, the better to see the pyre open the doors of the Heavenly Fields. The motion made her dizzy; she was far more unsteady on her feet than she should have been. Black shadows swept in from the edges of her vision, and an ocean roar filled her ears as if she were buried in tidal sand. Cinnamon surged again across her tongue.

She felt Mair grip her arm, and she leaned against her friend, murmuring, "I'll be fine. Just give me a moment." She forced herself to swallow hard, to fill her lungs with air. Hal looked at her, his dark brown eyes filled with concern.

Father Siritalanu was suddenly standing over her, blocking the sun. Rani could make out his green robes, impossibly fresh. The priest took her other arm, providing a tower of support. "Stand easy, my lady. The ladanum can be overpowering in the summer heat."

"It wasn't ladanum," she protested. The effort to speak made her bring air into her lungs; at least she was returning to some semblance of normalcy.

"Of course it was. You know the way of the priesthood.

You know the efforts that we make to purify the bodies, to make them joyous for the gods."

"I know the smell of ladanum, Father, and that was not it. I tasted Vir."

"Quiet!" The priest looked about, as if he feared that the Briantan Curia had penetrated to the very core of Morenia.

Rani saw Hal's curious glance; she watched the questions form on his lips. She would have to explain later. "You cannot silence the truth, Father. When Berylina and I Spoke—"

"That was my mistake," the priest hissed. "I should never have given in to her request. I should never have left the two of you to play at your games in that cell."

The priest's resistance gave Rani strength. When she straightened her spine, she scarcely realized that it was the first time in days that she had drawn a solid breath. "Berylina Thunderspear was not playing games, Father. She had mastered something new and powerful. She knew the gods in ways that we can only imagine, in ways that I am only beginning to comprehend." Father Siritalanu started to interrupt, but Rani silenced him by laying a firm hand on his arm. "No, Father. Do not speak against her here. Not at her pyre. Instead, think on the lessons that she taught us, the riches that she brought. There was strength in Berylina. There was power. There was the grace of all the Thousand Gods."

The priest might have intended to respond, but he never got the opportunity. Instead, he was interrupted by a page who came running into the cathedral close. "Your Majesty!" the boy cried, and his voice was sharp.

Rani's heart tightened inside her breast. There was no good reason for a messenger to interrupt worship beside a funeral pyre.

Hal turned to the child. "Aye?" There was a desert of command beneath the word. The child collapsed into a bow, actually touching his forehead to one crimson-clad knee before he bobbed back upright.

"Sire, the master of the mews sent me! Two messages have arrived!"

"Two?"

"Aye! Two pigeons, come within ten heartbeats of each other!" The boy's eyes shone with excitement. He proffered up a pair of tiny metal tubes, cradling them in his hands as if they were fashioned of precious stones.

Rani suddenly realized that she was still clutching Mair's arm. Back in Brianta she had left a pigeon with Master Parion. Weeks had passed. Surely the Glasswrights' Guild had completed their judging. . . . Surely they had evaluated the journeymen's masterpieces. Surely they had found the strength to act, separate and apart from the Fellowship, from Crestman's threats.

Rani forced herself to stand tall, to pull air into her lungs, to watch, watch, wait, as Hal fumbled with the metal tube.

A scrap of vellum was curled inside, scraped thin so that it could be rolled into the smallest flexible curve. Hal extracted the scrap and unfolded it gently, taking care not to drop it on the cathedral's green grass. He glanced at it and brought it closer to his face. He started to read, then stopped and turned it upside down. He blinked hard and brought the vellum closer still.

Rani waited, frozen. Even the shudders that had become her body's constant exercise seemed stilled. She could hear her heart beating a thousand leagues away. She watched Hal's face, waited for his brow to contract in pity or for his lips to curl in congratulations.

He retraced the message as if he were committing it to memory, and then he read it one more time.

And then he handed it to her.

Her fingers shook as she took the vellum. So this was what her guildish life came down to. Nine years spent laboring as an apprentice, struggling as a journeyman. Three months working in a foreign city, designing a masterpiece. One day creating the reality from the image in her mind.

One moment waiting to read the verdict. She unrolled the parchment and brought it closer, tilting it to better catch the light, to translate the tiny perfect letters.

> *The Glasswrights' Guild regrets that the Work of Ranita Glasswright is not judged to be the Quality of a Master, as she relied upon Tools not sanctioned by the Guild.*

Not sanctioned by the guild! Master Parion had watched her pick up the diamond knife! He had nodded at her to continue! He had seen her use her tools, and he had said nothing, done nothing—he had not stopped her in any way.

Rani knew that she needed to breathe, needed to speak, needed to take some action to break the spell of the message in her hand. All of those days working in the guildhall . . . All of those hours grinding colors, preparing plates of glass . . . All of the time wasted pounding metal into foil . . .

Gone. Worthless. Wasted.

Rani looked up to the Heavenly Fields, wanting to cry out against the Thousand Gods. Why did they hate her so? Why had they abandoned her?

As she gazed skyward her attention was captured by a window high in the cathedral wall above her. It was the newest of the stained glass there, yet it was already more than eight years old. It had a background of cobalt blue and a single fine figure, picked out and accented with lead-black stippling. Even now, more than eight years after its completion, Rani knew the design as well as she knew the lines on her own palm.

The Defender's Window. The design that had begun her strange journey. The window that Instructor Morada had been completing on that fateful day when Rani had climbed the scaffold, had entered the cathedral, had cried out and drawn Prince Tuvashanoran to his death.

Now the window stood over her like a stern parent admonishing a naughty child. Rani blinked, and she suddenly remembered standing in the yard of the Morenian Glasswrights' Guild, stoking the kilns. She had been a loyal apprentice. She had been a dedicated journeyman. She had learned all the skills that were required of a master.

She had wasted her time with the guild's test. She should have ignored the trappings of a house that had been ranged against her for years.

After all, the guild was more than its parts. It was more than an embittered master, more than journeymen who worked with leather and silken Hands. The Glasswrights' Guild was an ideal—a community of scholars and artisans who gathered together to create works of beauty.

It was a memory, and it could be a future. Rani could build it here, in Moren, even if she did not have the blessing of the old masters. Surely there were glasswrights who would come to her! There were guildsmen who would rebel against the unfair ways of the Briantan clique.

She *had* made friends in Brianta. Perhaps she could even encourage Belita and Cosino to join her here in Moren.

There were other glasswrights out there, others whom Rani could call. She could create her own guildhall. She could create her new life. She turned to Hal, ready to tell him of her discovery, ready to take her oath to build a future guild, free of the taint of Master Parion, free from the history of the old masters.

Only then did she realize that there was a commotion about her, a noise that rose above the pounding of her heart, the crackling of the pyre. Mair was down on her knees, a mass of spidersilk puddled on the grass. Farso knelt beside her, his arms struggling to enfold her, to gather up her raging grief.

The Touched woman fought off her husband as if she were a wounded beast. She looked to the pyre, and she cast her head back, howling like the wolves that stalked outside the city gates. Terrified, Rani took the second slip of vellum from Hal's stiff fingers.

In the name of Jair, Laranifarso is dead.

Rani felt the words like the edge of an iron sheet digging into her chest. She tried to swallow, tried to eke out a response, but she was unable to think, unable to move.

The Fellowship. Rani's failing her glasswrights' test had nothing to do with her using the player's tools. The Fellowship had executed Crestman's threat. They had failed her, and they had murdered Mair's son. No one had been fooled by her machinations. No one had been duped by Hal sending Mareka away.

Rani looked up at the sky, and a chill tripped down her arms. How had the Fellowship learned so quickly? They must keep pigeons here in Morenia, birds trained to home in on their mews in Brianta. And in Brianta they kept birds for Hal's own court.

That knowledge should not have frightened her more than anything else that the Fellowship did. After all, she was thinking about an organization that had murdered a *child,* an innocent babe who had no say in all the politics of the land.

Murdered Laranifarso.

"I'll kill them!" Mair's voice rose over the crackle of the funeral pyre. "I'll rip their cursed masks off! I'll expose their lying faces to the people of Brianta, and Morenia, and all the rest of the world! I'll see them stripped naked and staked in the road, with only the summer sun for comfort! I'll see their bones picked clean by winter ravens!"

Farso struggled to get his arms around his wife, fought to smother her vicious vows against his chest. The nobleman's snow-frosted hair bobbed as he fought against his own sobs, and Rani's belly grew heavy as lead. Mair's threats were all the more horrible because they were uttered in her official court voice, in the cultured tones that she believed would serve her better with Morenia. Even in her shock, even in her grief, Mair worked toward careful revenge. She plotted with all the cunning of a Touched girl and all the resources of a noblewoman.

And what would she do if she ever learned that Rani had held the power to save her son? What would she do if she found that Rani had been offered a choice—slay the queen or sacrifice the child?

Father Siritalanu moved to Mair's side. He whispered his platitudes, attempting to calm the grieving mother. Mair would take no comfort, though; she shrieked as he laid a hand on her back, screaming like an animal in pain.

"Farsobalinti!" Hal's voice cracked with authority, with a determination that Rani had not seen in years. "Take your wife away from here. Take her to your apartments, that she might mourn in peace."

The nobleman glared at Hal. Of course that was what he should do. Of course that was what he was attempting to do. Attempting and failing miserably.

Rani knew that she was responsible for all of this. She had made her choice; she was now reaping all that she had sowed. She had failed as a glasswright, failed even as a conspirator in a secret organization bent on conquering the world. Failed as a friend.

She stepped forward, easing up to Mair's side. She gently laid a hand on Farsobalinti's arm, urging him to step away. She saw the sorrow blooming on his face, knew that his loss must be worse, even more terrible, because he did not know why, he did not know how, he did not know what had caused his son to be taken from him.

"Come, Mair," Rani said, kneeling beside her friend.

"No! Do not tell me to come! Do not tell me what to do! They murdered my son! They stole him, and they killed him, and they never told me why! They never gave me a chance!"

Rani tried to breathe past the pain in her belly, tried to

find some word of comfort. What could she say, though? She had had a chance. She had made a choice.

She looked at Hal, begging him, pleading with him to say something, anything. After a moment's hesitation, he took a step closer, resting his hand on noble Farso's arm, as if he respected Mair too much to reach out to her. "My lady. My lord. I promise you this. I will find the people who have done this. I will find them, and I will bring them to justice. They will pay for the life that they have stolen. By First Pilgrim Jair and all the Thousand Gods, they will pay!"

Now, Hal did hold out a hand, helping Mair to her feet. "Go now, my lady. Return to your apartments with your husband. Turn to him in your grief, and prepare yourselves for yet another pyre, for yet another offering to the Thousand. But be of good spirit, my lady. This matter does not end here. By my crown and all my kingdom, this matter is not yet done."

Mair let herself be handed off to Farso, but she bared her teeth in a lioness's snarl before she turned away. "I will not forget that oath, Your Majesty. I will not forget the promise that you've made."

And then the grieving parents walked away, leaning close to each other to share their sorrow and their strength. Rani's eyes filled with tears as she remembered the nights that she had sat up with Mair, nights that she'd been kept awake by Laranifarso's fussing. She had held that child. She had nurtured him. Not as a mother, certainly, but as a woman who had loved him. The flame of outrage that flickered beneath her breastbone could be nothing compared to the inferno that Mair must feel.

Rani's anger was substantial enough that she missed Hal's first words to Father Siritalanu. She did hear him say, though, "And I thank you for your concern. I know how hard Berylina's passing must have been for you."

"Thank you, Sire. Of course I grieve for the death of any innocent creature." Rani heard the stiff formality of the

words, but she understood far more. The man had loved
Berylina. He had loved her with the helpless passion of a
priest, with the forbidden power of a man. He had loved her,
knowing that she would never, *could* never, return that love.

And when he lost her, he felt as if he had lost his bride.
His bride, his child, his dedicated worshiper—all had perished in the Curia chamber in Brianta. Rani heard the distant
rush of a waterfall, and she recognized the voice of Rul, the
god of pity.

Siritalanu was oblivious, though. He heard no god, saw
no god, tasted no god. He held his faith through tradition,
through the repeated mechanics of worship. He had feared
Berylina's strange rapport, and he would be entirely undone
if he knew that Rani had inherited that communion.

"We will leave you, Father, to finish your worship in
peace." Hal's words were a mercy; he managed to sound as
if he had not seen the tears welling up in the priest's eyes.

"Thank you, Your Majesty," Siritalanu said, bobbing his
head. For once, his boyish face looked aged; weariness
stretched his flesh, and it seemed that his skin was dusted
with some grey powder. He moved his fingers in a holy sign,
first in front of the king and then in front of Rani.

Hal nodded his appreciation, and then he turned away
from the still-burning pyre. Lacking a specific command to
the contrary, Rani followed him back to the palace. They
walked through the gates, through the corridors, up the
winding staircase to the tower room where they had been re-
united only a fortnight before.

Hal sent away his attendants, declining offers of food and
drink and a new-built fire. He insisted that he had accounts
that he must review; there were matters that he needed to
discuss with Ranita Glasswright.

As the door closed behind the last of the servants, Rani
said, "That is not my name."

"Glasswright? And what else would you call yourself?"

"The matter is not what *I* would say. It is the title that they would grant to me. Or not."

"And who are they? The glasswrights of a distant kingdom."

"My lord, they were *your* glasswrights once. They once lived in Morenia."

"Some of them, aye. But I do not recognize them now. And I wonder that you do."

Rani blinked, and she saw Larinda's masterpiece behind her eyes, the old guildhall in all its glory. "They were a mighty power once, the Glasswrights' Guild."

"Aye."

"They work to be a force once again. They labor to honor every one of the gods with their glasswork, to decorate every shrine dedicated to one of the Thousand."

"And there is a chance that they might succeed. If they free themselves from outside forces. If they learn to act on their own, without undue influence from the Fellowship."

Rani wanted to believe that. She wanted to believe that she had failed her test only because the Fellowship had decreed it so. She wanted to believe that Master Parion had found mastery in her glasswork, that he himself had recognized her creation as a worthy offering to Clain.

She shook her head. "It is not as easy as that. If the guild had wanted to raise me to master, it would have defied the Fellowship."

"Would it? Knowing the price that it once paid for getting caught in politics beyond its walls?"

Hal had not been in Brianta. He had not seen the open anger, the yearning, the loss on Larinda's face. He had not seen Master Parion's single nod, his silent acceptance of the players' tools that Rani had employed.

Still, she had fought with Hal enough. She offered up a token of agreement: "It is impossible for me to say, my lord. Impossible for any of us to know."

Hal sighed, as if he had not wanted her concession after

all. "I'm sorry, Rani. I know how hard you worked. I know what you sacrificed in traveling to Brianta."

"I did not lose as much as some." There. Someone needed to speak of the deaths, of Berylina and Laranifarso.

"Rani, you did not cause their deaths."

"That is not what you said when I arrived home, my lord. You blamed me for Berylina."

"I spoke in anger then." He looked directly in her eyes. "I was afraid. I feared what Liantine will do, what Berylina's death will mean for me and my people and all of Morenia in the months to come." She knew that he could admit his fear to her. He could admit anything to her. "I did not mean those words, and I should not have said them."

She offered up her own apology. "I did not intend to add to your troubles. I did not want to make you afraid for Queen Mareka's life."

He nodded, and she wondered if he was remembering the feel of that glass vial beneath his fingertips. She swallowed away the taste of metal as he said, "And so."

"And so," she repeated, and then she found the courage to go on. "You know that the queen remains in danger." He nodded. "If the Fellowship does not find her, Crestman might."

"I know. If not for him, I would send her back to her spiderguild. They might have the power to protect her from the Fellowship."

"Not from Crestman, though. Not from a man who served as their slave." She pictured Crestman's wasted leg, his twisted arm. "She would not last a month there."

"And last she must," Hal said with a sardonic twist to his lips. "For she remains my lawful wife. And in seven months, she'll be the mother of my lawful heir."

Rani's heart clutched inside her chest, and even in the secret spaces of her own mind, she could not say if she reacted from fear or loss. If Mareka succeeded in carrying this child, Hal's life would be in danger from the Fellowship. And if she failed, Hal would need to answer to his people. "I offer my congratulations, Sire."

Hal looked at her steadily, and she knew that she must hold his gaze, must keep her face from expressing her doubt, from unfolding her private pain. He would know, of course. He would know precisely what she thought and how she felt, because he was her king. Because he had fought beside her for over a decade. Because they had shared in the birth and the rebuilding of his monarchy.

"I accept them," he said at last. "On behalf of my lady wife and myself, I accept them."

"And the queen is in good health in these early days?"

"As good as she has been at any other time. She called an herb-witch to her this time, when my own chirurgeon refused to aid her in her quest."

"An herb-witch?" Rani could not keep from twitching as she thought of the accusations against Berylina.

"Aye."

"Your priests must have been furious."

"Mareka gave them no cause for that. She went to the cathedral every morning and called the herb-witch every night."

Rani nodded. "She was successful, at least."

"So far." Hal shook his head, as if he disagreed with someone. "So far, she succeeds. But she will not stay safe in Riverhead. She must travel somewhere else. Somewhere secret. Somewhere where Crestman cannot reach. I think that I will send her—"

"Do not tell me!" Rani could not keep panic from her voice.

"You know that I value your counsel, Rani."

"Do not tell me where you send the queen!" She stumbled over the words in her haste to get them out. "Crestman and the Fellowship have tested me, and twice I have failed. I paid with my trial for the Glasswrights' Guild, and I paid with Laranifarso. Do not tell me where you send Queen Mareka so that our enemies cannot use me again."

She saw the battle on his face. For all his faults, for all his uncertainties, Hal was a good man. He wanted her to stand beside him; he wanted to include her in his kingdom.

Or maybe, Rani thought, he did not want to be alone. He did not want to stand on the tip of the arrow.

He said, "You know that I must declare myself against the Fellowship now. It is not enough that I fight Crestman, who was only their instrument. I must take them down, or die in the trying."

She knew. She must do the same. She had known when she heard that Laranifarso was murdered. She had known in the long pause between her heartbeats when she read that she had failed the glasswrights' test.

But she had known for longer than that. She had known when she saw Crestman in the dimly lit street outside the Gods' Midden. She had known when he had pressed poison into her hand, when he had bid her kill a queen.

As a child, she had acted blindly, taking a life when she was bidden to do so. She had watched innocent blood pool beside her, watched shock and horror spread over a good man's face.

But she was not a child any longer. She made her own choices now. She took on her own missions, accepted her own burdens, assumed her own responsibilities. She chose to act for justice, for right. So she had spared Mareka's innocent life.

"I know that you must declare war on the Fellowship, my lord. And I will be there by your side. I will fight them, as long as I am able, and I will aid you in your quest in any way that I might. That, at least, I can swear. That, at least, I can promise today."

Hal looked at her. She wondered if he saw the dark circles beneath her eyes, the lank strands of her hair, the tired lines around her mouth. She hoped that he did not. She hoped that he remembered the glasswright who had journeyed out from his court to escort a princess, the woman who had taken up her burden, who had promised to nurture and support a lost pilgrim, a hopeless cause.

He nodded, and she knew that it did not matter which vision of her he saw that day. He knew her then, and he trusted her now, no matter her appearance, no matter the changes that had come over her.

She broke the connection between them first, looking away with eyes that suddenly stung with unshed tears. She glanced down at the brooch upon her breast, at the tangle of metal that had come to seem like an extension of her own heart.

Her Thousand-Pointed Star. Sacred to her still. Despite everything that had happened in Brianta, everything that she had witnessed, everything that she had done. Everything that she had not done.

She unfastened the clasp on the Star, and she held it out to Hal. He hesitated only a moment, and then he folded his fingers over hers, over the gold, over the ancient symbol. "By Jair," she said. "By Jair, I'll work with you to bring the Fellowship to its knees. We'll destroy that twisted body so that it can never work its secret evil again."

His fingers tightened around hers for only a moment, and he repeated, "By Jair!"

And then he was gone. She knew that he went to speak to soldiers, to guards, to arrange for the transport of his wife and queen to some safe place.

Rani crossed to the window of the tower. As she looked out over Moren, a breeze sprang up, lifting her hair from her face. Heavy clouds now filled the sky, great lowering banks of grey that seemed ready to fold over the top of the cathedral. A growl of thunder rolled across the city.

Thunder. The voice of Shad, the god of truth.

A brilliant fork of lightning split the sky, and rain suddenly broke, sheets of water pouring down from the Heav-

enly Fields like the blessings of all the gods. For just a moment, Rani could smell the dust of the streets, the hot breath
of summer. Then that dry scent was lost, drowned, washed
away in the torrent.

Rani leaned out of the window, cupping her hands in the
downpour. Her palms filled almost immediately, and she
laughed as she brought the water close to her lips. As her
tongue touched the rain, she knew that it had a power, a
sweetness, a force. She let it flow over her lips, across her
teeth, down her parched and aching throat.

No metallic taste.

Nothing but water. Warm, clear water.

Automatically, Rani offered up a prayer to Mip. The god
answered her before she had completed her thought—his
nightingale song filled her ears, painfully sweet, gloriously
perfect.

Berylina had brought her this. Berylina had taught her
how to reach out to the gods, how to feel them stir within
her. Somehow, through the power of Speaking, Berylina had
opened Rani's eyes and ears, her nose and mouth, her flesh.
Berylina had awakened her to the power of all the Thousand
Gods.

"Thank you," Rani whispered to the princess. "By Jair, I
thank you for this gift."

And then the Pilgrims' Bell began its tolling, calling to
the frightened and the brave, the faithful and the lost, summoning all of them home to Moren.

About the Author

Mindy L. Klasky lives near Washington, D.C., which has been her home since she took her first professional job as a trademark and copyright attorney at a major law firm. After six years of working as a litigator, Mindy became a librarian, and now she manages a law library's reference department. In her spare time—when she is not reading or writing—Mindy swims, bakes, and quilts. Her cats, Dante and Christina, make sure that she does not waste too much time sleeping.

RoC   (0451)

Mindy L. Klasky
THE GLASSWRIGHTS' SERIES

THE GLASSWRIGHTS' APPRENTICE
If you want to be safe...mind your caste.
In a kingdom where all is measured by birthright, moving up
in society is almost impossible. Which is why young Rani
Trader's merchant family sacrifices nearly everything to buy
their daughter an apprenticeship in the Glasswrights' Guild—
where honor and glory will be within her reach.
45789-7

THE GLASSWRIGHTS' JOURNEYMAN
Rani Glasswright is home in her native Morenia, and her
quest to restore the glasswrights' guild is moving forward
again. But there are those who benefit from having the Guild
shattered—and Rani is a threat to their plans...
45884-2

THE GLASSWRIGHTS' PROGRESS
Living in the palace of Morenia's new king, Rani Trader
struggles to rebuild the banished glasswrighs' guild while an
enemy of the kingdom assembles a very unusual army
45835-4

Available wherever books are sold, or
to order call: 1-800-788-6262

R418